GAMES OF MIND

DENNIS QUILES

iUniverse LLC
Bloomington

GAMES OF MIND

iUniverse books may be ordered through booksellers or by contacting:

iUniverse
1663 Liberty Drive
Bloomington, IN 47403
www.iuniverse.com
1-800-Authors (1-800-288-4677)

ISBN: 978-1-4917-0552-0 (sc)
ISBN: 978-1-4917-0554-4 (hc)
ISBN: 978-1-4917-0553-7 (e)

Library of Congress Control Number: 2013917165

Printed in the United States of America.

iUniverse rev. date: 11/11/2013

To the gallant and courageous people of Nome, Alaska.

CONTENTS

ACKNOWLEDGMENTS

I would like to thank all those around me whose words of encouragement kept me going. I wrote this book for all of those who believed that the only boundaries that enclose our imaginations are made by us—that although barriers may look menacing, strong, and threatening, it only takes one step forward to realize that we can break them all.

I thank those who believed in me, like Holly, Joe, and Henry, who in one way or another not only helped me with complimenting the contents of this novel but gave me encouragement and direction and kept me focused on my North Star. To them and many others (a list of whom is longer than this book) I extend my appreciation and heartfelt gratitude.

PROLOGUE

The door to my cell screeched as it opened, and I saw Colonel Harman with a smoking gun in his hand. As a trained operative, Harman showed no facial expression, making it hard for me to read his thoughts or anticipate his moves.

Was he going to kill me quickly, or was he was going to enjoy torturing me first? This thought alone sent chills up my spine. His movements were deliberate and calculated, and as far as I could read, he was in predator mode. And that scared the shit out of me, especially when I was not in a position to defend myself, bound to a butcher's chair three floors below ground level.

I didn't know what to think, and no words came out of my mouth. I had made peace with my maker a long time ago and knew that, when my time had come, well, it had come. I quickly glanced at the opened door area and noticed a man in a white coat covered in blood.

I could see that he had been shot in the head, and blood was still pouring out of the hole between his eyes. A warrior like Colonel Harman was trained to be lethal, efficient, and swift, and in my current position, I was counting on him to remember the latter. I looked back at him straight in his eyes and said, "Let's not waste time. Go ahead; get it over with—no pity and no remorse."

1

FOR ALL GOOD TIMES

It was a noisy and hot late June afternoon at the office; business was booming, and money was no longer a concern of mine. After solving the mystery of the journal, the whole world learned about Connor, Steele, and now Harrison Private Investigation Agency. Many high-renting clients hadn't stopped knocking on my door. Martha Harrison, my lover and now my business partner, and I had done well in the last year.

As I touched my face, I noticed that I hadn't shaved today. I remembered the old days when this was not even a concern of mind. But now, with all the consulting cases, new high-profile clients, and exposure, I guess I have to look more professional.

I glanced to my right and stared at my reflection from the new glass display cabinet. For a moment, I didn't recognize the new me. My black, wavy hair was manicured and cut. I was wearing a fricking suit for crying out loud! And if this was not enough, I may have put on a couple of extra pounds. My blue eyes looked a bit tired, but they couldn't hide the satisfying sense of accomplishment. I was another man; finding and exposing selected contents of Marilyn Monroe's personal journal had definitely changed my life for the best.

I was enjoying my new office, compliments of the US government, if I may say. It was the least they could do after my office was blown to pieces last year. Over the years, I had learned that the government was cheap, but I stood corrected after a crew with lots of construction materials showed up last year and started working on what was left of my office.

I missed my old dusty chair; I just couldn't get used to this new leather-smelling thing I sat on. The government may know a little bit about decorating, but comfort, well … that was another thing. The office looked just as I remembered but without the dusty smell, the squeaky door, and chipped desk. But that was now ancient history. I had been so immersed and busy with all my new cases that I had forgotten that I was working alone.

Martha, my red-haired, silky-skinned lover, was nearly six thousand miles away in Beijing, China, working on a high-profile case for a multinational corporation whose branch network was compromised by local professional hackers. When she was asked to help, she hadn't even blinked an eye or questioned herself for a minute. She immediately replied, "When do I leave?"

Oh my God, I think that I've created a monster!

Martha had been in China for nearly two months, and my last conversation with her was two nights ago when she woke me up in the middle of the night just to share with me how spicy her steamed fish was. I was thrilled to hear from her and how she was slowly but surely getting the hang of it. She told me the contract would most likely keep her in China for another two weeks or so. But if she could wrap it up quickly, she would be back in a week.

Music to my ears, I thought.

The pile of mail on my desk caught my attention. From one of the envelopes on top, I clearly identified a name I hadn't heard of in a long, long time. I pushed myself forward, picked up the envelope, and focused on the sender's name. Marie, as I recall, was married to Uncle Jimmy, my father's brother. The last time

I saw Uncle Jimmy was at his wedding in Anchorage, Alaska. I remember it well; it was just before I graduated from Annapolis.

I was intrigued; I wanted to know more. My uncle was not the type of person I could call a family man. He kept a distance from all of us, even my dad. Uncle Jimmy was what I called a lonely soul. Even after he married, he didn't want children, and although his passion was flying and dancing with the clouds, the rest of the little time he had was spent alone in the wilderness hunting, fishing, or just glancing at the stars in the middle of nowhere. As I recalled, Aunt Marie didn't care much, as they were in love, and my guess was this still was the case; I could imagine them nearly twenty-five years later, still holding hands.

I opened the envelope and slowly pulled out a well-folded, single-page letter. I glanced inside the envelope, but apart from the letter, it was completely empty. After dropping it on the desk, I started to read it:

Dear Jack,

Hope that these short lines find you well.

I know that we haven't talked to each other in a while, and I recognize that this is my fault. At this time, I will ask you to keep our past from preventing you from completely reading this letter without tossing it away first.

It is unfortunate of me to say that your uncle is in trouble, and I have no one else to turn to for help. The last few weeks, he has not been himself, and I don't know what is happening to him; he is not the man I married. I am afraid that he may be in real danger and fear for our lives ...

I didn't know what to think. Given all these years without a word, my mind was running at a hundred miles an hour. I felt like it was trying to put together a huge puzzle at the speed of light, but none of the pieces seemed to fit.

Uncle Jimmy was a professional pilot. I can still hear Uncle Jimmy narrating stories about operation Rolling Thunder in 1965. He was one of the first F-11 pilots out of the Seventh Fleet carrier who dropped countless ordinances on Vietnam. Uncle Jimmy's face would change each time he told his stories. It was like he was there once again, living each and every moment.

I could hear him saying, "Yep, you bet, after many preparations, high hopes, and huge confidence we lifted from the Seventh Fleet carriers in our new F-4 Phantom II multirole fighters. We were not the only ones who wanted air supremacy; the Soviets tested their MiG-21 interceptors against ours, and in the end, the Soviets had to rethink their engineering to keep Kremlin opinions from thinking that their MiG-21 was a very expensive mistake. These guys had no chance against our F-4. I tell ya, boy, even with the F-4's disadvantage of displaying black smoke from its roaring engines, during this campaign, the F-4 fighter pilots shut down eighteen out of fifty-five Russian MiG-21s that came to say hello."

His passion changed, and at times, I'd catch a glimpse of him dropping a tear over the face of defeat when he'd mention that none of the three objectives of this campaign had ever been achieved.

I would ask Uncle Jimmy what he meant that the three objectives were never achieved, and he'd look at me and say, "Jack boy, when we rolled into Southeast Asia, we had three objectives in mind—to boost the South Vietnamese morale, which was at an all-time low; to show the North that the South was determined; and to persuade the communists of the north to cease their support to the insurgency in the South. But we did not achieve any of those either, hear, boy? None!"

It took me several years to learn what Uncle Jimmy wanted to say to me over and over every single time he narrated this story. But when I became a man, wiser and taller, I remembered that it is not the amount of thunder and roars you make trying to achieve your goals but that determination, strategy, and patience are the true principles of success.

My uncle was a man of integrity, strong spirit, and valor. The Uncle Jimmy I remembered would never be what Aunt Marie described. He was a strong man, with deep convictions and lots of determination. The Uncle Jimmy I knew didn't know the words *can't*, *afraid*, or *never*. He was one of the most interesting people I had ever met and yet one of the most kind and gentle people of all. Something was wrong, very wrong, and I was determined to find out for old time's sake what it was. I would not dare to let my own blood, much less a veteran in need, hang in the wind. After the war Uncle Jimmy became an aircraft mechanic and then moved to Alaska, where for sure he thought he would be able to have it his way.

The moment I picked up the envelope from my desk, I knew that I was about to enter into waters I should have avoided sailing. But my loyalty to family blood was stronger than my gut feeling.

My uncle liked the wilderness, airplanes, and being away from the family. I'd always thought that he liked to be alone after witnessing the atrocities of war, and I kind of understood and respected that. The last thing that I remembered from Uncle Jimmy was that he was working at Anchorage Alaska Airport, but his address was from yet another town called Nome, Alaska.

I checked my caseload and decided that I could easily take a week or two to visit America's wilderness and still return in time to follow up a very mysterious theft case from Kindler & Carper Company Inc., which was begging for my attention.

Jim Butler, Kindler & Carper Company Inc.'s CEO, had called me a couple of days prior and shared with me that he thought that his chief financial officer was stealing from him. But every time the firm audited the vault, all the sheets somehow balanced and all was in order.

Butler indicated to me that he trusted his CFO, who was a good man and friend, but somehow his friend's recent behavior was giving him enough suspicions to believe that the CFO was on to something shady. So my contract was to prove it.

Piece of cake, I thought because this is a classic case of hide-and-seek, and in doing so, I was the best. But for now, blood was boiling harder than money, and I had to make some travel arrangements.

***

It was now 8:10 a.m., and the plane was reaching cruising altitude. Next to me was a very interesting old businesswoman from New York. The gracious flight attendant gave me a warm mixed nuts cup with a chilled cup of white wine. I was doing well, until the pilot announced that he was expecting a little turbulence and we should keep the seat belts on. All of a sudden, I stared to ponder how I'd gotten here.

I recalled calling Ms. Montgomery at the travel agency on the first floor below my office, and after back-and-forth negotiations, she'd booked me on the next flight out, leaving at 8:10 the next day.

Suddenly, I found myself smiling as I recalled last night's events at Tony's Club. Sheela Madison's performance was, once again, spectacular. Even Tony, my trusted protector, father figure, and friend, had stood still in a corner watching Sheela as she performed like the diva she was.

My thoughts were interrupted by a sudden bump caused by the turbulence. Now I was back to reality; the old lady next to me started to tell me her life story.

What the heck? I thought. *I have a lot of time to kill.*

I glanced at the stewardess, lifted up my now-empty cup, and saw that she understood the message loud and clear; from now until the end of the flight, she had a mission, and it was to keep my cup full of the tasty spirit at all times.

***

Marie was leaving the sheriff's office again, after speaking to him about Jimmy's situation, but again she was disappointed by the town's Sheriff Michael Lindblom who, as usual, had brushed her off with his typical phrase, *"Don't worry, Marie. Give time a chance. You'll see that all is going to work out."* As always, Marie placed her trust with the local authorities, but she knew that, in spite of the sheriff's good intentions and thoughts, she was sure her husband was in trouble. Sheriff Lindblom was a good neighbor and friend to most of the local citizens, but he was also a politician, and as such, everything he did revolved around this trait.

Sheriff Michael Lindblom was a true Swede descendant; his heritage line went as far as the first settlers of the town. He was a tall, white-haired, bearded man with broad shoulders and medium build. His presence was well noted everywhere he went. His uniform was always pressed, and many said that, if you touched one of his shirts' creases, you would cut your finger from the sharp lines.

The sheriff's family used to own half the town, before they slowly lost interest and moved out after the gold rush. But those who stayed felt the obligation to also police it. The story went that, back in 1898, three adventurous gold seekers found their dream in Anvil Creek. One of them was a young Swede called Erik Lindblom, the sheriff's family's ancestor.

From those three original settlers, Nome, Alaska, had grown to be a beautiful, four-thousand-resident regional hub. This remote little town could only be reached by boat or airplane, but both tourists and residents preferred the main and faster way to get there, which was by airplane. To this day, the two main industries were gold mining and tourism.

Nome was a vintage little town that Marie had learned to love. When she and Jimmy had originally moved there, it was all about Jimmy's job. He'd finally found a place where he could do what he loved—fly, fix planes, and hike the wilderness of pristine, untouched country. He was in heaven, and so he reminded Marie all the time.

As Marie stepped off the front porch of Nome's sheriff's department, in her heart, she knew that something was very wrong with her Jimmy. She had learned to tolerate, nurture, love, and care for him for too long, and she knew that he was not the same. Although he continued to come home every day, he was not the same lucid, talkative, caring man she used to know.

Jimmy was withdrawn, and at first, she'd thought that he might have been having an affair. However, after extensive inquiries and doing what every woman knows how to do best, she realized that what was happening to him was not external but, rather, internal. She reached her old, rusted Ford Bronco, and out of hope, drove back to her log cabin to prepare supper for a man who was unknown to her—a man who was no longer the person she'd fallen in love with. She was going to prepare dinner for a total stranger, and that bothered her the most. She knew that Jimmy was in trouble, that something had overtaken him, but what it was had haunted her for over six long months.

Back home, Marie stood at the counter, a knife in her hand, an onion on the cutting board. She gripped the handle of the knife harder and harder as she thought about her husband, how he had changed over the past months. She didn't know what was wrong, only that something was definitely not right—not right at all. Slowly, she began to methodically cut the onion into little slivers that made her eyes water.

That night, as she prepared a nice grilled deer steak, she recalled all the good times she and Jimmy had had together as two young lovers arriving in unchartered territory without money or any belongings. The only things they'd owned they'd carried inside their backpacks. However, they hadn't felt poor, as they were rich with love, purpose, and hope.

Jimmy was so eager to enjoy the opportunity of flying every day between Anchorage and Nome that nothing else really mattered. Marie was so content to have him all to herself in a place away from wars, away from the hurdles of a big metropolis and a place that gave her what she wanted—a place to start from scratch. Here, they could build and plan their lives as they wanted and not as the family would have engineered for them.

She'd thought in terms of *engineered for them* because Marie's family was as wealthy as royalty. They came from a silver-spoon cradle. Her grandfather was a self-made millionaire who'd made his millions during the California Gold Rush, where he'd established himself as the gatekeeper for most of the gold claims.

One of his many sons and Marie's father, Arthur Slenker, was grandfathered into the family business, taking over his father's legacy.

Marie didn't know hardships or hunger. She'd had all her heart's desires and was the only female sibling.

At least Marie had had it all until she'd come of age and her mother had wanted to arrange her marriage to a Californian oil tycoon. Any other young woman of her age would have jumped in the relationship as a gift from heaven, but not Marie.

Marie was well educated and not an airhead as many other young girls of her age. She had her own will, and no one was going to run her life. Given her deep regard for her father, mother, and brothers, she made several attempts to change her family's minds. Sadly, in spite of those attempts, the family remained certain, and she eventually realized that all her efforts were futile. She had to change strategies, and at this time her only option was to escape as far as she could from her dominating and wealthy family.

One Monday morning, she said good-bye to everyone. But this was the day she emptied her bank account and ran as far as possible from her well-meaning but overbearing family. It was like an adventure she'd never before had; to her, it felt as if she was breathing air for the very first time.

Marie hired a boat to Anchorage, and off she went. While walking the boat's top deck, she felt for the very first time in a long, long while that she was able to smell the air; she noticed the many shades of the sea and could really enjoy looking at the shapes of the clouds. At last Marie was free, but deep in her heart, she knew that, in spite of her heroic and foolish efforts to stay away from her family, her father was never ever going to leave her alone. The trip to Anchorage was long and tedious to say the least even though the crew in the boat she'd hired, who were all fishermen, behaved like gentlemen in front of her.

The boat she hired was an old crab-fishing boat—the perfect getaway if you wanted to keep under the radar and also if you wanted no one to know where you were. The trip was a bit rough for her taste, but the feeling of freedom was, by far, worth it. Upon leaving the boat, she took some advice from the captain to stay away from certain areas she as a lone woman should never visit. But the captain also gave her the name of a place where she could find help in case she needed it—a bed-and-breakfast near the pier; there, he assured her, she could always find refuge.

As the deer steak slowly cooked on the grill, Marie continued to remember how she'd gotten to Nome and how much Jimmy meant to her. She recalled that, without hesitation, she'd headed for a small bed-and-breakfast and registered under the name of her grandmother, Georgina Slenker.

She'd paid cash and also told the innkeeper that her husband would be joining her soon. With very little luggage to carry with her, Marie went up the stairs to a small and dirty room. She placed her luggage on the table and walked over to the window and peaked outside. As far as her eyes could see, there was nothing but desolate streets full of trash Dumpsters and a couple of homeless Dumpster divers attempting to find something to eat.

For the first time in a long, long time, Marie felt alone and helpless; for a moment, she realized the huge mistake leaving her home had been. But deep within her heart, Marie also understood that liberty had a price, and if being lonely was her cost for freedom, she was all right with that and was willing to give it a try.

That night, Marie felt hungry, and she put on a pair of jeans and a coat and walked down from her room to the street, looking for a place to eat. She was frightened by the dark streets near the pier and also the fact that nearly no one was around. She turned to a street and saw a sign that gave her hope. It said, "Pizza & Pub." She'd started heading to the place when she noticed some noise behind her.

Marie turned back and noticed two men following her. She stepped up her pace, and finally, she made it to the pub, which she entered and quickly found a seat. She looked back and saw the two men no more and, with relief, ordered her dinner. When it was time for her to leave, it was already past 9:00 p.m.; she paid the waiter and waited for a couple of backpackers to leave going in her direction and followed them closely.

Marie constantly looked back for the two men but was happy to learn that they were gone.

The backpackers turned left on Beech Lane, and she found herself once again alone. Marie stepped up her pace, and soon she saw the bed-and-breakfast and went in as quickly as possible. Upon entering, she did not see the front-desk attendant, an old, white-haired Alaskan man who, to her quick assessment, had probably done this job since his youth.

Marie continued on to her room, entered, and closed the door. She walked over to the restroom, and she froze in her tracks. One of the two men who were following her was

11

waiting for her in her restroom. She closed the door and turned back and landed in the hands of the second man. She was terrified as she struggled as much as she could to get away. During her attempt to run away, she bumped into the night table, and the lamp fell to the floor and broke in pieces.

She then tried to grab the phone in an attempt to strike one of her attackers on the head, but her effort was futile, as the attacker overpowered her and took the phone away from her, throwing it so hard against the wall that it left a hole in the drywall. Marie tried to scream, but one of her attackers had placed his hand over her lips and prevented her from alerting anyone. In her mind, she was doomed, and at this time, she realized that her odds of coming out of this ordeal alive were reducing by the second.

Marie turned the steaks over and, having finished cutting the onion, scraped the onion bits into a bowl next to the cutting board. She sighed, trying to shoo away the memories of the night she was attacked within hours after arriving in Anchorage. She could feel the man's hand clamped down hard over her mouth. She could taste his skin, smell his body odor, and feel the hard muscles of his chest as he pulled her close from behind. She trembled with anger and hatred. Even though the horror was long over, the sheer emotional impact of what had happened remained fresh in her mind, as if the man and his friend had tried to rape her only moments ago.

Marie tried to shake the memories away from her mind, but as she stared at the smelly smoke emanating from the steaks, the ugly memories she now called nightmares came back to her mind again.

She recalled being tied up to the bed frame with one of her attackers' belts. The left side of her face felt swollen and in pain. Next, the second men ripped her coat off like it was butter to a hot knife; she could see their faces full of lust and rage.

One of the men took the jacket away from her with a skill

that only told her that he had done this many times before. The second assailant pulled out a pocketknife, and she felt her delicate silk blouse slashed to pieces. She struggled as much as she could, but every time she tried to stir away from the hands of her assailants, she felt the cold, sharp blade push harder into her throat.

Marie did her best to prevent her fragile body from going through this violent hardship. But soon, her will was broken, and she found herself not able to fight anymore. In her mind, this rude awakening to reality gave way to darkening the last hope of mercy to herself. In her mind, the word *horror* was beginning to have another meaning; she no longer fought; she no longer felt; the only thing she wanted now was to end it all, and she found herself wanting to feel the hard, cold blade slash her soul from her mutilated body once and for all.

Her eyes were no longer asking for mercy but rather fixed on the discolored ceiling paint. Marie felt her eyes wet. They were not sharp anymore; a blurry sight inundated her spirit like a way to block the pain, as the savage thrust of the first attacker was giving way to an end. She realized that her blurry eyes were caused by the pool of tears coming out of her eyes. In a way, Marie found some comfort in not having to clearly see the rough faces of her attackers anymore.

She found comfort knowing that her last moments alive would turn into a blurry reminder of such a nightmare. As the first attacker found his satisfaction, the second man slowly fixed his eyes on such a beautiful bounty and started to drop down his pants when, all of a sudden, a loud noise interrupted the ritual and the old, stained room door was ripped in pieces, giving way to her salvation.

A determined man, with fire in his eyes and without mercy, discharged all his hate, rage, and violence on the two men inside the room. The first one received a deadly stroke on his nose that killed him right away, while the second man could barely move, given that his pants were halfway down his legs, and this one received a punishment far worse than the second.

Marie tried to focus on the action, but her body had given way already, and her vision remained blurry. She could see two dark silhouettes bouncing from wall to wall as noises of pain and splashes of blood inundated the room.

Marie finally was able to focus her vision as glimpses of hope started to flourish through her painful thoughts. She noticed that the stranger was hitting the face of the second attacker over and over until the second attacker no longer moved. Marie was almost in shock, and as she saw the stranger getting closer, her fear took over and she fainted into the dark.

Two days later, she awoke in the Alaska State Hospital. Upon waking up, she tried to fight back as if she was still under attack. Marie tried to take off the IV on her left arm, as she only wanted to run away from her hospital room. But a man in the room held her down to the bed, while a nurse gave her a sedative that relaxed her, surrendering her body to rest back in bed.

She remembered that, a couple of hours later, she slowly opened her eyes to see a man seated next to her. The man's face was soft and easy; he was looking at her with kindness, and his look gave her comfort. For the very first time after leaving her home, she felt safe. Marie took a few minutes to internalize what was going on around her, and she felt comfortable for a couple of minutes until her horrific ordeal came alive. The man next to her held her hand gently and tried to calm her down.

She would never forget the kind words this man said to her: "I am here now. Don't you worry; nothing bad will ever happen to you again. I am here for you."

At this moment, Marie had a very hard time talking; deep inside her heart, she felt dirty, deeply hurt, and helpless.

This was the first time in her life that something so devious and violent had ever happened to her. She was always protected by her family, and she'd grown up without discomforts, hardships, or pain. She had entered a phase of her life that was new to her; she was experiencing a rude awakening in another part of life that she didn't know, another part of life she didn't want, and yet was living every moment of it without warning and alone.

Marie suddenly awakened from her thoughts to the smell of burning flesh from the grill. She immediately pulled the deer steaks out from the grill, preventing dinner from charring by a few seconds. She guessed that her Jimmy would have to eat his deer steak well done tonight.

From what Marie remembered and was told by the hospital staff, Jimmy Steele was the man holding her hand while she was lying unconscious in bed. Jimmy had stood right next to her from the moment he'd brought her in until both walked away from the hospital two weeks later, and this was how the story went.

Jimmy had later told Marie how he'd known that she was in trouble. Upon arriving in Anchorage, Uncle Jimmy had found a bed-and-breakfast close to the airport and rented a room until he could get his bearing and make his mind on what it was he wanted to do next. Lucky for Marie, the place he'd chosen happened to be the same place where Marie was staying.

Right before Marie was attacked, Jimmy was returning to the bed-and-breakfast from the grocery store. As he passed by the lobby, he failed to see the old man standing behind the front desk. He had been there for a week, and it didn't matter time or day; someone was always there until 11:00 p.m., available for the guests. After eleven, there was a black and white sign that said, "For service call 555-56-5500." But when he passed by the desk, he saw no one and no sign, and the "trouble" light inside of his brain lit up.

Following this, he walked to his floor to see two thugs hovering in the hall. They didn't make eye contact with him, and they looked like they didn't belong. But to Jimmy, if they didn't bother him, he would not bother them, so he walked past them and entered the room past where they were standing.

Uncle Jimmy placed his groceries down and sat down and turned on his television set, but the sense you get under your skin when something is wrong bothered him so much that he walked outside the room and sprinted down the stairs. He opened the door leading to the small front-desk office and found the old man lying on the floor with blood dripping from his head.

Jimmy pulled the battered attendant up and tried to wake the man. Shortly thereafter, the innkeeper gained consciousness and told him that two men had forced him to give away the room of the young lady staying upstairs. Jimmy asked him to call the police, and with rage in his blood, ran upstairs to Marie's room.

Upon arrival, he heard through the door the noise that clearly identified the acts of violence taking place inside the room. This was more than enough for him to break the door down and put an end to it right away, even if it cost him his life.

Marie eventually recovered from her ordeal. After she was released from the hospital, Jimmy never ever left her alone. He became her protector; her confident; and subsequently, her lover. Marie told him once that his soft eyes, warm personality, and humanity won her heart after he told her in the hospital, "Nothing bad will ever happen to you again."

2

LOSS OF FATE

Upon entering the house, Jimmy Steele found that all doors and windows were wide open; the strong smell of charred steak inundated the house. Once again, as always, he was greeted with, "Hi, honey. How was your day?"

"Fine," said Jimmy.

"Are you hungry? Dinner is ready."

"Fine," he said again.

Jimmy didn't have to ask what was for dinner, as the intense smell he'd learned to recognize was clear enough for him. Although he noticed that he had not recently been as talkative as in the past, in his mind he felt his actions were as normal as taking a shower before going to bed.

Jimmy sat at the table and, without saying a word, started to eat dinner; he was hungry. As Jimmy ate his meal, he glanced at Marie, who took the opportunity to start asking questions. All the questions she asked were about his behavior. Jimmy saw no reason for the questions, as deep inside him, nothing had changed. He was just tired and focused on his job. But his wife, Marie, appeared to be uneasy, as he could clearly define through her puzzled face. Upon finishing, Jimmy stood up and walked away to take a shower and then went straight to bed.

In the morning, his wife prepared him breakfast and a takeout lunch before he left. To him this was normal—a routine he'd learned to live since he married Marie. What bothered him was that his wife, all of a sudden, was asking questions, making comments, and behaving as if something was wrong with him. The constant questioning bothered him. However, he felt that her allegations and questions about his behavior were overrated and unfounded.

Deep inside, he also worried that he may be getting sick, like many of the other residents of Nome he used to know. He felt no sickness, had no symptoms; he was fine. However, he did recognize that many other people in town had felt sick only just before ending in tragedy, either by taking their lives or dying in mysterious ways. But not him. He was fine, and the thought that nothing like that would ever happen to him was soothing. He ate his breakfast, took his lunch, said good-bye to his wife, and just drove away as he always did, toward his office.

***

"Jimmy, so good to see you again. How are you feeling today?" asked Seward Soule, his direct supervisor at the Nome Airport.

"Just like an old mukluk—no more, no less," said Jimmy.

"I know the feeling," said Seward. "Hey, Jimmy, are you still taking that gig Galway offered you way back?"

"Are you kidding? I wouldn't pass that one up for all the gold in Alaska. I couldn't pass up the opportunity to get behind the controls of old CM," said Jimmy, looking up to see the red-and-white aircraft, his pride and joy, resting inside the hangar at Nome, private fixed-base operator (FBO).

The Martin Mars was the one of the five original planes copied from a navy prototype that flew countless successful missions throughout the Pacific Islands during World War II. Most of the planes were destroyed, and so was the Caroline

Mars almost lost in 1962 by Typhoon Freed off the coast of the Marshall Islands.

The Caroline Mars was later recovered by a private company out of British Columbia, Canada, and rebuilt as a passenger plane, imitating the splendor of its predecessor constructed by Glen L. Martin Company called the PMB Mariner patrol prototype XPB2M-1Mars. This plane was very successful during World War II, ferrying troops to the Pacific theatre. The Caroline Mars was powered by 3,000-hp Pratt & Whitney R-4360 engines. In 1949, this beauty set a world record by flying 269 passengers from San Diego to Alameda, California.

Now restored to its original beauty, it was the official dignitary transport from Anchorage to Nome, Alaska, and Jimmy was its official mechanic, historian, and pilot. "If you have to travel to the ends of the world, do it in style." That was the company motto scribed large enough that you could read it right above the plane's hangar doors. In a place you could get to either by plane or boat, having the luxury of both at the same time was a no-brainer. Jimmy had flown many VIPs through his tenure in Nome, and flying old CM was never a burden to him. He knew that, if a VIP was flying in or out of Nome, CM was the most likely choice of travel, and the most qualified pilot was Jimmy Steele. It was his game, and no one was going to take this away from him—no one.

Jimmy turned to Soule and, after shaking his head, continued with his daily chores, which needless to say were many; not too many aircraft mechanics liked to work in a cold and desolated Nordic environment. Jimmy sat down for a moment and looked at the desk calendar, which was on top of his desk. He then looked very closely at a date circled with red ink and lost his thoughts. Soule, who was working at his office, walked nearly sixty feet to shake Jimmy awake.

"Jimmy, Jimmy, are you all right?"

"What are you talking about?" asked Jimmy.

"Well, for one, I don't pay you to daydream on the job?"

"What are you talking about, Soule?"

"You have been staring at that calendar for nearly ten minutes! What's up with you? Are you daydreaming again?"

"No, I'm fine. I just looked down for a minute, and I was blank! But it was just a minute, no more than that," said Jimmy.

"No, no, my friend. I counted ten entire minutes. I thought you had a heart attack ... for crying out loud!"

"I am good, Soule, not to worry about me. I am fine. Thanks for the heads-up."

"Heads-up? I tell you heads-up. We handle delicate work here, Jimmy. I don't even have to tell you that. Be careful, take some time, and go see Dr. Anderson. He is very good with this kind of thing, you know."

"Soule, I don't need a doctor. What I need is to get back to work."

Jimmy stood up and walked outside of the hangar. He raised his hand, took off his Alaskan beanie headgear, and slowly scratched his bald head, and whispered out loud, "What has happened to you lately, Jimmy? What is going in on with you, old friend?"

Jimmy stopped right outside the hangar doors and sat on a pile of wooden pallets. His hands were shaking, and his nose bleeding. He was as scared as a deer who just realized that he was in the crosshairs of a hunter's carbine. He felt a sudden urge to go to the local bar and have a cold, white-dressed, made-in-Alaska amber beer. Jimmy dropped his stained, oily rag and headed down to the airport liquor front store to quench his sudden urge.

Shortly after his arrival, Jimmy walked over to the bar and asked Boyd for an Alaskan Amber. Jimmy grabbed the cold, moist bottle, opened it without hesitation, and quickly placed the bottle to his mouth, smelling the spirit and feeling the soothing cold on his lips. He tilted the bottle up, allowing

20

the sparkling liquid to find its way into his belly in a couple of large gulps. The local patrons stopped what they were doing to see how a real man drank Alaskan beer, and all of them clapped their hands, congratulating and cheering.

But to Jimmy's despair, the shaking of his hands and his worries and recent distractions were not going away, no matter how many Alaskan Ambers he drank. Suddenly, he noticed, to his right, a heavily dressed man with a white hat who was sitting at the back of the room, and without hesitation, Jimmy joined the man at his private table. For Jimmy, that was all he remembered; and then it was night, and he found himself opening the front door at his home.

***

Behind the bar, Boyd, bartender and owner, had run this operation for a long, long time. He was not a native from Nome. Boyd had come from Canada eleven years ago when his grandfather, Aston, had died, leaving him the bar and all his properties, which included a gold mine claim that Boyd had never visited. He had seen too many people losing all they had in the mining business, and mining was not one of his priorities, at least not for now.

Aston, Boyd's grandfather, had been in the bar business for a long time and decided to move to Nome, Alaska, when he turned fifty. He bought a small pizza joint and converted it into what it is today. His grandson was the only relative old Aston had, and when he died the only living relative was the sole owner of all his land, properties, and a bar. Upon being notified of his grandfather's death, Boyd, who was a hustler in Vancouver, immediately bought a ticket to Nome and had remained there ever since.

Boyd had inherited the bar and, with it, "the hole"—a set of secret rooms located three floors under his bar. As far as he could remember, he did not have any recollection of how

21

the hole had come to be—who'd built it, who'd owned it, and how his grandfather had come to be the guardian of such an obscure and uncanny place. As far as Boyd was concerned, his curiosity was restrained as long as he had beer to serve; a place to sleep; and the steady, uninterrupted hush dough he received every first of the month.

Boyd had lost both parents in a plane crash and had been left to the mercy of his only relative—his grandfather, who could not stop him from roaming the Vancouver streets and hanging out with the town's many backpackers. When Boyd had come of age, Aston had left his grandson alone in Vancouver and had flown as far away from him as he could, to a place he hoped that young Boyd would never find him … That place was Nome, Alaska.

Young Boyd only cared for a quick buck and free money. When he occupied the bar, he noticed that, every single month, he found that his bar earnings grew by $50,000. Over the years, he figured out that this untraceable increase to his bank account came from the tenants in the hole, so he asked no questions and raised no hands. As long as the money continued to supplement the meager bar earnings, he would keep quiet. He blessed his grandfather and was happy to enjoy the fruits of the old man's life work.

No one was going to take that away from him; he was going to continue milking this cow as long as he could, even if, in the process, he would have to suffer some pain here and there. He was at peace with himself as long as "the means justified the end," and Boyd could live with that.

Boyd was ambitious and motivated by his primary love—money. As long as the price was right, he would look the other way, and as a hustler, he would never miss the opportunity to make a buck. This was his motto; it was his passion and his way of life. His charisma, street-smart attitude, and jovial personality all contributed toward his moneymaking mastermind.

Boyd was good at his game and enjoyed what he did, making him the ideal candidate to be Lindberg Research's test subjects' official recruiting master. Boyd's duties were simple; he would talk to his patrons and identify those who had no relatives, were just passing by, or were vagrants. Boyd would make his recommendations to the heavily dressed man, his untraceable extra monthly income would increase, and it was not his duty to question any further.

3

GLANCE OF HOPE

The conversation with the businesswoman was getting as old and tired as she was, and I couldn't wait for the flight to end. I looked at her, pretending to listen, but my mind was at Tony's.

I recalled entering the club's double doors and noticing that the dimmed lights and cigarette smoke made seeing what was going on around the room hard. However, even from where I stood, I could see that the place was full of well-dressed customers. After greeting my old friend at the door, I walked ahead toward my favorite table.

A spotlight at center stage illuminated the long, thick, red-velvet drape, indicating that Sheela was about to start her show. Chatter and sounds of clinking glassware inundated the place.

The bartender approached me and greeted me as usual with a kiss on my lips. *Oh, how I love this place.*

She complimented me on my night attire, which, needless to say, fit me as good as it looked; my light blue button-down shirt felt very comfortable under a navy-blue cotton suit. I had to hand it to her; she had good taste in men.

Next, she asked me if I wanted the night's special, which I loved very much. My answer was, "Yes, I'll have New York City's most famous fettuccine Alfredo," which later I drowned with my favorite Chilean white chilled wine, Marques de Casa Concha 2009 Chardonnay. I was not in a hurry, so I took the time to smell and taste and enjoyed the fresh smell of vanilla, kiwi fruit, apples, and pears that I tasted with each sip I took.

What I like about this particular wine is the fact that it is aged for eleven months in French oak. I enjoy the French oak in combination with the fruit and acidity in perfect harmony to produce a silky-bodied Chardonnay. Every time I taste it, I can feel the wood on the palate without it being too overbearing. The French do know how to make wine, and so do we, the Americans, as do the Chileans with their Casa Concha, which stands as a true testament of how far they have come in making the great juice of the gods.

Back in reality, the old lady was, by now, sound asleep; she'd apparently talked herself to exhaustion. I took the time to read all I needed to know about Nome, Alaska. One thing I was sure I had learned in the intelligence file back in the day when I was a naval intelligence officer was that you had to be well informed and aware of what it was you were dealing with and what was around you. So I had Googled and printed out all I needed to know about Nome before I'd left, and now, I had all the time I wanted to read about this fascinating piece of land.

***

Back in Washington, DC, young Danny, the vice president's personal aide, walked the corridors of the national observatory greeting staff as he made his way to the vice president's office. After greeting the Secret Service agent standing at the vice president's office door, he barged into the office with an agenda in his hand. "Mr. Vice President," he burst out, "allow me to revise your itinerary again." He looked at his boss briefly before continuing. "We are departing at zero six hundred hours from Washington on July third; we fly directly to Anchorage, where we are staying the night at the Millennium Hotel. And, Mr. Vice President, just as you like it, the Millennium is located on the shores of Lake Spenard, one mile away from the airport.

"Alaskan Governor McKenzie will meet you at the airport and have dinner with you before departing on the fourth to Nome. Local ground transportation will be provided by the governor. As you know, your Secret Service detachment will take care of the usual details. On the fourth, they will depart at ten hundred hours from Anchorage, and you will fly in style on the original Martin Mars plane, whose pilot is Jimmy Steele, a veteran from the Vietnam War. Think about the media saying, 'Vice President Farmer arrived at Nome in legendary World War II plane.'

"Forget about the Boeing C-32. You can fly the jet any day you want, but a unique and rare water landing in a vintage Martin Mars whose pilot is a Vietnam-era veteran is something else entirely. Just imagine this for a minute." Danny beamed at his boss. "Vice President Farmer supporting local veterans— whether in DC or in Nome, Alaska, Vice President Farmer walks the talk when it comes to supporting our American Veterans."

"Stop it, Danny, stop it. I feel your drift. Make it happen. We can always ask my pilot to follow the Martin Mars to Nome, just in case things don't work out, you know!"

"You got it, sir. I love the way you think."

"Let's continue with the itinerary, your arrival is expected to be around eleven hundred hours, and this gives you time to refresh at the airport lounge before you meet John Stafford, Nome City mayor, at the City Hall. Then you will be on your duties to present the trophies for first, second, and third places on the annual Fourth of July, twelve-and-a-half-mile run to and from Anvil Mountain. Mr. Vice President, any questions?" asked Danny.

"No, Danny," the VP replied, "but I am sure I will later on.

"To tell you the truth, Danny, I'd rather stick around DC

and watch the fireworks at the park rather than freeze my butt off in Alaska, you know!" he added.

"Yes, Mr. Vice President, but you promised Governor McKenzie … Do you remember, during the previous presidential campaign at the party headquarters?" said Danny.

"Yeah, yeah, I know, Danny, that I promised the Alaskan governor, but it was under the influence of one-too-many shots of vodka," said Vice President Farmer.

"Mr. Vice President, if I recall correctly, it was an ambush. There was no way to deny the offer when Governor McKenzie mentioned it in front of the party leaders, noting that you will be the first vice president in history to visit Nome, Alaska, the 'land of the last frontier.' What was it he said—that you'd be immortalized and become the city's most prominent visitor ever? And he went further to say that a statue may even be erected to commemorate this visit!"

"Yeah, yeah, Danny, I know. Politics as usual, don't you think?" remarked VP Farmer.

"Mr. Vice President, we all do what we have to do. Remember, you must give your people what they want," said Danny.

"And yet, Danny, the people must give us what we want in kind." VP Farmer paused for a second and looked pointedly at Danny, holding his gaze. "I like free enterprise. Don't you think so, Danny?"

Returning his boss's eye contact, Danny said loudly and clearly, "Indeed I do, Mr. Vice President, indeed I do."

Danny viewed his boss with admiration and was devoted to his service and to doing that service well. He was proud of the fact that Vice President Brad Farmer was selected for the position by the newly elected President William (Bill) Mitchell, who was the second-party option after the tragic death of the main presidential candidate, the late Hugh Lynderman. Vice President Brad Farmer was an honest, good, and feared politician.

They don't make them like this anymore, Danny thought.

The current GOP administration was about to launch a major offensive against stem-cell research, and the vice president was going to dedicate his term to enforcing the presidential campaign platform to push legislation and executive orders to prevent this type of research. Around the White House, a lot of speculation and rumors surrounding the shady and tragic death of former GOP candidate Hugh Lynderman still circulated.

Many dirty tongues are saying that he was a victim of an organization called Verum, that Lynderman overstepped his boundaries and hindered the interests of this corrupted and criminal organization, and that, because of his actions, he was killed. The newspapers were saying that Verum always strikes first and asks questions later, so on the issue of stem-cell research, both the president of the United States and his vice president were expecting heavy opposition from this lobbying group.

Verum was known to be the first and the best in all new profitable government projects, and unfortunately, Verum had let everyone know that it was pro-stem-cell research. Danny knew that the current administration would have to put a lot of resources behind this project and that, sooner or later, it would have to face this deadly and corrupted organization.

Danny had already confronted some of these lobbyists, as they'd already tried to buy the administration with countless bribe attempts, trade-offs, and intimidations, but his boss, VP Farmer, would not budge. Danny was afraid that his boss could face the same fate as Senator Lynderman once the new Verum chairman, Mark Jones, had extinguished all his options to bribe his way in and had no other recourse but to, let's say in fine words, "quietly and intelligently eliminate one of his obstacles called Vice President Brad Farmer."

Danny had the chilling thought that the VP traveling to a remote location like Nome, Alaska, was too tempting an opportunity, which Verum could not let pass. He speculated that Brad Farmer's death would most likely have to look like a tragic accident, so he could go away and be forgotten before he was buried away. Historically, this organization was very smart and clever; this was why it had been operating for so long without government intervention. And what it didn't own, it destroyed. This group didn't want investigative reporters, US Secret Service agents, or any other conspiracy theorists to find its north and create even more problems than they needed.

So Danny speculated that, if Verum's stronger arm was going to make an attempt against the VP's life, the organization would have to be quiet and swift—accomplishing the task in the best way, as Verum had done for decades.

The buzz in Washington and around organized crime snitches was that Mark Jones had given the word to eliminate obstacles that were preventing stem-cell research, that a plan was in motion, and that Verum Chairman Mark Jones always achieved what he set out to do. A multibillion organization like Verum would have the tools, the expertise, and the perfect plan to make it happen, and this made Danny feel uneasy.

Furthermore, and most alarming of all, the intelligence agencies agreed that billionaire Maynard James Lindberg, through his research company, was already lining up for stem-cell research mass production and that he was sanctioned by Jones.

These fears remained lurking in Danny's mind and would remain awake as long as this administration remained determined to stop stem-cell research. Danny knew that, and it was his duty to continue working under these conditions as if nothing would happen. He often took refuge in his work and trusted that his luck would not soon run out.

A LEAP OF TRUST

After a long flight, I left the comforts of a controlled environment in the plane for a chilly and cloudy day. The air was moist and damp, but it could have been worse. I was glad that I had let my blood dictate my feelings and had traveled to Alaska, rather than allowing my logic to rule and stay home and neglect Aunt Marie's request for help. After walking down to the gate, I could hear the native music getting louder and louder, and after a couple of turns, I could see a group of about six natives wearing their traditional local outfits while playing and dancing their local music; what a warm welcome to such a cold place.

I took a moment to acknowledge the group. Many other travelers also stopped to listen to their music and observe their dancing; it was a well-choreographed combination of movements and sounds that was subliminally enticing me to start dancing and stay for a while longer, but I had other, more pressing issues I had to attend to.

So without hesitation, I walked toward the luggage room to pick up my suitcase. On the way to the luggage room, I saw a number of animals on display in glass cages—from large, black grizzly bears to one of the tallest white polar bears, which to my conservative estimation, I would say was nearly ten feet high and weighed nearly nine hundred pounds. *What a wonder of nature*, I thought before continuing on my way down to the luggage room.

After retrieving my luggage, I looked for the hotel shuttle. I knew that Ms. Montgomery had booked me in the hotel closest to the airport. And a minute later, I spotted the Coast International Inn van. I was fortunate enough that the shuttle was waiting for me, and a few seconds later, I was on my way to the hotel. I was glad to feel that the heater was on, as it was kind of windy and chilly outside the terminal. After tipping the driver, I was outside the small hotel. In front of the porte cochere, I could see two large animal spirit totem poles. I was amazed by the architecture and colors. I entered the cozy lobby and headed toward the front desk, where I could see a beautiful native already smiling at me.

I approached her, and after I'd given her my last name, she said, "Mr. Steele, welcome to Anchorage. We have been expecting you. I take it you've had a very long day, so I took the liberty of upgrading you to a junior suite. I hope you don't mind?"

I immediately glanced at her nameplate and responded, "Well, Nukka, with this type of service, I guess I owe a world of gratitude to my travel agent, Ms. Montgomery!"

The front-desk attendant smiled at me once again.

"Well, doesn't Nukka mean little sister?"

"Ah yes, Mr. Steele, you know your language well," said Nukka with a smile.

While she was booking the room, I glanced at the bar and saw several continental tourists sipping their beers and talking out loud. Even a blind man could see that they were having a good time in a place far away from home.

"Here is your room number." Nukka pointed with her index finger. "If you need anything at all, please call me."

"Nukka, perhaps I will ... I am already tempted."

She opened those thick lips of hers into an ear-to-ear smile, as she knew that I'd understood and read between the lines. I was tired, so I went up to my room, with the intentions of taking a quick, cold shower and resting. I knew that, when I got up in the morning, it was going to be a long day.

***

Once again, Jimmy came downstairs to eat his breakfast; he looked like he'd had no sleep at all, with red eyes, bumpy under-eyes bags, and a slow pace. Marie didn't say anything; she loved him, and it was her duty to provide for him. But she was so afraid that some kind of harm would come to him or to her. While she prepared his lunch, she wondered where he spent so much time recently.

In the past six months, she had called work and been told that Jimmy had left earlier, but he was not home. Sheriff Lindblom told her that Jimmy was spending a lot of time at the Airport Liquor Front Store but offered no other explanation as to why Jimmy had suddenly chosen to spend time at the store drinking with his buddies rather than spending time with her at home as they used to.

Marie was still puzzled, and the worst of it, what bothered her most, was that there was nothing she could do to fix the situation. Feeling helpless was her worst enemy, and she hated living like this. "Here you go, darling, your lunch box. Shall I expect you at the same time tonight?"

"Of course, why wouldn't I be on time?" he replied. He then picked up his lunch and walked away. What he didn't realize was that, for the last six months, he had never returned home as usual; he'd lost sense of time. And that he would lose his way home was one of Marie's concerns.

Marie watched as Jimmy walked out to his SUV and drove away, not sure if she would see him again. She sat on the window seat and was drawn back in time six months. She remembered how Jimmy would always be home on time for dinner. He would bring her something special at least twice a week. Whether it was a simple love card or a nice gift from the airport, a post card, or even a candy, her Jimmy, she remembered, was a man of many details. Now it was a tragedy that the person she loved was slowly drifting away from her. "What in the world happened?" Marie said out loud. "Where is my Jimmy? Where is my love …?"

***

As early as I could, I went to the hotel restaurant for breakfast. I choose the buffet; I had no time to waste. It was a quick bite and then on with business. Private investigators don't have time to wait for orders a la carte when we are chasing someone or expected to move at any moment's time. I had gotten use to buffets at least when I was on the job, although Martha doesn't forgive me if I take buffets when I am with her. This is a no-no; she is about taking the time to enjoy the moment. For her, a meal is an experience, while for me, it's just food.

While eating my juicy pancakes with butter and honey, I spotted a subject who appeared to be out of place. This subject was not eating, ordering, or drinking. He was seated at a table pretending to read the morning paper. He was up to something, and I had to know; after all, I am a detective. And I like detecting things for my own good. I don't like surprises, and I knew that this subject in the corner table was up to no good. I didn't move my head, but with the corner of my eye, I picked and tried to identify his target.

Bingo—there it was. He was dead-centered on a briefcase that was left on a chair. I hated it when this happened; not even in Alaska can one have the chance to enjoy a hot meal without having to be worrying about one's briefcase being stolen. No matter, I just couldn't let this happen; so I checked the subject's escape route options and, voilà, he had no escape strategy that didn't require him to pass by my table. So I just waited to see if the shady subject would have the cojones to actually steal the briefcase. I finished my pancakes and drank my favorite cup of tea with brown sugar. And when I was halfway through my second cup, I saw that the subject had gained the courage to do it.

He took the only opportunity he had, which was waiting until both businessmen from the table stood up to replenish their plates. One went for more strawberry preserves across the room and the other for more fresh fruit at the buffet station, which was about ten feet away from the table. It was a matter of seconds before the subject stood up, put his coat over his right hand, and walked by the chair. He reached the table, picked up the briefcase, covered it with his coat, and walked away. It was brilliant; I had to hand it to him.

The thing is that I hate thieves, as they can ruin your day, especially when they take your business plans, corporate secrets, or just an old book you haven't fully read along with your briefcase. Either way, this crafty thief was not going to get away with it, not on my watch.

As the subject sped up his steps, he bumped into one of the chairs left halfway out at the small corridor between tables. The noise alerted both businessmen, but only the businessmen getting the jelly noticed the briefcase gone and yelled, "Stop that man. He is stealing my bag!"

Just as one of the businessmen shouted at the thief to stop, with the corner of my left eye, I saw the guy to my immediate left drawing what appeared to be a an automatic pistol. The adrenaline rush allowed me to flip my table over, which made the man with the briefcase stumble and fall to the floor. A shot rang out, echoing loudly in the small dining room. Hearing screams and shattering glass and the sound of running behind me, I rolled over on the floor, hoping I hadn't been hit, and in seconds, I was on my feet and charging the shooter to my left.

I saw surprise register on the guy's face as I slammed my right fist into his throat, causing him to drop the gun. I grabbed his neck. He made wet choking noises, and I decided to hit him again straight to his jaw to put him out of his misery. The second thief was already trying to stand up and was reaching for a weapon. Before the thief was able to aim his gun, I had picked up the weapon from the floor, aimed and shot twice; the only thing that followed was two bodies falling down to the floor.

The businessman at the fruit station immediately ran to attend to his friend, who had been shot. His actions told me that he had some previous experience handling this type of bloody situation. I immediately bent down and checked the shooter next to me; he was knocked out but alive. Then I moved over to where the thief was and checked him; he was still breathing. I pulled him close to me and asked him why, why he had to pull a gun on me.

He only said to me with his dying breath, "Eco Free First." And he expired, looking at me with a smile. *What a sick bastard*, I thought as I pulled the briefcase away from his hands.

I walked over to where the two businessmen were, and upon approaching, I could see the injured businessman was going to be all right. It was a clean, in-and-out shot, and his friend had already stopped the bleeding. Both of them thanked me emphatically. The injured businessmen looked at me and said, "Gee, mister, I owe you my life."

"What do you mean?" I asked.

At this time, hotel security came running to the restaurant, weapons blazing, and I said it was all right, that one of the shooters was dead and to secure the second one, who was still lying on the dining room floor, and to call the police right away. The security guards looked confused, but one of them drew his radio and started to call for help.

I looked around the restaurant. All other customers had run away as the first bullet was shot, and the place was empty. The only other people remaining in the restaurants were the stiff, sleeping beauty, the businessmen, me, and the cook behind the omelet station; at the time, I could only see his long, white hat starting to emerge from behind the grill.

The security officer came through the door with a first-aid kit and headed toward the two businessmen, asking for those not injured to step away. This was my cue to find out what the hell was going on and why stealing a briefcase involved such an elaborate plot. I pulled the non-injured businessmen to a corner and seriously asked him what was going on. He looked at my eyes and, dead serious, whispered to me, "Mister, we are doctors from the Centers for Disease Control and Prevention, the CDC. Thanks for your help, but now we need to go."

Rage came to me, and with both my hands, I grabbed the front of his manicured blue jacket and pulled his body hard toward me. His face must have been half an inch from mine, and I asked him one more time what was so important inside the briefcase that a man was lying dead on the floor. I could see from the fear in his eyes that he knew I meant business, and with my face one inch away from his, by now, he would have registered in his brain the seriousness of the moment.

The subject then hesitated; apparently he feared more what was in that case than my big, sweaty face so close to his. So I pulled the briefcase away from him and tried to open it; it had a combination sequence. I just looked at him like I meant business, and he spelled out, "two, nine, three, five, four, and two again."

I looked around before opening the briefcase and saw that the two security guards were preoccupied with the injured person. I slowly opened the case, which was well insulated and padded, and in the center were four vials that I recognized as trouble—not the kind of trouble you can get rid of right away but the kind of trouble that sticks with you and gets you killed. I looked closely and read the inscription:

"Lot 667, vial 233, CDC Spanish flu, active specimen."

I saw my life flash in front of me like I hadn't in a long

time. I could fight a man or a few with knifes, guns, and even swords, but bioweapons … I took a deep breath to calm myself down. Nothing I knew or had trained for could protect my old skin from the Spanish flu, so I closed the case and spun the combination. I looked at the geek in a suit and asked him why he had this deadly virus with him, and he looked straight into my eyes when he answered.

"What you saw in the briefcase are a couple of examples we are showing at a local convention. We are the keynote speakers at the bioweapons of mass destruction convention here in Anchorage, which is sponsored by the Alaskan Department of Health and Social Services," he said.

"Well, I guess that we owe you after saving our lives," he added, "but please don't tell anyone. And if you do, we'll deny it. Agreed?

"Now it all makes sense," I whispered to him. "The thief I shot, before he expired, said to me 'Eco Free First.'"

When I said this to the good doctor, his knees became weak, and I had to hold him in place.

"Are you sure that is what he said?" asked the doctor.

"Yes, that is what he told me," I responded.

The doctor thanked me, turned around, and started walking toward the door.

I held him by his shoulders and said to him, "Now you have to explain a little more to me."

And he responded, "Don't you see? Don't you get it? 'Eco Free First' is an organization made up of a bunch of crazy individuals who want to eliminate men off the face of the earth.

"Their goal is to allow earth to be reborn again. They want us dead, and if they had gotten their hands on these samples, they could have very well done so. I have to take this briefcase to a safe place. I'm sorry." And with that, he left in a hurry.

He didn't even tell me his name. Nor was I able to share mine. But who cares?

I glanced at the other businessman, who was well taken

care of by the trained security officers. As I look around, I saw it was time for me to fade away in the gray before the police arrived and wanted to take me downtown for further details. The police could get their story from the sleeping beauty and the injured doctor, who later would have all the time in the world to tell police all the details they wanted, as he'd just missed his keynote speaking opportunity. Today, I may have inadvertently saved half of the United States from suffering a slow and fatal death. If memory served me well, back in 1918, Spanish flu killed over 21.5 million people.

Now I saw the connection as to why this happened here in Alaska. If my mind served me well, I recalled a bio-weapons course I'd taken several years ago, in which I'd learned that old viruses have been considered by terrorists as bioweapons for mass murder. Among the potential viruses discussed was the Spanish flu. The story went that half a century ago, a retired pathologist, under the name of Johan Hultin, was able to retrieve samples of the virus from the lungs of dead victims, whose bodies had been preserved by the Alaskan permafrost at the village of Brevig on Alaska's Seward Peninsula. This is what the conference was all about—to prove that the virus had originally jumped from birds to humans. I wished them good luck, but if I was them, I would have had an armored car and hired a couple of guns for protection.

Even these amateurs were nearly able to steal the samples. God save us all if professionals knew that these two keynote speakers were bringing here the real McCoy.

I could hear the police sirens approaching and needed to get out of Dodge before they arrived. I had no time to waste in a downtown interrogation room. Well, so much for a quiet morning breakfast, but I had a plane to catch and had no time to wait spilling my guts to local law enforcement.

I walked outside the restaurant, and as I knew that the whole area was going to be a mess very soon, I walked two blocks away from the hotel to catch a cab to the airport.

Shortly thereafter, I was at the airport. I had to be careful; if Anchorage police and local FBI got wind of the real bioweapons' threat, they would close the airport and start looking for me to answer a few questions about the dead tree-hugger terrorist lying on a restaurant's floor. So I ditched my coat and bought a new one and a local hat that said, "I Love Alaska," or something of that sort. I looked like a tourist now.

I headed up to my gate, and all appeared to be normal. I guessed that, in small-town Anchorage, things didn't move as quickly as in NYC, for example.

I boarded a small commuter plane that took me to Nome. I looked and saw that there were no suits inside the plane—no ties and no briefcases, not even a first-class section. What I saw were a few youngsters and tourists, couples, and a one of the friendliest flight attendants I had ever encountered. I felt relaxed and in control. I was back in my game; my mind was working better than ever, and my instincts were as sharp as they could be.

I sat down, buckled up, and started reading a magazine article I found inside the front seat pocket, titled, "Things to Do in Nome, Alaska." After perusing the magazine, I noticed a pattern on every third page. I observed how a name kept on appearing in different ads. To my analytical mind, this told me a lot about Nome; someone was having all the fun, owning most of the town's important businesses.

The name *Lindberg* resonated in my mind like an alarm clock sound in the morning after trying to wake up with a hangover. I recognized at least seven town industries, which were owned or operated by the Lindberg subsidiaries—the Bank of Nome, the largest tourism agency, the Gold Exchange Corporation, and St. Francis Heritage, the main hospital in town, among others. In addition, the airport was leased to the town by the same person, and also Lindberg owned the fishing industry.

My mind was running at a hundred miles an hour. How was this possible? How could a single person own so much in this place. I knew that, somehow, it was inevitable that I would have to bump into one of the Lindberg family members while I was in town. I made some mental calculations to ensure that I did not forget the name of Maynard James Lindberg, which could come handy while I was there.

The flight attendant announced that it was time to pull the tables up and prepare for landing. I immediately looked out the window and enjoyed the beauty of this place.

Upon arrival, I didn't have to wait for my luggage, as it was unloaded from the plane right in front of me! Talk about efficiency. After securing my suitcase, I walked to the front terminal and hired a taxi. Believe it or not, it was not as cold as I expected. The average temperature was in the low fifties. *What a relief*, I thought because cold weather and I were not on the best of terms these days.

After I'd given the address to the taxi driver, he looked at me and said that he could see the resemblance.

I looked at him and said, "Come again?"

"Steele, right? You are going to Jimmy and Marie Steele's house aren't you?"

"Yes. How do you know?" I asked.

"Mister, there are only a few taxis in Nome, and this is a very small town. We know everyone. By the way, my name is Larry." He turned around and started driving out of the airport.

Larry drove the taxi on a road next to construction and then on to Center Creek Road; the view was fascinating. This is what I needed after a long day. He gave me the tourist treatment and drove a couple of roads until, finally, we yielded at Nome Bypass Road. I didn't know why he had chosen to give me the tourist treatment. Was it because I was visiting Uncle Jimmy or because of my "I Love Alaska" tourist hat? Either way, I was enjoying every moment of it. A couple of minutes of driving and we were at 12 Unalaklet Six Street.

Larry took me to a small but good-looking house. From the

41

taxi, I could see that the side stairs were covered by a rustic roof and the walls appeared to be a nice vanilla color. To my surprise, the house was lifted on wooden columns that stood at least four feet high. As a matter of fact, most of the houses I saw had been built this way. The house looked as if it were floating in air. I bet that, if I looked under it, I would be able to see through to the other side.

I waited inside the car while the driver pulled out my suitcase. I looked at Larry and asked him, "Larry, my friend, tell me something. Why are these houses lifted from the surface? Is it because of flooding or what?"

"Sir, in Alaska, the winters can be brutal, so to prevent the warmth of the interior from melting the snow and then converting it to ice, the builders prefer to keep the buildings high to prevent the ice from breaking the foundations."

I thanked Larry, gave him a big tip, and said good-bye to him.

Uncle Jimmy's narrow balcony out front was telling me that summers in Nome were short; no time to sit, sucking rays, sipping beers, and telling stories.

Before I was able to close my fist and knock on the door, Aunt Marie opened the door and hugged me hard. Her tears and worried eyes clearly told me how much she appreciated me coming. Her tight hug told me how desperate she was and that I was about the last chance she had for help.

I had grown old in body but clever in sensing, and this woman was living a proverbial hell. Although Aunty Marie was now about sixty years old, she looked as I remembered her twenty years ago—five eight, dirty blond, slender body, and nice female attributes. Her athletic-looking and marked Anglo northern features told me that time did slow down in Nome. She held me by the hands and pulled me inside the house. "Jack, my son, how good to see you. I have no—"

"You don't have to say anything," I interrupted. "I'm here to help you and Uncle Jimmy in any way I can."

"I am so relieved to see how much you have grown; you

are the pure image of your father, but you have your mother's eyes," said Marie.

"Come on, Auntie Marie. You are making me blush," I said.

"Nonsense, son. Here have a seat. Let me make you some hot tea. I know that you must be tired from your trip. Just relax for a minute, and I will be right with you."

As Marie left the living room, my analytical mind was already working at full speed. If I didn't know that I was in Nome, inside this home, I could very well mistaken this house for any other in the New York suburbs. Jimmy and Marie had a very nice, large, wood-burning fireplace, and I could tell that it has been used a lot. How many warm nights must they spend here reading a nice book or just playing a table game between two old love veterans?

I got up and walked close to the fireplace mantelpiece, where I could see several family photos. One was of my dad, Uncle Jimmy, and me at Coney Island, New York. I was holding a blue-colored cotton candy in my hands while standing in front of Dad and Jimmy. My dad was dressed in military uniform, and Uncle Jimmy wore a white polo with a golden plane propeller embroidered on the upper portion of his left pocket and a pair of khaki pants.

I remembered this day well. I'd had so much fun and had eaten so much that I was sick to my stomach for three days. But I'd loved every single minute that I got to spend with my dad and Uncle Jimmy.

To my immediate right, I could see a photo of my first birthday—in it, all the ones I loved were still alive and smiling—a moment captured in a single photo that had transcended time, family quarrels, divorces, and death. But every time I saw this piece of hidden history, it made me believe in the power of family values and togetherness. To my left, I could see high on the wall a 12-gauge double-barrel Remington shotgun. I had to hand it to Uncle Jimmy; he really knew how to muster trust and power in a single piece of equipment, whether it was a plane or a weapon.

The house felt cozy and warm; there was wood everywhere. I saw wooden floors, walls, and ceiling. The floor also came with the distinctive sound of screechy wood every time you took a step. When I looked to my left, I saw Aunt Marie approaching with tea.

I quickly sat and looked at her as if I've been waiting for her for a while. She was not stupid; she noticed all my moves. Perhaps I was getting too old, or she was still as sharp as a blade. She said, "Jack, those photos are what have kept me alive and well all these years. There is nothing stronger than the invisible force that unites families. The memories, the love, and the ability to quickly forgive one another are as strange as time itself but as much a comfort as water to the thirsty."

I looked at her with admiration. She was a world of wisdom and experience all by herself.

"And talking about that, here is your tea. If I recall, you take it straight, right? No sugar and no milk? Am I good or what?" said Marie.

I glanced at her eyes and replied, "As always, you are right again—although, these days, my old body is asking for some brown sugar once in a while," I added.

We laughed for a second as I sipped my tea, but things changed in a dime of time. Marie could not hold it anymore, and she opened up to me as she had never done before, spilling out her sorrows.

"Aunty Marie, I am here now; stop worrying about it and let me help. I promise I will get to the bottom of this, one way or another. Don't you worry. I am here for you—for both of you."

After listening to her and attempting to construct this difficult puzzle inside my head, I came to realize that her fears were not unfounded but that she had a genuine concern about Uncle Jimmy. And if her assumptions were right, Uncle Jimmy was in a lot of trouble. After a long conversation with her, I had enough information to start my inquiries. And my inquires would definitely have to start with a visit to Uncle Jimmy's shrink, Dr. Anderson, to find out specific behavioral pattern trends and how deep Jimmy was into his problems. From there, I would do what I do best—just follow my instincts. I still had a few hours left before Uncle Jimmy came home. I wanted to see him in a place where he had mastered himself, rather than off balance in another place completely unfamiliar or threatening to him. I wanted him to be at his best in all angles before I talked to him.

I asked Aunty Marie to stay home and to call me the minute Uncle Jimmy came home, if I wasn't back before dinner.

I took Marie's car and drove to Dr. Anderson's office; this town was easy to navigate and was too small for you to get lost. All the streets ran like those in any other US city— parallels, one up and one down—so I just interrogated the map, and in a matter of minutes, I was parking in front of the shrink's small office.

I entered and found several locals sitting in the waiting room. All of them appeared to be from different social class levels. To my left, I saw a nurse, a fireman, and what appeared to be a banker by the way he was dressed. To my right, I saw a local café employee and what appeared to be a city's public works worker. The shrink's walls were decorated with positive messages illustrated with photographs. To my right, I saw a large photo of the sea and, on the lower section of the photo, a phrase that read, "Seas can be treasonous but an experienced captain can still muster his vessel."

Next to it was another smaller frame, displaying a photo of a white polar bear floating on a small piece of ice and the message was, "To survive in life, use all available resources." On the other side was another photograph of a dogsled, and the message was loud and clear: "Teamwork." Enough of this psycho blah-blah shit; this sounded like brainwashing to me.

45

I wondered what was going on in this little town. And why did so many people need to be visiting a shrink?

These and many other questions were still lurking in my head when they were scared away by the receptionist, whose name on the desk plate read "Annie Ketcher." "May I help you Mister ... Steele?"

I said, "Jack Steele. I would like to see to Dr. Anderson if I can."

"Allow me to check his schedule ..." Annie looked at the computer with intensity and purpose before she told me that the next available appointment she had was in two weeks.

I told her that it was a matter of importance. I followed by saying that it was about seeking his professional opinion on a very special project that had to do with the mind and that it would only take him a few moments of his time.

She again, without looking at the computer, told me the same thing.

I was about to lose my patience when a tall, medium-built man with a long, white ponytail walked in and stepped in front of her and gently told me, "Good morning, Mr. Steele. I was expecting you!"

Ms. Ketcher stepped aside without a word and, without hesitation, allowed Dr. Anderson to take over. Deep inside, I was surprised by the way Dr. Anderson defused the situation but equally puzzled as to how he knew my name.

"Now what seems to be the problem?" the doctor asked.

"I wanted to talk to you about—"

"Say no more," interrupted Dr. Anderson. "Mr. Steele, please step into my office."

I was once again uncomfortable with the way Dr. Anderson was not only handling the situation but also handling me; this was something that I didn't like. I was a person who did not like surprises, and yet in my line of duty, surprises were something that I could count on. Dr. Anderson was as closed as a book that I had to open and scrutinize in detail if I wanted to find answers to my many questions.

We walked through a series of halls, and at the end of a long, stretched corridor, we entered a room that led to a very small and cozy office. On my way to the office, I made some mental notes about the building's layout and security features.

It didn't surprise me to see the usual "I-love-me" wall, when I entered his office. The wall behind his desk was full of medical certifications and university diplomas. This was not the thing that caused me concern; what caused me a lot of curiosity was the door that was located to the right of Dr. Anderson's desk.

Dr. Anderson continued to his chair and sat like any other professional would. But he also had an aura of confidence and mastery that was getting on my nerves. Perhaps it was the fact that I had never visited a shrink's office before. But I knew people; I had learned over the years to read people's behaviors and use this skill to my advantage. Today, it appeared that Dr. Anderson was able to read all mine and use that to his advantage. I sat down on a very comfortable couch, which, seconds later, felt as if it was swallowing me and holding me tightly in place.

Dr. Anderson looked directly at me and told me in a very soft and gentle way, "Mr. Steele, you are wondering why I know about you. You would like to know why I know your name. But also you would like to know why I insisted on talking to you now instead of having you wait for my next available time. Am I right, Mr. Steele?"

"You think that you are a very good shrink because you can even read people's mind, don't you?" I quipped, buying myself a moment.

"No, Mr. Steele. I wish that this was the case. Please allow me to explain. Nome is a very small town, and word on the street spreads very fast. You are not a tourist like many others but, rather, a family member visiting relatives. When you mentioned your last name to my assistant, I had to make an intelligent assumption that you are related to one of my very own patients who has the same last name. You are related to Mr. Jimmy Steele. Am I correct, Mr. Steele, or should I call you Jack?"

"You are doing well so far with Mr. Steele, thanks," I said.

"Very well, Mr. Steele. I'll do as you wish. You know, my patients and I have no secrets; this is one of my professional fundaments. What they know, I know so I can clinically evaluate their current states of mind and offer possible solutions to effectively manage their internal, shall we say, conflicts."

"Tell me, Dr. Anderson, do all the people who come to visit you have internal demons, or do they get them after your initial sessions?"

"Now let's not get ahead of ourselves, Mr. Steele," said Dr. Anderson.

"Dr. Anderson, it's fascinating that you appear to have all the answers. So let's see if you can start by answering a simple question that has been bothering me all along. Allow me to ask you why you were expelled from the department of psychiatry and bio-behavioral sciences at UCLA?" Before leaving the house, I'd spent some time on Marie's computer, Googling Dr. Anderson's background; after all, one doesn't just go face-to-face with the devil without first knowing something about hell.

Dr. Anderson's face changed from predator to prey in a matter of a second. He even shifted his eyes from me and looked at his desk and then at his I-love-me wall. I had touched a pressure point that Dr. Anderson was not prepared to argue.

Dr. Anderson looked down at his desk and then back to his I-love-me wall and said, "Well ... that's not the truth. I ... I ... was ..." He was dismantled by my question and looked as guilty as a little kid who'd been caught by his mother with his right hand in the cookie jar.

"You see, Dr. Anderson, I was not the only one who did

his homework. Just like you, I am a master in what I do. And you can relax. What happened at UCLA will stay there for all I care, but what is happening here is my concern. And I want to know what is happening with my Uncle Jimmy, yes, Jimmy Steele."

"Mr. Steele, do you know of the HIPAA privacy rule?"

I'd had it with this monkey in a white suit. I had no time for games. So I got up, walked around his desk, and got very close to him. "Look, Dr. Anderson, I've traveled far and have come here to look for answers."

The doctor looked at me and said, "I have come to terms with my UCLA dismissal. I am sorry I was so rude."

"UCLA is of no importance to me," I repeated. "What bother me are assholes like you who hide behind rules and medical regulations to get away with murder. I do know what HIPAA rules are, but as you may also know, I did not come two thousand miles to be lectured by you! What I came here to do is to find the truth about what is happening to my uncle and to this town.

"I'll tell you what, Dr. Anderson, sooner or later, I will find out the truth about your twisted mind games here. I'd rather you come clean and share what you know. Or I promise that I will have no mercy toward you when I find how you are implicated in this charade. I promise you that I will find out what is happening in this little town of yours, do you hear me?"

"Ha, yes, Mr. Steele, I understand you. Please leave my offices now ... Please know that I pose no threat to you, Mr. Steele," said the monkey in the white jacket.

I knew that I'd let my resolve take over, but when pukes like this tried to manipulate the system to get advantage over others and profit at the expense of the mentally ill like the people of this town, I just couldn't get a hold of myself. In a second, I realized that I'd overstepped my boundaries. The doctor was sweating, cold.

Annie Ketcher appeared to have heard the commotion and ran inside the room asking if everything was all right.

The good doctor told her that all was right and that I was leaving. She looked at me with a puzzled face but made no comments of any kind.

Before leaving the room, I told the good doctor that I was coming back for answers. I looked around the room and then back at him, and I saw how, in a microsecond, Dr. Anderson looked at the door to his right. I made no other gesture but said the right thing before I left: "I'll be back." As I left the room, my adrenaline was running high, and I swore I could feel smoke coming out of my ears.

Ms. Ketcher walked me all the way to the door and, with a forced smile, said out loud, "Have a nice day, Mr. Steele. See you next week."

At that moment, I did not know what her final words meant, but later I learned that this was the same phrase she told each and every one of the patients right before they left the room. It was a phrase that told all the others in the waiting room that everything was normal and that they would be expected back. Everyone who heard her expected me to come back the next week, but I had other plans—to come back later tonight when it was dark.

As I walked outside the doctor's office, I walked straight to Marie's car, a faint red, old Ford Bronco, which was parked on the street under a nice, large, and shady evergreen. All of a sudden, a black shadow in wheels accelerated toward me and almost ran me over. I jumped onto the sidewalk to prevent the demon driving the black pickup from making me a permanent addition to the cold, black asphalt.

By the time I recovered and tried to read the license plates, it was over. The demon driving the pickup was gone. *What a morning*, I thought. *I haven't even been in town for two hours, and someone wants me dead already? I think I have to work on my manners.*

My guts were telling me two things—that I was on the right track and (something I didn't want to hear) that it was near lunchtime and I had to have something to eat. So I drove back to town and stopped at a nice local diner called the Midnight Sun. I entered and found a seat where I could see both doors and the bar.

This place was like any other diner—old, worn-out, and simple. This was my kind of place. The chairs were made of wood but covered with plastic. I guessed that, during snow days, customers didn't want to sit on a wet seat. The tables were raw wood and stained with burger grease, pizza oil, and sauces. But I glanced at the food, and it matched the smell and sure looked inviting. The walls were covered with decorations from the sea. From where I was sitting, I could see old wooden items hanging on the wall. I also saw a ship's brass compass and a large ship's sail decorating the ceiling.

The rest of the decorations were photographs of gold miners, dating back to the town's foundation. The bar featured mostly local beers, but I'd bet that, if I wanted an imported beer, I could get it but it would cost me dearly. So I thought that I would just stick with the local flavor in the meantime. Everyone in the bar was minding his or her own business, and I thought that I would do the same.

After all, I'd had a hell of a first day. Since I'd arrived, I'd insulted a doctor, delayed the daily psychological therapies, and almost gotten squashed by a black pickup. Now that I was a lot more relaxed, I wondered if the pickup was an accident, a youngster joyriding, or a deliberate act to murder me. These circumstances affirmed my thoughts that I was on the right track—that someone with power, resources, and initiative didn't want me snooping around his business in town. But who?

All I wanted was to find the answers to the many questions lurking in my mind and, in the process, try to find out what was wrong with Uncle Jimmy. *Is that too much to ask?* I wondered. And if so, was there something going on in this town that was not only affecting Uncle Jimmy but also half of the town?

If I was not careful, I feared that I could be next. I had come here for answers, and I would get them, even if I had to steal, maim, or cheat.

5

EVIL LURKS

S pecial Agent Grant Landis, US Secret Service, lead agent for the vice president's detail, received a secure e-mail from VP Aide Danny Bedford detailing their intentions to visit Nome, Alaska, for the Anvil Run and Fourth of July speech. While working at his desk, Landis opened the e-mail and read all the details of the trip. In this brief, he also read a short intelligence briefing stating that the National Security Agency had picked up some chatter about a possible attempt on the vice president's life in Alaska.

Well, time to go back to work, he thought. He made a mental note to pack warm and some written notes and continued with his work.

Agent Landis came from a small family in Tennessee; he had one brother who was a US Air Force pilot and had died in Afghanistan supporting the fight against terrorism. Although his brother was not a fighter or bomber pilot, he was one of those pilots who flew pickups for special operations, under the disguise of a cargo plane. His brother's plane had been destroyed by a surface-to-air missile as he was leaving Afghan airspace to enter Pakistan six years ago.

As for Landis, he'd grown up in a small town outside Tennessee, gone to the UOT, and studied law. This is what his parents had wanted him to do, and as soon as he'd completed his degree, he'd returned home, handed his parents the college certificate proving that he'd become an attorney, and told them that he'd done what they wanted him to. He further said that now that he had followed his parents' wishes he could follow his true calling. He told both parents, while seated at the kitchen table and before walking out of the house, that his true calling was to protect the president of the United States.

With sadness in his eyes, his father had watched him leave, knowing that it was his doing that had forced the only son he had left to leave the safety of home to work in a risky and dangerous business. After losing his eldest son, Landis Senior did not want his wife, Simone, to suffer the hardships of losing not just another son but the only one they had left. So Landis Senior had planned his son's career away from a dangerous life.

Landis leaned back in his seat and let his mind wander. Soon, his thoughts ranged far back in his past, to when his dad had shown such ambivalence upon learning that he wanted to go into the Secret Service. Landis knew his dad's first marriage had suffered, in fact self-destructed, because he'd felt compelled to fight in Vietnam. Simone could not bear the thought of receiving two uniformed officers at her door telling her how sorry the secretary of the army was because her husband was dead.

So he'd sworn that he would not allow this to happen to Simone or their two sons. Unfortunately, Landis Senior could not keep his promise to Simone, as both of his sons had chosen for their careers fields of glory, instead of desks of boredom.

US Secret Service Agent Grant Landis had become one of the best agents in the academy, and during his tenure, he'd been able to challenge and change several teaching methods and processes that had been in place since the academy first opened its doors in 1865.

Immediately after joining the US Secret Service, Landis had met with lots of senior USS agents and had carefully planned his career path, following it to the point. He'd learned from the best, and he knew that his last step before reaching the position of lead agent for POTUS was completing this assignment as lead agent in charge of the protection of the vice president of the United States.

So far, his record was immaculate; his actions, many achievements, and attitude were true testaments of his chosen path to reach his dream. He just had to wait four more years until this VP assignment was over, so he could start his new job. He knew the incumbent on the POTUS detail was going to retire at the end of this cycle, and he had already applied for the position and gotten the blessing of the top brass. All he had to do was play the game for four more years, and he would be able to satisfy his childhood dream.

Secret Service Agent Landis looked as his watch and noticed that he had three more hours before landing. He checked his e-mails, noting that Agent McAllister was waiting for him and everything had the green light, so this was the only time that he had to relax a little bit. He knew that this trip would be hard, but to reach his goals, he would have to climb the ladder one step at a time. Although he didn't like to start a mission with such limited resources and the odds against him, in this particular case, he knew he'd have to swallow hard and do his job well and with pride.

Although the vice president had an office at the White House west wing, his official office was located at Number One Observatory Circle. At the old naval observatory building, the vice president's Secret Service agents performed most of their service details at a small office in the building, which was where the vice president also had his official residence.

Going to Alaska required help from the Anchorage Secret Service office, which would need to do the advance work and provide local logistical and manpower support. The vice president of the United States, as many may think, did not receive the same level of protection as his boss, the president. Although the VP and his family were provided with protection, the details were nearly one-third of what the president got. Of course, things changed when there was a clear and confirmed danger. Vice presidential protection protocols had not changed since the moment vice presidents were granted protection back in 1902.

Agent Landis prepared his usual paperwork to request resources and start coordination with the office of the US Secret Service for full support, and for that, he made sure to followed proper procedures. At this point in time, he knew that this was going to be a low-threat, low-risk visit, but it was his duty to worry about things that "regular" people, such as the vice president and his aides, would never be suspicious of, so he went to work.

***

Verum Chairman Jones received a very disturbing notification from a distant source he hadn't seen in a long time:

> From: Verum agent USSS-32NCC
> Outpost NACUSA
> Zulu Time-Date: 1230, 2007-06-25
>
> ***Break***
>
> Message: Jack Steele arrived in Nome, Alaska, early this morning. Subject contacted local asset ID-D198. Local resource attempted to eliminate threat but was unsuccessful.
>
> ***Break***
>
> Plans for J-4-VPV still on schedule. We are confident that mission has not been compromised. Waiting for further instructions.
>
> ***End***

Damn you, Jack Steele, Jones thought. *Why is it that you continue to interfere with this organization?* This time, he resolved, he would finish what his predecessor had failed to achieve. This time, he would kill Jack Steele.

Chairman Jones pressed a button and gave specific orders to his staff about how to handle Jack Steele, and when he finished, he realized that a drop of sweat was sliding down his sideburn. He reached inside his Armani suite and retrieved a Kanchipuram Indian silk handkerchief and slowly allowed the drop to soak into the fabric.

Chairman Jones did not realize that he was repeatedly tapping the floor with his leg in a fast motion, indicating that he was very distressed by the message. He was thinking that he would do all in his power to ensure the success of his mission, even if that meant exterminating the entire population of Nome, Alaska. He was a Verum chairman, and he would never be stopped or persuaded from completing his wish, because otherwise, he would no longer be able to continue enjoying the perks that came with this high office. He could not fail.

So Chairman Jones summoned his Nome, Alaska, project team leads—the world renowned two-time PhD and head of his medical psychiatric division, Dr. Harris Harjo, and billionaire and CEO of Lindberg Research Corporation, Mr. Maynard James Lindberg—for a brief meeting.

***

The small-town diner was similar to any typical diner you could find in any small town USA. A beautiful, young, long-haired, native-looking waitress approached me and said to me "I haven't seen you before, good-looking. What are you having today?"

"Your lunch special and a local beer will do," I replied.

The waitress pulled out her small notebook and wrote my order down and then looked at me and asked me if that was all for today.

I was tempted to follow her flirt, but I was too busy thinking about my next move. So I just ordered and let her take her leave.

As was routine, I turned my head to scan the bar. Behind the bar, I noticed that a strange-looking, middle-aged bald man was looking at the waitress like she was his property; perhaps he was her father or a platonic lover, but either way, I got the message. The place was all right. I could see a few locals sipping their beers and watching sports on a small, flat screen. To my back was a young couple having pizza, and to my left, I could see the town's main street.

Through the window, I observed a lot of activity on the streets—too many people walking around for a small town of under four thousand people. *What could be the special occasion?* I wondered.

In front of me, I observed an old man sitting down and staring at his soup. I recalled that the old man hadn't taken a sip since I'd walked through the café's main doors.

The man looked like an Alaskan Inuit; I noticed that he had been beaten by the years and that he did not take too much care of himself. Immediately, I assumed this was why he was sitting alone in the front corner.

My thoughts were interrupted when the young waitress approached the old man, and both started to talk in the local language. I could tell that she was a bit upset, but the old man was handling the situation with some authority, which led me to believe that he was a figure of authority in her life or culture.

I heard a bell ring, and the young waitress turned around and headed back to the bar. Seconds later, she returned and headed right for my table. The special of the day was a supreme pizza with all the ingredients you could imagine, including some steak. I could tell that it was smoking hot. In her other hand, she was holding a precooled, oversized glass mug with what appeared to be beer.

She'd placed the food on the table and started to leave when

I told her that I knew it wasn't my business but the customer sitting at the front (referring to the old man) appeared to be upset. I further asked the waitress what was going on.

She snapped back, asking me to promise not to make fun of the old man.

"Not in a thousand years," I replied. I glanced at her nametag and called her by her name, "Sora," and then softly told her that I would never do something like that.

But the waitress had her reservations and looked at me with suspicion as the stranger I was.

Once again, I politely asked her to tell me the old man's story.

Sora turned and looked back at the bar to see that no one was there. She appeared to be a lot more comfortable, now that her boss was not manning the bar and opened up to me. "The man there is our village counselor. He is a Sani-Shaman, an elderly wise man. But when the town started to grow, our religion and customs were no longer what most of my generation wanted; they wanted progress and money. Our ways became second to money and Sani-Shaman turned from a respected elderly man to the mockery of everyone in town.

"He was considered a person of influence, and the Lindberg Research Corporation used his influence to settle here next to sacred lands. And when they were settled, they kicked him out and never delivered anything they promised. Sani-Shaman didn't have anywhere to turn. As far as our people were concerned, Sani-Shaman had disgraced the village by allowing the white men to settle in our lands and take everything we owned and considered sacred. Because of this, he felt he could not turn to his own kind or the Lindberg Research Corporation, as they needed nothing else from him.

"Since then, he has not been the same; he became an alcoholic and a nomad and even rejected his own family because of all the guilt that lay behind all his doings."

Sora heard a person clearing his throat and looked back; it was the man behind the counter again.

I asked her, "What it was with that man, Sora?"

"He is Bob, my boss," she told me. "He owns this diner, and he also thinks he owns everyone else who enters his domains, including the waitresses." She further mentioned that her boss was a major pain in the neck but that her job paid the bills and there were very little options for her in Nome. She then excused herself and started to walk away.

"Thanks, Sora. It was nice catching up with you," I told her, sincerely.

Sora took her leave and went back to the bar area. By now I was hungry and started to eat my smoking lunch. To my surprise, the pizza was excellent—just like the ones I used to eat at Little Italy. This pizza tasted slightly different and had thinner crust; however, I approved.

Just after I'd enjoyed my third slice of pizza, three men entered the door. By their appearance, I guessed that they all worked in the same place.

One of them reached the bar before the other two and immediately placed his right hand on Sora's butt. She moved the hand away and asked him what he wanted for lunch. He looked straight into her black eyes and said, "You!"

From my table, I heard Sora reply, "In your dreams, Taylor."

"Well, guess what I dreamt last night?" said the young man named Taylor. "That we were in the back of my truck—"

At this time, the man behind the counter came out from the kitchen. "Enough of the mind games with the waitress, Taylor. Order your food or get out of the diner," yelled Bob from behind the counter.

Taylor apologized. "Sorry, Bob. I'm just having a nice conversation with Sora."

In the meantime, the other two young subjects were at Sani-Shaman's table making fun of him. One of the youngsters was pouring salt and pepper on his head, while the other was challenging his manhood and inciting him to a fight.

The old man didn't react to the insults; he just sat there and took it all as if he deserved it.

I took a sip of my cold beer and continued eating my pizza, but deep inside, I knew that my lunch wasn't going to end well.

Taylor ordered three cold Alaskan Ambers and continued trying to get his way with Sora. She moved away from the counter and headed to the back of the dining room to attend to her other customers. Bob quickly served the three beers, and Taylor paid for them, picked them up, and headed toward the old man's table.

A few minutes later, the youngsters intensified their verbal abuse, as if the cold beers they'd consumed had given them permission to act this way. The verbal abuse turned to physical, and the three young jerks were having their fun.

I didn't want to get involved; I assumed that Bob would do his civic duty, and all would remain within the family.

Seconds later Taylor, the big bully that he was, poured his half glass of beer on to Sani-Shaman's head and soaked his face and long beard with the white bubbly liquid. I was about to stand up when Bob yelled from the counter, "Enough, Taylor. You three get out of here."

"Bob, don't get your balls in a twist," replied Taylor. "You know that Daddy owns you and your diner." He continued, saying that he might go complaining to his father and suggesting that Bob recall what happened to him the last time he'd had an encountere with Taylor's father. Bob lowered his head and remained quiet. It was evident that he did not want to experience the same punishment again.

Taylor and company felt empowered, and one of the other bullies picked up the bowl of soup and said, "This old man needs his nourishment, but he is not eating. Maybe we should help him." He then threw the bowl's contents at

Sani-Shaman's face, and the soup splashed all over his face, hair, and torso.

I saw Sora passing by me, running to the old man's rescue, but when she arrived, she was grabbed by Taylor, who started to touch her voluptuous feminine attributes while the other two continued to pull the old man from his seat and drag him to the corridor.

I'd had enough. I stood up, moving in closer to the action, and said, "Taylor, is that your name? Taylor, this old man has had enough of your fun. Now please leave him alone."

Taylor looked at me with disbelief written all over his face and said, "This is not your fight, stranger. Get the hell out of here before you join this old man on the floor." Immediately following these words and without hesitation, he swung at me with all the strength he could muster.

Lucky for me, I ducked, and he only managed to mess up my well-manicured, black hair.

The adrenaline came to me just in time for me to grab Sora away from Taylor and return the favor. Gathering my strength, I hit Taylor the best I could, breaking his nose. A splash of blood covered his red-and-white checkerboard shirt.

"You broke my nose, motherfucker," Taylor said as he held his nose with both hands and started to hump up and down like a little girl. Then he commanded his two companions, "Get him, boys."

The other bullies, without hesitation, left Sani-Shaman alone and came after me. The first one, as I suspected, was eager to get a hold of me, but as he came onto me, I used his speed to push him away, and he landed on one of the tables and hit his stomach hard.

The other saw what happened and said to me, "You are going to pay for his." He pulled out a pocketknife and charged at me like a maniac.

I knew his type of bully well; they intimidate people, they

hardly know how to fight, and they are often scared when their intimidation tactics fail.

So I said to him, "Where do you want your pain—in the stomach or face?"

He stopped dead in his tracks and asked, "Come again?"

I repeated the question. "Where do you want your pain—in your stomach or head?"

He looked at Taylor, noting his swollen and bloody nose, and then at his other friend holding his stomach as he convulsed from pain in the middle of the floor. But without thinking, he continued and charged at me. So he had made his choice, and so did I. Both areas it would be.

As my attacker raised his hand with the pocketknife, I took the opportunity to get closer. I punched him hard in the pit of his stomach and raised my fist to punch the tip of his nose, which started bleeding. The bully followed the same childish behavior as the other two.

I looked at Sora, and she apologized for their behavior. As I was walking back to my table, I saw the town sheriff, dressed in his impeccable uniform, entering through the main door.

The sheriff was not alone; he was in the company of two deputies. The two deputies picked up Sani-Shaman and walked him outside, while the sheriff approached the scene and, without a word, took a very good look. He walked up to Taylor and saw his bloody nose and then to the other two and said out loud, "You three get out of here now."

Taylor looked down at the other two boys and, without hesitation, ran away from the establishment in a hurry.

The sheriff then turned to me, looked at him, and then looked to Bob, who was still behind the counter. "Bob, would you like to tell me what happened here?"

"Sorry, Sheriff, but the boys came here and started to mess with the old man, and the stranger here intervened and made this mess."

"So, Bob, what do you estimate the cost of damages here?"

"I would say at least four hundred dollars."

The sheriff looked at me and said, "Well, mister, once in a while, we get to work with foreigners who think that they can take over law enforcement duties. Are you one of those?"

I looked the sheriff straight in his eyes but said nothing.

"Well, stranger, I guess that you heard Bob. You owe him four hundred dollars." He gaze at me with an icy stare. "Will that be cash or credit?"

I knew there was no way I could win here. I looked at Sora, placed my hand in my pocket, pulled out four bills, and put them on the counter.

"Will there be anything else, Bob?" asked the sheriff.

"Yes. He hasn't paid for lunch yet!"

Sora looked at Bob and opened her eyes and said, "Are you for real?"

Bob looked at my table and said to the sheriff, "It's thirty dollars plus tips, which makes it about fifty dollars."

Sora looked at me, shaking her head in disbelief and shame.

I dropped my hand again and pulled out a hundred-dollar bill. Placing it on the counter, I said, "Twenty dollars is not enough for what this young lady has to put up with." I then said to her, "I'm sorry for the mess, Sora."

The sheriff looked at me. "If you are so eager to pay, why don't you come with me to the police station and pay a fine for disorderly conduct, and then you can be on your way."

I don't believe this guy, I thought to myself. But I also realized that I was a stranger there and that the sheriff looked after his own, and I respected that. It didn't matter who'd started the fight, as the newcomer was always guilty. As far as the sheriff was concerned, it was his duty to protect his own little community, and I understood that. I had to play by their rules if I wanted to get to the bottom of what was going on in this place.

The ride to the police station was short. I did some mental calculations so as to remember its location, as I had the feeling that, before I left this town, I would have to visit this place at least once a day. The sheriff took me inside the station and asked me to sit in his office. From there, he called a person who showed up in seconds with a ticket, which he filed right away, for the amount of five hundred dollars—the local charge for disorderly conduct.

I was pissed off beyond imagination, but I guessed this was a way the good sheriff established his authority and made strangers pay for their mistakes. I didn't want to let the sheriff know that he'd pushed some of my buttons, so I patiently and quietly paid my fine right away.

To mitigate the situation and looking at it on the bright side, I was glad to find that no fingerprints were taken, no mug shots were required, and no judge was called. I realized this was the way little towns like Nome took care of local, minor issues. They hit you where it hurt you the most—in your pocket.

The sheriff handed me a receipt and said, "Nice doing business with you, Mr. Steele!"

As I took the receipt, I looked at the sheriff and said, "I am at a disadvantage. How do you know who I am?"

"Mr. Steele, from the moment you arrived here in Nome, we knew who you were. It is our duty to know, and we know that you are Jimmy's nephew. Nevertheless, this doesn't give you permission to start busting heads, kicking doors, and taking names."

I asked the sherriff if he had learned about my earlier encounter at Dr. Anderson's office.

"Mr. Steele," replied the sheriff, "we run a very quiet and tight operation here in Nome, and regardless of who they are, we hate it when strangers stick their big noses in our town business. Do you understand?"

"Loud and clear, Sheriff," I told him.

"Now, why are you in Nome? What brings a private eye here to this town?" the sheriff pressed.

I assured the sheriff that I was not working and that my visit to Nome was strictly personal. "Aunt Marie—"

The sheriff interrupted me, saying, "Marie Steele is a fine woman, but she tends to exaggerate things. She came to me on a few occasions with her concerns about Jimmy's behavior. But we can assure you that Jimmy is all right and that her suspicions are based on pure speculations."

"Sheriff, please let me be the judge of that," I said.

"Yeah, we know about the letter," the sheriff added.

"What letter are you talking about?" I asked, sure that the surprise had registered on my face.

"The letter that Mrs. Steele mailed you a few days ago. You think that we don't know that? As I say, this is a very small town, and there are no secrets here in this community," said the sheriff.

I glanced at the sheriff's desk and took in his nameplate. "Sheriff Lindblom, is it?" I asked, though it wasn't really a question. "You seem to know everything, Sheriff—which means you must also know that I won't leave this town until I can change her mind or find out what's going on with my uncle."

Sheriff Lindblom urged me not to test his patience today. He continued, saying that perhaps he would not be lenient the next time and warning me that, if he heard about me raising hell in any other part of this town again, I would have to respond directly to him, and closed his comments with a question. "Do I make myself clear?"

"Crystal," I responded.

At this time, Sheriff Lindblom asked me to leave the office. In lieu of what had happened, I realized that I did not have any means of transportation back to the diner and asked if I could call a cab.

The sheriff responded, telling me not to bother looking

for a cab when my car was parked right outside his office. He further commented that one of his deputies had driven it back to the office while we were getting to know each other. "After all, this is a very friendly town, and we often take advantage of the many vehicles that are left open with keys hanging from the ignition."

"Most appreciated," I said. "With your permission, I would like to leave now."

With his right index finger, Sheriff Lindblom touched the tip of his cowboy hat, remaining seated at his desk.

I walked outside the office and into a corridor, where I passed by a missing persons' board. To my surprise, the board covered the entire wall. Photos—some dating back to the sixties—alongside personal messages from friends and family members of the missing persons, filled the board.

I focused my attention on one of the photographs, which featured a local Alaskan Inuit woman who must have been in her early thirties. It was not her face that made me stop and look but, rather, the written message printed under her photo. The handwriting appeared to that of a young child, and the message read, "Mom, I will wait for you. It doesn't matter how long it takes. I will be here when you return."

Something very odd was going on here in Nome. I didn't know what it was, but my trained mind told me that something very shady or even disturbing was taking place in this town, and I sincerely hoped that what had affected those many missing people wasn't also affecting my uncle.

I found Marie's Ford Bronco right where Sheriff Lindblom had said it would be—keys in the ignition and ready to go. I also noticed that the car had been searched. The reason for the search didn't matter; what mattered was that I was on to something important enough for the sheriff to show interest in what I was doing.

I had to give it to Lindblom; he was doing his job, but for whom was he working? Yet to be determined was whether the good sheriff was part of the problem or part of the solution. Was he working for the people of Nome or for his own benefit? Or was he under the payroll of the town's owner—Maynard James Lindberg?

My mind was quickly asking the right questions—the ones that would lead me to finding the right answers. Who was the driver of the black pickup who wanted me dead? And why? Dr. Anderson was terrified to tell me the truth about Uncle Jimmy, but why? These were questions that I would have to answer along the way—and quickly if I wanted to get to the bottom of what was going on with my uncle. What concerned me the most was that whatever was happening was larger than my uncle, and this thought was deeply disturbing to say the least.

Before driving away from the police department, I glanced at a road map and noticed a place that caught my attention— Lindberg Research Corporation. I made a few mental notes about the location, as I knew that, sooner or later, I would have to pay a visit to this place if I was unable to find the answers I wanted in downtown Nome.

But for now, I had to go back to the source of it all—my uncle's house—and get firsthand information from him. So I put the Bronco in gear and started to drive.

After driving for a couple of blocks, I detected through the side and rearview mirrors that an unmarked car was following me. Based on the model, driving, and distance, I determined my tail had to be law enforcement. I guessed that the good sheriff wanted to keep tabs on me, and that was all right. I would be doing the same thing if I was in the sheriff's shoes. Today, I would play the game and give them what they wanted so tomorrow they could leave me alone.

***

Jimmy was running maintenance on the Martin Mars. He wanted to make sure that it was in optimum condition for the

VIP visit. This was one of the few occasions that Jimmy got to fly this master of beauty and also a time that the hangar would make additional cash that was much needed.

He was interrupted by a heavily dressed man with a white hat, who greeted him. "How are you doing, Jimmy?"

"I'm good, Galway," Jimmy responded. "What about you?"

"Hanging in there, old man, hanging in there," Galway answered. "Hey, Jimmy, how's the old Mars holding up?"

"Just fine, Galway." Jimmy continued, saying that, since he'd been asked to take this gig, he hadn't thought about anything else.

"Good for you," replied Galway, indicating that he figured Jimmy was the right man for the job. "Furthermore," he added, "my employers are glad they chose you, Jimmy."

Galway suggested that Jimmy make sure that "this red-and-white beauty" was in perfect flying condition, saying they wouldn't want to disappoint Mr. Lindberg, if, all of a sudden, the Martin Mars was not in shape to fly.

"No, Galway, we don't want to disappoint Mr. Lindberg. But you haven't told me yet who the VIPs are you want me to transport here from Anchorage."

"All in good time, Jimmy," Galway replied. "We don't even know ourselves, but when we know, you will know." Galway got close to Jimmy and said to him, "Let's take a break and go and get a couple of Ambers at the airport bar. What do you say, pal? I'm paying. Well ... are we going or what?"

Jimmy was still conducting his preventive maintenance checks and was halfway down the list, but he couldn't resist Galway's offer and dropped his oily rag, hung up the checklist, closed the plane's door, and took off his working overalls; with a smile, like a trained puppy, he willingly followed Galway along to the place he didn't really want to go.

6

INTELLIGIBILITY

As I parked at the house, Marie came out to receive me. She was still anxious and nervous. I guessed that she was kind of afraid about Uncle Jimmy's reaction when he saw me. She wanted to make sure that he thought my visit was a surprise visit, rather than requested. I understood and respected her wishes, so I played along.

After having the afternoon tea, I asked Marie several questions about the people disappearing in town. I asked about the large board full of photographs in the sheriff's office. She mentioned that it had been that way since the day they moved in to town.

Most of the disappearances were attributed to disorientation in the snow, getting stranded and dying because of the elements, and a large consumption of alcohol getting in the way of making road and driving decisions. Other people had left their homes for the States and were never heard from again, and a few disappearances were chalked up in a different category altogether. "Oh yeah, Jack, other disappearances that the sheriff's office can't catalogue yet are attributed to local folklore," explained Marie as she smiled and sipped her hot tea. "You know that the people of this town are well known for these types of things, believe it or not.

"I personally always pursue factual information," Marie added. "Folklore is not my forte."

I was perplexed, but in my line of duty, you learn not to confuse fact with fiction, and Marie was right; when people don't have the facts, they tend to lean toward the unexplainable, the supernatural, or the bizarre. And this was when devious minds took advantage of the weak.

After a few hours, Marie and I heard the door open. Shortly thereafter, Jimmy's figure came into the light. I stood up from the living room sofa and waited for him to see me. To my surprise, Uncle Jimmy didn't seem happy at all; he acted as if he had seen me just an hour ago.

"Uncle, it's me, Jack!"

"It's been a long time, boy."

"Yeah, Uncle, it's good to see you too."

I wanted to get close to him to read him better, but he changed the conversation and faced Marie, asking for dinner.

"Jack, boy, I trust that you are staying for dinner, right?"

I didn't know what to say, so I said, "Yes, I will."

"Good, Marie, please set another plate; Jack is staying for dinner. I'll be right down." He continued walking upstairs, leaving a scent of beer in his path.

I looked at Marie and didn't know what to say. I felt sad but also relieved to realize that Aunt Marie was not making this up and that her concern was as genuine as my curiosity to know more and discover the truth about what was really taking place in my uncle's mind.

During dinner, Uncle Jimmy didn't say much, other than that it had been a busy day and that he had to make sure that the Martin Mars was in top shape for the Fourth of July.

Marie mentioned to me that, on the fourth, the town was hosting the Fourth of July celebration, the town's yearly Anvil Mountain Run, and that the mayor as well as the governor would be surprising everyone in town, as they would be bringing a VIP, whose name was to be determined.

After dinner, I had to find some answers, so I asked Marie for a key to the house, and she replied that they used no key. The door was always open, so I should feel free to come and go as I saw fit. I told her that I was going to take a little evening walk. It was nearly ten o'clock. I dressed in black, put on a balaclava, and gathered my usual toys of trade—my trusted lock picks, mag light, mini-electrometer, batteries, cables, cutters, screwdrivers, magnetic card readers, and the like. After all, you never knew what you would have to face out there.

I didn't want to wake up Marie; after the heavy dinner, both she and Uncle Jimmy were sound asleep. After the many beers Uncle Jimmy seemed to have consumed, I figured it would take an act of God to wake him up tonight. So I pushed the Ford Bronco a few houses away and then got in and let it ride for a block down the street before I started the engine and headed to the offices of one Dr. Anderson, town shrink.

7

IMMINENT RUSH

"**R**ight this way, Dr. Harjo. The chairman has been expecting you," said the chairman's personal butler, a well-manicured, middle-aged livery man, whose overall appearance was impeccable.

Dr. Harjo entered a large office through large, tall double doors, which emulated an old Capistrano church entrance and were opened by two sentries inside the office. Dr. Harjo observed the back glass wall displaying a magnificent view of the White House and the Washington Monument; the view was breathtaking. It seemed as if no glass separated him from this impressive view.

Between the walls was an eighteenth-century mahogany desk large enough to serve three desk chairs. It was immaculately clean; the only thing on top was an antique candle brass phone, a computer screen, and a pen holder. The room was spacious. From the entrance, no one could miss the dark leather sofa, two chairs, and a center table, all of which only matched the opulence of the desk. The office had high, well-crafted, decorated ceilings, depicting historical battles of the world, accentuated with reds, gold, and royal blue. The office decorations were impressive, for lack of a better word.

To the right of the room was a mahogany and white marble bar decorated with back mirrors that anyone would have bet supplied any type of liquor one could think off. The floor was pure, polished Italian marble for all one could tell. It showed an elegant, custom water jet–cut design with an elaborate and exquisite Giovanna marble floor medallion in the center.

"Dr. Harjo, please join me here and have a seat."

Dr. Harjo immediately acknowledged by moving his head up and down and sitting down on one of the dark leather chairs.

"I've taken the liberty of fixing you a drink that I hope will be to your liking."

"Thank you, Mr. Chairman. It's very thoughtful of you."

"You are quite welcome," said the chairman. "Dr. Harjo," he continued. "I summoned you here to learn directly from you how our program is progressing. I will encourage you to be short, precise, and to the point. You know that I am a busy man. I want to have a quick report of the overall project and how you are planning your strategy. But as you explain, I would ask you to choose your words carefully. We are not alone here. Do I make myself clear?"

"Of course, Mr. Chairman, I will—"

"Then proceed. I am all ears," responded the chairman.

Dr. Harjo looked at his drink and took a sip. He then gently let the glass rest on the table and looked directly at the chairman, before saying, "The plan is going according to schedule. Our test subjects have been responding well to treatment, and I have high hopes that they will not fail."

"Hope, Dr. Harjo?"

"Sorry, Mr. Chairman, I meant to say *surely* ..."

"Proceed, Dr. Harjo. Please don't mind my interruption."

"As I was saying, one of the test subjects, NA-JS-2004, has responded well to treatment. In less than three days, he will be able to perform as programmed," said Harjo.

"Dr. Harjo, what guarantee do I have that he will perform as you very well put it as 'programmed' and won't have a mind of his own—for lack of a better word, let's say 'fuck up' our plans at the last minute?"

Dr. Harjo hesitated, and Chairman Jones waited for the man to collect his thoughts. "Well, Doctor?" Jones asked. "What do you have to say?"

Harjo still didn't speak.

Jones picked up a pen and tapped the end on the top of his desk.

"I assure you that this subject will perform as expected. You have my word."

Jones noted that Harjo seemed frightened. Harjo kept biting his lower lip, and his hands shook. Jones smiled, knowing he had the doctor right where he wanted him.

Finally, Dr. Harjo mustered his thoughts and said without hesitation, "Mr. Chairman, I am well aware of your concerns." He then explained that they were implementing a new intense hypnosis therapy through a serum that had been perfected under his direct supervision. Dr. Harjo continued his monologue, saying that the serum was capable of inhibiting the emotions and reprimanding adrenaline on test subjects. Furthermore, he indicated that the serum had been tested several times on local residents, yielding nothing short of expected results. To end his spiel, Dr. Harjo looked straight at the chairman, assuring him that the current test subject would perform as expected.

"Dr. Harjo, this is very good news, indeed, very good news. Remember that I want no ties to our local operation or any ties to our organization period." He added that he would personally hold the doctor directly responsible for the success of this operation and looked directly into Harjo's eyes when he said to him, "Do I make myself clear?"

His reply was as Jones had hoped, for Jones noticed that the doctor, out of fear, could not hold his gaze as he replied, "Yes, Mr. Chairman, I understand that failure is not an option."

The chairman took this moment of weakness, fear, and direct alignment with him and said, his voice firm and determined, "Dr. Harjo, there is another pressing matter that recently came to our attention that perhaps you can help us with. May I suggest you test your serum with another subject?"

The doctor replied that he had never refused a subject—that he was intrigued by the chairman's request and eager to please the organization. He followed up by asking Jones to please tell him more about this test subject.

The chairman slowly and methodically explained that there was a new visitor in Nome, one Jack Steele, and that Harjo could have him for testing. But he also looked into the doctor's eyes and warned him that Steele could be a worthy adversary, to be careful, and not to underestimate him.

Dr. Harjo, like the madman he was, thanked the chairman for, as he well put it, "such a delightful opportunity." Harjo assured Jones that he would consider his new mission a top priority and would, upon his return to Nome, request the local staff to start working on Mr. Steele immediately.

Music to my ears, the chairman thought. He told the doctor one more time that Mr. Steele was not like his conventional test subjects and that he was a very dangerous individual—resourceful and, without a doubt, determined. Furthermore, he told the mad doctor that he'd received reports that suggested Steele may want to interfere with the organization's mission at Nome and emphatically suggested that he, under no circumstances, should let that happen.

Without hesitation, Dr. Harjo reached for the edge of the table; picked up his glass; and, in a natural motion, downed the remaining spirit in a big gulp, saying, "Not at all, Mr. Chairman. Consider it done."

From the chairman's desk, he could sense Dr. Harjo's inner evil, greed, and devious nature. He was sure about one thing when it came to the mad scientist sitting and sweating in front of him—that as long as he provided the doctor with test subjects for his research and the lavish life of his, Harjo would be under his control and do as he said regardless of what he requested. Clearly, the man's actions were measured only by his loyalty to the cause; how many people he got to kill; and his selfish, pathetic life. Finally, Jones asked him, "Dr. Harjo, I trust that my intentions are clear? Do you have any other questions for me?"

Without thinking, Dr. Harjo, filthy rich, brilliant scientist and murderer, responded, "Mr. Chairman, I'll get right to it." He stood up and thanked the chairman for his time before turning around and starting to walk out.

The chairman looked at the clock hanging from his left wall and whispered as Dr. Harjo opened the doors, "I hope you have a pleasant trip back to Nome. It was nice to know you."

***

As Dr. Harjo walked outside the chairman's doors, the ego inside him took over and he flashed back to how he'd become one of the nation's top scientist. He walked with pride down the marble stairs surrounded by roses that complemented the chairman's office. He continued walking straight to his waiting stretch limousine, whose rear door was opened by the chauffeur; from the happy look on Dr. Harjo's face, the chauffeur could clearly discern that the doctor's short visit with the chairman had been a complete success. Harjo entered the limo with a purpose, and soon his head rested upon the comfortable leather headrest, where he got lost thinking about his past.

He went back in time, recalling his two PhD completions. Self-regarded as the best pioneer in mental-control programming that the nation had seen, he thought that the methods and techniques he had perfected through the decades of study and research were infallible. He was a scientist, a professional, whose ambition lay on breaking new mind-control frontiers, and he had repeatedly succeeded where many other peers had failed.

As the driver drove forward, Harjo's humble beginnings came alive in his mind. He recalled that he was not born corrupted and evil; he was a man of science, and in 1953, as a young boy, he had once taken a trip to the University of Harvard. His father was a professor at the university and dedicated his life to research in psychology, specifically on multiple personality disorders. Many claimed that the doctor's father's research was backed by CIA background funding, but no one ever could prove that.

Harjo had become obsessed with the idea of completely controlling someone else's mind since his youth. He'd desired the cheerleading captain at his high school so much that he was willing to sell his soul to the devil or take the easy route of stealing his father's research to learn the tricks of the trade. He spent countless nights trying to understand the process until, one day, he was able to effectively hypnotize the girl he desired to do whatever he wanted. He thought that he had struck gold.

From there, Harjo used his advanced techniques and, of course, his father's influence to muscle his way into Harvard, and he became, along with his father, one of the most brilliant psychologists that the school had ever produced. Through the many hypnotic sessions he conducted, he found success until one of his earliest experiments test subjects took her life. This incident had devastating consequences for those working under Harjo's control. The event destroyed him emotionally but also made him realize a taste for the power of mind control.

It was at this turning point that Harjo's mind had ignited like gasoline to fire. He had reached a state of hypnotic ability superior to that of his father. He had reached the inner mind control that was stronger than the "human will." He had found the key to preprogramming the human brain. He had reached and unlocked the innermost intimate mind keys that would persuade a normal human being to take his or her own life without regard to self-preservation.

Back in 1968, as his experiments started to become

popular, he had been approached by a CIA official who asked him to continue his studies in a project called "Project MK-Ultra" or "Mind Control Ultra." This was a project that his father had developed and worked on for many years before him.

Professor Harjo worked with the CIA until the CIA director, Richard Helms, put an abrupt stop to all funds and closed the project after intense pressure and, possibly, facing a formal inquiry from a congressional commission in 1973.

After the project was closed, Dr. Harjo found himself alone, with no funds, and unable to continue perfecting his theories. The only thing he had were the many victories he'd achieved while working for the CIA and building on his father's original research. While on the CIA's payroll, Professor Harjo was working for the government intelligence services, which clandestinely continued to work on Project MK-Ultra.

Since then, Harjo had dedicated his life to developing the perfect weapon, and soon, his achievements were noticed by other organizations, like the US military. They secretly used his methods and techniques to create a unit of mind-controlled warriors. His technique was similar to the extraordinary work done by the chairman of the department of psychology at Colgate University, Dr. George Estabrooks.

Dr. Harjo took advantage of Dr. Estabrooks's advanced hypnosis program based on three major program areas. The first step was "disguised mind control or reprogramming induction" to prevent the test subject from knowing that he or she had been used or programmed. The second phase was to "suggest amnesia," to make sure that the subjects never learned that their brains had been reprogrammed. Last but not least important was "sealing" against future hypnotic competition.

This was achieved by giving an instant "posthypnotic suggestion" to the subject, for instant reinduction by cue. The technique was brilliant. Dr. Estabrooks's research was nothing short of genius. But luckily for Harjo, the results of Estabrooks's

81

work fell into his lap one day. This was the beginning; from there on out, many test subjects would consider Dr. Harjo their worst human nightmare.

Harjo immediately dedicated all his spare time to learning this new hypnosis process. To him, it was very simple; in his mind, he was perfecting the techniques of Dr. Estabrooks and his father by administering the subject with a serum that dismantled the subject's "inner will" to fight back through emotions. This allowed Dr. Estabrooks's technique to effectively take its course. It was simple; it was easy. The road had been paved for him. He only had to walk one step at a time and the rest would come to bear:

- First, he covertly identified a test subject who had the propensity to go into a deep amnesiac trance. Dr. Harjo had developed a process of identifying these subjects through a series of behavioral analysis indicators. These included, for example, the subject's tendency to submission, acceptance, and sadism, all of which were prime qualities for accepting his mind-control technique.

- Second, he used the induction-by-disguise method. This process gave his test subjects posthypnotic suggestions for the subject to become deeply hypnotized again, and whenever the hypnotist give him or her a certain cue, such as touching the tip of the nose with the small finger or repeating a phrase, the subject would reenter the hypnotic trance without even knowing or realizing he or she was acting according to a predetermined set of instructions or commands. The subjects would only respond to the hypnotist's voice and cue, even if others would provide them with the same instructions, orders, or cues.

- Third, he also gave a posthypnotic suggestion that denied the subject any posthypnotic knowledge of this hypnosis or any subsequent one—a brilliant insurance against any future mind-regression techniques that could definitively reveal that the subject's mind had been tampered with. The subjects would never know nor would their minds accept that they had gone through this intense hypnosis process, providing total deniability of the mind programming in the first place and making the subjects totally responsible for their past, current, and future actions.

- Furthermore, Dr. Harjo developed a technique that would give a posthypnotic suggestion that no one else could subsequently hypnotize the test subject, sealing the subject's mind and creating hypnosis insurance, a very clever way to "cover the asses" of those who would practice such surreptitious mind-control manipulations. A couple of these harsh and inhuman insurance processes were that, if anyone else attempted to hypnotize the subjects, they would respond to a preprogrammed trigger telling them to kill themselves or to seek refuge in a mind-control loop—such as an unreal thought or past-life memory that the subject was unable to ever leave and that would render their minds worthless—or giving any number of other preprogrammed instructions that would ensure that the would-be posthypnotic professional would believe the subject had gone insane. This was a clever way to seal his macabre work.

- Finally, to mask the process, Dr. Harjo used the most ingenious hypnosis of all, which was to give the subject the posthypnotic suggestion that the subject would act in a trance, just as if he or she were wide awake normally, also known as a "walking hypnosis." The combination of his effective, swift techniques would allow Harjo to place a subject into hypnosis through a casual conversation and reprogram the subject without the subject's knowledge while in this conscious state—a brilliant aspect of his research that made him the best at what he did and a very dangerous predator in our society.

This was a very ingenious hypnosis technique used by spies, in which the conscious mind was loyal to its country while the subconscious mind would be loyal to the foreign country who'd recruited the subject. Several incidents through history serve as examples in which this technique could have been used to successfully reprogram minds to do horrendous crimes, such as Sirham Bichara Sirhan, Lee Harvey Oswald, James Earl Ray, and many others. All the subjects had in common that they had a first, middle, and last name. Using a subject with three names would help project managers discern at a glance those crimes committed by people under their treatment and differentiate between them and other crimes committed in the United States by people who were simply criminally insane (and had just a first and last name)—those who were not part of the program.

These subjects were prime examples of how regular citizens were able to carry out acts under a hypnotic state that they later retained no memory of. It was virtually impossible to determine that the subject was under hypnosis unless he or she was immediately examined by an expert on hypnotic control, and yet the hypnosis would still be very hard to detect if the subject had been "sealed."

The limousine driver accidently passed over a pothole on the road, and Dr. Harjo's head bumped back from the leather headrest, awaking him from his trance. He was quick to curse, and the driver followed quickly with apologies. Dr. Harjo slowly placed his head back and took back his line of thought right where he'd left it.

He recalled the time when the military's black op had embraced this system, and so had the US government. But when his methods started to scare the politicians in 1973, the hypnosis masters were cut from all funding and left in the streets to rot. That was when the Verum organization took notice of the mind-control scholars, and by flashing cash, impressive grants, and deception, reeled them all in into their world of service.

This was the time when Harjo started to lose the little conscience he had left.

By the time he and his staff realized the true Verum intentions, it was too late. He had already sunk too deep into their games of mind that it was nearly impossible to get out without going feetfirst. So he took advantage of the grants, the endless supply of test subjects, and the world-class facilities and developed what the Verum organization called "the ultimate mind-control weapon."

Dr. Harjo prized himself for having perfected a mind-control technique that was virtually impossible to detect. To keep this control rooted in the subject's mind, he used the perfect insurance—an anti-emotion brew Dr. Harjo was very proud to call his "victory serum." In his mind, Dr. Harjo considered himself a pioneer, a genius who was able to beat two brilliant minds by perfecting the ultimate mind control technique, which was his and his alone.

***

I had to wait until about 1:30 a.m. before the sun set. I silently drove closer to Dr. Anderson's office and parked the Bronco in an alley a block away, near the Nugget Inn hostel. I walked in the shadows to Dr. Anderson's office. It was a single-story office, narrow but long. I found my way to the back door.

The street was quiet, with hardly anyone in sight. The cold weather and time were ideal for the locals to be either asleep or keeping themselves warm with whiskey at the local bar. Good news for me. I had with me all I needed to get inside this office—my pry tools, a small flashlight, and a smart tool. Before trying to open the door, I did my homework, scouting around the building and looking for signs of an alarm system. Fortunately for me, I saw none and then remembered Aunty Marie saying, "Here in Nome, we use no keys. We sleep with the doors unlocked." So why would the local shrink bother installing an alarm system at his office?

I stopped what I was doing and listened for any background noises, but all I heard was the sound of the waves pounding the shore. I love it when a plan comes together; the sounds of the waves also hid my own noise.

Upon looking at the door, I could see the lock, which I recognized; lucky for me it was an easy one to pick. I placed my hands on deck, and in less than a minute, the door was open. I eased myself slowly and tried to make as little noise as possible. I had my face covered with the balaclava. I was dressed in black and used my favorite pair of spy gloves, which were good for concealing my fingerprints but were doing a lousy job protecting me from the cold weather.

But today, the weather was the least of my concerns. I stopped dead in my tracks before taking any step farther. I recalled my mental notes from my previous visit and positioned myself accordingly. I was able to quickly figure out where I was, and within a few moments, I was at the doctor's office door. I again looked for any evidence of an alarm system, but I saw none. I glanced at the corridor corners but saw no camera system. *So far, so good*, I thought.

I placed my hand on the knob and gently moved it right, but it didn't turn. I proceeded to try it to the left with the same results. I had to hand it to Dr. Anderson; he was serious about keeping his patients' information confidential, and he was not kidding about HIPAA. As a master in the trade, I tried to push the tension wrench in and push the pick, but the lock did not budge. When I examined the lock more closely I noticed that it was a Medeco lock; the internal tumblers, pins, and key groove were different from conventional locks, so I was out of luck.

Then I remembered Occam's razor: "The simplest explanation is most likely the correct one." In many instances, people simply made the same mistake over and over again. They never thought twice about compromising security for convenience, and this was precisely what had happened here. I shifted my light to the doorframe and noticed that the door hinges were exposed to the outside rather than the inside. Convenience, for the good Dr. Anderson, appeared to be more important than security. This was his loss and my gain.

Many architects and floor-plan designers use these techniques to make the door open to the hall rather than to the inside of the room, allowing for small room interiors to be used without completely having to lose space to allow the door to swing inside. In many cases, like hospitals, schools, and other public buildings, the same concept is applied for safety. In case of fire, people inside the room can push out, instead of opening the door toward the inside of the room.

Now in Nome, Alaska, Dr. Anderson's definition of "convenience" would help me enter into his private retreat. I pulled out my smart tool and unscrewed all three hinge pins. Then very careful and slowly, I picked up and removed the door from its frame. It was as easy as taking candy from a kid.

Now I was inside the room. No alarms or police seemed forthcoming, and I was as happy as a groom on honeymoon. I glanced at the file cabinet that was inadvertently pointed out to me by the good Dr. Anderson and, out of courtesy, tried to pull it open. It was locked. I had to hand it to the doctor; he followed protocol well.

I used my prying tool again, and the cabinet opened like magic. I perused through it and found a file identified as

"Steele, Jimmy A." I pulled it out to look at it. It was pretty much empty—strike one. All I could see were a few therapy dates and some medications that were prescribed to him. I read the notes along the interviews, specifically the first and last interview. What I read remained consistent with ... *Oh my God*:

"Patient consistently reflects the same collective symptoms as the rest of the town's patients; patient displays acute paranoia. The patient has a tendency for self-destruction, and in my opinion, the patient will end up taking his own or someone else's life ... Subject believes that he is slowly losing his ability to have feelings, to love, smile, and experience pain ..."

I could not believe what I was reading. Aunty Marie was right; this was the same strange sickness that had ended the lives of many good people in Nome and had driven many away from their homes.

When I closed the file, it hit me. Why hadn't I seen this before? The file displayed the Lindberg Research Corporation logo. I opened the record again and, after a closer look, found that, when I moved the paper against the light, I could clearly see that all the papers displayed the Lindberg Research Corporation watermark.

What the hell did this mean? As far as I knew, Lindberg did not openly own any psychiatric organizations; they were not engaged with any tests ... *Wow, wait a minute*, I told myself. *I know that Lindberg does research.* But did this mean? In the plane, I had noticed that one of Lindberg's subsidiaries was the Nome St. Francis Heritage, a medical facility, which all the local residents had to visit one way or the other. *Oh my God ...*

I didn't even want to consider what I was thinking.

I had to do something about this, and I had to do something fast. I scrutinized the file page by page and photographed each page, including the cover and logo, with my mini-camera. I didn't want to disturb any of the pages or take them out of the file.

As soon as I took the photos, I placed the file back in its place and locked the cabinet, leaving everything as it had been previously.

My curiosity was killing me, so I walked behind the desk and looked at the metal door to my right. The door was a challenge, as it had no visible locks or handle, so my pry tools were useless. The door hinges were inside, so how was I to open the fricking door? I decided I needed to think like an old and lazy doctor, so I sat down in Dr. Anderson's chair and placed my hands on the desk.

I want to leave in a hurry, where do I have to ...? Wait a minute ... I glanced under the desk and used my flashlight to help me search for a button, but there was none—strike two. I opened the top shelf and found nothing but pens and rubber bands. The rest of the desk drawers were closed and locked. I pried the locks, and soon all drawers were open. But the only interesting thing I found was a bottle of cheap R & R whiskey. Shit, someone should teach this doctor how to drink.

It was getting late, and I wanted to see what was behind that door, so I played a trick I learned in spy school. Most of these doors had an internal motion sensor, which when activated, immediately released the door so good, lazy people like our beloved doctor didn't have to push an exit button.

I picked up a few sheets of white paper from the copy machine and found my way to the upper door space between the door and the doorframe and pushed the bunch of papers in together. I put my finger on the door; closed my eyes; prayed; pushed; and, voilà, like magic, the door opened. I looked and saw a set of wide service stairs leading to a room below. The lights automatically came on, and I could clearly see my way down the stairs.

Without delay, I walked down the stairs to find the whole room full of archives; all of them were locked with high-security locking devices, which I didn't have the time or the equipment to crack open.

But what interested me the most was that half of the files headings were listed as "Nome Mental Health Patients" and the other half as "Lindberg Research Corporation." What the hell was taking place here? What did Lindberg Research Corporation have to do with Dr. Anderson's files? What was the connection? And how did this connection affect my uncle?

The files were listed in alphabetical order, so I looked straight at the ones listed from R to T, which I thought might contain Uncle Jimmy's records. Unfortunately, when I touched the handle, all hell broke loose. An alarm sounded as loud as thunder, blinking lights came alive, and I knew that it was time for me to leave.

I picked up the white papers that I'd used to active the door sensor from the floor, stuffed them in my cargo pockets, and fled the area as quickly as my legs allowed. I used the rear beach way, circled around to my car, and drove away with purpose. I reached Aunt Marie's house, parked the Bronco, and eased myself inside the house. I walked to my room and, upon opening the door, noticed lights reflecting at the house like a vehicle was passing by.

I slowly moved the curtain aside and saw Sheriff Lindblom stepping out of the cruiser and touching the front hood of the two cars parked at the house. I watched as he went directly to Jimmy's Jeep and then toward the Bronco. He quickly pulled up his hand. He glanced at the house, but to my surprise, he returned to his cruiser and slowly drove away. I had been made—strike three.

It was nearly 4:00 a.m. I was tired and wanted to catch a couple of z's before dawn. In summer, the sun in Nome comes out at about 4:30. I knew that I had a busy day ahead and wanted to start early.

RED-HANDED

It was 6:00 a.m. I tried to sleep, but my search for answers kept me awake and looking at the ceiling. I tried to pull all the puzzle pieces I had collected together, but even with all I had, it wasn't enough to really make up a picture of what was happening. Only one thing was constant in this town, and that was the Lindberg Research Corp.

I had to find out more about the men behind the "Lindberg Empire," so I turned my laptop on and started my research, and what I found made a lot of sense. According to several news articles, Lindberg practiced no principles, morals, or conscience; all he cared about was money and power.

Money was his prime motivation and had been from the very beginning, since he'd learned that, to get ahead in life, all you needed was money, influence, and power. During an interview with a prominent national journalist, Lindberg narrated that, when he was a little boy of no more than eleven years old, he was at school, and the most beautiful girl he had ever seen was buying soda pop at the vending machine. She was short by a nickel, and she turned to him and said, "If you give me a nickel, I will share half of my soda with you!"

The young Lindberg reached into both his pockets and realized he had not a single penny.

"Too bad, you lose," said a voice behind him.

He turned to see Brat Morris pulling out a nickel from his pocket and dropping it in the slot. Morris then pushed the button, and a soda was dropped into the lower compartment. The girl picked it up and looked at young Lindberg with pity and laughed as she walked away holding Brat Morris's hand. From that moment on, Maynard James Lindberg had grown to become an insatiable money machine.

By age fourteen, he already owned the garbage collection contract for his community. Police investigated but could not prove allegations that by eighteen, before graduating from high school, he had murdered, stolen, and extorted money just like a Mafia don would. Lindberg apparently realized that there was more money to be made by playing the good guy than from behind the scenes. By age twenty-five, he'd invested all his money in the stock market and was fortunate enough to make millions. Needless to say, FBI investigators speculated that Lindberg had insider, confidential information from the Verum organization, but in spite of the rumors, he was never officially charged.

By age thirty-five, Lindberg had earned his first billion dollars and created the Lindberg Research Corporation, and with a hefty contract from the government, he had become one of the richest men in the United States. By age forty, he didn't want to be just the richest man in the United States, so he expanded his empire across the pond and bought any other business that could pose a threat to him. His strategy was clear; he was going be "it."

Between cheating, exhorting, and lying, he acquired the name of the tenth-richest man in the world. His empire extended from the United States and touched all seven continents. As a result of his childhood incident and the rejection by the little girl, Lindberg turned his back on any woman who came near him.

Information leaked by Lindberg's shrink revealed that, as a young adult, Lindberg had rejected the opposite sex in order to protect himself against rejection, and he enjoyed imposing his dominance on other men. But with all the money in the world, he was a lonely man; he dedicated his life to making money, and this he did well. The shrink also hinted that Lindberg despised animals, had a hard time maintaining relationships, and had never learned to love. From my research, I'd learned that many business partners agreed that Maynard James Lindberg didn't have a conscience—that little voice most of us have that talks to us and keeps us out of trouble. The only true friend to him, which also became his worst enemy, was piles of cash that continued to fill the big abyss deep inside his heart.

Although Lindberg later denied it, he was once quoted as quoting Machiavelli's "the means justified the end."

After learning a bit about the mind behind it all, I walked down stairs and left a note for Aunt Marie. I slowly opened the door and carefully glanced outside. I didn't want to have to face the Nome Police Department deputies or the sheriff. After making sure that that coast was clear, I got in the Bronco and drove away.

I knew that I would have to gather more information in order to connect the dots, and a good way to start was by getting to know the opponent. I glanced at the map one more time to refresh my memory. Although this was a small town, I knew that I didn't want to end up on the wrong part of the fence at the wrong time.

During my short drive away from town, I could see several athletes and other sportsmen exercising and getting ready for the big run two days away. The morning's temperature was so cold that you could see steam coming off of the warm bodies as they were doing their daily calisthenics. I noticed a lot of advertisements all over town reminding tourists and locals about the Anvil Mountain Run and fireworks.

I wondered if the peaceful and nice people of Nome ever knew what was transpiring right under their noses. When you are used to seeing the same pattern over and over, you kind of lose your perspective and become one of the many in the same primordial soup. As an outsider, and thanks to a trained mind, I could see the pattern from miles off. This town had a cancer, and unfortunately, it seemed that I was the only one who could come up with the cure, for Uncle Jimmy's sake.

After driving for about thirty minutes, I started to see an eight-foot-high, reinforced fence. This fence was regulation, suited to protect a military base. I noticed a sign on the fence every one hundred feet, clearly indicating that "This is Private Property and Deadly Force is Authorized." What the hell? *Was this another Area-51?* I wondered.

This had to be the place, as it was the only one marked with these warning signs and also the location of the town's largest and most important industry—"fear," also known as Lindberg Research Corporation. I could see that more cameras were located in this place than the rest of the town put together. Something very important and valuable must be happening here—something that Lindberg did not want anyone else to see.

I stopped at a safe distance, parked the Bronco, secured a pair of binoculars that were in the glove compartment, and climbed to the top of a hill, from where I could see most of the complex. And I have to tell you, it was impressive. It was a series of connected buildings that had a lot of green, energy-saving features, including large glass walls, glass ceilings, and other energy-conservation features.

From my strategic position, I could see little activity outside the buildings; only a few trucks, some cargo carts, and some workers in dark blue overalls came into view. I had to hand it to the man; the security setup was impressive.

Lindberg Research Corporation had security guards in dark suits posted in the right tactical places; this place looked like Fort Knox. It was double fenced, and between the fences, I saw guard dogs with their handlers. It would be challenging for me to enter but not impossible. I knew a trick or two, but I would need all the help that I could get. Unfortunately, today this was a solo mission.

Regardless of how good a security operation is, you can always find service inconsistencies, thanks to one common factor called human nature. Security elements are designed to be effective and proficient in what they do, but they are also human, and we are creatures of habit. Thus, the first of many mistakes I noticed was that the guards left parts of the fence open for short periods of time, allowing me to learn most of the guards' routines in less than two hours. As I said before, breaking in to this place was going to be challenging but not impossible.

I went back to town to prepare for tonight's break-in. I needed a couple of things before I did my damage. So I slowly walked down to the Bronco and started to drive away. All of sudden, I saw a black pickup in my rearview mirror. "What the hell?" I said out loud. Who could this good-for-nothing be so close to my six?

I pushed the pedal to the metal, and so did my pursuer. I was using all the skills I had just to keep the vehicle on the road while negotiating its many dangerous curves. I had to be careful because, although Marie's Bronco could negotiate well in snow and off road, it was not designed for high speed and curves. The black pickup gained on me very quickly and hit the Bronco's rear bumper. I felt the impact in my spine. I tried to see who was driving, but to my bad luck, the front windshield was tinted black.

Again I was negotiating the curves. I could not see the edge of the road, so I was in big trouble. After I'd used all the evasive driving I knew, the road came to a long stretch. The pickup came close to me, and in a second, it was side by side with the Bronco. We were doing nearly seventy-five miles an hour. I could hear the pickup's roaring engine. I had to hand it to the owner; that vehicle could move.

The pickup driver tried to push me off the road, but I

anticipated his move and blocked hard with the Bronco's left side. I tried again to see the driver's face, but to no avail. I pushed back and slowed down the Bronco so I could hit the pickup's rear fender and force him off the road, but the driver was good. And before I could complete my maneuver, he pushed me hard, and I was off the road and landing in a ditch dead center with a huge, thick mountain evergreen.

The last thing that I remember was looking at my right-side rearview mirror at the black pickup, which came back and stopped on the side of the road to ensure that I was done. Once the driver had parked the pickup at the road's edge, the driver roared the engine a few times like a chanting of victory. Blood was staining my vision, and I could not move a muscle. As I tried to open the door, I lost my strength, and everything went black around me.

***

Nome was in full swing for the upcoming Fourth of July celebration. Streets were blocked, stores were doing a brisk business, and the Midnight Sun diner was crammed with people who lived in the far reaches of the Seward Peninsula and hardly ever came into the town. Police were running scarce as the chief started to implement his public safety plan. Police had set up the Nome baseball field as a camping ground for those who wanted to enjoy nature and camp near the event. Others were staying with friends, and some took advantage of the local entrepreneurship and stayed in locals' homes, for a not-so-cheap fee of course.

Once again, the city looked healthy, like when it was young, fresh, and full of hundreds of camping tents; the view was spectacular. Preparations were underway for the twelve-and-a-half-mile Anvil Mountain race. Helicopters were ready, first-aid stations were set up around the route, and resources were quickly scattered all over the race grounds.

WHAT COMES AROUND GOES AROUND

I woke up looking at a dark canvas full of smoke and native paintings on the wall. What in the world had happened to me? I could not move and, all of a sudden, lost consciousness again. I felt cold and, in the background, heard a faint jabbering I could not make sense of. I wanted to wake up but was unable to open my eyes. I had a strange dream that I was lying in bed trying to wake up from a strong hangover, but this was somehow different.

What had happened to me? I was desperately trying to muster every single drop of energy to open my eyes and join the world of the living. Suddenly I slipped, and it all went dark again. The next thing I knew, a strong aroma was penetrating my lungs. I opened my eyes, grasping for air again, this time with the strength of a bear and the agility of an eagle. I was alive and strong, but where the hell was I? To my left, I could see Sora the waitress. She was smiling at me like an angel. And to my right was Sani-Shaman.

"Be careful, Jack," said Sora softly. She reminded me that I had been in an accident and filled me in on the rest. She also explained to me that Sani-Shaman had found me and carried me to his place and brought me to life from the hands of hell.

Sora also mentioned that the old man had had to cash in many favors to the underworld to bring me in, as when he found me, I was nearly dead.

With difficulty, I looked at Sani-Shaman and bowed in gratitude, but I had many things to do, and my time was running out.

Finally, and for the first time, the old man spoke to me and said, "Cheechako."

I looked at Sora, and she explained that Sani-Shaman was welcoming me back to life and to his land.

I felt like shit; my body ached even in places I didn't know how to pronounce. I felt that I had no time to waste. I wanted some answers and had to leave.

Sani-Shaman spoke in clear English and said to me, "A burned child dreads fire," which I fully understood.

I had no choice. I had already started a chain of events, and it was inevitable that I follow this lead. "Sani-Shaman, I understand. However, it doesn't matter what you say to me. I have to go back and finish what I started."

He looked at me with compassion, but with a firm expression said, "Don't count your chickens before they hatch, Mr. Steele. If you must do this, I will help you any way I can. The spirits still owe me some favors, and they appear to be generous paying me back today, but don't let your eyes be bigger than your stomach. You must make baby steps before you can run; you are in no shape to do anything now under your current condition."

Sani-Shaman thanked me for saving him from pain and humiliation at the diner and explained that singling him out for "fun" was becoming a habit of those three boys. However, Sani-Shaman clarified that they were young and stupid, and they would soon learn their lesson—perhaps not from him, but life always delivered retribution eventually. He further explained that the spirits had told him that his time was short and he already had a written ticket to the underworld. With deep serenity, he thanked me, not for saving him but for saving Sora. Sani-Shaman was feeling sorry for himself; he was ready to endure every pain and humiliating minute he could get before he died. For him, the more he cleansed his soul here, the less karma he would have when it was time to face his ancestors in the afterlife.

When he thanked me again for my actions in the diner, I assured him that neither he nor Sora owed me any gratitude—that I had just done what any other man would have.

He stopped me and said firmly, "Nonsense, Mr. Steele, you were not alone in the diner, and yet you were the only one who cared enough to end it. You are special; you have a strong spirit inside you, and the spirits are telling me that you are the one who could quash the evil that is hovering over this small town."

I didn't understand what he meant, but who could with the sharp pain that was consuming my thoughts?

I looked at Sora for answers, and her serene face told me that she understood what Sani-Shaman was talking about. With a very polite and soft voice she said, "Jack, what Sani-Shaman is talking about is the old fight between good and evil. He sees you as the person who could, once and for all, put an end to the town's curse, the problems that curse has created, and the Lindberg Research wrongdoings."

Although I did not understood the "hocus-pocus" about good and evil, I did understand what she was saying about LR Corporation, and I intended to do something about that tonight.

"Okay, you win. I will rest tonight and then you will take me to Lindberg Research where I will do my worst."

Sani-Shaman looked at Sora and moved his head from side to side, expressing his fear, but he also whispered, "More knows the devil because of age and experience than for what he is. You know what you want to do and help you I will."

Sani-Shaman picked up a small bottle, opened it, and

asked me to smell it. I took a deep breath of the aroma, and immediately, my eyelids felt like they weighed a hundred pounds. I lay my head on the improvised pillow and fell in to a deep, deep sleep.

***

Marie gave Jimmy his lunch box and, once again, watched him leave the house. She took a very good look at him, as if this was going to be the last day she saw him. For the last six months, she had learned to live with this routine. However, the situation was killing her, and in her mind, the uncertainty of not knowing what was happening to her husband was becoming unbearable.

With every day that passed, watching her husband slip away was taking a heavy toll on Marie. Every single day, the intensity of Jimmy's rejection and lack of feeling was a burden that she felt she could no longer bear. It was like Jimmy's humanity was slowly draining away, and she was afraid that the Jimmy she had been in love with more than half her lifetime was never going to come back to her.

Her biggest fear was that Jimmy would end up disappearing, like the other strange cases in town. She was terrified to think those years of love, good memories, and caring were going to disappear in seconds under the sounds of a discharged weapon or the deadly silence of a hunting knife. All of these demons were haunting her day and night; Marie was on the verge of a nervous breakdown.

Jimmy was going to therapy, as were many of the other victims of Nome. She had alerted the sheriff, their many friends, and coworkers, but the more she shared with them, the more Jimmy's symptoms appeared like those of others who'd met with tragic endings. She thought that the only hope for normality rested now in her nephew's hands.

This morning, when Jimmy had left, Marie had felt like he'd

walked past her as if she was someone he'd never seen before. This hurt was particularly poignant, as forgetting the people who were important to him was one of the many symptoms Marie's friend Fred had displayed before committing suicide in front of her boss.

Marie had the feeling that Jack was in trouble because she hadn't heard from him in more than twenty-four hours. But she didn't want to entertain the idea that he would not come back. Perhaps if she waited a little longer and gave it time as the sheriff always advised her to do, Jack would be back in the house for dinner. She thought of going to the market for a few groceries and making a quick stop at the sheriff's office to ask him if he could help. She felt that he owed her an update as result of their earlier conversation, and until she got one, she would continue bugging the old sheriff to death.

After Jimmy left, she made a call, picked up her bag, walked outside, and waited for a cab ride.

It was Larry who came to pick her up.

"How are you today, Marie?" he asked. "How's your morning?"

"Good, my dear. How about you?"

"Fine," said Marie

"Where to?" asked Larry.

"To the market, Larry, to the market," said Marie.

Mary glanced at the photo of the driver attached to the rearview mirror; in it, he was wearing a green military utility uniform.

Marie knew Larry very well. Larry had told her his story so many times that Marie knew it by heart. She recalled that Larry had come back from Vietnam so proud, having completed his tour and bearing the scars of a hard and bloody war. The first thing that he was confronted by at the airport was a group of hippies blaming him for the death and destruction he'd inflicted on the innocent people of Vietnam, calling him words like *war criminal, assassin, warmonger*, and worse.

Larry had told her that he hadn't asked to be there; he hadn't volunteered to fight. But when America had called him, he had done his duty, and had done everything he could to do it right. Nevertheless, in spite of his efforts, medals, and scars, the very same people who had called him to action, the very same neighbors he'd grown up with, were waiting for him on his return to call him a traitor, a war criminal, and a heartless soul. Larry had not been expecting this, but evidently, to Marie's assumptions, his pain was his reward for surviving a heartless war.

Larry had told Marie that he'd left in search of the farthest place away from so-called civilization he could find and had landed in Nome, Alaska. Upon arrival, Larry'd had nothing but a green duffle bag full of dirty uniforms and a lot of anger against the antiwar demonstrators.

Marie recalled Larry's favorite tale about having found the American dream by settling in Alaska, where he now had a wife, two beautiful children, and a God-honest job.

Marie was proud to have him as a friend and proud of what he had achieved in life and what he had overcome. One of his pains, he once said, was watching his fellow countrymen die and seeing the many innocent Vietnamese people slaughtered by violent Vietcong. But what really scarred his soul was seeing the hippies' hatred of the uniform, and Marie had no doubt that the memories Larry bore deep inside him would stay with him until the moment he died.

She was suddenly brought back to reality when Larry told her that they had arrived at the market.

"Thanks, Larry. Please keep the change and say hello to Helen and the kids."

"Will do, Marie, Have a happy day!"

For a moment, Marie Steele felt alive and part of the community again, but soon this moment would be taken away by the burning reality that was bugging her existence. She stopped by the bakery and purchased some fresh bread and then walked by the fresh produce. As she was about to purchase some milk, she spotted Sheriff Lindblom. *Oh good,* she thought. *This will save me a trip to the police station. Perhaps my luck is about to change.*

She walked right up to the sheriff and told him all she knew, but she got back nothing from him. Marie had to listen one more time to the sheriff's all-purpose phrase: "Don't you worry, Marie. Give time a chance; you'll see that all is going to work out."

Marie was tired of the sheriff's laid-back attitude and said to him, "You know, Sheriff. I hope that this was not the same thing you said to the Parkers, Kens, and Morrises. They followed your recommendations and gave time a chance, and you know all of them lost a husband, a father, and a son. So, sheriff, you can take your 'give time a chance' and shove it, you ass."

Marie Steele turned her back and resumed her shopping at the busy street market, leaving Sheriff Lindblom standing there with the words on his lips she didn't care to hear anymore. The sheriff, she realized, was merely a public official who was part of the problem and not the solution.

***

Danny found himself standing in front of the vice president's office located at the Naval Observatory. He paused for a second before he knocked on the door and entered once VP Farmer had invited him in. He greeted VP Farmer.

"Sir, we have prepared the stem-cell research restriction policy for your speech in Nome. Remember that, after you hand out the Anvil Run ten top awards, you will have the opportunity to tell the world the administration's stem-cell policy. I have summoned the usual supporters and the usual key journalists who closely follow your work. And, sir, the Alaskan governor has endorsed your initiative and will meet you in Anchorage."

"Isn't that something, Danny? It's easy to jump on the bandwagon when things are already in motion, rather than getting out and pushing when stuck in a hole," said Farmer.

"Mr. Vice President ..." Danny paused a moment to take a deep breath and then looked at the vice president. "Politics as usual I guess; politics as usual," he concluded.

"You can say that again, Danny. This will make him look like a hero, having me in his land, saving thousands of neonates and providing hope for humanity. I have to say that, in a world ruled by technology and by the powerful, sometimes peoples' consciences seems to be obscured by money and blinded by the undying thirst to play God. I believe in technology and progress, but humanity is not ready yet for this kind of research, and I am going to put a stop to it. Someone has to take a stand and do what's right for America.

"I don't want this great country of ours to be remembered in the history pages as a savage, heartless, selfish country that would kill the young to serve the old. Just saying it doesn't make sense, does it, Danny? The president is clear and certain that stem-cell research is not going to be endorsed by this administration."

"Sir, I would like to caution you; you know you have one of your worst opposing forces right in Nome, Alaska!"

"Oh, you mean that old fart, James Lindberg? He is powerful and owns most of the lobbyists in DC, but he can't buy this administration, and he knows it. He is no threat to us, Danny, and we are not afraid of him."

"Sir, if the millions he's spent in advertising and lobbying pro stem cells raises awareness for the stem-cell issue, this may help us achieve our goals and get more endorsements for the opposition bill. I guess it wouldn't hurt to give him some credit; would you agree?"

"I guess I have to agree, Danny. So are we ready to fly to Alaska?"

"Yes, sir. We leave tomorrow morning as scheduled."

After running through his speech, VP Farmer was confident that his new and aggressive initiative would be quickly endorsed by Congress, as quickly as a fat woman sliding down a waterpark slide.

Danny felt his cellular phone vibrating. He looked at the screen and saw that the caller was US Secret Service Special Agent Landis. Danny excused himself from the vice president.

"Yes, Agent Landis," he answered.

"I wanted to make sure that we go over the details one more time before we go," said Agent Landis.

"Yes, of course," confirmed Danny. "Are there any changes from the last time we spoke?" he asked.

"No, Danny. There are no changes. We leave tomorrow as scheduled from Andrews AFB, and we'll be using the Boeing C-32. We'll pick up the VP at zero eight hundred hours from USNO and drive directly to Andrews, board the VP plane, and fly directly into Anchorage."

Danny understood the plan details as explained by SA Landis over the phone. At this time, the trip was a go, and everything was going to be all right. Throughout the conversation Danny had felt as if SA Landis was at ease knowing that he understood the plan. To this effect, Danny highlighted the show's flow over the phone as Landis carefully listened. "Let's see if I got it right, Landis; we'll fly to Anchorage, stay there for a day, and go to a fundraising dinner, where the VP will meet with the city mayor and governor.

"Vice President Farmer will receive the key to the city and, the next day, fly to Nome. VP Farmer will give his speech and schmooze with the local cream and close the day by presenting the top Anvil Run awards.

"Simple, got it," said Danny.

***

Landis was pleased with the simplicity of the plan but also worried that it was not going to be easy to execute, especially when the intelligence he'd read earlier about the possible assassination attempt was still lurking around his head. He was not about to tell Danny or anyone else about his concerns, not unless he had more concrete intelligence confirming or supporting the initial bulletin. He thanked Danny and hung up the phone.

Following the call, Landis started to gather his trip resources and soon got frustrated with an Anchorage, Alaska, FBI field office after the office confirmed that it was short of agents because most of them were on leave; the other excuse was attrition.

"I can't believe this!" said Landis as he slapped the top of his working desk, located at the small command center next to the vice president's residence. "What a bunch of crap. I have never asked Anchorage's field service for any assistance, and the first time I need them, they back out and come up with this shit. How can they expect us to protect this principal? This is bullshit!"

Following this, he called SS headquarters and complained to SS Operations Director Peter McAuley.

Landis's boss gave him the score, saying the local cops would carry the load and that Landis was to use his full detail.

Agent Landis hung up his phone, lay back in his chair, stared at his office ceiling, and exclaimed, "What have I done to deserve this?" He then turned to his computer and retrieved the Anchorage and Nome, Alaska, police departments' phone numbers and started to beg for more resources.

Anchorage was not a problem; he could have as many as the department could spare. Nome was another matter. Chief of Police Lindblom could only assign three more men to the SS detail, indicating that most of his resources were already committed to the Fourth of July celebration. Agent Landis took all he could and thanked the chief for his assistance, but he knew that protecting Vice President Farmer was not going to be a walk in the park, especially when he had to protect the vice president in the Fourth of July crowd in Nome as VP Farmer delivered the administration's message to the rest of the world.

After the call, Agent Landis started to coordinate working schedules using all the resources within his reach. He prayed and crossed his fingers that nothing would happen. He had to make a plan. He picked up his usual template and started to fill in the blanks. Let's see—logistics support, zero; resources, limited; communications, good; intelligence, low; threat, low risk; transportation ...

Agent Landis was a professional protective agent who knew his work well, but he also knew the repercussions if his security plan failed. And even without confirmation, the new bulletin about the possible attempt on the VP's life changed everything about this trip. If everything went as planned and nothing happened, he would not get even a simple "attaboy," but if the shit hit the fan, he would have to face an official inquiry at the home office and his job could be jeopardized; this was something he was not ready to face.

The first thing that he would do was send one of his agents immediately to Anchorage and then to Nome for the advance work. He would then have to use the remaining agents to accompany him from the VP's residence in DC all the way to Anchorage and then to Nome.

"Business as usual; let's start the show," he whispered as he stared at the computer screen. Landis was sweating hard as he contemplated the logistical details in his plan, how he was going to effectively execute it in a place he hadn't gone before—a place where the current administration had a very strong adversary—and above all, how he was going to get the VP back to DC in one piece.

10

THE JOURNEY

I swore I could hear faint chatting around me, which prompted me to open my eyes. And when I opened my eyes, I felt a lot better. I was back on my game, but the body aches and pain, although faint, still reminded me that I was not a young man anymore. I mustered all the strength I could and thought, *Ready or not, I have no choice.* I had to be ready for action.

I sat up in bed to see Sora and Sani-Shaman looking at me. The old man had a smile, as if he was looking at the miracle he had created. Sora was not as impressed with the miraculous recovery, but my heart was palpitating knowing that I was alive because of whatever Sani-Shaman did, and I was grateful.

I had work to do and asked Sani-Shaman to take me to the Bronco because I needed the tools I'd left behind. He smiled again and looked to his right. I followed him with my eyes to see that all my tools were inside the tent—along with a shelf full of other pieces, like C-4, detonators, pineapple and smoke grenades, and the like.

I have to recruit this guy to work for me in Little Italy, I thought. I took the time to explain my plans to Sani-Shaman and Sora. It was a KISS plan (I had intentions to keep it simple and stupid).

I knew that I was working against the clock, and I couldn't

get the word *suicidal* from Uncle Jimmy's file out of my head. I knew that it was only a matter of time before Jimmy would lose whatever it was that was keeping him alive and take his own or perhaps others' lives with him. I knew him; he was a determined and very able man, and if he wanted to do something, no force on this earth would prevent him from doing it.

My plan was to use the little nighttime left tonight to find my way in to Lindberg Research, discover what the corporation's plans had to do with Jimmy and this town, and stop it before it was too late. I knew that, by now, I could not go back to Dr. Anderson's office for answers, as after my little incursion, I bet that all the important files must have been taken out of the office and moved into the only secure location in town, Lindberg Research Corp.

So the three of us mounted three amphibious Argo ATVs and headed toward the complex. The route was exquisite. It was full of nature and green as it could be, with the clearest ravines and lakes I had ever seen. I was beginning to understand why people came to this place. Experiencing nature at its best was amazing. To my left, I could see a group of caribou drinking water along the lake. An eagle soared above us so majestic with his black silk feathers, looking like he owned the skies. Sani-Shaman bowed at him with respect as he passed high above us. I couldn't even begin to understand the close relationship and respect that the natives had for the wildlife and nature. *Wouldn't it be nice that if those on the mainland also had the same type of respect for nature as the locals do here?* I thought.

The path was treacherous, so we chose to follow one behind the other. Sani-Shaman wanted me to get there in time, so he took us through a shortcut he knew well near the mountain range he called Kigluaik Mountains; he told me that they were the highest peaks around here. As we cleared the narrow path, Sora drove ahead of us to scout out the path. I pulled alongside Sani-Shaman and asked him what her story was.

"Jack, there's not much to tell; she's just a small-town girl," he said.

"But a small-town girl wouldn't turn to face three men to defend a vagrant at a diner; she would just work there."

"Jack, she lives with a chip on her shoulder," said Sani-Shaman.

"What happened?" I asked.

From Sani-Shaman, I learned that Sora had studied at the University of Anchorage. She'd earned her degree in social work and had been recruited from the university by Lindberg Research Corporation to work in its research and development department. She was very good at what she did. But as she was getting more and more involved, she had started to discover things she didn't like. She'd decided to resign and leave before it was too late for her. Lindberg Research made sure that she could not get a job anywhere close by, so she'd had to become a waitress.

I had to ask Sani-Shaman what he meant by "things she didn't like."

He told me that, one day, she'd heard a conversation between the director of research and development and another person she'd identified as Dr. Harjo on the speaker phone. The two were talking about the development of more resources to accelerate the town people's assimilation process. Sani-Shaman told me exactly what Sora had heard as she kept quiet and continued to work. She'd relayed the details of the conversation verbatim:

"Dr. Harjo, I am glad to report that patient twenty-six is responding well to the serum. Twenty-six is acting normal; his ability to interact with others is amazing; and, although he is fully programmed, he doesn't realize it. Dr. Harjo, I think we have perfected the serum; this batch is a complete success."

"I take it that congratulations are in order."

111

"Thank you, sir. We appreciate your gratitude."

"Then let's get to work and start mass production right away."

"When? Now?"

"Yes, I mean now."

"We will go into mass production right away as you wish, sir."

With that, the R and D director had disconnected the speaker phone.

Shortly after that telephone conversation, Sora was asked to step up her game and to start convincing locals to participate in LR Corp's free psychological counseling, telling them it would help them get rid of anxiety, stress, and other mental illnesses.

Throughout the process, Sora realized that, once many of the participants had enrolled in the free psychological counseling, they started to develop other inexplicable tendencies. Many sold their land and properties to what was later discovered to be a realtor who worked under LR Corporation's pocket. Others locals abandoned their traditions and, once in the program, were encouraged to endorse LR Corporation and help it gain control of the local sacred lands.

Some committed suicide; others killed their families. Once Sora started to suspect that these strange occurrences were related to the corporation's psychological counseling program, she confided in Sani-Shaman. As an elder, he used his tribal council position to check on her allegations and treated the information as his own. He'd brought it to the attention of Lindberg Research Corporation management, and within weeks, he'd been approached by high executives within the corporation who had made him believe they cared and assured him they would look into the situation.

As expected, this never happened. Sani-Shaman pushed harder to find answers, until one day he was accused by one of his own tribal members, who was obviously under LR

Corporation control, of accepting bribes, and Sani-Shaman was disgraced by his own council members.

Through a series of key questions, Jack was able to reconstruct a very good picture of what was happening in this town. Almost 80 percent of the town's able-bodied worked at LR Corp. And, of course, after working for LR Corp, none of them were ever the same.

"Tell me, Sani-Shaman, when did all of this mental illness and the problems start?" I asked.

Sani-Shaman told me that the mental illness started even before LR Corp came to town. In the beginning, some of the natives started to experience out-of-body experiences. Many said that the gods had come and taken them. Others mentioned that the ancestors had come and spoken to them during the night. Some also testified that their inner spiritual animal had spoken to them and asked them to do things.

Sani-Shaman further explained that, as this phenomenon started to develop, many psychologists came to town and tried to help, but they saw no progress. Then LR Corp came and bought St. Francis Hospital and created its mental illness program. It was free of charge, and at first, the locals thought that the program was helping. So with open arms, they embraced it, endorsed it, and surrendered their faith to medical science.

Eventually, and without reason, many of the locals started to do things that were against their faith, beliefs, and folklore. People behaved in ways that had never been seen in these parts of the country—fights between brothers and sisters, youngsters against elders, and many ended up either missing or committing suicide.

In this beautiful place, how could people ever have enough problems to commit suicide, let alone kill their own families?

Sani-Shaman continued to explain that, for years, their people had consulted with their ancestors; they had lived their lives by the pure counsel of Mother Nature through their inner animal strength. And for centuries, they had never witnessed the behaviors they were experiencing today.

Now I understood why Sora had left the organization. Everything that was touched by Lindberg Research Corporation seemed to result in death, destruction, and blatant disrespect for nature.

Sani-Shaman also said that other things had happened to Sora, but that it would be up to her to tell me, as he didn't see it was his duty to break her trust.

Then Sani-Shaman slowly raised his head to the sky and said to me, "A man who disrespects his past and nature is bound to live a meaningless life of scarceness and sorrows."

I realized that what he was trying to say was that, based on the present, no future was left in Nome. I could see that we were getting closer to Sora, so I looked at the old man with respect and thanked him for the information.

Now I understood that there was more to this company than meets the eye. I was convinced that there was a correlation between LR Corp and the collective psyche of the town. LR Corp was responsible for many lives, for stealing away the land, and for hiding its true intentions behind local legends and folklore.

To me, LR Corporation's true intentions were clear, but how would I prove it? I had to put an end to this before Uncle Jimmy became part of this local sickness, and I knew the solution was there, behind the barbed wire and high fences. Tonight, I was determined to find out one way or another.

Sora looked at us and pointed her finger to the north. In the distance, I could see a well-fortified place. Sani-Shaman then took off his boots before stepping on holy land and performed a short ceremony.

Sora later told me that it was his way of honoring the ancestors and asking for permission to enter their holy land. I respected this. "Without traditions and respect," she added, "man is bound to find his way to an empty soul."

As I stood there watching Sani-Shaman, I felt my mind running at a hundred miles an hour. I had a hard task ahead of me, and I hoped that, within the unfamiliar words that Sani-Shaman was chanting, he had found a way to ask the trusted ancestors for help—as I was sure that we were going to need all the help we could get to complete our goals tonight.

Sora looked at me as if she knew what I was thinking, and I felt that, somehow, the ancestors did too. To bring down this company, it would take a lot more than one woman, an old man, and a burnout PI. We would need all the help that we could get.

11

BUSINESS AS USUAL

With the dawn's early light, Danny got up and looked at his watch—showtime. He'd had a chance to pack the previous day, and the only thing he needed was a nice shower and a hot cup of black coffee.

It was a nice, warm morning as he rode on DuPont Circle, following the turns on Massachusetts Avenue. From there, with the sun on his face, Danny continued a few more minutes to Number One Observatory Circle. He reported to the main gate and then drove directly to his right and continued on until he was able to see the white structure with gray shingles at 34th Street. This well-kept-up 1893 mansion was an impressive sight to see. The three-story house was made of bricks and, later, painted white.

The Queen Anne–style home was a mansion (although no one liked to call it that) at nearly 9,150 square feet. Historical records disclosed that the building had been the official home of the chief of the Naval Observatory since 1929. But in 1974, Congress had decided that this would be a better home for the US vice president, and so it had been ever since.

Since then, many vice presidents had lived there, including the first VP Ford and his family. The only vice presidential family who had not lived in the house were the Rockefellers, who only used this mansion for official dinners and other lavish parties but never considered it an official residence.

Nevertheless, since 1974 the mansion had been the official residence of all vice presidents, including the Mondales, the Ford's or Rockefeller's every other vice presidential family after them.

What Danny liked was that he had his own undercover parking garage for his Ironheads motorcycle, and this to him was worth more than anything. He hated leaving his precious ride at the mercy of the environment at a regular parking space at Andrews Air Force Base.

Danny was greeted by the US Secret Service detail stationed at the house, and after going through the daily inspection routine, he was allowed access to the VP's home. Danny found his way through the back door and decided to follow the strong smell of eggs and bacon.

Soon afterward, he found the employees' dining room, which was his favorite breakfast spot. He liked light eggs and turkey bacon in the morning, followed by a large glass of freshly squeezed orange juice.

To his surprise, he found the vice president there and immediately greeted him. "Good morning, Vice President. How are you today?"

"Just fine, Danny, just fine. Would you care to join me?"

"But if it's okay with you, I'd prefer not to have breakfast today."

"Whatever you say, Danny, whatever you say," said VP Farmer.

"Are you ready for a little ride?" asked Danny.

"Do I have a choice?" asked VP Farmer.

"I'm afraid to say that's entirely up to you, sir. But I already know what you are going to say."

"Yes, you know me, son, but I have no choice, right?"

"Then ... I guess we are going to Alaska, Mr. Vice President. With your permission, I would like to check that Gordon has packed all you need for the trip, including some warm garments."

"Very thoughtful of you, Danny. I will be ready in fifteen minutes. I know that the protection guys left me a message saying that they will be leaving at 9:00 a.m. sharp."

"Yes, Mr. Vice President, you are right; 9:00 a.m. is the departure time on the schedule they gave me as well. I am sure you don't want to miss our departure window," said Danny.

Shortly after that, Danny walked upstairs and met Gordon, the vice president's butler. "Good morning, Gordon," said Danny.

"Good day to you, Danny. How was the Harley ride today?" said Gordon.

"Like a dream, Gordon ... like a dream," said Danny.

"I thought so," replied Gordon. "I can assure you that Mr. Farmer's luggage is complete, and I also put in a couple of warm garments for him. I know he doesn't enjoy cold nights. I know that the climate in Alaska could change on a dime, and I wanted to make sure that he is dressed appropriately for any occasion," said Gordon.

At this time, Vice President Farmer's wife, Lenora, entered the room, looked straight into Danny's eyes, and clearly said, "Brad is in your hands. Please make sure that you bring him back—in one piece. Do you hear me, Danny?"

"Yes, Lenora. I promise," Danny assured her. "As always, I will bring him back to you."

Lenora took a sip from her refined china tea cup, raised her left eyebrow, smiled, and turned around and walked toward her room.

Danny never understood why the vice president chose to sleep in separate rooms from his wife, but he guessed that it was a matter of tradition within the mansion.

Both the vice president and Lenora still looked in good shape, they were very healthy and loved each other, but in this mansion, they chose to sleep in separate rooms. Just thinking about it bugged Danny. To Danny, love was about passion, togetherness, and feeling the one you loved right next to you. Sleeping in separate rooms meant, to him, separation and distance, and in his book, this was not right. But again, he was not part of the Farmer family but just another aide, and what he thought was not important to them. And although he'd learned to care for the family, this thought was not something that he would dare to share with them anyway.

***

A buzzer sound came out of the room, and Gordon recognized it immediately as the ten-minute warning before departure. As he pushed the intercom, acknowledging the call, he saw VP Farmer's figure walking upstairs and heading toward the room. He knew that, in less than ten minutes, his boss would be boarding the car and heading to Andrews Air Force Base and that he would not be returning for the next three days or so.

***

Danny headed downstairs to make sure that all the vice president's luggage, his briefcase, and his special documents were in the vehicle before departure.

Danny had already discussed details with SSA Landis, and all was in place. Landis gave him a brief security report for Vice President Farmer to read on the plane during the trip. As usual, the report contained the weather in Anchorage and Nome and key facts about both places that he should know as a political, economic, and social thermometer about both places, which included key names, people's photographs, and issues. Finally, the report had a complete list of emergency contacts that Landis had added just in case.

Music to my ears, thought Danny.

SA Landis, as well as others, believed that the president

or vice president read these reports when, in fact, people like him were the ones who spent countless hours reading them so they could advise their bosses.

It was true that what made great leaders and great men were people like Danny, who were the true heroes assisting people in positions like the vice president. It was his duty to know his job well, to think ahead, and to take the blame when things didn't go the way they were expected—in other words, to ensure his boss's success at all costs. Danny knew and accepted the responsibility and, thus, the perks that came with the job, such as flying on the VP's plane and going to Alaska, a place he had never visited before this trip.

Seconds later, VP Farmer was escorted by Gordon to the front porch, and Danny took over from there.

After opening the door and seeing to it that VP Farmer was comfortably seated, SA Landis closed the back door and, as usual, sat in the front passenger seat. It was a well-rehearsed and choreographed routine—the motorcycle escort, the front and chase car driving from 34th Street. During this time, both Danny and VP Farmer were immersed in details and briefings about the trip.

Danny could never take for granted the amount of detail involved in transporting the vice president from point A to point B. From the back of the limousine, Danny could hear SSA Landis providing details about the vehicle's occupants— special pass codes that allowed the gate to swing open for them as they continued their trip toward the hangar.

Agent Landis went through the hangar's open doors and was welcomed by the air force support staff directing him where to go. The plane, as always, looked magnificent and impressive. The majestic, iconic colors screamed US government all over. This plane was a true testament of power, authority, and majesty.

Shortly after boarding the plane, the Secret Service agents followed the take-off routine. Landis never left the sight of the

121

VP while the other two agents still on the ground supervising the bags and special equipment they always carried with them had all been loaded onto the plane.

Minutes later, the plane started to taxi onto the tarmac, escorted by AFB military police.

The pilot and captain called the tower and requested permission to take off. Both the airspace, as well as the tarmac, had been cleared just for this plane to take off. In less than five minutes, the plane was airborne and heading northwest toward Anchorage, Alaska.

Danny looked at the front storage where he'd left his coat, knowing that he may need it upon landing.

He noticed VP Farmer standing up and walking toward his office. Danny changed seats and sat near the VP's office entrance to make sure that he was readily available in case the vice president needed him. He then opened his briefcase and started reading the Secret Service brief before he become sleepy and tired. He knew that he had at least six hours ahead of him before he would have to discuss the post-landing details with Vice President Farmer.

***

The room was noisy; loud music and the sound of clinking beer jugs filled the air. A group of men were playing pool and talking about the deer one of them hunted a few days ago. At the bar, a few men were drinking their regular brew and talking about women. Pizza, sandwiches, and beers bottles filled all but one table. The back room table only held a couple of beer jugs; one was full and one almost empty, and Jimmy Steele was holding the latter. He was sitting comfortably at the table, talking to the heavily clad man with the white hat.

To Jimmy, the man with the white hat seemed to be the answer to his questions—the light in the dark and the path under his feet. Jimmy Steele should have been in his house

122

holding his wife tightly, and yet he was in a bar drinking beer. The problem was not that he was drinking his favorite brew or that he was talking to friends; the problem was that he did not know why. Like many other men in town, Jimmy felt like life was passing by, and he was missing it. He could not recall the last time he had gone fishing, the last time he'd camped in front of the beach alongside Marie to see the whales' migration, and yet he didn't know why.

As he sipped his beer, he looked around and was amazed to see family men who were drinking their lives away in the bar. *But why?* he thought. *What has changed? And what mysterious poison have they drunk?* What forces a family man to leave the woman and children he loved and cared for to gather in this diabolic tavern?

What bothered Jimmy the most was that he was one of them, and in spite of his many questions deep inside him, Jimmy could not find an answer that would satisfy his quest. His mind only brought him back to the cold, soothing flavor of the local Alaskan Amber beer that recently he'd learned to love so much.

Jimmy felt that something was wrong, very wrong with him. He feared that, soon, he would not be able to remember the last time he'd been intimate with his wife, and this was driving him crazy. He understood that something was off, really off, but what it was he didn't know.

To him, he was living a normal life and yet Marie didn't see it this way. So what had changed? He grabbed his cold glass and stared at its contents, focused on the foamy, yellowish liquid and thinking through his options. In his mind, he could only see the past and the present, but it was very difficult for him to picture the future, and he was terrified to think that there was none.

Jimmy, as well as most of the men in town, was drinking his life away in this little establishment, and yet the men didn't even know it. Nor could they explain how they'd got

123

there. Many of them left work in the middle of the day, others gathered after work, and some could even be seen having a few drinks during the early to mid-morning. This phenomenon, or rather, gathering had taken place since the sports bar opened, but it seemed that this activity had intensified during the last six months.

The man with the white hat had made this little sports bar table part of his permanent office. He didn't bother anybody; he just sat there, and as many regular patrons said he was the beer god. He talked to people, bought them as much beer as they could consume, and even drove them home when needed. What a guy! Many said he was a true pal. A man sent from heaven to help lessen and forget their daily worries. The beer and chat helped them to ease their daily burdens, especially as they didn't have to spend their meager weekly wages to get to enjoy the juice from the gods. It always seemed to taste even better when it was given to them for free.

From where Jimmy was seated, he saw Sheriff Lindblom enter the main door, take off his hat, and make his way slowly toward the bar. As always, the interior of the building was dark. Boyd kept the lights down for various reasons; first of all, he didn't want to pay a large power bill. In addition, he didn't want people to see the dust he didn't have time to clean. And lastly, the low lights kept an atmosphere of secrecy and discretion.

And this last part was what the young lovers enjoyed about the sports bar. They liked to hang out in the dark, and other than the woods, this was the ideal place to make out away from their parents' homes. The bar was full of locals; at any time, you could find airport workers, fishermen, and even the fearless firemen. This was the place to quickly grab a cold one, play some pool, and hang loose.

***

As the sheriff walked to the bar, he could see that the three pool tables were full of locals making their wagers. He was not particularly interested in bothering anyone placing a few hundred dollars or even a few ounces of gold on top of the table, as long as they honored their responsibilities and made no trouble. At one of the pool tables, Lindblom saw a high-caliber Winchester, which told him that at least one of those locals should be out hunting instead of drinking. He wondered what this local had told his wife before leaving home with his rifle. He took a wild guess that it was something along the lines of, *Honey, I am going hunting with Bob.*

That was the couple's problem, and he was not about to make a big fuss about it.

To his right, he saw a couple of young locals throwing darts at the red, green, and white target. Most of the time, the darts landed on the tables, chairs, and even the ceiling. Nevertheless, a few customers were lucky enough to, once in a while, hit the bull's-eye of the colorful target nailed to the right wall. The sheriff knew that, to Boyd, this translated to more consumption of beer and food to celebrate the occasion. As for the damage to the establishment, that was worth the aggravation, as long as his customers consumed his beer, drank his liquor, and ate his pizza.

Lindblom had almost made it to the bar when a couple of tourists acknowledged him with a "Howdy there, Sheriff."

He nodded at the tourists and concluded from their appearance that they must have flown in from either Alabama or Texas. They must have wanted to have an adventure and take some photos to bring back home, making them heroes in their local tavern.

Lindblom directed his focus back to the bar.

"Sheriff." Boyd nodded a hello. "Will you be having your usual poison?" An old Canadian man, Boyd proudly displayed a few threads of salt-and-pepper hair on his head. He also wore a long, white goatee and a shiny, black-leather jacket

125

over a white T-shirt. He was frozen in time and looked like a character from *Happy Days*.

"You know it, Boyd," said the sheriff, taking a seat on his preferred corner stool.

"Right away, Sheriff. One cold Amber on the way," said Boyd.

Lindblom looked around the room to see that everyone was having a good time and thought to himself, *Why should I prevent myself from enjoying the same pleasures I swore to protect?*

Boyd came close to him and said, "Sheriff, here you go—a cold one dressed in a wedding dress for you." The beer was served in a large, frozen glass jug, and some of the beer was spilling out, making a white line dripping down the glass, which at a glance looked like a wedding veil.

Sheriff Lindblom stared at it with a watery mouth and replied, "Just as I like it, Boyd, just as I like it. Thank you." The sheriff took a couple of sips and glanced at a young couple in a dark corner making out. He moved his head sideways with disapproval but knew that this type of behavior was expected in places like this. As far as he was concerned, as long as no one complained, he hadn't seen anything.

As he continued to look around the room, he saw three men making noise over a bet, and immediately in front of him was a local native dressed in furs who appeared to have had too much to drink. "Hey, Boyd, what's up with this one?" asked Lindblom.

"Nothing, Sheriff. The native's in the animal fur business; he comes here every week, sits down, and drinks his whiskey. He bothers no one, and on occasion, I see him crying in the same dark corner. He's harmless.

"On many occasions, I listen to him talking to himself about having seen a huge laboratory full of bodies enclosed in glass cages, but then he starts to cry again. The only thing that calms him down is a fresh Alaskan Amber. What a character.

If you ask me, Sheriff, I think that spending time in the woods hunting has done a number on him."

Sheriff Lindblom sipped his beer, and as he felt the cold and bitter liquid running down his throat, he labeled this man as no threat—just another antisocial crazy who preferred the hardships of Mother Nature over the comforts of town life.

He panned the room and stopped when he spotted one Jimmy Steele and recognized Billy Mayer, the man with a white hat. Seconds later, Mayer saw the sheriff looking. For a split second, the two men's eyes met, before Mayer dropped his gaze and concentrated on Jimmy. Billy Mayer and the sheriff shared some unpleasant history, and it was clear to Lindblom that Mayer preferred to avoid him at all costs.

He watched Mayer place his beer on the table and stand up; Jimmy followed suit, and both men started to walk toward the back room. Sheriff Lindblom took another sip, and when he was about to stand up, Boyd stopped him and asked, "Sheriff, are you going to have a deputy in the bar during the Anvil Run? You know that last year some tourists got a little rowdy and broke a few things. Sheriff, it's hard to find replacements here, and I don't have to mention that they are very expensive to get! I would like to prevent vandalism if I could."

Lindblom looked him in the eye and said, "Boyd, how long have you owned this bar?"

"Let me see, Sheriff, I have been here for over eleven years now. Why do you ask?"

"Now that you've answered me," the sheriff replied, "I ask you, for how many years have I assigned deputies in or near the bar before, during, and after the Anvil Run?"

"Hard to say, Sheriff. Let me see—eleven years."

"So I wonder, Boyd, why do you ask me now? Not to worry; a deputy will be close by at the airport, and since it's just a couple of minutes away, if you need him, he will be here at once."

127

Sheriff Lindblom started to walk out when Boyd call him again, "Sheriff, your beer!"

Lindblom looked back at him and responded, "I'll be back in a minute, Boyd. Keep it cold for me, will you?"

Lindblom took a stroll toward the back room and entered through a double door into the back bar storage. At a glance, he saw no one as far as his eyes could see. He walked toward the back and opened the rear loading door. To his surprise, there was no one in sight.

Lindblom entered the storage and looked around. To his left was a rack of canned food, water, and other dry products. To his right were a few silver-colored CO_2 tanks, a freezer, and a stack of boxes.

Where did they go? he wondered. This was a very small area. Lindblom calculated that Boyd's distraction had delayed him for less than thirty seconds; he should have caught up with Jimmy and Mayer.

He turned toward the bar doors to find Boyd looking at him steadily.

"May I help you, Sheriff? Is there something you want?"

"Yes, Boyd, as a matter of fact, there is. I thought that I saw old Jimmy Steele and Billy Mayer walk out through the back door, but they seem to have disappeared into thin air."

"Sheriff, as you can see, there is no way they could've disappeared. I mean, look! There is only one exit here. Did you look outside?"

"Yes, Boyd, I did, but they were gone."

The sheriff walked into the bar and stood right next to the table where both men had been sitting, only to find a spotless clean table. Looking at the table, the sheriff noticed that no beer glass water rings left a trace of any presence here and the chairs were neatly positioned. He shook his head with disbelief; he could swear that Jimmy and Billy had been sitting down at this table and that they'd walked out the back door.

"Perhaps you are right, Boyd," he finally said. "I think that the beer is having a strange effect on me today. Never mind. Have a nice day, Boyd."

With that, Sheriff Lindblom walked out of the bar, without paying or leaving a tip.

Sheriff Lindblom was a man who was seldom confused or imagined things. He prided himself on being a very detail-oriented man, but today, things didn't add up the way they used to. As he entered his official vehicle, he sat down, moved the rearview mirror to his face, and stared into his eyes. Something was wrong in his head; this was not the first time this had happened to him recently. Not too long ago, he could have sworn he was at home sleeping, and he'd woken up in his car under a bridge, the car still running, and he had no clue how he'd gotten there and for what reasons.

He was beginning to remember people he had never before seen or been introduced to. What's more, strangers were calling him by his first name. It was public knowledge and widely advertised that he preferred to be addressed as either Sheriff or Lindblom and didn't tolerate the use of his first name. Although these unexplained circumstances were bothering him, the most disturbing of all was that he didn't know why and this, for the first time, started to scare him; he felt that those feelings were messing with his sanity, and keeping his sanity was a key ingredient to continuing his duties as the sheriff of Nome, Alaska.

12

HANDS ON

After the short ceremony, Sani-Shaman decided to stay in place until after dark. He feared that, if they got much closer to the LR Corporation, either the sentries or their technology would detect them. I knew that our best ally was darkness and needed no further convincing.

In the meantime, Sani-Shaman was explaining to us the mechanics of the complex, all he remembered from his time as local tribal liaison to LR Corporation, and I was plotting the best strategy to get in and out in one piece.

After about forty minutes, I came up with a plan based on our observations.

Then, without warning and out of nowhere, a patrol helicopter passed near us, roaring with a purpose. We all buried our noses onto the cold tundra, hoping that we had not been seen. My heart was pounding hard out of my chest. I looked at Sani-Shaman, who was still trying not to move. To our doom, the helicopter stopped, circled back, and came slowly toward us. "Holy shit, we got canned," I whispered.

Not waiting for the helicopter to get closer, we were able to slowly move to the edge of the hill; lucky for us, the hill had a couple of medium-sized pines that had concealed the ATVs, but we were exposed to the elements and helicopter view. We moved closer to the tree as quickly as we could and tried to be part of the edge of the hill as much as possible. As the helicopter was hovering almost in front of us, we saw a group of caribou scare from the noise and run down the pine areas toward the meadow.

The helicopter stood still, hovering almost on top us. When the gunner opened fire, the caribou fell one by one in front of our frightened eyes. Seconds later, the smell of burned powder engulfed the area, and down in the meadows, what was once a group of healthy and warm caribou now was a heap composed of blood and fur.

Sani-Shaman wanted to stand up and unleash his anger at the helicopter gunner, but I was quick enough to pull him down and hold him under me in an effort to save our lives. The helicopter pilot turned the bird around and made a quick descent toward the well-fortified complex.

I looked at Sora, and she was in tears. The killing of those innocent animals was a cowardly act by people who do things not because they are right or wrong but because they can, and this was what I could read on her wet face.

Sani-Shaman crawled away from me and looked with hatred at the bird making a quick descent toward the well-fortified complex called LR Corporation. He started to say something I didn't understood, but one thing I picked up for sure was, "You'll pay for this. I promise you will pay."

After our adrenaline levels receded and we had recovered from the near-death experience, we got back to our plan. I pointed out that the complex's most fragile place was its northeast section, where a wall faced the mountains. To the south was the road leading to and from town, and to the east, there was nothing but open tundra. Anyone coming from a mile away would easily be spotted as the approach offered no places to find cover or hide. Sani-Shaman agreed with my assessment that the northeast section would be the least protected.

After finishing our incursion strategy, we went over it once again to make sure that we had it memorized. First, we would approach the complex from the northeast fence. I would cut the fence open and walk in at precisely the moment when the guards were in the middle of the shift change. I would walk in with Sani-Shaman, and Sora would remain as a lookout, feeding us intelligence and covering our exit. The plan was KISS again, and I liked it.

We lay down to wait for sundown, and I found time to ask Sani-Shaman to tell me what he knew about the town's missing people. He said that, in the beginning, Alaska was a big land of ice and the animals roamed free and were friends with his ancestors. The people understood animals, and the animals didn't bother them. Sani-Shaman added that people only killed for food, not for sport or to boost their vanity.

He continued his monologue by saying that the land was clean and free, but as the white men continued to expand their search for Mother Nature's precious metals and killing the animals for sport, the land turned against them. The ancestors' way of life, which saw a balanced relationship between man and nature, changed from harmony to chaos. The mysterious disappearances had their roots back in the sixties and continued to this day. That was right when the Lindberg Research Corporation came and promised prosperity for Nome and that they would respect the ancestors' land. But soon, the locals realized that the Lindberg Research Corporation was pursuing hidden agendas, against local traditions, beliefs, and values.

Many, like Sani-Shaman's father, fought the corporation with everything they had. But they soon realized that LR Corp used magic on those who opposed them. Eventually the corporation's opponents either mysteriously changed their minds or vanished in the middle of the night.

I asked him what he meant by "mysteriously changed their minds."

He told me that many strong, hard-core advocates for land and culture started to support progress and the white man's ways of life that were offered by the LR Corp. Many abandoned their ancestral beliefs and way of life. They changed their hunting ways for microwave dinners; they forgot to pick wood to burn during winter in favor of paying for gas. They no longer fished like the bear and now bought frozen fish from the market.

Sani-Shaman recalled that his father called for an elderly village council to evaluate why their youth and brave citizens were no more a part of the vibrant, sustainable community focused on their traditions, beliefs, and tribal lifestyle. They traded ancient beliefs for cars, money, and women. Many of their own people became one with the white man, and the majority of their young adults left the tribe to embrace the white-man's lifestyle. Others walked out in the middle of the night, leaving their families, personal valuables, and loved ones and disappeared forever.

Sani-Shaman said that this corporation used magic because only magic could encourage a native out of his land and livelihood without explanation or trace. Nothing short of possession by the underworld could explain people who had wives, children, and traditions taking the eternal walk and never coming back. He further said that the LR Corporation had sided with the underworld and cast a spell on Nome and the surrounding villages against their will and way of life.

From Sani-Shaman's stories and from my research, I'd come to realize that LR Corporation was the common denominator when it came to the troubles of this town's people. Because of the corporation's powerful position and vast resources, no one in his or her right mind would dare raise a voice against Lindberg; one way or another, someone would end up either missing or committing suicide.

It all makes perfect sense—that Aunty Marie was so worried and that Uncle Jimmy's recent behavior was unusual, I thought.

"Tell me something, Sani-Shaman. What does the sheriff have to say about all of this?"

He told me that the sheriff had an unusual way of dealing

with these issues. He would handle each case by telling the families of those who were physically and emotionally affected, "Don't worry. Give time a chance. You'll see that all is going to work out."

I glanced at the large, secure complex and felt that my intuition was more in tune than ever. My guts were telling me that not only was something wrong, something was very wrong and this town was not only under the influence of a magic spell, as Sani-Shaman had called it, but this magic spell was developed and masterfully deployed by the Lindberg Research Corporation.

Everything seemed to be so methodic—so predictable that it was unbelievable. I knew that Lindberg Research was in the middle of it all somehow, and tonight was the time to confirm that. But to what extent were they involved? If the theory I was working on was right, I feared that our actions tonight could jeopardize the livelihood or even the lives of all the locals, including Jimmy and Marie Steele.

But I had to do what was right; I had to get to the bottom of this and pray that, in doing so, I'd be able to stop this monster before it destroyed all of us, including me. I knew that I was outmanned, outgunned, and out of my environment and felt that, if this were a game of chess, we were virtually at checkmate. Nevertheless, Sani-Shaman's determination and valor gave me strength. As I looked through his tired and deep eyes, I could see the light of hope; and this was all I needed tonight to do my worst.

***

After Boyd observed Sheriff Lindblom driving out of his parking lot, he walked back to the storage, where he stepped in front of the freezer, opened a door, and walked to the end of the far wall. He pushed a code on a hidden keypad, and a back wall moved to the left and revealed an elevator.

Boyd took the elevator three floors down, and when the elevator opened, he could see a heavily dressed man wearing a white hat sitting next to Jimmy Steele, who was restfully lying down on a comfortable divan. Dr. Anderson was next to him, holding a small replica of the Martin Mars plane in his hands.

Boyd took one glance at the man with the white hat and quickly returned to his bar upstairs. Boyd normally knew better than to go down stairs to "the hole" unless he was invited. Boyd was in big shit, and he knew it. His tenants paid well for two things—space and privacy—and, today, Boyd had violated one of the clauses. Boyd thought that his actions were justified, that he had an obligation to check on his tenants and to warn them that the sheriff was lurking around.

He walked out of the elevator, and as soon as the elevator's doors closed, so did the freezer doors, sealing the secret passage. Boyd stepped to his left to pick up a pizza case and noticed that both of his hands were shaking. He stopped for a second to get ahold of himself, held the pizza box tightly, and walked out of the freezer.

Upon his entering the bar, some of the tenants stopped what they were doing to glance at him, but seconds later, they all continued sipping their drinks and socializing, as if nothing had happened. Boyd placed the pizza boxes in a small cooler he had next to the bar and looked at Sandi, his barmaid, who handed him a note with a couple of drink orders. Without delay, Boyd went back to work as if nothing had happened. Well, at least nothing yet. Over the years he had learned that the rules of his partners in the hole were not flexible and nor were they.

Boyd soon buried himself in the job at hand and tried to forget about the issue. In the meantime, he had a bar to run, and it appeared that half the town and its tourists were in his place, which he was glad about.

13
THE PATH

Through the open door, Danny observed VP Farmer picking up the trip portfolio he had given him earlier. The vice president appeared to be practicing his speech. Danny saw this as very favorable, as he knew that, once they'd landed, the vice president would have little time to rehearse, and he knew that the VP hated to improvise. Danny understood that his boss didn't like surprises and that he wanted to know everything before it happened around him. Although Farmer was very demanding, Danny had learned to respect him and tolerate his indulgences. His controlling and obsessive behavior drove Danny crazy, as his boss's demands were, in many cases, extremely difficult to please. But Danny's determination to make his boss happy made him one of the best at what he did.

Danny knew that it was going to be difficult for him to please his boss in Alaska like he would in DC, where he controlled most of their surroundings. But Danny was relying on Agent Landis and other staff to do their part, to cooperate, and to make this trip as painless as possible. Danny knew that, to achieve great things, you have to suffer a little; and this job came with a share of that "little pain."

Danny was a young man but was mature enough not to let inexperience and stupidity rule his life. Even though he had not lived long enough to be considered a seasoned aide, he prided himself on learning from the best to ensure that his boss was kept from any embarrassing moments that could end the good-standing positions both of them enjoyed today.

After a few hours into the flight, Danny had finished reading through all the detailed plans, revised every speech, confirmed every appointment, and tied up all the loose ends that he would have to face upon landing. He'd also answered and sent a couple of e-mails before the toll of the flight got the best of him and he felt himself nodding off.

Danny was smart enough to let himself fall asleep. He knew that, upon landing, he would not have a moment to himself until the VP went to sleep, and then he'd have to revise, check, and recheck the next day's event. Danny figured that, if he was lucky, after the landing, he would only be able to have about four hours' sleep. So he let himself have a nap.

***

Agent Landis, who was across from Danny's seat watching the VP's door, noticed Danny surrender to the comforts of his seat and the monotonous but constant plane engine noise. Agent Landis also wanted to do the same, but for him, his duty was not about checking schedules and speeches; it was about protecting lives. He knew that he had to be prepared for everything and anything that might cause his protectees harm, embarrassment, or pain. Agent Landis was a professional; he liked what he did and also, unlike many of his coworkers, enjoyed and felt proud of who he was and what he did.

***

Marie Steele was at her home dusting when she received a phone call. Immediately, she picked up the phone and answered, "Hello. This is Marie!"

"Mrs. Steele, this is Deputy Sheriff PJ Marshall. You have no idea how relieved I am to hear your voice!"

"What do you mean, PJ?" asked Marie.

"Are you okay, Mrs. Steele?"

"Well, yes. I am well, PJ. What is going on?"

"You see, Mrs. Steele. Johnny from the shop is trying to retrieve your car from the Mountain Road ditch near the stone bridge."

"My Bronco? What do you mean? Is Jack okay? Oh my God, Jack; is he—?"

"Calm down, Mrs. Steele. The vehicle was empty, but who did you say was driving your car?"

"It's Jack, my nephew. He was driving the Bronco. PJ ... is he all right?"

"Although he may have been injured, there's a good chance that he made it through the crash, since he must have walked away on his own. We have instructions from Sheriff Lindblom to bring the hound dogs in to attempt to find him before it's dark. When we do, we'll bring him back to the hospital, where you can go and see him later. I promise."

"Oh, PJ, I know you will. I just pray that he is alive. I am going there right now."

"No, Mrs. Steele, I can assure you that we're doing everything we can, and it makes no sense for you to leave the comforts of your home to drive out there. There is nothing that you can do at the moment, and you're better off waiting there, in case Mr. Steele returns or calls. I will personally call you the moment we have a lead. Remember, you must stay home and wait for us there. I'm sure that Jimmy would like you to stay home and wait for us."

Marie looked at her empty bed and replied, "I should hang up now."

"Yes, I think that's a very good idea," the deputy agreed. "You can come down to Johnny's garage to pick up your car tomorrow morning."

"I will make sure I do," said Marie, and the phone went dead.

Marie was a nervous wreck. She put down the phone and sat on her bed. Through the window, she tried to look outside, in the hope that she'd see Jimmy or Jack on their way back home.

Marie felt afraid and guilty; she would never forgive herself if something happened to Jack. She could not face him becoming another statistic among the town's mysterious disappearances.

Her mind often went back to when it had all started— when Jimmy had returned home from a regular day's work and hadn't said a word to her. When she'd kissed him that day as he'd entered the house, his expression had been dry and cold. She'd thought briefly that he may have been having an affair, but this was a very small town, and something like that would have made the local gossip in less than a week, so she knew that this was not the case.

At night, she would turn to him and seek his marital deeds, but again, Jimmy would turn his back to her, clearly attempting to make her believe that he was sleeping when, in fact, she could sense that Jimmy's eyes were wide open. Marie knew Jimmy like the palm of her hand, and she could tell just by the way he was breathing whether he was awake or asleep.

Jimmy started to forget important dates and previous agreements, and he failed to bring her flowers like he used to. Marie's conversations with her best friend made her conclude that Jimmy was, in fact, falling victim to the town's curse. Jimmy no longer walked with her during the midsummer nights. He no longer held hands with her while they sat on the balcony enjoying a late-afternoon sunset or looked at her with the passion that would start her inner feminine urges, and this devastated her to the point of insanity.

Marie's mind was inundated with doubts, conjectures, and fear; she had so many questions and so few answers. And this bothered her a lot. Now a new series of questions flooded her mind: How would the sheriff's office catalogue Jack's disappearance now? Would it be another animal attack? Or perhaps the story would go that Jack had become disoriented and lost his bearings after one-too-many drinks and had become a victim of the elements? Would Jack be found dead? Or even worse, would he never be found again?

Marie was too frightened to even think about it, but she knew better, and her faith in Jack soon put her mind at rest and gave her reassurance that everything was going to be all right. She knew that Jack would not fail because failure was not a word in his vocabulary.

Nevertheless, these thoughts did not prevent her from covering her face with both hands and crying. As she lowered her head and tears wetted her fingers, she began to wonder whether asking Jack for help may have been a very bad idea, as dark clouds of guilt started to cast a shadow in her mind.

She should have followed Sheriff Lindblom's and Dr. Anderson's advice and left things the way they were; there was no reason she should fight the system and the town's curse and challenge the local authorities with her unfounded allegations.

Marie was not at her best, but the only thing that kept her from losing her sanity was what Jack told her when he'd first seen her: *Aunty Marie, I am here now. Stop worrying about it and let me do my job. I promise I will get to the bottom of this one way or another. Don't you worry; I am here for you—for both of you.*

Those words sounded loud and clear in her mind; they were like a ray of pure morning sunshine piercing through the dark shadow that had obscured her thoughts. She believed that, if anyone could put this town back in place, it was a Jack. She raised her head and wiped her face, and deep within her soul, she could sense a small light of hope that was starting to come alive.

***

Sheriff Lindblom took off his hat and wiped the sweat from his forehead as he watched Johnny pulling Marie's Bronco from the bottom of the mountain road ditch. Many of the locals watched the tow truck pull the car up the slope. It was not very often that accidents like this took place, and the weather cooperated for everyone to see.

From a distance, some black uniformed men in a Hummer were observing from a nearby hill. The reflection on their binoculars gave them away; Sheriff Lindblom could clearly identify them as Lindberg Research Corporation's Special Security Detachment. What bothered Sheriff Lindblom was that the LR Corp's security team enjoyed more sophisticated, equipped, and trained men than the local, small-town, ten-strong sworn police officers he had under his command. Even with all the police officers, the law enforcement training, and every weapon he could muster, the Nome Police would never get close to matching the corporation's security team.

Among its force, the LR Corp had a small but highly effective SWAT team, along with a couple of EADS North America AAS-72X helicopters, Hummers equipped with military-grade equipment, and many automatic weapons—ranging from AR-15 assault rifles and 9mm Glock 23s to .45 pistols, MAC-10s, and Ingram pistols, to name a few.

The sheriff always resented that he had to put up with Lindberg's security department—to tolerate this small army in his own backyard.

Johnny interrupted the sheriff's thoughts as he alerted him that the Bronco had now been pulled all the way up to the road's edge.

Sheriff Lindblom approached the car, and after making sure that it was secure, he opened the door to find blood spatter all over the instrument panel, steering wheel, and internal door panel. *Jack, I think that it was very painful, but what are you up to?* he thought.

The sheriff observed the vehicle and noticed that the door

had been pried open, as if someone had opened it from the outside.

He took off his hat again and looked around to the south, north, and west, as if someone was watching, and whispered, "Mr. Steele, you just arrived in Nome and you seem to have a very peculiar way of making new friends."

He neglected looking east because he knew that, if Jack had gone east, he was heading back to the LR Corp, and those at the top of the hill may already have caught up with him. That said, if they were still looking downhill to the crash site, it could only mean one thing—that Jack was not in their custody.

As he closed the Bronco's door, he noticed several black scratches. He knew immediately that this was not a simple accident but a murder attempt. Lindblom made some mental calculations as he walked to the middle of the road. He looked at the street and noticed skid marks; he then followed the skid marks' direction and their correlation with the Bronco's crash. He looked at the two paramilitary security operatives on the hill. The sheriff had figured out what happened, but he was going to keep it to himself, at least for now.

His thoughts were interrupted when a small pickup parked next to him. It was Anyo, a local native who had brought two bloodhounds and asked the sheriff where he should start.

Sheriff Lindblom pointed toward the Bronco with his right index finger and said, "Anyo, as soon as possible."

Anyo immediately parked his pickup and, with the help of a fireman, opened the cage, and let the two dogs out.

Anyo, whose native name meant "one who hunts for food or knowledge," was today hunting for men. The sheriff gathered a few local hunters and three deputies, and after the pure bloodhounds found the scent, they spread out and went through the woods. The noise of the dogs' barks and crushed dry wood shattered the quiet and pristine countryside.

Sheriff Lindblom remained topside next to his patrol car,

manning a rustic command center and listening to the radio while looking at the two dark Hummers, which were still parked at the top of the hill as quietly as a kite in a mid-April sky.

14

THE PERFECT TALE

A ir Force Two's captain heard the cockpit alarm, indicating twenty minutes out to Anchorage Airport. He looked at his copilot and nodded and then picked up his microphone and announced, "It's time to land."

With this notice, all passengers began to put their paperwork away, close the service tables, buckle up, and straighten their seats.

Danny knocked at VP Farmer's door and, after being granted permission to enter, found the VP sitting at his desk signing papers.

"Here, Danny, make sure these get to the right people," said VP Farmer as he handed a few envelopes to Danny.

"Yes, sir, I'll take care of it. Do you have any questions before we land?"

"No, Danny. I am as ready as I can be. This is a walk in the park. Alaska is one of our strongest allies, and a big chunk of our party's funds come from this golden state.

"This is going to be quick, direct, and in no time, we'll be back in DC," said Farmer.

"I wish I was as much of an optimist as you, Mr. Vice President," responded Danny.

"Don't worry about it, son. When you have done this as long as I have, all of this becomes routine, just routine."

And with this, the pilot's voice interrupted the conversation, instructing all passengers to take their seats and fasten their seat belts.

"Okay, Danny, that's our call. Let's do what Major Parker requests. I don't want to upset the pilot! Do you?"

"No, sir, absolutely not," responded Danny as both of them started to walk toward their assigned seats.

From the front, Danny scanned the VP's crew and entourage. Danny loved the action, the thrill, and the excitement, so he couldn't wait to land. Just before finding his seat, Danny glanced at Agent Landis, who had been monitoring everything that was taking place. Danny nodded at him, indicating that all was all right from where Danny was sitting. He could see that Agent Landis was getting ready for landing as well.

From Danny's experience dealing with the Secret Service, he knew that an agent was supervising the control tower, and he was correct; this time, it was USSS Agent McAllister who was stationed at the tower to ensure that all procedures were followed and that no surprises would be awaiting Air Force Two.

Danny felt the plane starting to circle for landing as pilots often circled the outer markers until they received the final clearance to land, and shortly, the plane started its final descent to Anchorage. Danny could feel the pilot start his controlled descent, and in no time, he felt the plane's tires touching the landing strip. From his window, Danny could see the ground security and airport police escorting the plane. The plane was directed to an isolated area within the southwest section of the airport. When the plane had come to a stop, Danny saw three vehicles waiting for them next to a very long red carpet.

From the plane, Danny recognized Alaskan Governor Theodore McKenzie stepping out of his state limousine and walking toward SS Agent McAllister, who stood next to the red carpet straight and firm waiting for the vice president to disembark the plane. It was amazing to see the same procedure over and over.

As Danny moved closer to the last window, he observed Agent McAllister looking everywhere, as if he was checking to see that the police officers were positioned in key areas. Next to Agent McAllister, he saw a man he later identified as Captain Grimes, the local police operations support commander on site. *So far, so good*, thought Danny.

***

The plane's doors opened, and the first person out was Agent Landis, who waited for a minute as he assessed the overall conditions of the airport before he allowed anyone else to leave the safety of the secure plane. He touched his earpiece to listen to Agent McAllister's assurances that the landing zone was secure and that he was waiting for him at the end of the red carpet.

Agent Landis looked back and nodded to the crew, who immediately directed the vice president forward and began to disembark. As he walked behind the vice president, Agent Landis saw Agent McAllister give a hand signal to all of his officers, signaling everyone to move a bit closer to the red carpet as the VP walked down the stairs.

Agent Landis moved closer to the vice president as he greeted the Alaskan governor and his small entourage. In the blink of an eye, Agent Landis was next to the vice president and walking two steps back and to his right.

He acknowledged and approved that Anchorage police had created natural barricades so the Alaskans' guests could freely walk to a reception building where the city mayor and a local police band were waiting to welcome him.

Landis saw Agent McAllister stepping up his pace to meet Captain Grimes, who was making sure that the preestablished vice presidential path remained intact and was holding airport employees and others bystanders from blocking the vice president's path to the reception area.

As the group approached the reception building's sidewalk, the music started and the doors to the reception building opened. Nearly three hundred persons occupied the building, among them city employees; local politicians; party officials; and, of course, reporters. Landis could see that Vice President Farmer was enjoying every moment of it, as any politician should.

Agent Landis was in hell, thinking about the many things that could go wrong; he did not want to live with the memory that it was his lack of duty, or rather "resources," that could have led to the tragic death of the vice president of the United States and the destruction of a promising career. Although the temperature was barely fifty degrees, Agent Landis could feel the drops of sweat dripping down his spine.

Shortly after the principal was in a secure and controlled building, things became a little calmer, as the politicians were "holding babies and kissing ladies."

It's all about the photo opportunity, thought Agent Landis. It didn't matter whether it was a big or small city, village or metropolis; it was all about looking good for the media. Landis observed that Danny was front and center, making sure that every single photo counted and that he could get the mileage he wanted for the man and office he served.

As soon as the VP was inside the building in a secure location, Special Agent Landis instructed McAllister to leave and execute phase two of the security operation. His next stop was the hotel where the VP was going to be staying for the night. Agent Landis gave him the green light, and both Captain Grimes and McAllister left in a cruiser "lights ablaze and sirens buzzing."

After forty-five minutes of photographs and chatter, VP Farmer recited a short speech. Despite the shortness of the speech, it was so politically correct that people's applause interrupted him on several occasions. Agent Landis's impression of the speech was that it was like being at the State of the Union presidential address to Congress.

Danny looked at Landis and nodded, giving him the signal that his boss was ready to leave. Agent Landis raised his hand and pushed the earpiece on his right ear and called for the vehicles. Thanks to Agent McAllister's and Captain Grimes's advance work, the vehicles were right in front of the back entrance of the building facing the secure tarmac.

Moments later, three vehicles drove up and parked right at the designated spots. SSA Landis signaled Danny, and without delay, Danny and the VP, who at the time was kissing babies, began walking toward him. From there, Danny followed Agent Landis to the vehicles.

Just before boarding the official limousine, Landis observed Vice President Farmer standing next to the limousine door and taking a very good look at his surroundings. Landis felt like the VP was absorbing the moment; he figured that this was the way VP Farmer felt his glory, his time; he bet that the VP was having the most wonderful feeling a human could have—being wanted, needed, and accepted. From Farmer's expression, Landis discerned that the crowd, the music, and the media's camera flashes in his face were his fuel and that he could do this all day long. However, it was now time to go; so he turned toward Danny, who asked him to enter the limousine. He did so, as did Danny and a couple members of the VP's local entourage.

***

A number of the Anchorage Police Department and, of course, SSA McAllister and the VP's entourage were already waiting at the Millennium Hotel. Although they'd tried to keep things under wraps, they'd had to use hotel security to assist local law enforcement to help set up a secure perimeter for the VP's arrival.

As McAllister inspected the room, he was reminded of the wife of the prior vice president being embarrassed and upset after her husband had returned from a trip outside the Unites States, and when she'd opened his luggage, she'd found a pair of woman's underpants. She'd raised hell and almost divorced her husband. It had taken the removal of her husband's detail lead agent and two others, along with a long explanation of what had happened for her to let it go.

What had happened was that the prior occupants of the presidential suite had used the room for a corporate CEO bachelorette's party. Twelve beautiful females were staying in the room, raising hell or, rather, having a good time under the heavy influence of alcohol. The noise was so disturbing to other guests that, after several warning attempts, the hotel management had asked them to leave. In the midst of the circumstances, the dozen beauties had left some of their clothes lying all over the room, including some in the room's dresser. The maid who'd cleaned the suite had apparently not paid attention to details such as opening the drawers all the way to ensure they were empty and, as a result, a piece of underwear had remained tucked between the top drawer and the back of the dresser's wall.

The VP had placed his clothes in the upper drawer, causing the female undergarment to be pushed down to the lower drawer, which was already full of clothes. When the VP had packed, he hadn't noticed that one of the white dressing jewels was not like the others. To the VP, who'd been packing in a hurry and doing so without using his prescription glasses, things like this went unnoticed, but for a thorough wife sorting through clothes for the laundry service, this was a detail that would never be missed.

After the agents conducted a detailed investigation, they'd found the truth, which they'd quickly shared with the VP's angry wife. Although she had managed to forgive her husband, she was not so forgiving of the agents, and this had caused their dismissal from the vice presidential detail.

After this incident, Secret Service agents paid attention to details and learned to be thorough and meticulous when they inspected a room before and after their principals occupied and/or left a room. This included taking with them all the garbage that was discarded in the room and making sure that nothing was left behind so that it didn't appear on eBay as the "hot item of the week" or, rather, TMZ celebrity news.

Things like empty prescription bottles, what type of chocolate the principal ate, and what type of books the principal liked to read should be kept private at all costs. Public officials were people too, and they didn't want everyone knowing the many things they kept under wraps to protect their image—things that, if people knew in detail, may mean they would never give them their vote. So agents had to protect their principal's private and public lives and keep details like this from reaching public domain, which could embarrass their principal, the political party, and possibly the government of the United States.

As expected, the master suite was inspected, readied, and guarded by local police as SSA McAllister had directed.

The limousine slowly came to a halt and stopped right in front of the Millennium Hotel's main doors, where a red carpet had been placed. In addition, shiny bronze statues stood at attention on both sides of the red carpet, marking the path for the vice president to the main door in testament of the place's heritage.

SSA McAllister had carefully positioned all hotel staff and management to stand to the left and right of the statues dressed in pristine uniforms. The uniforms were starched from top to bottom and the shoes shined to perfection. To the left, the hotel management were next to one another smiling and welcoming the top VIP; their shiny brass nameplates were a true testament of a well-manicured operation. On the right side of the carpet, the staff ranged from chambermaids to cooks and waitstaff filling the space to prevent other unwanted visitors from getting too close to the VIP.

***

Agent Landis opened the limousine door and immediately assessed the situation. He looked for Agent McAllister, who gave him a positive nod, indicating that all was clear and to proceed entering the hotel.

SSA Landis moved slowly to the rear door, where he opened the door to allow the vice president to leave the vehicle.

VP Farmer's smile was worthy of an Oscar when he saw how many people were gathered at the front of the hotel to greet him. Loud applause and cheering filled the space. As was true for every politician and man or woman in office, moments like this boosted one's image, and this VP really enjoyed being recognized by his constituents and was not shy about it.

He slowly raised his hand to greet everyone and was closely followed by Agent Landis, who was one step to his right as US Secret Service escort protocol dictated. Agent McAllister walked immediately in front to protect the vice president.

Agent Landis was a professional; he knew that, given that he'd never received confirmation of the bulletin warning him of a possible attempt on the VP's life, this trip remained a relatively low-risk, low-profile visit. However, he also knew everyone he saw around him had a potential for darkness, and he also knew that he couldn't dismiss the bulletin altogether. As always, he took nothing for granted and was operating under full US Secret Service protection protocols. He was determined that nothing would happen to his protectees during his watch.

VP Farmer was greeted by the hotel's general manager, who insisted he personally walk the vice president to his suite. And who could blame him for doing so, as this was an unwritten protocol practiced by all hotel managers around the world.

McAllister was ten feet ahead with a couple of plainclothes local police officers making the way for the VP, as many of the patrons wanted to shake his hand and others were standing in the way applauding. VP Farmer looked like a polar bear on ice, doing what he loved, and as they walked toward the elevators, VP Farmer began complimenting the hotel's GM on the premise's antique decor and elegant look. Various walls displayed bear and deer skins elegantly. The head of a caribou was mounted ornately the top of the lobby's rear bar wall.

***

VP Farmer liked the decor of the place. To him, the hotel offered a warm and welcome atmosphere, which was one of the feelings he experienced the least outside his own residence. After shaking the hand of locals and other states' visitors, he was directed to the elevator, where the general manager punched the third-floor button and the elevator started to lift.

Shortly after the elevator doors opened at the third floor, the entourage headed toward the only police officer standing at attention at the very end of the corridor. The officer, upon noticing the party, quickly opened the door and allowed them in. Once in the room, the hotel's GM opened the curtains, revealing the best view of Lake Spenard, which, needless to say, was breathtaking.

The VP thanked the hotel's GM by saying that he would be sure to let him know if he needed anything and expressing gratitude for his kindness before the GM made his exit.

***

On the way out of the room, SSA Landis looked at the closet to make sure that the VP's suitcases were there, and then he checked that the room's connecting door was closed and locked. Seconds later, he closed the door and stood next to McAllister, shaking his hand while thanking him for a job well done. Following this, SSA Landis asked Agent McAllister to join him and Captain Grimes to ensure that everything was prepared for their departure tomorrow.

15

THE EYE OF THE STORM

The sun had set, and darkness covered the tundra. Sheriff Lindblom called Anyo. "Anyo," he said, "it's getting dark. Let's call the search party back."

"But, Sheriff, the hounds are following the trail; they've got the scent. Let's continue," pleaded Anyo.

"Anyo, tell me, in what direction is the trail taking you?"

"Well, Sheriff, northwest so far," said Anyo.

"Anyo, what is in that direction?" asked Lindblom.

"Not much, Sheriff. The only things northwest of us are a few local homes, Peter's Chip's wood barn, and—"

"Sani-Shaman's cabin, right?" the sheriff interrupted.

"Yes, Sheriff, his home is also in this direction."

"Anyo, your services are appreciated, but before you start to trip and fall in the dark, let's go back to town. Tomorrow is another day, and we have a marathon to run. I am sure that, if we haven't found Mr. Steele thus far, he must be enjoying the company of a few new local friends," said the sheriff.

"As you wish, Sheriff Lindblom," Anyo said. "Let's go home, boys; it's time to eat some delicious sea lions," the sheriff heard him say to his team before his handheld radio clicked out.

Sheriff Lindblom lit a green flare and let it go high in the sky. He knew that the rest of the search team would look at it and recognize the signal, which would tell them that it was time to go back home.

Sheriff Lindblom thought that, with the amount of blood he'd seen in Marie's Bronco, if Jack Steele hadn't had help, he would already have been prey for the wolves or the bears. Since no pieces of body had been found yet, he must have found some local help, either from Peter the hermit or from crazy old Sani-Shaman. Either way, searching in the dark was not going to bring him back, but rather, may put the search party at risk.

Tomorrow is another day, he thought as he walked down the small, rocky hill. He felt in the pit of his stomach a very strong feeling that, very soon, he would be hearing from Jack Steele. And his gut feeling was telling him that the encounter was not going to be pleasant.

***

We'd concealed the ATVs and walked down near the fence; in front of me, Sani-Shaman stood up and felt the wind. He wanted to make sure that we were standing against the wind and not in its direction so that the trained dogs patrolling could not pick up our scent. I was beginning to appreciate the wisdom of this man. He didn't have a college degree, nor had he any former military experience, yet he was as masterful as any "Specwar" trained element.

From my previous observations, I knew that the fence was protected by very sophisticated sensors—the kind that, if touched, would immediately send an alarm signal to the security operations center inside, which would subsequently dispatch patrol vehicles to check the troubled zone. I was about to test their systems ...

I picked up a rock and waited for the speed dome camera to turn left. I threw the rock as hard as I could against the fence. We hid behind a nearby rock covered by medium-sized bushes and looked at my watch, counting the seconds.

Yes, I was right; in less than a minute, a patrol vehicle arrived, and two security operatives stepped out of the vehicle and floated the area with very powerful, handheld floodlights. I peeked through the bushes to look at the camera position and had a scan of the entire area. One of them picked up the radio and reported in, and then both left the area. I waited one more minute and again threw another rock toward the same area.

I looked at my watch and waited. I counted again; in one and a half minutes this time, I saw the same security officers who'd arrived previously. This time, one stayed behind, opened the back door, and released a large dog. The animal, held by a strong leash, was pulling the guard toward the fence. But after sniffing around, the dog found nothing and just lifted up one of its back legs and urinated next to a bush at the fence pole.

Both officers returned to the SUV patrol vehicle with the dog and left. I waited another two minutes before throwing my third rock. This time, when I observed my wristwatch, I found that it took the guards three minutes to respond. The same two officers, who this time didn't even get out of the patrol vehicle but rather slowly cruised by and only used the vehicle's spotlights to check the immediate vicinity, left after not finding anything untoward.

My plan was working; this was the type of reaction I was looking for. During the last two attempts, I'd observed the cameras and had noticed that the camera was placed back in the routine observation task thirty seconds after the officers' departure. This was exactly what I was expecting. This time, I waited five minutes and threw another rock. I glanced at my watch and took the time. I waited for five minutes, and no one came. The camera moved back and forth once and then was placed back in routine mode. This was, once again, the type of behavior that I was looking for. This was great for us and bad for LR Corp's security team, but that was their punishment for being lazy and not following procedures.

The technique I was employing was widely used by bank
robbers to test law enforcement's and private security firms'
reactions when responding to triggered alarms. We are all
human and cut from the same cookie dough. Usually, guards
will respond to the first alert as if the world is going to end. The
second time around is usually met with suspicion and doubt.
The third alert is considered a burden, and investigating it
seems a waste of resources.

Rationalization is the psychology behind this response;
after a few alerts producing no results, we come up with
explanations for what's happening. It may be a glitch in the
system, we reason. Or we tell ourselves that the system's too
old and needs fine-tuning. We conclude that, since nothing
is actually happening, we don't need to respond immediately
and, instead, take our time to get out there. After all, it's just
another false alarm. This type of reasoning is what gets us in
trouble each and every time.

Tonight, I was counting on this psychology to make
my plan work, and so far the predicted behavior of these
professionals was similar to that of those wannabe cops and
Uncle Sam's fine soldiers in the military I had seen all my life.
They all behaved in the same predictable manner.

This time, I waited fifteen minutes and threw another rock
as hard as I could; again I watched the time. And no one came.
After fixing my eyes on the camera, I noticed that the camera
didn't even blink.

LR's security team had taken the bait, and now it was time
to make a hole in the fence and ease ourselves in.

I didn't want to make the same mistake that many other
fence-breaking amateurs do—like making a hole large enough
to fit a truck through and then risk someone seeing it from a
mile away. Through many years of experience, I'd learned that
cutting the fence behind the support pole would be the best
place to help us conceal our entry.

Just then, Sani-Shaman, who'd momentarily disappeared,

158

came back with a handful of bushes. I told him it was a little late for him to think about camouflage.

He looked at me as if I was a little slow and said, "Mr. Steele, this is not for wearing but to cover our entry."

I gave him a puzzled face, and Sora whispered, "Jack, those are the bushes the dog pissed on. Sani-Shaman wants to use them to cover your steps, so when the dogs come back to patrol, they'll get confused by their own scent, which will camouflage your natural body odor."

"Sani-Shaman," I said, "are you sure you weren't a special-warfare warrior in your past life?"

Sani-Shaman and Sora started to laugh as I continued cutting the fence.

After I'd completed the hole and we'd entered the facilities, I made sure to close the fence hole with plastic tie-downs to cover our tracks.

Tie-downs were strong enough to keep the fence together but also easy to cut if you were in a hurry when you were coming back out. I had to make sure we had a good exit plan, especially if, when we came back running, we were being chased by the facility's security.

I had to consider the possibility that, during our escape back to the tundra, security elements could be following us. If this proved to be the case, I had to assume that the security elements who came after us would be wearing their security equipment—pistol belts, large weapons, bulletproof jackets, and everything else they could carry. Thus, it would be virtually impossible for them to clear the hole as fast as we could, giving us the extra seconds we would need to clear out to safety. You never knew what could happen, so being prepared had its benefits.

After securing the last tie-down, I saw that Sani-Shaman was looking at me with his mouth wide open; I could see his warm, white breath coming in and out. I asked him why he had his mouth open.

And he responded to me with a very assertive, coherent voice, "Mr. Steele, the wind has changed, and we are now downwind. We must move quickly if we want to enter these facilities tonight."

"You are right, my friend. Let's move. But first, I'd like Sora to stay here and be our lookout. Sora, make sure you keep warm and don't move from here."

"Don't you worry, Jack. I'm fine. This is my backyard, remember?"

Under the dark of the night, two silhouettes moved slowly toward the second fence. Sani-Shaman was dusting the pavement with the moist bush as we walked, covering our scent. I had used my bolt cutters to open a small opening right behind the pole. Putting the fence back in place was easy, and once we were inside, I used the dark plastic tie-downs to close the fence back behind the poles as planned. I doubled back and handed Sora the cutters. I didn't want to leave them behind for a dog or guard to find, and I didn't want to have the extra weight with me either.

Every couple of seconds, I eyeballed the speed dome camera, but as predicted, it did not move. Again, doom on Lindberg's security force. You could select the best officers money could pay for and give them the best deadly toys to protect the premises, and yet, what it comes down to is just common sense, which is the least thing humans have; and tonight I was counting on this old saying to also be true.

I went through the plan again in my head and checked all the places where the cameras were supposed to be. I also ran through the ground patrols' routines, and we were making good time. The guards' shift change and what they call in this industry the "guard mount" didn't end for another fifteen more minutes. This meant that all security officers on shift from midnight to eight in the morning would have to endure a thirty-minute block of instructions, training, and post-order updates.

All officers had to put up with this guard mount. They had to listen to all twenty-nine minutes of bullshit and just one minute of real post-actionable instructions. It was the same everywhere you went, regardless of whether it was a powerful, well-funded organization like the one we'd just easily infiltrated or a mom-and-pop small business. *Good for me*, I thought and immediately signaled Sani-Shaman to follow me toward a set of stairs located at the back of the main building.

From my observations so far, I could see that the Lindberg Research Corporation was using all of the above techniques and probably had many other surprises I was yet to identify. That said, without these challenges, my incursion today may become, let's say, boring ...

Typically, all security would be dedicated to the ground level, and very few would be used on the second floor or above. Tonight, I was counting on the security designers for the LR Corp having made the same mistake. Sani-Shaman and I climbed the stairs to the second floor, and it was easier than I thought.

The back of the building didn't even have any security cameras. The only cameras I saw were at first-floor level. I had to give the security engineers credit; the cameras were positioned facing out, as if they were expecting to spot a polar bear breaking down one of the lower doors or windows. However, the top floors appeared to be camera-free, just the way I liked it. Security engineers had no respect for eagles like me landing on their roof; this pissed me off. But luckily for me, this was their mistake and one I would exploit tonight.

As we walked along the second-floor wall, I spotted a light. We ducked and hid in the shadows. I thought that we had been spotted. We waited for a while, but no action ensued—not a peep sounded and no guards came shouting or running toward us. So I slowly peeked from behind an A/C unit box, and to my surprise, it was an employee dressed in what appeared to be a white lab jacket who opened the door.

Sani-Shaman and I stayed behind the A/C box observing the individual, who took his sweet time smoking a cigarette. From where we were hiding, outside the second floor behind the A/C unit box, I could see that he smoked it all the way to the filter. Before going back to the building, he threw the cigarette butt, which landed next to my boots; what a nasty habit, I might say!

I wondered if he knew how much I hated cigarette smoke! I made a mental note to tell his manager about him later. As the door slowly closed, I grabbed the door's outer handle and held it ajar very close to its frame. I then waited an additional thirty seconds until I heard another, inner door slam close and slowly opened the door to see a large room full of stacked boxes. I asked Sani-Shaman to follow me closely as we both entered the room. I was careful to close the door to prevent anyone from hearing us.

These days, most major corporations followed a nonsmoking policy in the building and employee smokers were forced to smoke outside the building or windows to comply with these new rules. The fact was that these rules had nothing to do with employee health but with preventing employees from burning the building down. Police and fire department statistics clearly confirmed that more buildings were burned down by employees' careless smoking habits than by any other cause.

If corporations allowed employees to smoke inside the premises, they were exposing millions of dollars of equipment and risking the loss of lives in the process, which could mean the end of their organization as they knew it. It had happened before and could happen again.

That said, many corporate offices also had their own smoking sanctuary, where senior executives could smoke at leisure inside the building; this is usually somewhere on the executive floors.

But of course this did not apply to the other, less fortunate employees, who had to smoke outside the building doors or even outside their campuses' main entrances on the sidewalk; what a sight. But tonight, this policy was on our side, and I had just exploited it to the max.

Once inside, the room looked to me like a long, narrow storage room. It was about twenty feet high, with many exposed metal beams on the ceiling, and the walls were made of both wood and metal. The room was filled with metal shelving one next to the other, leaving space in between for what would be logical to assume was an industrial lifter. It was very clever use of the space. The metal shelves extended at least fifteen feet high, and all of them were full of white boxes.

Before Sani-Shaman could take his first step toward the inner door, I extended my hand in front of him and stopped him from walking the step. I panned the room, looking for sensors, cameras, and other hidden gizmos that could alert security of our presence. One thing I had learned over the years was to never assume anything. As I've said before, "assumption is the mother of all fuckups," and thus far, this Old World proverb had worked in my favor; I was not about to take any chances—at least not until we had what we'd come here for.

After scanning the whole room, the only things I could identify were a couple of smoke and heat sensors; so far, so good. But just as I was lowering my hand in front of Sani-Shaman, the lights when out. I raised my hand once again and continued to keep holding Sani-Shaman from walking forward. I stopped dead where I was and realized that a building of this caliber would probably have energy-conservation lights, meaning the lights would turn off after a period of inactivity. I hoped that my theory was correct, but if not, we would soon be surrounded by several uniformed men with angry faces and large weapons.

I took the first step forward and then allowed Sani-Shaman to do the same, and the lights came back on. Bingo—this was what I was expecting. We carefully continued past the center aisle, and before heading to the door, I stopped to see if I could identify the contents inside one of the many white boxes resting on the metal-shelved aisle.

After opening a few boxes, I soon realized that this was a supply room and that some of the boxes contained a drug called Amantadine or Tetrabenazine. If memory served me well, these drugs were widely used to control body movement. This trip was starting to get interesting. I took a sample of both, placing them in my trouser cargo pocket and continued on. We carefully walked toward the door, and upon reaching it, I saw something that would be of use.

I loved building engineers and safety professionals. They were always so concerned about employee safety that they placed floor maps everywhere for us to see where we were and where the nearest exits were, so people could find their way to safety in case of fire or any major evacuation. Tonight, this map was going to lead me to where I wanted to go, which wasn't out but, rather, farther into the building; what an irony. I grabbed the floor plan and carefully located the room we were in, which, as expected, was marked with a big, red star saying, "You are here."

According to the floor plan, the second floor had several hallways and rooms. Upon further examination, I located the place I wanted to get to next. It was a large room labeled in large writing, "Restricted."

I looked at Sani-Shaman and whispered, "Since we are not employees or visitors, I feel that this warning does not apply to us. Do you agree?"

Sani-Shaman looked at me and smiled.

I took it that he agreed.

Sani-Shaman then looked back at me and said, "Mr. Steele, be careful what you wish for …"

He didn't have to say anymore. I understood his warning. But this was what we were here to do, and we would not leave the premises without the answers to the many questions we had.

Sani-Shaman pointed at the room with his index finger and immediately knew what I meant, nodding in an affirmative way. Before opening the door, I placed my ear next to it and listened, trying to recognize any possible threat to us before we left this safe location. I heard nothing, so I opened the door slowly and peered from between the door and the doorframe along the empty corridor.

But as I opened the door, I faced two large, black-dressed security officers standing right next to the door. I could see in their eyes the expression of surprise and fear—like the one you have when you are caught red-handed or doing something wrong. Unfortunately, for these two, in a matter of seconds, I pushed Sani-Shaman back into the room and took advantage of the fact that the guards' hands were busy with cigarettes and a lighter; right away, I kicked one in the pit of the stomach as hard as I knew, and as he bent down, I took the opportunity to grab the other by the neck and slam his head hard against the concrete wall.

He fell like a rotten apple, not to move anymore.

As the first guard was starting to straighten himself up, I introduced my right knee to his face, and I guess that he didn't like it because he bounced back like a slinky, landing flat on his back.

I called back to Sani-Shaman to help me get both bodies inside the room. Once we had them inside, we used their belts to tie them to the farthest corner we could find and bound their mouths with their socks, which I guessed they would hate me for later.

I looked for weapons and electronic keys, but the only thing we found were two worthless RFI cards, which we took right away. Doom on us again; perhaps these two irreverent cigarette smokers hadn't taken their shifts yet and wanted to take a smoke before they started it.

Sani-Shaman looked at me and said sarcastically, "Well, they say that smoking is harmful to your health." Now was our time to make a move. I saw sensors on the walls, which I knew were used to identify employees and visitors without an escort, and lucky for us the guards we'd ran into had "volunteered" their RFI passes for us to walk the halls. So we should not have any issues passing through. One thing I had learned from the Special Operations Warfare Academy is that, when walking along unknown corridors, you should follow the "mouse" technique. Always walk close to the walls and never through the center of the corridor. So this is what we did; we became rats.

As we approached the corner at the end of the corridor, I glanced at my map and noticed a closet room. I opened the door and, inside, found some cleaning supplies and a cabinet containing freshly cleaned white coats. I reached for one and handed it to Sani-Shaman and pulled out another for myself. I have to say that efficiency may have been LR Corp's biggest curse. The coats came with their own embroidered names and departments. "Good to meet you, Dr. Baker," I said to Sani-Shaman.

And he responded back, "And to you, Mr. Roberts, maintenance and cleaning crew."

I wondered if my luck was leaving me as I donned the coat and felt like one of the cleaning crew. But I was hoping that this disguise would somehow come in handy in the near future. As they say, when in Rome, do as the Romans do, or alternatively, it is polite, and possibly also advantageous, to abide by the customs of a society when one is a visitor. And tonight in Nome, I was following uniform policy by dressing like a Lindberg Corporation employee; I mean this was the least we could do.

Again we exercised caution before leaving the supply room and heading to the restricted room. So far so good; I checked my pocket phone to make sure that I hadn't missed any text messages from Sora and to ensure that the phone was on silent mode, as I didn't want to alert our hosts that we were in the building—well, at least not yet.

I quickly sent Sora a text, telling her not to call me at any time but to remember to text me if she needed to get in touch. Believe it or not, sometimes corporations of this caliber, especially those engaged in research and development, didn't allow employees to carry any personal mobile phones at all while on duty. Many others even went to the extent of ensuring that employees complied with their policy by implementing "cellphone jamming technology" to prevent personal phone use.

This was a way to control communications. Only the phones that were authorized in the system could generate or receive signals as long as they were within the confines of the building. This type of technology was often used in highly sensitive buildings and widely used in many maximum security prisons.

I was hoping that this was not the case. I wanted to keep technology on our side and hoped it would work with us, instead of against us, tonight. Text messages tended to generate such a small signature that, in most cases, they would go through the system without detection.

No contact from Sora was a good sign, so we continued to move toward the room, and soon, we were standing right in front of it. As I was about to grab the doorknob, the door opened, and an old gentleman with a white beard like Santa Claus's slowly walked out of the room in front of us.

I greeted him, and he looked at me with anger and asked where the hell we'd been. "I've been waiting for someone to clean the mess inside for ages! Hurry up and do your job!" He had an accent that had hints of German. I hadn't heard this kind of accent in a long time. He was not American or Canadian, as were the many people I had encountered since I'd arrived in Nome.

"I am sorry for the delay, sir ..." I glanced at his name

tag, which read "Jensen MD." "I will get to it right away, Dr. Jensen," I assured him.

Without looking back, the old man continued walking down the corridor as if he owned it. We followed his example and entered the door like we owned it too.

Once inside, we found ourselves in a small reception area with four doors round us. *Now what?* I thought.

Sani-Shaman looked at me and said, "Well, you're the cleaning crew; isn't it your job to know where we're going?"

"Well," I responded, "you have the PhD. Don't you know where your lab is?"

Sani-Shaman smiled and pointed his finger to the door to his right.

I looked and agreed with him. This was the only door that had a secure lock. Furthermore, the door was made of solid metal and had reinforced frames. All the others appeared to be made of hollow wood and had large, see-through, tempered-glass sections from their middle to their upper portions.

I could see a camera pointing at the door. This was definitely the door we were looking for. However, I didn't want to get in trouble by putting ourselves in front of the camera. As we considered our options, the main door was opened by a cleaning man. He was pushing a cart with what appeared to be some biohazardous plastic containers.

To my surprise, Sani-Shaman generated an angry face and said to the man, "Where the hell have you been? I have been waiting for you for a while. I don't have all night, you know. Open the door at once and clean the dammed mess."

"Yes, sir, at once," he replied. "I'm so sorry for the delay."

He got close to the opposite door, and I said, "Man, have you already forgotten what we called you for? It is the other door where you need to go."

Sani-Shaman said out loud, "I refuse to go in that room until you clean that shit." He turned toward me and said, "You go in and show him where it is. I will wait right here."

I replied, sounding as if I was intimidated, "Aaah! Yes, sir, at once."

All was going well until the cleaning crewman clearly said out loud, "Sir, I have no access to this door. You will have to call security to let us in."

"Do you know who you are talking to? Let me see your name. Sammy Warner, you call down and get security to let us in, or I will hold you responsible for any damages in there," said Sani-Shaman.

The technician reached for his radio and called in the request.

The control-room voice asked for the name of the person asking permission, and as I heard this, I moved right to block Sani-Shaman's embroidered name tag and said to the crewman, "Tell them that Dr. Jensen is asking and that he is very pissed about it."

"Yes, right away."

"Control, the person requesting the service is Dr. Jensen."

The wait for a radio response took about thirty seconds, but to us, it seemed like an eternity. Then all of a sudden, a radio call interrupted the silence. "What are you waiting for?" the voice on the other end of the radio said. "Do as he says. Stand by the door and wait for the buzzer."

In just a matter of seconds, the door sounded a buzzer, and Crewman Warner opened the door. We followed behind. As we walked behind the cleaning man, we made all efforts to keep our faces away from the camera placed at the door. To our surprise, we saw that a cup of coffee had been spilled on top of a desk.

Both of us looked at each other and then back to the cleaner, who without delay, started to clean the desk. Sani-Shaman and I split in order to search the room; he took the right while I took the left side and found myself facing a rather large amount of long cabinets full of records. Five minutes later, the squeaky cart left the room, and with that, the door closed. We were now alone.

I found several file labels dating back to the early seventies; the files were named name "Project Hera." If memory served me well, Hera queen of Greek mythology and wife of Zeus, used mind-control techniques to force Hercules do things he didn't want to do …

The room door opened again, and this time, from behind a file cabinet, I could see one guard entering the room. He was calling out for Dr. Jensen.

I immediately stepped out and said to him, "He is busy now. What do you want him for?"

The guard pulled out a flashlight and illuminated my face.

I asked him to get the darn light away from my face, and he pulled a pistol and pointed it at me.

I closed the distance slowly and said to him that he should not take offense from my words, but he asked me to slowly walk toward him. As I walked forward, I went by Sani-Shaman who was hiding behind a cabinet and aware of the situation. I continue walking toward the guard. He asked me to stay quiet and to raise my hands.

Again I was in a difficult position. This guard knew what he was doing. He asked me to stop and to kneel in front of him and interlock my fingers behind my neck.

I complied like the very good employee I was, and immediately, the guard called, "Doctor, please step forward."

The man with the Santa Claus beard and the Germanic accent from earlier—the real Dr. Jensen—stepped out and stood in front of me. "Who the hell are you?" he demanded.

I told him that I'd been helping one of the other doctors move some files and that the doctor had stepped away from the room for a minute.

Dr. Jensen told me coldly that no other doctors worked in this area. He further said, "I own this vault, and you have no authorization to lay a finger on a file in this room. You are not a member of my staff."

I told him that I was new and that I had the company identification with me.

He replied, "The hell you are."

The guard was puzzled for a minute, and this was the right time for me to act.

I said to the guard, "Allow me to pull my ID card. I have it here in my pocket."

The guard told me not to move and closed the distance between us. I tried to move my hand to reach for the RFI card I'd stolen from the guard, but the guard cocked the pistol and asked me not to move. He then put the pistol muzzle right between my eyes and reached for my pocket.

He pulled out the card without taking his eyes away from me, so I waited for when he looked at the card to validate the photo, and this was when I made my move. With my left hand, I pushed the pistol to my right, and as I moved the pistol I moved my right hand and was able to pull it out of his hands as if he had buttery fingers.

The guard knew that he had committed a huge mistake, and now both the guard and Dr. Jensen had their hands up. As I moved forward toward the guard, he made an effort to take the pistol away from me, and I had no choice but to shoot him center mass. I didn't have time to waste tonight playing games.

As he went down, I whispered, "Sorry, man, but taking weapons away from people's hands only works with hard training and when done by professionals."

He dropped to the floor immediately. Upon landing, blood spilled from his wound, and Dr. Jensen, who had a front-row view of the situation, slowly knelt down and started begging for his life. Sometimes life squeezes your neck just enough for you to feel it but not to choke you. What I mean is, moments earlier, I had been kneeling down about to be shot and now I was holding the gun and the PhD who owned this vault and had full access to all it contained was ready to grant all my research desires.

Sani-Shaman walked back out to the hall and stood next to me and said, "Jack, we have been blessed and cursed at the same time because they will be looking for this guard."

I looked at Sani-Shaman and told him not to worry, as we would cross that bridge when we got there.

I directed my eyes to Dr. Jensen, whose eyes told me that he was about to pee his pants. "Now, Doctor, I recall you saying that you own this vault, and we have a few questions for you." As I pointed with my finger, I added, "Let's start by you telling me about the contents of those files over there."

The doctor told me that, if he said any word to me, he would be killed and he had worked hard for his job and position.

I looked at him and told him that his problem was not what the corporation would do to him but, rather, what I would do to him if he didn't speak to me and soon. I picked him up from the floor and walked behind him. I pressed the cold muzzle to the back of his head until I heard him take in a big gulp of air and exhale it slowly. He told me he'd talk if I promised him I would spare his life.

I directed him to turn around to look at me and said, "I will spare your life as long as you are telling me the truth. The moment I realize you're lying to me, I will shoot you without mercy and without warning. Do we understand each other?"

He said, "Yes."

And at this time, I had him right where I wanted him. I pushed him over to the file cabinets area, following closely behind.

"Now start telling me what 'Project Hera' is," I demanded.

He indicated that this was a project that had started back in the seventies and was focused on controlling the human mind. He continued talking about the project until he focused on Sani-Shaman and said to him, "I know you."

Sani-Sham said that he did not recognize the doctor at all.

Under my pistol sights, Dr. Jensen walked to a file about a

hundred feet away and, by punching in a sequence of numbers, opened a set of files. He pulled out a file and handed it over to Sani-Shaman, who immediately started to read.

A couple of minutes later, Sani-Shaman motioned for me to look at the file. I realized he had tears in his eyes. I pushed Dr. Jensen to the floor and trained the gun on him before taking the file from Sani-Shaman's hands. At a glance, I recognized the faces in the photographs the file contained. I had seen them on the sheriff's office's corridor wall.

"Jack, please meet my daughter and wife," said Sani-Shaman.

I looked into his eyes and said, "I am sorry, Sani-Shaman. How long have they been missing?"

He confirmed that his wife had been gone for over twenty years. "My daughter, Aala, would be a university student if she were still with us today. Twenty years ago, I went out to work, and when I came back, they were both missing. I searched around, called local friends for help, and used dogs to try to pick up their trail, but they were never found. I even trusted big brother, the federal government, and with all their technology and training, we were not able to find them. It was like they were banished from the face of the earth and had gone to live with the spirits, taking their bodies with them."

Sani-Shaman could no longer speak, as his throat had given way with pain and anguish.

Dr. Jensen took up the story from where Sani-Shaman had left off. "Dr. Harjo and his team brought them here to the corporation; they didn't vanish from the face of the earth."

I extended my hand to Sani-Shaman and placed it on his shoulder as Dr. Jensen cleared his throat, seemingly having trouble finding the words to continue. His voice sounded full of remorse and shame, and he could not look Sani-Shaman in the face. Rather, he looked at the floor before he managed to find the strength to continue his monologue. "The local hospital, under the control of Lindberg Research, needed some fresh test subjects.

"They needed a female, and given the mental aptitude of your wife and the fact that she had just given birth and they were experimenting on breaking the bond between mother and daughter, she was the ideal candidate." He was looking into the distance and seemed far away as he continued, "But it seems the spirit is stronger than the mind. Dr. Harjo's team could not break her spirit." He cleared his throat. "So he commanded that the test subjects be terminated. But believe me when I say that I had nothing to do with that."

Dr. Jensen seemed as if he was about to cry when he added, "These experiments take place in Section 8. And I don't work there and never have."

Sani-Shaman looked at me with a pain so poignant it was hard to bear. "Jack, this happened at the same time I went against the corporation and started a campaign to get them out of the sacred land," he said. "It was me who killed them; it was my foolish fight against the white man that killed my family."

I could see that Sani-Shaman's guilt was tearing him apart. A grown man was in tears at this point, and I had to say something to him. "It's not your fault, Sani-Shaman, but it all makes perfect sense," I said to him.

Sani-Shaman looked at Dr. Jensen. "Why?" he asked.

The doctor's reply was chilling in its simplicity. "This is the technique the corporation uses to tell everyone that it owns this town."

Sani-Shaman was looking into a past that LR Corp had denied to him as he looked at the photographs of his late daughter. He looked at Dr. Jensen with hatred and spat out a question, the answer to which he probably both wanted and didn't want, "How many days were they here?"

Dr. Jensen clearly didn't want to answer, so I pointed the pistol at him and said, "Speak. Answer the questions."

Dr. Jensen looked at the shiny floor and said with sadness in his voice, "Section 8 kept your daughter alive for many years, carrying out mental and other experiments until she and your wife were finally disposed of. That's when the file was marked as 'closed' and sent to me. I read all the files before storing them, and it was clear that your wife didn't fully assimilate the new mental programming. In the meantime, they used her as a surrogate to give birth to five children who were later used for stem-cell research."

Sani-Shaman's devastation as he internalized all this information all at once was written all over his face and body. He appeared to be engulfed in a cloud of guilt and sadness I haven't seen much since I was in combat. He looked like his reason for living had been taken away from him.

Sani-Shaman leaped from where he was standing and grabbed Dr. Jensen by the throat. He squeezed hard, until the doctor's eyes started to roll back.

I had to intervene, as I had one and a million questions that needed answers, and this doctor seemed to know a great deal about what was taking place at this facility. I pulled Sani-Shaman's hands away from Dr. Jensen just in time for the doctor to take one large gulp of air before dropping to the floor coughing.

Sani-Shaman broke down in tears as he slowly slid down the wall to his knees. "Jack, all these years, and she was still alive; these bastards tortured my wife and daughter and then killed them like animals. And what about the babies? What did they do with the babies?"

I could have asked Dr. Jensen to answer the question, but I refrained, as I was not going to add to Sani-Shaman's pain. Instead, I placed my hand on Sani-Shaman's shoulder and told him to take all the time he needed. I handed him the file with his wife's and daughter's photographs. I knew he needed time alone, so I pulled Dr. Jensen from the floor and moved him toward another set of files.

Upon arrival at this section of files, I saw that to my right and left were hundreds of filing cabinets, each identified with a different state. However, I concentrated on those nearby marked with "Nome, Alaska." I didn't have to ask Dr. Jensen, as he quickly opened the cabinet for me.

As I perused other files, I recognized many faces from the sheriff's office wall. What in the world was this corporation doing to the people of this town? Most of the women's files also showed baby photos, and as I read deeper, I came to realize that these were featuring the children they had given birth to in captivity.

I showed the files to Dr. Jensen, and he told me that Lindberg Research Corporation was using these test subjects as guinea pigs, experimenting with their minds and bodies as part of a mental-control program. New methods and techniques had been developed thanks to these experiments and were currently being used by many psychologists worldwide. They also used women to produce babies for stem-cell research, and most of the key laboratories around the world were lining up for orders from LR Corp. He continued for about another ten minutes before I asked him to stop and take a breath. I realized that I had stopped breathing. What he'd told me was horrifying. Most of the babies didn't make it to six months of age, as their brains, kidneys, lungs, hearts, and liver tissue, among other vital organs, were extracted. The corporation was playing God with stem-cell experiments.

Dr. Jensen had also told me that, in the process, LR Corporation's research scientists had discovered that stem cells could replicate themselves many times over and could be used to replace decaying organ tissue for new tissue.

This was what LR Corp was doing. The corporation was controlling people's minds to have them behave as they pleased and raping women of their fertile eggs, which they used to grow babies through in vitro fertilization. LR Corp was monitoring women's ovulation process, and in many cases, removing all the eggs from their fallopian tubes, killing their owners in the process.

Dr. Jensen further explained that the women's ovaries would be fertilized by sperm in a test tube in the laboratory located near Section 8 and they would grow as many babies as they could. Those women who served as surrogates were used to continue pregnancies, and even the baby's umbilical cord was used as a supplement of stem cells so nothing would go to waste.

It was all about controlling the minds of men and women for reproduction in any way they could. They wanted to perfect the technique of giving birth to babies that they could use as guinea pigs for stem-cell research. Dr. Jensen looked at me. "Who wouldn't pay thousands or even millions of dollars for a new heart, kidney, or lungs?" he said simply.

Whoever controlled this market would be rich beyond imagination. I found my hands shaking from anger, frustration, and a little bit of fear, knowing what these people were actually getting away with it. That so many innocent people had been affected in the interest of "science," or rather, in the interest of money, by the unscrupulous people working here was nearly unfathomable. It was a truth so overwhelming and so much to take in all at once that I decided not to share it with Sani-Shaman.

But I hadn't realized that Sani-Shaman had been listening all along. At this time, Sani-Shaman walked toward Dr. Jensen and hit him with a pipe several times on the head as hard as he could; Sani-Shaman did not stop until the doctor's brains were splattered all over the file cabinets. I wanted to stop him, but he had earned the right to, as the good doctor Jensen had put it, "dispose" of this body.

I waited for Sani-Shaman to vent his anger against the corporation—against what this cold-hearted institution had done to him and his family. After he stopped, I pulled him up and looked into his eyes. "After witnessing the destruction, pain, and anguish this corporation has inflicted on so many innocent people, I swear to you that I will sink this Lindberg to its foundations if it's the last thing I ever do," I promised.

I realized that the tears in his eyes were no longer tears of anger but rather pain.

We had been lucky for too long, so I only glanced at the rest of the files on top of the filing cabinets. As far as I could see, these people were not only experimenting on the small town of Nome but also had been conducting similar "research" throughout the United States. This was even larger than I had originally thought.

I then fixed my attention on one particular filing cabinet, which was labeled, "Beyond Stem Cells." Dreading to think about what I was going to find, I opened the cabinet, picked up the first file, and began reading. The first page was so graphic and Machiavellian that it gave me chills up my spine and made my hands shaky and sweaty again.

16

RUN, JACK, RUN

A s always, Marie was waiting for her husband like the good wife she was; dinner was ready, the house was impeccable, and she had dressed for him. Finally, after Marie had waited a whole day for him, Jimmy found his way home at the usual time.

Marie tried to explain to him what had happened to the Bronco and to Jack, but he was emotionless; it was like she was speaking to a wall. The only thing he managed to say was, "All will be all right."

To further add to her frustration, Jimmy ate his dinner and went straight to bed without even noticing her new dress and hairstyle.

As was usual lately, Jimmy was not making a lot of sense to her. To Marie's impression, Jimmy was under some type of spell.

She prayed that Jack was still alive and that he would be able to help them. Otherwise, she was afraid that she could not hold onto her sanity any longer. She made a mental note to call Deputy PJ Marshall in the morning to follow up on the results of their search for Jack. At least this was what she had been told to do.

Every moment was excruciating for her. At home, she was living with a man she barely knew anymore. Her only hope and sanity rested on knowing that Jack was on the case chasing a solid lead that could lead to some understanding of what was going on in her husband's life. Of course, she didn't know where Jack was, and this uncertainty was really affecting her sanity. Marie felt that the life left in her was slowly being sucked out of her body minute by minute. If this agony didn't end soon, she would entertain the idea of ending her own life.

Much later that night, a weird feeling awakened Marie. She opened her eyes to see her husband lying next to her. She noticed that his head was facing toward the glass window. She felt like Jimmy was waiting for something, but what that something was, she didn't know. As she attempted to focus her tired eyes on Jimmy, she wondered if he thought of her anymore, if he'd at least had one or two thoughts about her today or if he would tomorrow. Did Jimmy recall anymore any of the happy moments that often flitted in her mind several times a day?

Marie stretched her imagination, searching in vain for a reasonable explanation for her husband's behavior. What was going on in his mind? What could she do to rescue him and bring him back to her? Marie's worst thought was that she didn't know if she still had time to do something to bring Jimmy back to her—back to the way he was six months ago. Was it too late already to bring back the person she had fallen in love with and had vowed to spend the rest of her life with?

***

As Maynard James Lindberg was entering his Silver Spur Rolls-Royce, he glanced at his two-hundred-years-old summer mansion. Maynard James Lindberg was never shy about his properties, and although he stayed in this house only two months out of the year, he liked the power that this property—one of the most expensive houses in Anchorage— gave him. Lindberg's house was impressive; he owned an

1870 Ames-Webster mansion with French-style architecture, brownstone walls, and a grand staircase—a thirty-thousand-square-foot property.

The thirteen-room home boasted fifteen fireplaces and a grand foyer specifically designed for entertaining. The well-kept Brazilian redwood floors complemented the main reception area, and they were so shiny that you had the feeling that you were walking on polished glass. The many European features included a large, stained-glass skylight designed by the artist Eugène Viollet-le-Duc. His designs always stood as a true testament of time and wealth. Lindberg was passionate about owning the finer things in life, and this house was one of them.

Dressed in a tight, black-and-white suit and a well-manicured bowtie, Lindberg peacefully enjoyed the quiet and comfortable ride in his Silver Spur Rolls-Royce. Tonight, the cream of Alaska was going to rub elbows with him during a banquet. The keynote speaker for the night was the one and only Brad Farmer, vice president of the United States.

Lindberg wanted to be where the action was, and to run all his enterprises, he needed to have strong allies who could help further his agenda. Although many thought that the small suggested contribution to attend this event was a bit high, for Lindberg, $50,000 per person was just pocket change.

He was looking forward to talking with people who, just like him, were not afraid of spending a little to gain a lot. Upon arrival, his driver was directed by valet parkers to the front porte cochere, which was decorated to look like an enchanted castle entrance. The bellboy's jacket buttons were as shiny as Christmas lights as he opened the door for Lindberg and welcomed him to step onto a nicely placed red carpet. Lindberg noticed that behind the Rolls-Royce were several other expensive cars waiting to drop off their anxious, wealthy passengers.

Lindberg didn't hurry at all; he didn't care about holding

anyone else up and wanted to take it all in and to enjoy his short moment of fame. He was not married, and he didn't care about what other people said about him. Rumors in the upper classes were that Maynard James Lindberg was sexually attracted to members of the same sex. It was rumored that he especially enjoyed the much younger, muscular type. He often chose them as his personal assistants and, in many cases, even introduced them as distant family members.

But everyone knew that he was not bound to anyone in particular, and like sailors, he had what he wanted in every port, only Lindberg's whatever he wanted was the best that money could buy.

Lindberg graciously walked the red carpet like a king. His smile and elegance were second to none. The local and national presses turned all their attention to him, and flash after flash illuminated his gracious figure as he walked his way into the building.

**

SA Landis was going crazy trying to keep things safe and secure. His lack of manpower was making things difficult but not impossible, as he'd found lots of help from Captain Grimes and his team. Grimes's men were so helpful, interested in the task, and detail-oriented that Agent Landis felt as though he was working with a full complement of US Secret Service detail.

Agent Landis's mission was to secure the vice president and prevent any type of incident from affecting the VP staff. So far, things were going according to plan. A couple of hours more, and phase II of his plan would be done.

When dinner ended, the men moved to a section of the room for a cigar taste, courtesy of Cabana Tobacco Products Inc. (CTP), a Dominican Republic tobacco company with ties to the Castro regime that was trying to make its covert way in to the US market.

The dinner was sponsored by yet another lobbyist who was advocating for exploitation of Alaskan oil reserves. The facilities were sponsored by the local Chamber of Commerce of Anchorage, whose very own governor chose to award VP Farmer the keys to the city.

At his earliest opportunity, Governor Mackenzie found an opportunity to ask the vice president to help endorse the national governors' conference for the following year, the location for which the board had not yet decided on; of course, the good governor wanted it to take place in Anchorage.

That night, everywhere policymakers and politicians went, the lobbyists followed very closely. Lobbyists were doing their best, luring each and every one with exquisite and expensive gifts to attract attention to his or her cause. Whether the gifts were money, expensive perks, beautiful women, or votes, lobbyists in the United States had mastered the art of "giving" like a science. They had engaged psychologists, academics, and other politicians alike to learn the needs of humankind and had developed the best lures possible to attract new clients.

If by chance they were lucky enough to find a true boy scout—a clean, motivated politician who really wanted to do the right thing—the interested parties generally found their way to the "scout" through coercion or intimidation, forcing such resource to do as they please. Many trade old-timers even said that, occasionally, if trying these dark tactics didn't work, then the lobbyists were required to dispose, eliminate, or discredit what started out to be a very promising, clean American politician of the people and turning him into a dirty, discredited, and untrustworthy human being.

Cabana Tobacco Products was featuring its newest products from the Dominican Republic, which they called the "Great White." This was a cigar line that offered a greater variety of flavors, giving the company's Cuban neighbors something to envy (as its marketing propaganda claimed). The variety of aromas and colors distinguished these cigars, bringing them head-to-head with Cuba's counterparts. Cabana Tobacco Products had flown in a team of cigar makers from the Dominican Republic, along with the company's best products, to exploit the many urges and satisfy the clients' desires.

The ten different cigar flavors and aromas were spreading way beyond the smoke room, overwhelming the grand ballroom. For the non-cigar lovers, the mild tobacco aroma was pleasant and enjoyable, as it wasn't accompanied by the heavy and intoxicating burning smoke often despised by nonsmokers.

For the smoking guests, the hotel management had arranged an open terrace overlooking the lake. A cigar, a glass of cognac, and the lake view were incentives enough to pay not one million dollars but ten times the amount or more a seat. Although Cuban cigars were well recognized around the world, the Dominican Republic cigars shared some of the same seeds. Variants such as moisture, terrain, altitude, and drying process may vary the final product, but overall, if you gave a DR cigar to anyone but a confirmed expert and told him or her that it was from Cuba, it would pass with flying colors; or at least this is what Cabana's marketing campaign claimed: "Cabana Cigars, setting the new world standard."

***

Vice President Farmer was trying to keep an eye on Maynard James Lindberg, who was in a corner of the terrace like a preying tiger waiting for the right time to strike. His avoidance strategy was working thus far, but he knew that, sooner or later, Lindberg would make his debut, and Farmer was doing everything he could to avoid this encounter. He took a second away from focusing on Lindberg to ask Danny to start preparing for his departure, and when Farmer turned back, Lindberg was already next to him introducing himself.

"Mr. Vice President, allow me to introduce myself. My name is—"

"Yes, I know who you are," VP Farmer interrupted. "You are Maynard Lindberg. Which of your many interests do you represent tonight? I hope not the stem-cell research industry because—"

"No, Mr. Vice President." This time it was Lindberg who interrupted. "Tonight, I am just another guest supporting your fundraising," he said.

"Well, in that case, welcome to my party."

"No, Mr. Vice President, it is me who has to welcome you to Alaska; you see, this is my home and the home of many other fine things in life waiting to be exploited for the benefits of pursuing and achieving the American Dream."

"Mr. Lindberg, I know very well what you are trying to drag me into, and this is not the venue or the time to discuss this matter. The president of the United States and I are very clear that we are not going to allow the integrity of our country to be jeopardized by endorsing your indiscriminate research. This is not what we have in mind for the legacy of this country, and as long as we can, we will continue to be advocates for the restriction of this research.

"Don't you see, Mr. Lindberg? We have to step in to the twenty-first century, but not by ripping apart and stepping over our morals. We are responsible for starting a new millennia with hope and respect, not only for the lives of others but ours as well," said VP Farmer.

"I am so sorry to hear that, Mr. Vice President. I live one day at a time, and today, stem-cell research is vital for those suffering from cancer and lung and heart disease. Today, we have the cure—the ability to put an end to the suffering of so many, and yet you are denying us this blessing? I came here to talk some sense into you and ask you to reconsider your campaign. I thought that, perhaps, I could persuade you to change your mind, put aside your so-called 'morals,' and join my efforts. I know that, together, we can change this nation and, tomorrow, the world," said Lindberg.

Lindberg took a sip of his champagne, taking a moment to savor its crisp and delightful flavor. Clearing his throat, he added, "Mr. Vice President, I know you don't support my position on stem-cell research, but can you at least bear with me for another minute or two?" Lindberg could practically see the wheels turning in Farmer's head as the man obviously thought through his response before saying anything.

Farmer crossed his arms over his chest, a bad sign. His body language told Lindberg everything. Farmer was closed up tight and said to Lindberg, "Whatever you say to me, it won't change my mind. I am going to announce tomorrow that America is not selling its soul to the devil of stem-cell research. We are going to revamp the faith, hope, and beliefs of our treasured Founding Fathers. Thanks for attending my fundraiser and for your gracious welcome—"

"Mr. Vice President, Alaska is as dangerous as it is rich. Please be careful while you are here." He looked over the balcony toward the ground level before continuing. "We wouldn't like anything to happen to you; it would be uncivilized."

VP Farmer was about to explode as he got very close to Lindberg's face and said to him loudly and clearly, "Just who do you think you are? One word from me and your ass will be in deep shit with the Secret Service."

SA Landis, along with Danny, was at the vice president's side almost immediately. "Mr. Vice President, your car is ready to take you back to the hotel," the agent said.

Farmer backed away from Lindberg and in a very aggressive tone said, "Good evening, Mr. Lindberg. Please don't take it personally, but I hope that I don't see you again."

Lindberg bowed to the VP as he said, "May you have a safe flight to Nome tomorrow, Mr. Vice President."

Vice President Farmer looked at both SA Landis and Danny and nodded to them, a clear indication that they should lead the way out and that he would follow. In a matter of seconds, billionaire, philanthropist, and madman Maynard James Lindberg was left in a corner holding his drink with a face full of defeat and hatred.

***

As VP Farmer left the room, another man approached Lindberg and asked what had just happened. "Are you trying to antagonize the vice president of the United States in front of all these guests? What is wrong with you?"

Lindberg gently tried to produce a smile to save face, as if all was right, and responded, "Mr. Jones, I am trying to recruit a new asset, but in spite of my tempting lures, the man just won't bite." Lindberg, a man who was not used to receiving negative responses from people, had been defeated tonight, not by a man but by his morals, and he didn't like that at all. "I am just trying to save lives, Mr. Jones, but it appears that Vice President Farmer wants to die for his beliefs, and that leaves us with no choice but to make his dreams come true."

"Mr. Lindberg, now that you put it that way, he deserves what is coming to him," said Jones. "And speaking of that small venture, how is it going so far?" he asked.

"I thought you'd never ask!" said Lindberg. "Allow me to say that the Verum leaders will be please to know that things are going according to plan and that hopefully all—"

Jones interrupted, correcting the billionaire in a very direct manner, "*Hopefully*, Mr. Lindberg?"

"Sorry, Jones. I meant surely. Vice President Farmer will not have a chance to present his plan in Nome," Lindberg concluded.

"You see, Mr. Lindberg, sometimes it is very important to choose the right words and communicate clearly to ensure mutual understanding. I am sure that Dr. Harjo has a way with words," said Jones.

"You are right, Mr. Jones. As we speak, Dr. Harjo has Mr. Jimmy Steele eating from the palm of his hand, and I can assure you that VP Farmer will never reach Nome, or should I say, at least not alive."

Both gentlemen laughed out loud, until they were approached by a young man who stopped next to Mr. Jones. "Mr. Lindberg, it is my pleasure to introduce you to Clark Michael Stratfor III. He is the son of the late billionaire Clark Michael Stratfor II and sole heir to the business of his late father, may God rest his soul."

Lindberg looked at the young man, reached for his hand, and kissed it. Lindberg was grateful that this night was not a complete loss.

Young Clark's eyes glittered with flirtation and desire, and Lindberg knew how to read between the lines. For him, the message was loud and clear. Lindberg took Clark by the hand and headed toward the main door as proud as a prom-night senior who was about to finally expand his wings with his high school sweetheart.

***

Verum Chairman Mark Jones observed Lindberg and the young man walking out of the room. He knew how to exploit his friends' and enemies' weaknesses, and this was one of the traits that distinguished him as a true Verum leader. He didn't have to pay for Lindberg's loyalty to Verum. As Lindberg had it all, he didn't have to extort, pressure, or torture him, but instead, he attacked and exploited the most common of human emotions, which is self-gratification.

Chairman Mark Jones was very good at his game; he had worked his magic not only on Lindberg but on many other powerful individuals in the political and economic game that night. Whether it was a beautiful women, young boys, or young girls that the individuals desired, for Mark Jones, the sky was the limit. He would use his skills to his advantage and offer the best money could buy. In doing so, Mr. Jones ensured his own fame and the adoration of his many clients—or rather, targets.

***

The more I read, the more questions I had. This was larger than I could begin to comprehend. Lindberg had developed a program to offer all predisposed clients an insurance policy for growing stem cells for them. This research was not about saving millions of lives; it was about money, control, and power. The contents of this insurance policy was about mining hospitals, medical specialists, and other insurance programs to obtain information on all ill patients.

Once Lindberg had the information, the corporation would contact the prospective clients and offer them a way out of their illness or sickness by having "ready-to-use tissue" developed by pre-harvesting their own clients' sperm or ovaries. This process would ensure that the product would be ready for them when needed. For a modest price of one and a half million dollars, a contact would include the product, aftercare, and confidentiality.

Of course, this cost was for the wealthy, but LR Corp also had a plan for the economically challenged citizens. For those who could not pay the premium feed all at once, the LR Corp had already lined up a complete line of insurance programs that a family could start paying into upon the birth of a child, so the family would have a complete life policy to pay for the much-needed stem cells, helping its members to live longer.

Either way, the LR Corp was not going to put the product to waste. The corporation's researchers were already working on a preventive maintenance pill that would be developed by Lindberg Pharmaceuticals and Research, LLC. This pill would have two hooks. First, those who would need the stem cells would have to purchase a pill through the medical plan. The pill would have to be consumed at least three times a week to prepare the body for the procedure and stem-cell acceptance. Furthermore, once the customer had endured and survived the stem-cell insertion procedure, the customer would have to switch pills, taking one a day for the rest of their life to ensure success and prevent further tissue deterioration.

These bastards would not only cash in from the insurance but also for the rest of the customer's natural life. The plan was Machiavellian and yet brilliant and yielded no space for losses. The bottom line was about earnings and profits. The icing on the cake was the last sentence. I read it twice: "The beauty of the program is that stem cells don't need any medication either before or after the procedure. They'll work through the natural growing process and are very resilient; using the X-2915 substance we develop in our European lab, we are programming the stem cells to become addicted to this drug and, subsequently, addictive for the user."

These guys were really starting to piss me off, and I promised that they would pay for what they'd done and were about to do to the American people and the world.

It all made sense. James Lindberg had secured and protected all research-and-development files in a remote and secluded place called Nome, Alaska. It occurred to me that I'd struck gold. This organization was the root of all evils—it was playing with people's minds, causing atrocities during early stem-cell experimentation, and tampering with human lives. I was surprised and pissed off that, for so long, the corporation had gotten away with such a scheme and no one had come forward to expose what was going on.

I observed Sani-Shaman, who was still staring at Dr. Jensen's body. I could see a tear running down his left cheek. It was Lindberg and his cohorts at the hospital and private practices who had helped program most of the people in Nome and steal their bodies to use them as surrogates.

I walked over to Sani-Shaman and handed him a file that had his name on it.

With shaking hands, he opened it up, and I got closer to see what was inside. To my surprise and as I glanced at his photograph, I read the classification under it: "Project Threat."

He read out loud, and what I listened to was disturbing. His introduction to the program had started when he'd gone to the hospital for appendix surgery.

"Now, it all makes sense!" said Sani-Shaman.

Before he'd gone in for the surgery, all had been going well for him and his family, and right after he'd surrendered his body to the local doctors, all hell had broken loose. After his medical procedure, he'd lost everything, along with his will, his family, and his power over his people. The corporation had taken advantage of his condition. When he was sedated, they'd reprogrammed his mind so they could do as they pleased. It was no wonder that, after he was dismissed from the hospital, he intensified his focus on convincing his tribal leaders and his people to endorse a company they had learned to hate and repudiate over the years.

Sani-Shaman turned the page and shared with me a list of people he recognized. He told me that most of them were still alive and actively supporting the corporation. The others had disappeared and had never been found. He pointed one out to me and said, "This name, I remember well."

He explained that the man—Gerald Cox—had been the town's former sheriff. Sani-Shaman went back to the file cabinet and pulled out Cox's file. He handed it to me, and after we'd read the first page, we both realized what had happened to Sheriff Cox. According to the file, Sheriff Cox had rejected reprogramming, and after several attempts, Dr. Anderson had submitted his name to LR Corp for immediate termination.

Sani-Shaman whispered to me that the sheriff's death hadn't been an accident as the town had been left to believe.

Sani-Shaman didn't have to read the file to tell me what had happened. He explained that a 9-1-1 call had come in from the Anvil Mountain Correctional Facility, and the sheriff had left the station and headed up the hill, but he'd never returned. Two days later, he'd been found frozen inside his patrol car at the bottom of a ravine.

The only reasonable explanation was that his patrol car had skidded from the road and landed on the riverbank. Half of his face and left shoulder had been eaten by wild animals. The town was devastated, and since then, his second-in-command, Deputy (now Sheriff) Lindblom, had been heading up the office.

***

Outside the corporate facility, Sora was freezing. All of a sudden, she heard the sound of a dog growling behind her. She knew she was in trouble and didn't even have time to alert her two partners before the corporation's special security canine force lifted her off the ground like she was weightless. The dog was ready to rip her apart, but the special unit followed protocol and kept the dog at a distance.

She remained quiet and played the game; unfortunately, on the way out, the security patrol saw two more ATVs next to hers. She was doomed, but even worse, so were her two friends, who were trapped and blinded inside the corporation's belly. The officer handling the canine asked the animal to seek and follow the scent left by Jack and Sani-Shaman.

The officer illuminated the fence area with his flashlight and noticed that the fence had been repaired. He immediately reached for his handheld radio and reported, "Code Red, Intrusion Alert."

Sora could not do anything at this time; she was at the

mercy of a superior force, and she knew it. Her best chance to stay alive was to play the game and hope that somehow she would be brave and strong enough to slow the interrogation process until both her friends could clear the premises.

***

The sound of the general alarm ripped through the compound. Red lights came alive in the room, and an annoying alarm that sounded like those Jack had heard when the submarines were going down on an emergency dive pierced the air. Jack thought that it was as annoying as hell; this was why the navy used those piercing sounds—to make sure that everyone was facing a state of emergency. But the sound was the least of his problems.

Jack turned toward Sani-Shaman and told him it was time to leave. But before they did, Sani-Shaman took a couple of key files and placed them in both his cargo pockets.

Shortly after, both men ran away from the file vault, heading toward the storage room where they had made their initial entry.

17

TIME TO DIE

A phone rang, and Maynard James Lindberg reached out to his right to pick it up. "This is Lindberg. This better be important, or you won't have a job tomorrow morning!"

"Sir, this is Tom Harman, your chief security officer at the Nome facility. We have some intruders on the premises." Colonel Harman finished by asking if there were any instructions.

"Yes, of course, Tom Harman, chief security officer, if you still want to have a job tomorrow, you'd better detain the intruders and have them ready and conditioned for my arrival in two hours. Do I make myself clear?" Lindberg roared into the phone.

"Perfectly clear, Mr. Lindberg. You can count on me." And the line went dead.

***

CSO Harman placed his car phone in the cradle and continued his final drive to the main gate of Lindberg Research Corporation's Nome headquarters. The place looked like a high-security prison, with activity buzzing everywhere—patrol cars were everywhere, and the SWAT team was on

195

foot, bearing high-powered weapons and flashlights, checking the fence inch by inch, and searching everywhere, even on top of the building.

There was no way that anyone could slip through the heavy security protocols that retired Special Forces Colonel Tom Harman had established. As he reached the front gate, he was met by two of his most trusted front gate special police officers, who shoved a bright light in his face and asked him for ID.

When they recognized him, they apologized.

"You don't have to apologize for doing your job," he told them. "This is my ID, and I expect you to do the same for every single person who you allow access into my building. Do you hear?"

The two officers snapped to attention as he cleared the gate, and as soon as he'd passed through, the gate closed and they walked to face each other and then turned to face the front, holding at port arms specially designed M16 A-2 rifles with night scopes.

Colonel Harman was very proud of his command; although he was no longer serving in the military, he measured his people and his civilian job under the same standards he'd learned so well when he was in the service. Needless to say, he was now paid for results, and his employer was as ungrateful and unforgiving as an enemy's bullet.

The colonel parked his black, company-issue SUV and headed toward the operations room. The first thing he asked of his shift security supervisor was to cut the alarm. Or in his own, polite words, "Will you please cut the fucking noise? By now everyone in Nome and the whole of Alaska, let alone these premises, knows that we have an emergency here."

Shift security supervisor Levi Thomson picked up his radio and gave a command to the security operations room, and in a second, the premises were as silent as a cold cemetery at midnight.

"Now, where is the intruder?" asked the colonel.

"Sir, follow me. She is in detention cell fourteen," said the shift supervisor.

Colonel Harman followed Thomson through a long corridor toward the rear of the building near the loading docks next to the security detention area.

On the way there, the shift security supervisor explained the details to the colonel. Thomson was very nervous and speaking as if his life depended on it. Harman was not asking any questions; he listened to the detailed rendition of the night's happenings.

Once they reached the detention room, Harman saw a very scared young girl lying down on a bunk. "I am your worst nightmare," he said in a low growl. "This is how this is going to play. I ask the questions, and you answer them; if you don't, you will feel real pain, and if you do, I promise that your death will be quick. Do we understand each other?"

***

As Sani-Shaman and I were on our way back to our entrance point, we encountered a group of fully armed security officers. I learned that their intentions were hostile when the first couple of bullets whistled near my head. We ran back for cover, and as we ran, I heard who appeared to be the team leader spell out our location over the portable radio.

We ran for our lives down the large corridor. Sani-Shaman was keeping up with me, but as we tried to open the doors to our left and right, we found that all were locked. We took a corner that was identified as "Emergency Exit," and to our surprise, it landed us in a large hall with four intersections. To our back, the security team was getting closer; to our front, we soon heard noises that indicated that another security group was quickly approaching. You can't ever forget the sound of polished leader slamming against the floor with cadence.

Suddenly, the first group caught up with us, and they let us know their intentions, as a few bullets impacted the ceiling above us and pieces of dry tiles dropped on top of us.

As I recovered my bearings, I looked at Sani-Shaman, who was running toward the left corridor. I tried to follow him, but as I started to run, the second team was close enough to start shooting at me, and I was cut off from Sani-Shaman, who ran like there was no tomorrow. I had no other choice but to run toward the emergency exit door to my right and hope for the best.

I walked down the first set of stairs to the lower room. When I walked into the corridor and opened the door, I found a couple of men dressed in white coats. "Gentlemen, do you know what happened? What was going on with the dammed noise? I couldn't concentrate," I said.

"What is it to you, cleaner boy? Go back to your duties. This is no concern of yours."

As humbly as I could, I dropped my head and continued walking past them and headed toward the next room over. This seemed to be like a test room of some sort. It was full of electronic equipment, seats that looked like dental exam chairs, and a lot of headsets that looked like those you only find in science fiction magazines.

I passed right by the room but not without picking up a hard drive that was left plugged into the side of a laptop on the main console. Intelligence was my business and I knew that hard drives were used to carry current information one needed to keep handy at all times. I wanted to keep this one handy to study during my downtime.

As I tried to open the door, I saw a squad of four shooters in combat fully equipped and moving with a purpose. They were carrying what appeared to be a smart phone and looking at it. Based on my experience, I guessed that this device allowed them to tap in to the camera system so they could see what was ahead of them. *Very ingenious*, I thought, *very ingenious*.

I closed the door and looked inside the room. To my doom, I observed two infrared cameras staring at me. I locked the door from the inside and hid behind the wall.

Seconds later, the shooters stopped and tried to open the door. When they realized it was locked, they said something like, "This room is locked but let's take a look at the mobile-cam unit."

I ducked as fast as I could but, on my way down, brought with me a plastic water jar that bounced on the floor away from me. I was hoping that they couldn't hear the noise. Then I heard the door electronically strike open, and two officers entered the room.

I hid behind a large, long, thin cabinet, waiting for them to go or for the right time to strike. I saw one officer walking toward the plastic jar and the other covering him from behind. I had to give them credit; they did know proper search procedures. The officer picked up the jar and placed it on top of a table. He then hand signaled his friend to keep quiet and to start scanning the area.

Oh shit, here we go again, I thought. I waited for the right time, and when I saw the first officer's shadow getting close to where I was, I mustered all the strength I had and pushed the file cabinet toward him. As the file was moving away from me, I was exposed. I ran to a nearby table and dropped behind it for cover. Security officers in high alert tend to get trigger-happy, so when this happened, both of the guards were startled and both started to shoot. The first one near me was doomed, as he concentrated on me and not on the file cabinet, which fell on top of him, and the second one fully discharged his thirty-round magazine in my direction.

Pieces of chipped wood, plastic, and glass flew in different directions. The smell of burned powder soon inundated the room, and the whistling of rounds passing only inches from my body told me I was in deep trouble. However, discharging his full magazine was a tactical mistake for the second shooter.

199

When I heard the unique sound of an empty weapon, I rushed out of my protected, hidden place and immediately assessed my offensive options. My trained mind swiftly noticed that I didn't have enough time to reach the officer before he could either change his magazine or draw his sidearm, so I went for the first officer's rifle as fast as I could. I was determined and resolved and knew exactly what I had to do. Unfortunately for the second security officer, this was not the case.

He thought that I was dead, a fatal mistake that I read on his face when I picked up the rifle and sent a few projectiles up his way. The bullets quickly found their way into his chest, and he dropped with a look of disbelief and fear. But when you have a weapon and you are shooting at someone, you have to expect that the other party will try everything in his or her power to eliminate the threat. And this was what I had just done. It was kill or be killed, and tonight I had chosen not to die.

I felt a warm substance dripping down my left shoulder, and when I touched the area, I found that a piece of wood had found its way into my left upper shoulder area. I pulled the piece of wood out and was glad to see that it had only made a small wound. I would attend to the wound when I had time later. It wouldn't kill me, but the other armed, able, and equipped security officers would.

So I grabbed my phone and typed a text message.

***

After intimidating Sora out of her mind, Colonel Harman had left the room, forcing her to ponder the words he'd just spoken to her. This was a technique that Harman had used in the past with very good results. It combined the element of uncertainly with an expectation of maiming and death. He levied in Sora the same level of stress that a dead man walking feels as he walks from his cell to the electric chair.

Deep inside the interrogation room, the cuffs bit into Sora's wrists, and she felt like she was going to throw up. She tasted bile, and she had a strong need to pee. She glanced quickly toward the door of the interrogation room when she heard keys jangling outside. The door opened a second later, followed by a person who said, "Now it's time to talk.

"Tell me your name!" the interrogator demanded.

"Sora, my name is Sora."

"Wait a minute. I know you! You are a waitress at the diner. What are you doing here?"

"I am alone," she said. "I was looking for Sani-Shaman, as he disappeared yesterday, and I followed his ATV here. I'd just gotten there when your men arrested me. I demand to call the sheriff."

"Very clever lady, if I may say so. Do you care to tell me why you were near three ATVs instead of two and why you chose to take matters into your own hands instead of calling the police?"

"I didn't want to further humiliate Sani-Shaman, but he is already damaged goods, and on many occasions, he forgets his way home," said Sora.

"I'll tell you something, girl. I am a human lie detector, and you are lying through your teeth. Nothing you are saying makes sense, especially when we found our perimeter fence broken. Does your Sani-Shaman also have problems with fences?"

She did not respond and lowered her face.

"Hey, look at me when I am talking to you. I will ask again. What are you doing here?"

At this moment, the shift security supervisor approached Colonel Harman and handed him Sora's cellular phone.

Harman read the message and approached Sora. He showed her the message, which read: "Sora, please leave immediately and contact the local authorities. Ask them to bring all the firepower they have. We hit a gold vein."

"Now do you care to change your story? Or do you want to feel a little pain to warm up your cold body?"

Sora looked Harman straight in the face and could not help letting a tear drop down her cheek.

"What do you think I am going to do with you?" said Harman. "Do you think that I have pity for you because you are a girl and you can cry? Lady, I eat girls like you as snacks. Go ahead, gentlemen, give her to my son. Taylor and the boys can soften her up a little. We have two other rats to catch."

Harman turned around and headed for a room past the command center and picked up an HK 9mm hand pistol with two clips of ammunition. He then turned back to the security room and said to his men loud and clear, "Men, Maynard Lindberg is coming to these facilities in less than two hours. I suggest that all of you get busy and find the intruders, or I promise that one of you will be shot before sunrise today. Now go."

He stood looking at everyone, and with that, the two officers manning the security console cleared the room in less than a second.

***

Maynard James Lindberg's limousine arrived at his private hangar. His driver stopped right next to his jet's door and got out to open the door, allowing his master to leave the car. From outside the limousine, Lindberg could see his pilot at the cockpit getting ready for takeoff. His trusted flight attendant was ready, waiting to welcome him at the plane's main door. As he went up the jet's ramp, his driver picked up a suitcase from the trunk.

As Lindberg entered the plane, the flight attendant received him with a glass of his favorite drink. The flight attendant noticed that Lindberg appeared to be wearing a permanent smile on his face tonight. What had happened last night was not her business, but she made a mental note to ensure that this smile remained there for the rest of the flight.

Chief Pilot Andre Emerson walked to the main cabin and greeted Lindberg before explaining that it would take an hour and a half to arrive in Nome.

Lindberg appeared not to be bothered and asked not to be disturbed until it was time to land.

The driver dropped off his master's suitcase and wished him a safe flight before starting to walk down the plane's stairs.

Shortly after this, the flight attendant pushed a button, and the jet's door started to close. In no time, the plane was taxiing out of the hangar and heading toward the tarmac.

Lindberg knew that he was in good hands, so he was going to use the short flight to Nome to capture some rest. His trusted chief pilot, Emerson, had been employed by Lindberg Research for over ten years, and he had been a trusted employee. Lindberg sat down, buckled his seat belt, and lay back in his seat.

After asking the flight attendant not to disturb him until they'd arrived at Nome, he watched her going to the front cabin and closed his eyes, soon falling into a deep sleep.

***

Sora was, indeed, facing her worst nightmare. She was in a closed room with Taylor and the two other boys. She called for help, but no one came; she called for mercy, but none was there. She felt alone, frightened, and deserted; in her mind, she was experiencing the worst day of her life.

"Okay, okay. I'll tell you everything, but please don't hurt me," Sora pleaded.

"It's too late for that, baby, because tonight you are mine. I have been waiting a long time for this."

"Wait, Taylor, tonight she is ours, remember?" commented one of the boys.

"Yes, you can have her after I've finished with her," Taylor told his friend. "Wait your turn and watch and see how real men do it."

Sora screamed hard and long, but no help came to her rescue. Taylor, a big bully, came closer to her and grabbed her by the coat and ripped it open. She felt incredibly vulnerable, as if her fate had abandoned her. She hadn't felt so alone and frightened in a long time.

Taylor threw the coat to the boys, who started to fight for it. The big bully then grabbed her blouse and followed suit. In seconds, her tender breasts were exposed and vulnerable to the devil's intentions showing in Taylor's eyes.

Sora was by herself. She had to endure every second of torture as she tried to buy time for Jack and Sani-Shaman, so they could rescue her. She was praying that the torment would end soon as every second she had to look at her attackers seemed like an eternity to her. The two boys in the background were already discussing their turn.

When Taylor got closer to her and tried to hold her in his arms, Sora screamed from the depths of her soul, making all the noise she could muster.

Taylor looked at her and said, "Scream all you can, you bitch, because tonight you are mine." With that, he let out a long, hard laugh.

He stopped for a moment as he no longer heard the two boys chatting behind him. Turning, he saw Sani-Shaman holding a bloody knife in his hand and the two boys lying on the floor with their throats slit. Their blood stained the small cell walls and floors.

Sora observed Taylor moving behind her and grabbing her tightly. With one hand, he grabbed her hair; he wrapped the other around her neck. Sani-Shaman's face told her that he was at a loss as to what to do next. She had to do something. She moved left and right, to make sure that Taylor was holding her tightly, and when she was sure of it, she bent herself forward and catapulted Taylor upside down onto the floor. Taylor body followed the motion like an apple that couldn't resist falling down the tree. As he landed on the floor, he hit his head hard and became partially unconscious.

Sora raised her hand to stop Sani-Shaman, who was about to run toward Taylor. She walked toward Taylor, turned him face down, and sat on top of him; and with all the strength she could muster, she pulled his head backwards as far as she could until she heard his neck snap. Once she'd realized what she had done, she started to shake all over and began crying uncontrollably.

Sani-Shaman handed Sora her coat, and as she put it on, he scanned the area for any security personnel in the vicinity. "Sora, are you okay? Was I too late?"

"No, Sani-Shaman. I prayed to the spirits, and here you are. I am fine. Now where is Jack? Let's get out of here."

***

I waited for a couple of minutes until I heard silence and slowly opened the door. No one was in the hall, so I slowly and with purpose walked along, as if I belonged there. I walked to the left and spotted an elevator. As I passed by, I heard the bell ring; I was dead center at the elevator landing. I didn't have time to run, so I swallowed hard and waited. The elevator door opened, and five technicians and a security officer left the lift. They looked at me and said, "What are you waiting for? We are to report back to the assembly room. Don't just stand there! Follow us," they demanded as they turned their geeky faces away.

I followed the geeks down the corridor to find two security officers manning a checkpoint. I had no choice but to play the game and follow the group. They were stopping and finger scanning everyone before allowing anyone to proceed to the secure room. I let two of the geeks go first and then stepped beside the last one. I wanted to have him around because he was going to be my distraction.

I put my finger on the scanner; my hand was still moist from the blood from my shoulder wound. However, I had no choice. I had to play the game and look as normal as possible.

But my gamble didn't work, and a sound like those buzzers that go off after you score in a basketball game echoed around the narrow corridor. I guessed that this wasn't good because, all of a sudden, the security officers started to raise their weapons.

I pushed the geek against two of them and knocked the one behind me out cold with a roundhouse kick to his heavyset jaw. I turned back to handle the other two officers and grabbed the one closest to me and hit him hard on the throat. He went down without saying a word. Following this, I slid forward and grabbed the last security officer's M16, and as he discharged the weapon, the bullets impacted the fragile corridor walls and missed my torso by inches, if that.

I reached for the rifle's muzzle and pulled the weapon toward me as hard as I could. I could feel the hot muzzle burning the inside of my hand, but this pain was secondary to what those bullets would do to me if they hit me. The instant reaction of the officer was to pull back, so when I felt the pull, I just let go, and the officer tripped backward and fell on the floor. However, when I was going to counterattack, I heard the click made by the charging of an HK 9mm pistol.

I froze where I was standing and only looked back to see the faces of two security officers pointing their M16s at me. Between them stood a civilian man who was nearly seven feet tall, as strong as a mule, sporting a short-cropped haircut, and pointing the pistol at me. "I don't know who you are, but it's just a matter of time," he said. "Allow me to introduce myself. I am Colonel Tom Harman. You have created a hell of a mess for me tonight, mister. Now let's take a walk to my office ... Shall we?"

I had to say he was polite. I had to give him that. But his face was that of an assassin, and this worried me a lot—not for myself, as I was no stranger to pain, but for Sani-Shaman, who, as far as I was concerned, was still missing in action.

***

Sora and Sani-Shaman took a moment to consider their next move. They quickly dressed, using the uniforms from the two security officers Sani-Shaman had dispatched a while ago outside the control room as he'd found his way to her. They also picked up the officers' weapons and put on their hats. Looking like they belonged there was the best chance they had if they wanted to leave the premises alive. They headed toward the garage exits, which Sani-Shaman knew well from his previous visits when he was aiding LR Corp.

As they approached the entrance, they saw a lot of activity. They had no chance of getting away unless they created a diversion. Sora understood what she had to do and immediately pulled the emergency fire alarm. With that, all hell broke loose. This was going to be the only chance they had for a clean getaway. As the security personnel went into military operation mode, Sani-Shaman and Sora wasted no time jumping into an unattended black Hummer and driving away at speed.

***

"God damn it! Not again," said Harman.

He picked up his radio and called down to the command center, only to find static. "To all units monitoring this frequency, no one enters and leaves these premises unless cleared by me," he barked.

***

Sani-Shaman and Sora were making the black Hummer scream as they left the motor pool in a hurry. Sani-Shaman knew his way around, and he knew that they had no chance getting through the main entrance or rear service area. Both areas were heavily guarded and had anti-passing bollards, which he knew were challenging, even to a Hummer.

So he did what he thought best. He drove the Hummer toward the same fence they'd broken to come in. The fence gave way like butter to hot steel, and off they went under the rapid fire of the security guards, who completely discharged their weapons on the Hummer. Guards in two patrol vehicles who had been summoned to follow the Hummer were hot on their trail.

***

I found myself looking at the colonel's face as he discovered his two console operators lying dead on the floor, wearing only their briefs. He immediately headed toward a door marked "detention room 14." Inside, the two youngsters and their chief bully, who I recognized from the café the other day, were lying on the floor dead.

Harman knelt next to the leader of the trio and looked at him for a moment. The colonel's expression completely changed; pain, grief, and remorse were etched clearly on his face as he picked the boy up from the floor and gently placed the inert body on his lap. I realized that the boy had to be either a family member or a close friend; I assumed it was the first.

He stood up and looked at the night shift supervisor. "Do you remember what I said here tonight?"

"Yes, sir. You promised that one of us would be shot before sunrise today."

"Yes, that's right." And with that, Harman raised his HK 9mm pistol and shot the shift security supervisor dead.

The other security officer in the room stood silent, but I saw him breathe a sigh of relief. Colonel Harman then turned to face the second officer and said, "I lied. I will kill you both." Subsequently, he shot the second officer center mass. "This one is for Taylor, you sorry ass. Because of your incompetence, my son is dead."

In less than three seconds, the room was silent and more security officers had come to offer support.

Harman turned to me. "Mister, whoever you are, you chose the wrong night to mess with me. I am pissed off, tired, and my blood is boiling with vengeance."

I looked at him and swallowed hard, but even though the colonel was an intimidating man, I was not afraid. He was a man with vengeance in his heart, and to what he was feeling I could relate.

***

Sani-Shaman knew this terrain well. He'd used all the shortcuts and back roads he could remember. But just when he thought that he was in the clear, he was lit up by the intense reflectors of a privately owned AAS-72X assault helicopter.

"Oh shit, Sora; we are doomed." Sani-Shaman tried to steer the Hummer away from the light, but the helicopter soon found the bulky Hummer, which was difficult to conceal given the lack of trees.

***

Inside the combat helicopter's dark cockpit, the green, yellow, and white console lights provided the only source of illumination. Both pilot and copilot were actively looking down, like eagles trying to locate the Hummer below.

After they'd been in the air for several minutes, the pilot signaled his companion to look down and then used his right index finger to point in the direction where he'd spotted the Hummer below.

The copilot pushed a button in his helmet and reported to base. "Lima-Romeo-10 this is LR-1. Target in sight, request instructions, over."

The new console operator picked up the microphone from a military-grade multiband radio and said, "LR-1, this is Lima-Romeo-10 wait, over."

The new control-room operator immediately picked up his handheld radio and asked Colonel Harman for instructions.

The reply was, "Kill them all and leave no witnesses."

***

A shower of bullets landed at the front of the Hummer. "Oh my God; they're going to kill us," said Sora.

"Not if I can prevent it," Sani-Shaman assured her. "Listen, these vehicles are usually well prepared for emergency situations. Look in the back and see if you can find something useful."

"On it," said Sora. She unbuckled the seat belt and moved to the rear seat, where she started to open metal boxes. She was opening a box when Sani-Shaman drove through a ravine. Water seeped into the Hummer, making them both partially wet.

The helicopter, which was still on their back, unleashed another shower of bullets, hitting the Hummer's roof and missing Sora by inches. It smashed the rear seat's back support in to pieces.

Sora moved closer to the back and opened a large box, which was clearly marked on the side, "Stingers."

"Hey, Sani-Shaman, what is a stinger?"

"Do you mean to tell me that we have stingers in the back?"

"Yes, Sani-Shaman, there are two of them," said Sora.

As Sora attempted to grab one of them, the Hummer ran

into a small depression on the dirt road and jumped. She banged her head hard against the sunroof; the impact nearly knocked her out, and she was momentarily blinded by the pain.

Sani-Shaman had to think quickly and come up with a plan. Immediately, he put pedal to the metal and drove as fast as he could. The helicopter followed closed behind.

Sani-Shaman felt a third set of bullets hitting the rear section of the Hummer, and suddenly the Hummer felt lighter. The vehicle had lost its rear defense and part of the side fender. These were not ordinary bullets raining down on them; they were 40mm cannon bullets. Sani-Shaman and Sora were in big shit. "Sora, Sora, can you hear me? Sora," cried Sani-Shaman.

Sora, regaining her conscience, responded sounding very confused.

Sani-Shaman continued accelerating, and when he saw the helicopter lining up for the kill, he stopped right in his tracks; the helicopter flew right by. He stepped out, quickly pulled Sora out of the Hummer to safety, and went back to the vehicle to grab one of the stingers.

Sora observed that, by now, the helicopter had turned back and was spraying another round of bullets toward the Hummer, which lit up into flames and exploded in a big ball of fire. The helicopter kept its distance, keeping its powerful light beamed on the vehicle.

This was the pilot's fatal mistake, as Sani-Shaman pulled out the stinger, aimed, and fired. The surface-to-air missile locked onto its target right away and, in seconds, was finding its way to the head source hovering above.

***

Inside the helicopter, a red light came alive, indicating the impending missile. Right before the missile impacted the bird, the door gunner managed to squeeze the last bullet load toward a man standing next to the burning Hummer.

***

Sora watched the big explosion in the sky, which illuminated the whole area.

Following, Sora saw multiple bullets hitting Sani-Shaman's body. She ran toward him. His body was torn apart, and with his last breath, he murmured, "Sora, we made it. I have finally found closure. I can go now to join my loved ones. Now you must finish what we started." He pushed his hand inside his cargo pockets and gave her the files he had been carrying with him.

He could not hold on any longer. His breathing became shallow, and he was spitting blood from his mouth and nose. Sani-Shaman died in Sora's hands, and she could not hold back from breaking down into tears. "Sani-Shaman, don't leave me! I beg the spirits of the earth to spare you. No. No. Why did it have to be you, Sani?"

***

Back at LR Corporation, one of the security officers relayed the message to his boss, Colonel Harman. They'd lost contact with LR-1, and it was believed that the bird was down.

Colonel Harman, who was steaming with anger, shouted, "Get out of my face. Don't bring me more bad news! What about the mobile ground units?"

The guard responded, "Sir, the ground units in pursuit reported seeing a huge explosion in the sky right before we lost contact with the bird. They are heading there now."

"Don't come back here unless you can give me good news, you hear, good news!" snarled the colonel.

"Yes, sir, as you command," said the young security officer as he left the room.

I found myself tied up to a chair again, helpless and without a plan. This was just like three years ago when I was back in my office before it was blown to pieces,—a very serious déjà vu that tarnished my thoughts. But this time, I was facing a worthy adversary—a man full of hate and vengeance—and the problem right now was that the night was still young.

Colonel Harman looked at me, took a few steps closer to my face, and said out loud, "Mister, this is the way I see it. Now, if I am wrong, feel free to interrupt me at any time.

"Let's start with the ground rules. Whether you cooperate with me or not, you will not be leaving these premises alive. I ask the questions and you answer; you don't answer and you feel pain. If I feel that I've got all the information I need, I will kill you quickly. But if you play games with me, I will make it my mission to make you suffer a slow and painful death, so bad that you will still remember me in the afterlife. Do you copy? I repeat, do you copy me?"

"Crystal clear," I answered.

Based on what I'd overheard so far, I was sure Sani-Shaman had escaped and that he was giving them hell out in the tundra. I had warned Sora and hoped that she was safe as well and would be back here soon with company. I just had to wait for the cavalry to arrive and hold on a few hours more.

***

Sora saw two lights approaching on the horizon. She knew she had to leave immediately, so she pulled Sani-Shaman closer to the Hummer's driver's door and left him there. She then took the stinger and placed it in his hands and ran away as fast as she could in the opposite direction.

In no time, her two pursuit vehicles reached the Hummer, which was in flames. The guards immediately dismounted, and the patrol team leader instructed the others to search and destroy. Weapons in hand, the team secured the perimeter, and when they reconvened minutes later, the team leader went back to the lead patrol vehicle, picked up the mic, and radioed control. "Lima-Romeo-1, this is Lima-Romeo-5. Target destroyed; there are no survivors, over."

"Lima-Romeo-5, this is Lima-Romeo-1, secure the perimeter until daylight and stand fast for recovery vehicle, over."

"Lima-Romeo-1, this is Lima-Romeo-5, copy that, out."

***

I was quickly realizing that the colonel really knew how to produce pain; I was bleeding already. But he was getting nothing out of me. Colonel Harman was about to ask another question when he was interrupted by a security officer bearing the good news. "Sir, the stolen vehicle has been detected, the perimeter is secured, and there are no survivors."

"You see," said Harman. "This is what I am talking about. Good news. So, Mister, tell me now, how lucky are you feeling after hearing that both your friends are dead?"

I could not hide my disappointment and grief. I was sorry for both Sora and Sani-Shaman, but this didn't change things. I had to think of something quickly. I needed to get out of here and fast because no one was going to come to my rescue. I was on my own.

"Don't you see, Mister. Your situation is hopeless. You are in my domain, and there is no help coming your way. So are you ready to talk now?"

I was furious with this guy already. He had killed two innocent people who were my friends, and he would have to pay dearly for that. "I'll tell you what, Colonel Harman. I will tell you all you want to know, but you have to come closer."

Colonel Harman hesitated, but his curiosity was stronger than his caution.

When he got closer to me, I whispered, but he could not hear, so he lowered his head closer to mine. I whispered again, "Colonel Harman, eat shit and bark to the moon."

He paused for a minute as if he didn't believe what he had just heard.

I moved my head with all the strength I could muster, and I aimed for his nose. In seconds, blood poured out of his broken nose splatting all over my well-pressed and manicured maintenance uniform.

To my surprise, the colonel didn't scream, flinch, or show any pain. He pulled a camouflage handkerchief out of his back pocket and cleaned up the mess on his face. "Very well, Mister. Now it's time for you to die." He pulled out a flashy, black 9mm pistol, cocked it, and aimed the muzzle at me.

I had not been this close to death for a very long time. I was tied to a chair in the middle of Alaska, my friends were dead, and I had managed to piss off a retired colonel whose nose I'd broken and son we'd killed. I closed my eyes and waited for the sharp pain that would surely end my life for good.

18

THE MOMENT OF TRUTH

I was never so happy to see a stranger as I was to see the man in a white coat who arrived just before Colonel Harman was able to squeeze the trigger. I finally let the air out of my lungs, as I was going purple. From the center of the room, bound to the chair, and with a front-row view, I heard this man say (or rather, scream) the kindest words I'd heard all night. "Stop your madness, Colonel. This man is not to be harmed."

"Bullshit, Dr. Harjo, this bastard is the cause of all this mess and the death of my only son. He must pay for his sins, and I am here to collect!" barked Colonel Harman, still pointing the gun at me.

"Perhaps you are right, Harman. But I tell you that time itself has no end, but it takes time to get there! I promise you that he will die today but not here," the doctor added, his voice turning soft and gentle.

As if he was under a spell and like a good soldier, Colonel Harman slowly and with craftsmanship placed his right thumb on the pistol hammer and slowly released it forward; he then put his pistol in its holster. He was no longer looking at Dr. Harjo's face. "Very well, Dr. Harjo," he said. "To what do I owe the pleasure of your visit?"

I was amazed to see how easily Dr. Harjo had been able

217

to manipulate a warrior, a leader, and a man full of vengeance and rage. He had transformed Harman in to a walking zombie! I didn't know what to think. Who was this man and what power did he possess that enabled him to control men?

"Colonel Harman, this man is Jack Steele; our employer has other plans for him. Please untie him at once and bring him along to the lab."

When I heard the word *lab*, I didn't know whether I was going from bad to worse or, worst, to hell. I should have stopped dead in my tracks right then and there and asked Harman to kill me, rather than taking my chances that I might serve as guinea pig in Harjo's lab.

At the moment, I didn't know what to think. Would I be better off dead or serving as a guinea pig for this Harjo character? I didn't know whether to laugh or cry! Was my luck about to change for the better or for the worse? I felt a very dark cloud lingering over my head, and my heart was starting to scream, if I may say, very loudly.

Perhaps my luck was changing for the better because I was still alive, and this meant that I could still be able to find a way to escape. After reading all those files and knowing what these people were capable of, my mind started to play games with me, and I felt that I was starting to sweat for the first time.

Dr. Harjo calmly waited for the colonel to untie me and then extended his hand to me. "Allow me to introduce myself. My name is Dr. Harris Harjo, and I run this place. Please forgive the colonel. Occasionally he can be a little hasty. We don't enjoy visits from men of your qualifications and status around here too often, Mr. Jack Steele."

For a long time, I found myself at a loss for words. Finally I responded, "Well, it's about time someone offered me some courtesy around here!"

Without emotion on his face, Dr. Harjo nodded to me in an affirmative manner, turned around, and started to leave detention room 14. I and Colonel Harman followed behind, as did two heavily armed, tactical, fully equipped security officers. I felt honored to know that these guys believed I could pose such a threat to them that they had to impress me with all their hardware and escort protocols! After all, I was just another man.

We walked along a long corridor and passed several doors before we entered an elevator. Inside the elevator, Dr. Harjo swiped a card and pushed a code next to the elevator control box. With that, the elevator started its descent, going down at least three floors. I could feel the change in pressure every time we passed a floor.

When the doors opened, I could see what appeared to be a medical lab buzzing with activity, and I thought, *This part of the facilities was not on the emergency evacuation map I took from the storage room.*

A security officer was standing at attention next to the entrance, but after looking at Dr. Harjo, he stepped aside and allowed us in. As we walked along the main corridor, I could see several glass cages. I could see people inside the cages. Some were staring at the floor, broken and without life; one lady to my left was banging her head rapidly against the glass, and blood was splattered all over her forehead and the glass. I could only just make out her face. To my right was another young woman, who I guess was no more than twenty-five years of age. She was half-naked and bouncing her upper body back and forth in an endless but steady motion.

I could not bear to watch so much abuse and pain. The glass cages went on to my right and left for about a hundred feet, all of them showing a different psychotic case. So I switched my eyes to the opposite direction and was faced with an Alaskan Inuit woman who must have been in her midthirties and whose face seemed familiar to me somehow. It hit me. I'd seen her photo at the sheriff's office on the missing persons' board. She was the one with the message: *Mom, I will wait for you. It doesn't matter how long it takes.*

219

These were the words of a young child who was still waiting for her mother to return, and these motherfuckers had turned her into a piece of meat.

Dr. Harjo clocked my interest in the lady and said, "Sorry, Mr. Steele, that you have to see the fruits of our earliest experiments. But as you'll see, we have been able to perfect our techniques. Fortunately, now we are experts in the art of influencing others, and you will have the chance to experience it firsthand; I promise. By the way, I can make her love you if that pleases you ..."

I wanted to jump on his back and snap his neck like a cracker, but you have to learn to choose your battles, and my inner voice was telling me loudly and clearly to keep my mouth shut, as this was not the time or place to act. It was only a matter of time, but I promised myself right then and there that I would bring back with me as many of those poor souls as I could to their families, even if it was the last thing I did.

Farther to my left, I saw a large sign that said "Stem-Cell Research Lab." This was a place that even I was afraid to see, but I had no choice, as we were walking right to it. The doors were sealed with some kind of pressurized mechanical system. From what I could see, the first room we entered was a decontamination chamber, and upon entering it, we were sprayed with a white gas. The inner doors opened, and we continued with our tour.

"Mr. Steele, I wanted to show you our nursery."

I looked to my left, and I could count at least a hundred neonates. Many of them were still inside incubators, and others had some type of needles attached to their arms. I stopped in my tracks to take a closer look at the amber liquid, which was slowly dropping down the IV pipes.

"Mr. Steele, I see that you have taken an interest in our work. Good. In case you are wondering, this is our pride and our core business. The liquid that these neonates are taking is our newly developed serum. We use it to make sure that the infants acquire a taste for our drugs, so when we transplant their stem cells to the new recipients, they also become addicted to our preventive medicine. Ingenious, don't you think?"

I looked at him with rage and made no response. Dr. Harjo didn't even deserve my comments or acknowledgment—even to let him know that his plan was as perverse and mad as no other I'd ever encountered. Something like that would probably be a compliment to him, so I kept my mouth shut.

We continued farther, and to my right, I saw a lot of beds full of women who were being held down by metal restrainers and monitored by state-of-the art electronic bio-readers. I had no explanation for this. As I recalled from my earlier readings, these women must be the surrogates who were placed in comas so the "scientists" could harvest their eggs.

But upon further examination, I guessed that my first assumption was incorrect. Half of the women were pregnant. I could see the distinctive contour under their robes. As we reached the end of the corridor, I watched a couple of doctors operating on some female bodies that were resting on top of a metal table.

A couple of female bodies had been cut open right where their fallopian tubes were located. I assumed that this barbaric act was to extract their fertile eggs to support the experiments and develop in vitro babies. *What an atrocity. Are we back in the dark ages?* I thought. Who had given permission to these people to play God? With what rights were they taking a free life and making it into a vegetable?

I looked at Dr. Harjo and said to him, "Before the night is over, I will see you dead."

He looked at me with an expression that implied a sour taste in his mouth and swallowed hard; he must have taken my threat as seriously as it was intended.

After a short pause, Dr. Harjo mustered enough courage to say, "Mr. Steele, not even you can stop progress. Stem-cell

221

treatment is here to stay, and we are pioneers, just like the famous pioneer scientists of the past who resorted to stealing bodies from the cemetery to practice their theories. We, in kind, prefer to steal them from their homes, which is a more humane way to make a contribution to medicine and progress."

"You are mad. That is what you are—a mad scientist."

"Do you know, Mr. Steele, it is ironic that you say that because Bruce Feirstein once said that 'the distance between insanity and genius is measured only by success.' And at Lindberg Research Corporation, we have succeeded where other men have failed; we have pioneered the gift of life. A person like you should understand that, in order to make an omelet, you have to break a few eggs—you know that."

I interrupted Dr. Harjo with rage in my eyes. I stopped where I was and said to the doctor, loudly and clearly enough for him to comprehend my frustration, "That's how you treat innocent humans?" I demanded. "That's the extent of your humanity? You are mad; all of you are mad."

Dr. Harjo looked at me. "Don't you worry, Mr. Steele. In a few minutes, I can assure you that you will understand and will even be begging to join us."

And with that, I felt the cold muzzle of Colonel Harman's pistol pressed into my back as he pushed me to continue forward.

At the end of the corridor, we entered a room, which was full of electronic equipment and a couple of chairs that looked like high-tech dental chairs but a lot more refined. These actually had shackles for your neck, arms, and legs. I stared at the chair and dreaded to think what these madmen must have done to the people in them. Just thinking about it sent a chill down my spine.

What type of torture went on in this room? How many innocent people had lost their minds, souls, and lives in this cold, secluded room three feet under the earth? I was not even sitting on the chair, and yet I felt my spirit broken by just realizing that those poor souls incarcerated in the glass cages hadn't stood a chance once they were brought here and seated in one of those creepy chairs.

My trail of thought was interrupted when the two security officers left and the doors shut. Meanwhile, Dr. Harjo and the colonel were looking at me like the last piece of chicken in the bucket. I was about to be dinner, and I didn't even know it. Jungle guerrilla warfare, terrorism, and spy stuff I knew and understood well. I had no problem with that, but what frightened me more than anything was the unknown; and this situation, without doubt, clearly qualified as unknown.

Dr. Harjo looked at Colonel Harman and asked him to leave us alone. I could tell the colonel didn't like it, but like a good dog, he reluctantly moved his tail away from the room.

Dr. Harjo turned his attention to me and offered me a drink. I had to hand it to the doctor, he may have been pure evil, but he was still a complete gentleman. I walked over to him and reached out for a bottle of cold water, which was in the fridge.

Dr. Harjo looked at me with interest and whispered, "How interesting. Mr. Steele, from all the fine spirits we have here, you choose a bottle of water? You strike me as a man with a more refined taste."

I poured the water into an empty glass, and as I drank half the glass, I strategized how to play my cards right. I wanted to play his game and to let him know that I was not afraid of him. "Dr. Harjo, you are practicing on the good people of Nome here, away from civilization and away from the law that I understand. However, what I don't get is what is your end game?"

"Mr. Steele, I can assure you that we are not practicing with the people of Nome; we finished practicing several years ago. Our ... or rather my, program has been perfected for a while now. You know, with unlimited resources you can make leaps and bounds. What my colleagues and the medical community have mastered is both stem-cell research and the art of mind control. Nome is a cover-up; it's the perfect place for me to peacefully work without interruptions.

"Don't you see, Mr. Steele, as long as people believe in the local folklore, we have the perfect cover-up here. Peoples' disappearances here and our products' side effects have become part of the local folklore—just like that place in Mexico … yes, Ciudad Juárez—so it is the perfect place to conduct my experiments without much noise from the locals.

"We can use people to do what we want them to. And when they become, let's say broken, we just trigger the autodestruct mechanism, and they accidentally die," said Harjo.

"How poetic," I replied. "You mean to tell me that all those people who've disappeared and others who committed suicide in Nome and Ciudad Juárez were part of your pathetic experiments?"

"No, Mr. Steele, they are … how should I say … keeping the myth alive," responded Dr. Harjo.

"Humor me, Dr. Harjo. How do you do it?" I was trying to obtain as much intelligence on the subject as I could and buying time to plan my escape. Not in a thousand years was I going to drink his Kool-Aid. This guy was nuts for sure. But I had to dig deeper because, when I left this place, I needed to have a story to tell the authorities so that I could help drop this miserable, coldhearted operation to its knees. Unfortunately, for now, I had to play the game, and if Dr. Harjo was talking and willing to tell me the operation's details without me feeling pain, I was all for it.

"It's very simple, Mr. Steele. Sit down and enjoy the ride."

"No, Dr. Harjo," I replied. "I prefer to stand."

He then pointed to a flat screen on the wall and pushed a button. Immediately, I could see young Dr. Harjo, dressed in a white coat and looking maybe twenty years younger, running experiments with college students.

I watched him; he was in a white parka inside a van

looking through the window at a house from a distance. He picked up the phone and dialed a number. In the video, you could see a man inside the house answering the phone. He was holding a baby in his hands, and after the man answered the phone, Dr. Harjo said to him, "Time itself has no end, but it takes time to get there."

And with that, the man placed the baby down on the floor, reached for the wall, pulled out a hunting rifle, and shot his kid and wife before placing the rifle in his mouth and squeezing the trigger. Half of his head disappeared right before my very own eyes.

I looked in to Dr. Harjo's eyes, and with anger, I whispered to his face. "You are a murderer. Why do you have to kill these people?"

I rushed to him and grabbed him by his neck and squeezed as hard as I could, but immediately I was subdued by a couple of security guards, who quickly hit me behind my neck rendering me down.

As I came out of a short paralysis, I felt that the two guards were sitting me down on a chair, and then I heard Dr. Harjo saying, "Don't waste your strength on me, Mr. Steele. Soon, you are going to need it. Even if you kill me now, the plan has been put in motion, and the outcome is inevitable.

"Don't you know, Mr. Steele? Don't rush yourself because time itself has no end when you are making progress; but it takes time to get there."

I felt a little dizzy but didn't want to let him know. I didn't know if the dizziness was a result of the hit on my neck or what I'd heard and seen, but I played the game. I wanted to know more before I acted.

Harjo continued with his monologue. "I had to show Lindberg that my research was over and that I could manipulate minds at will, but it takes time to get there."

I felt like something inside of me was changing. I felt Dr. Harjo's voice claiming every inch of my mind. His voice was deep and controlling. It was nearly impossible for me to hear myself thinking. All kinds of alarms were ringing inside of me, telling me that something bad was about to happen. Whether I believed it or not, Dr. Harjo was trying to get inside my mind; he was trying to manipulate my thoughts, and it was becoming hard for me to even think.

"I understand now, Dr. Harjo. The means—"

"Yes, Mr. Steele, I know. You don't have to recite it back to me. I did what I had to do to prove that my program worked— just as I have to prove that I am able to control your mind as easily as everyone else's. Remember who I am and that what I do is for the good of the program, for the good of the people, and for your own good."

As he ended his last word, the door opened, and a person of authority and elegance spoke. "Greetings, Mr. Steele. I trust that Dr. Harjo has taken good care of you in my absence?"

I heard myself saying "Time itself has no end, but it takes time to get there. We serve Dr. Harjo for the good of the program and for my own good."

"Congratulations, Dr. Harjo. You have proven your weight in gold!"

"Sentry!" Dr. Harjo called out to the security officer standing right outside the door. "Will you step in the room, please?"

The obedient sentry came into the room as fast as he could and stood at attention. "Now, give your weapon to Mr. Steele."

And without hesitation, the sentry gave me the weapon; its weight told me that it was fully loaded.

"Now, Mr. Steele, kill the sentry."

The voice repeated in me—it was deep and persistent—and I spoke out loud, "Time itself has no end, but it takes time to get there." On my last word, I raised my hand, pointed toward the sentry's face, aimed between the eyes, and squeezed the trigger.

A small, round red circle appeared between his eyes, and

his body, pushed back by the bullet's impact, landed halfway across the hall, while I remained motionless, still pointing the weapon in the direction I'd just fired.

Dr. Harjo then commanded me to put the gun to my right temple and squeeze the trigger slowly. I followed the command as instructed and slowly raised my right hand and placed the gun on my right temple. And as I was squeezing the trigger, the gentleman at the door said out loud, "Stop, Mr. Steele. Stop."

Dr. Harjo asked me for the weapon, which I handed to him without hesitation, and then he said, "Time itself has no end, but it takes time to get there."

I blinked a couple of times and looked at him and then at Colonel Harman, who had just walked into the room and asked, "What happened?"

I looked at the blood on the sentry's body, which was lying a few steps in front of me and then at myself, covered with sprays of his blood. I then realized my worst nightmare.

"Mr. Steele, you just killed a man in cold blood," said the gentleman at the door.

"No, it's just not possible. I had ..."

"You were under Dr. Harjo's powers of persuasions," said the gentleman at the door. When I looked at him, he spoke softly, introducing himself as Maynard James Lindberg, and repeated again that I had just murdered one of his sentries in cold blood.

Colonel Harman looked at me with anger, but I could see in his eyes that even a cold-blooded killer like him still had a soft spot for justice, and this somehow comforted me. Perhaps there was still a chance that the warrior in him was not dead after all.

I looked toward the floor with submission and shame, knowing that, although this sentry was one of the bad guys, he never stood a chance and this was no way to die, regardless of his sins.

"Now, Mr. Steele, please sit down." Dr. Harjo pointed toward one of those funny seats.

I had no choice but to obey as helpless as I was.

Dr. Harjo wasted no time. He tied up my hands, legs, and neck. Next, he placed the funny headset on me, which covered my head and ears, and with that completed, he looked at Mr. Lindberg.

Before either man spoke any words, I said, "Tell me, what is your end game? Why are you doing this? What are your plans?"

Mr. Lindberg, full of pride and without hesitation, started his spiel. "You see the irony, Mr. Steele? Someone is going to kill the vice president of the United States."

I had to hold on tightly to the chair arms, as what I heard almost caused me to faint. "What do you mean, kill the vice president?" I demanded.

"Don't you see, Mr. Steele? In a few hours Vice President Brad Farmer will arrive in Nome for the Fourth of July celebrations, and it will be his last. You see, Mr. Steele, no one can resist me. Half of the town's leadership is under my control. I own this town's people and all of those who think they can outsmart me too—just like you and your pathetic quest for rightfulness and justice."

"I don't seek justice, you arrogant piece of crap, but when I see people like you preying on the innocent and getting away with murder, someone has to stop you," I spat.

"Mr. Steele, soon you will learn to appreciate my work, and you will see it unfold right before your own eyes, as you will become one of the protagonists of my work—just like the mayor, the sheriff, the doctors, and many other key people holding official positions that in one way or the other contribute to my success," said Dr. Harjo.

"We could use a man like you in our organization; with your skills and position you could bring a lot of good to my business. You can become my personal-interest protector; you can even replace this worthless piece of shit CSO and become my empire's chief of security. You can earn millions of dollars at my side. I will make you richer than you could ever imagine, and, Mr. Steele, we can even become good friends," whispered Lindberg.

Out of the corner of my eye, I could see that Colonel Harman's face was one of disappointment, as he realized that his boss no longer considered him a valuable part of the organization. I swore I could feel hot steam coming out of Colonel Harman's body.

"Do you need my answer now or right before I kill you?" I said, like I meant it.

Maynard James Lindberg moved his face away from mine and looked at Dr. Harjo. "In the end, Mr. Steele, you will do as I please anyway," he said. "Why fight it?"

I managed to say loudly and clearly, "You won't get away with it, Mr. Lindberg. I am not dead yet. And guess what? I had promised that I would kill Dr. Harjo first. But I guess you've just now made number one on my list."

"How pathetic you are, Mr. Steele. I just offered you the world—to be part of something great, to be part of history—and yet you not only turn me down but also manage to insult me. Dr. Harjo, do your worst."

***

Jimmy Steele got up early and had his breakfast as usual, but today, he felt especially disturbed. With an absent mind, he said hello to Marie and headed to the airport. He walked like he had a purpose, and inside, a feeling of anxiety was killing him. As he sat inside his car, he looked at his hand and saw that it was shaking. He could not shake away the feeling of helplessness and uncertainly.

Through his windshield, he saw his house but it didn't feel like home. *What the hell is going on inside me?* he thought. He felt like something was pulling him away from his life—like he was predestined to do something he didn't want to do today. But what was it? What devil's curse was pushing today?

He tried to get back out of his car and enter his home, but deep inside his mind, some unexplained force was controlling his acts, and yet he did didn't know how to control these impulses. He felt powerless. In his mind, he saw all kinds of images that just didn't make sense. He looked at the clock on the dashboard to make sure of the time and affirm that he wasn't going crazy.

He saw men wearing white lab coats, and then the image became distorted by a sequence of photographs he didn't understand and could not identify but could not get out of his mind. Jimmy glanced at the rearview mirror to see that his face was sweaty. Glancing back at the dashboard clock, he realized he'd just passed fifteen minutes sitting in an idling car but could not explain why.

As he tried to step out of the car, he heard a voice that was very familiar to him, yet he could not put a face to it. The words the voice spoke were very loud and clear: *Remember who I am and that what I do is for the good of the program, for the good of the people, and for your own good.*

Jimmy closed the door, and although he did not remember the face, he surely realized that he had something to do. And like the automaton he had become, he shifted the car into drive and drove directly to Nome's airport. But it was like driving on autopilot, if you don't mind the pun.

He reached the hangar and picked up his lunch bag, which faithful Marie had prepared for him, from the front passenger seat.

Upon touching the hangar's pedestrian door handle, Jimmy found, to his surprise, that it was already unlocked. He opened it and looked at his boss, Soule, who was working on some paperwork at his desk.

Soule heard the door squeak and looked up to see Jimmy

walking in the room. He raised his hand and signaled him to join him.

After greeting Soule, Jimmy accepted a cup of hot, watery coffee that Soule had prepared a few minutes earlier. "Drink up, Jimmy. It taste like shit, but it's hot!" said Soule.

"Just as I like it, Soule. What's going on today?"

Soule looked at Jimmy, stood up from his chair, and said, "You are kidding me, right?"

Jimmy, without any facial expression, said to him, "What?"

Soule sat back down in the chair and grabbed his bald head with both hands. "Jimmy, today is the Fourth of July. You are flying the Martin Mars to Anchorage to bring the vice president of the United States here."

As Jimmy was about to speak, a man wearing a nice, black trench coat and a hat came through the office door that led to the hangar and said, "It's truly a beauty, Mr. Soule. Thanks for allowing us to make a final inspection before takeoff."

Jimmy looked at the man and then back at Soule and raised both his shoulders in a gesture that said, *Will someone explain to me what this man is doing here and why he is inspecting my plane?*

Soule stood up from the chair again and, this time, walked in between the man and Jimmy. "Jimmy," he said, "allow me to introduce to you US Secret Service Agent Felix Mainer. He flew in yesterday afternoon from Anchorage and got here early today to make a final inspection of the facilities and plane before you take off today."

"What do you mean, Soule?" asked Jimmy.

"Not to worry, Jimmy. Agent Mainer indicated that all was well. What did you think would happen to this hangar when the VP of the United States is due to visit the most forsaken place on earth? Agents will ask questions and make inspections, and in less than an hour, two deputies will be here to supplement security," Soule concluded.

"What security are you talking about? We are in the

231

middle of nowhere, and nothing happens here. Even the local paper has nothing to print."

"Take it easy, Jimmy; all is well. I will be taking care of this. You just concentrate on getting to Anchorage before eight in the morning. Refuel at Manny's and get back here with the vice president. Just follow the flight plan you gave me."

Jimmy took a deep sip of the steaming coffee and looked at Agent Mainer and said, "Well, as long as I can fly the plane, I guess I have nothing else to say."

Agent Mainer nodded as Jimmy passed him by and headed toward the Martin Mars. As Jimmy walked away, he heard Agent Mainer ask Soule if Jimmy was always this cranky.

Soule could not hold it in anymore and laughed. "No. Jimmy only gets cranky when he has to fly the vice president."

And they both started to laugh.

Jimmy ignored them and continued walking toward his precious Martin Mars.

Jimmy got close to the wall and activated the hangar door, which immediately started to open, allowing the cold, early-morning air to seep into the hangar. Jimmy felt the rush of cold caressing every inch of his body and suddenly realized how cold it really was. Without further ado, Jimmy went back to the office to get his flight bag and flight plans and to sign out the Martin Mars.

As Jimmy walked back to the hangar, Soule called him to let him know that he had a call. Jimmy would normally have ignored the phone, but as his boss was calling him, he decided to go back to the office and take the call.

On the other line, a man spoke to him, saying only a few words: "Time itself has no end, but it takes time to get there."

Jimmy slowly placed the phone back on its cradle and walked back from the office and got into the Martin Mars.

Once Jimmy was in the plane, a crewman drove one of the tug carts near the airplane's front landing gear and hooked up the car. Then the crewman cleared the plane chucks, which were placed at the front and back of the landing gear tires to prevent the plane from drifting away from its parking position.

The crewman signaled Jimmy, indicating to him that all was good to go. And with that, Jimmy gave a thumbs-up, signaling that he was also ready. The crewman pulled the plane out of the hangar to the taxi area and listened to the tower and pilot's conversation.

At this time, Jimmy felt like a fish in water; he was in his environment. He took a minute to admire the beautiful flying machine, which would have been fit to take prize place as a main attraction at any Smithsonian Museum.

"Nome Tower, this is NUSMM-1 requesting permission to taxi."

"NUSMM-1, this is Nome Tower. Permission granted. You are free to start water takeoff procedures."

The tug operator slowly pulled the plane through the taxi area and headed toward the pier's port number two.

As the plane was towed through the airport, mechanics and other early-bird ground personnel stared at the magnificent machine. Jimmy felt like a canary in a golden cage as he finally reached the water. Slowly but surely, the tug operator maneuvered the plane one foot at a time toward the water. The plane slid into the water easily and immediately started to float. The tug operator anchored the plane by tying a rope to an existing pier anchor, and this kept the plane steady until he removed the tug away from the front landing gear. He gave the signal to Jimmy, who acknowledged him.

Jimmy, who sat in the pilot's seat, looked to his right to see the right engine starting to turn and then to the left, which did the same. Soon, the four engines were roaring, and Jimmy was feeling the distinct vibration that told him that the plane was alive, well, and looking for open water. He signaled the tug operator, who immediately released the rope, allowing Jimmy complete control of the plane.

Jimmy pushed the engine throttle forward, and the large aircraft claimed its place on the open water.

He masterfully managed the plane's throttles, and he felt the plane moving forward. It didn't matter to him how many times he had done this, flying this bird was a feeling Jimmy loved, and with the adrenalin rushing through his veins, it felt as if every time was his first. He throttled the engines to keep the plane straight and gently moved on the calm sea water. Jimmy positioned the plane away from the boats and, once he was facing open water, radioed the Nome tower.

"Nome FBO, this is NUSMM-1 requesting permission for takeoff."

"NUSMM-1, this is Nome FBO. Permission granted."

Jimmy held the yoke tightly and let the engines drive forward, but the fun had not started yet.

He faced the plane toward the narrow water channel and looked down the long stretch of water, which reached for half a mile away from Nome Airport. He made sure no approaching vessels or small boats were in his way. Patiently applying thrust to the engines, he slowly cruised the channel, trying not to make large waves, which could easily sink any small boats tied to the coastline. He waved to several fishermen and tourists standing on top deck, who waved to him as he passed by. He could see a few tourists taking pictures of the plane and others waiting for him to pass by so they could use the Martin Mars as background in their pictures.

Once he reached the end of the channel, he turned the plane around and secured a good takeoff position. Jimmy pushed the throttle forward, and all four engines responded with elegance and grandeur as the plane slowly started to gain speed. In no time, the Martin Mars claimed the channel, and as Jimmy negotiated between the sea's waves, the plane's velocity, and the takeoff distance, the plane responded as expected, and a few seconds later, the plane was claiming the skies and Jimmy's anxiety about today's flight.

19

WHAT CAN GO WRONG ...

Agent Landis answered his phone.

"Sir, plane inspected, pilot checks complete, and en route to you," said advance Secret Service Agent Felix Mainer.

"Music to my ears, Mainer. Please keep the facilities secured and do the best you can to maximize the two deputies. Let's take no chances."

"Very well, sir. I am on it. Have a safe flight to Nome."

"Thanks," said Landis, and the line went dead.

Landis was still worried about this trip. Something deep inside him was telling him that he should not chant victory until he got VP Farmer back to DC. Landis could not put his finger on the root of what was troubling him, but he would not rest until he felt satisfied that he had covered all angles and crossed all t's on this mission.

Peering through the window, Landis could see that the sun was out already. His watch displayed 5:00 a.m., but the position of the sun was telling him that it was already midday. He shook his head in disbelief and got out of bed.

Secret Service Agent Landis had the distinct feeling that it was going to be a long day. A couple of hours later, he would be escorting VP Farmer to the special breakfast prepared by the local Altruists chapter to collect funds for the homeless.

Just as President Franklin Delano Roosevelt had been, VP Farmer was slave to his wife's commitment to the cause and could not say no to his wife's request. In fact, she was the person who'd arranged this particular charity breakfast event from Washington.

***

It was nearly zero eight hundred hours, and Jimmy was getting closer to Anchorage. It was time to contact the tower. "Anchorage Tower, this is NUSMM-1, requesting permission for a water land."

"NUSMM-1, glad to hear from you! You are clear to water land. As usual, you can park in pier number 12."

"Anchorage Tower, this is NUSMM-1, roger; out."

Jimmy turned the plane three degrees to starboard, and the flying fortress responded with the elegance of a trained circus horse.

Jimmy was in control of the plane, and he knew every inch of it—how it felt and every vibration and screech it made, both on land and in the air. Jimmy looked out to the front and steered the plane, aligning it dead center with the pier 12 parking spot. He dropped the power in time to allow the plane to slowly touch the sea as he skidded forward without rush or hesitation. He knew that this one was going to be a nice water landing. He then sat back deep in his pilot's seat and let his hands do the rest, as he enjoyed every moment of the water landing process.

From the cockpit, which was almost three stories high, he could see lots of movement below. Police cars were flashing their red and blue lights, and Jimmy felt the reception committee below composed of suits, uniformed police, and airport ground crew was overstated.

***

McAllister was a seasoned operations agent who knew his stuff well, but the lack of resources was making him slightly nervous. In normal circumstances, he would have at least ten to fifteen Secret Service protection agents, and they would be augmented by several meticulously handpicked police officers. He wouldn't have to worry about all the details as he was forced to do today, but in the real world, the only thing he would have to worry about would be waiting for a site report from each of his agents every fifteen to thirty minutes.

Today, his best ally and support was Anchorage's Captain Samuel Grimes, who had been working alongside him each and every second since he'd landed the day prior. Captain Samuel Harry Grimes was a public service veteran with over fifteen years of service and commander of the Anchorage Police Department's dignitary protection squad. He was the person to contact for all dignitary protection detail and also was the training instructor for the local SWAT team.

McAllister made some mental notes to write up a decent thank-you letter to the Anchorage chief of police to thank the department for all their cooperation during this visit. He knew that a large part of his job was about relationship building and influence, rather than dictating or demanding services, and deep inside him, he wanted to keep it this way.

Agent McAllister continued to review his checklist, to ensure that his concentric rings of protection were as tight and waterproof as possible. After all, they were protecting the second highest person in office in the United States of America.

***

As Jimmy was maneuvering his plane next to the pier, again his right hand over the throttle became shaky, and anxiety took him over. He could feel the voices in his head telling him over and over the same mantra. But why? He asked himself

237

what was happening to him today. Why today? He had flown several very important persons to and from Nome. Why was he feeling so out of control for this one? What was special about this trip?

And yet, master pilot and seasoned operator Jimmy Steele could not answer those questions. Not even his local shrink could give him the answers he was looking for. The only thing that was keeping him sane was the face of his Marie—a face that came once in a while like a refreshing gulp of cold water, the face that he was holding onto to keep his sanity, but also a face that came and went, and he could not explain why.

Shortly, Jimmy regained control, holding hard to Marie's face. And once again, he demonstrated his expertise by positioning the plane right next to pier 12—so close that the pier crew effortlessly secured the plane to the pier in no time.

Through his pilot's window, Jimmy acknowledged the ground crew signaling that the plane was secured to the pier. He turned off the engines, shut down the master, and walked out of the cockpit with his flight bag.

Jimmy opened the door and felt as if he was a celebrity, seeing the two police officers who were already posted at the pier to secure his plane. As Jimmy walked away from the plane, two men in suits approached him. Each identified himself, the first as Secret Service Agent McAllister and the next as Anchorage Police Captain Grimes.

The two men asked him to follow them to a secure area. Jimmy followed his entourage toward the hangar but stopped to turn toward the big, red metal fortress to see two police officers and a man in a suit guarding the plane like a candy store owner facing a school bus full of hungry kids arriving at his front door.

Jimmy had made several trips with VIPs, but most of them had been corporate CEOs and local politicians. Today was different. He knew that, in a few hours, he was about to make a historical flight, and he was a bit nervous about that.

His Martin Mars call sign would no longer be NUSMM-1 but "Air Force Two."

As Jimmy was walking away from the Martin Mars, he could see a few airport workers taking pictures of the plane and an additional two Coast Guard boats surrounding the plane. He felt the intensity of the situation and hoped he didn't have to get use to this.

Jimmy was taken to the secure hangar operations office, where he was asked to sit down, offered a cup of coffee, and was asked several questions by Agent McAllister. In this small reception room, he also met Air Force Two's official pilot, copilot, and navigator. Unfortunately, he was also instructed by Agent Landis that the VP's copilot would accompany him on this flight, to make sure that Jimmy would have all the help he needed to fly the Martin Mars back to Nome.

Jimmy felt that he didn't need the additional help for this flight, but Agent McAllister's instructions were clear and final. There was no way in hell that only one person in the cockpit was reassurance enough for Agent McAllister to allow VP Farmer to ride in the plane. Rules were rules, and Jimmy understood and thought that having a copilot with him would only yield to a lot more chatting time during the short trip to Nome.

While he sipped his coffee, the three pilots went over the flight plan and Agent McAllister continued to check his list and reported his progress to his boss, Agent Landis.

***

Marie stared blankly out the kitchen window as she squeezed the sponge she'd just used to clean the counter from the day's breakfast residue. She squeezed tighter and tighter, her fingers aching from pain, her knuckles white from the effort. She felt like she was suffocating—that a heavy weight pressed down on her. Marie was worried sick about Jimmy, and on top of that agony, she hadn't heard yet whether her Jack was still alive. She hadn't heard from him in over twenty-four hours; if only she had some way to find out where he was and what he was up to. She knew that something was not right; she had a feeling that she may not see either of them again, and she was sensing that something really bad was about to happen.

Unfortunately for her, she was right.

The thought of enduring seeing Jack's photo as a permanent decoration on the sheriff's missing persons' wall each time she had to go there was squeezing her heart. Even as she was enduring these feelings, Marie still wanted to attend the Fourth of July event at Nome's main plaza in downtown Nome.

She figured that it made no sense to stay at home feeling miserable and, on top of that, miss the largest show in town, so she opened the door and took a step out. In her mind, she thought that maybe, if she was lucky enough, she may be able to find someone who could help her make sense of the way she was feeling. Marie knew that everyone in Nome would be there.

While standing on her front porch, she saw the morning sun, which was starting to clear the clouds. It was going to be a very nice day. But not even the energizing rays of the sun and the cold mist taking its leave would shake off the ominous feeling she was carrying deep inside her heart.

After walking a short distance along the road, she could see that many of her neighbors were starting to set up picnic chairs on their driveways, front yards, and sidewalks. They knew that the runners would soon be passing by. To her left, she saw Ms. Tattle, a woman in her mid-seventies, setting up a table with plastic bottles of water and what appeared to be a jar of freshly squeezed homemade lemonade. She was not surprised to see a sign that read, "$5 a cup," as lemons were hard to come by in this little piece of American land. *What a way to make money*, she thought.

As Marie passed by Ms. Tattle, she smiled and kept on

walking, afraid that, if she looked at the stand, she would be charged a few bucks as well.

After walking a little over a mile, Marie could see that, as always the sheriff and his team had blocked all access to the primary roads leading to Anvil Mountain and downtown. The sheriff was very thorough, and he did not want any accidents, incidents, or the like, especially when the vice president of the United States was coming to town.

And talking of the devil, there he was, staring her face. On a telephone pole was a poster welcoming the vice president and mentioning that the vice president would be personally handing out trophies to the top ten arrivals. The town was buzzing with cheers and an array of colors. Happiness permeated all over but in her mind, she was actively searching for her nephew Jack in every face she saw.

Marie took her time walking to town. Although she would have preferred to drive, her Jeep was in the shop, and Jimmy had taken his car to work today. She was not afraid to find herself without a prime seat, as, for the last twenty years or so, she'd enjoyed watching the event from the mayor's balcony. This was a perk given to the senior leaders of the community, and needless to say, she was also among the mayor's wife's best friends. She made her way to City Hall, and after greeting and being greeted by everyone, she climbed the stairs to the second floor, where she expected to find Gertrud, the mayor's wife.

After a short meet and greet, Gertrud asked one of the many volunteers to fetch a hot cocoa, as she knew it was Marie's favorite. From the second floor, Marie was able to see all the action through the large bay windows on the rear side of the building. The good thing about the City Hall building was that it was two stories high and was located in the best corner at the epicenter of the action.

Given all that was happening in her life, a drop of normality would not be a bad thing. From the large bay windows, Marie watched the many red, white, and blue banners; flags; and other draperies on show around the small town. The streets were bustling with activity, but despite her searching, she was unable to locate Jack. As she sipped the warm, brown liquid, the smell of the cocoa evoked memories of her childhood. When she was a little girl growing up in Virginia, her mother would always prepare her a cup of hot cocoa before going to bed. She was told that this would help her sleep better, and whether this was true or not, she loved drinking it.

Marie's reminiscing was abruptly interrupted by the mayor, who had received the good news that the vice president of the United States was departing Anchorage in less than an hour. Honorable John Stafford wanted Gertrud to help him rehearse the speech he had prepared for the occasion. He wanted this one, in particular, to be as presidential as it could be—given the company. Gertrud quickly excused herself and walked down the stairs to the mayor's private office to exercise her lawful right to make her husband look as good as she could for the cameras and the rest of the world.

Marie could see many media trucks and vans parked in a section allocated to them by the city. Parabolic antennas broke the soft sky highline, showing off their imposing disks, demanding respect, and demonstrating their power. What a huge amount of effort there was for a two-hour visit from the vice president of the United States. Despite all the commotion, Marie never stopped looking among the crowd for Jack.

20

A DAY TO DIE

"**Y**ou bastard, you can't do this. Uncle Jimmy never hurt anyone, he is—"

I was interrupted by Dr. Harjo, who said, "He is under my control, just like you were a moment ago and will be again soon. I promise. You see, Mr. Steele, we have already won, and there is nothing you or your uncle can do about it—that is, apart from following my orders."

"Enough talking." Dr. Harjo was abruptly interrupted by Mr. Lindberg. "It's time for actions, not words," he said.

"Indeed, Mr. Lindberg." Dr. Harjo turned my captive chair backward so that gravity would make it harder for me to move and slide the helmet's frontal visor over my eyes. A small visor was then placed in front of me. I saw a number of pictures displayed one right behind the other that were so intense I barely had time to process. I found myself no longer thinking but was fully engaged with the images. It was an overwhelming power that took me by surprise and was quickly taking over my own will.

My brain was beginning to accept the array of photos but didn't know what they meant. The only thing I could make out were sporadic words embedded between the colors. I began to realize that the pictures and forms were actually speaking to me.

243

From the headphones that had been placed over my ears, I could hear subliminal messages recorded with a voice I recognized as Dr. Harjo's. I understood what the voice wanted me to do; it was simple. I was to get close to the vice president of the United States, and when I heard the words, "My fellow Americans," I was supposed to raise my hand and shoot him in the face five times or until he was dead, followed by pointing the gun to my own head and squeezing the trigger as many times as I could.

It was simple; it was easy. It was something I had to do ... I could clearly hear the words over and over again: "Time itself has no end, but it takes time to get there." In my mind, I found this fascinating. I recalled hearing the words: "No one else has power over you but me. If someone tries to hypnotize you, it is your duty to reject it, and if such person reaches deep inside your mind, you are to swallow your tongue until you can't breathe any more. I was to "Remember who I am and know that what I do is for the good of the program, for the good of the people, and for your own good," because "time itself has no end, but it takes time to get there."

A few minutes later, all was silent and black. My head felt as if I was driving at 200 miles an hour, and all of a sudden, everything stopped, and I was surrounded by a motionless silence and darkness. The serenity of silence brought a lot of comfort to my confused head, and finally, I saw light again as the visor was taken away from me by a face I recognized.

"How do you feel, Mr. Steele?" said Dr. Harjo.

"You bastard, get me out of here, and I will tell you real close and personally."

"Tell me one thing, Mr. Steele. What was the last thought you remember before you sat on the chair?"

"I sat on the chair; you put a fucking visor on my head and took it off. What type of games are you playing here with me, Harjo? Get me out of here, and I mean now!"

"Good, just like the others," I heard Dr. Harjo whisper.

"Mr. Steele, you've responded well to my mental programming. Now allow to me to say that we have other plans for you. You are scheduled for termination in thirty minutes, so please don't go away. Stay right here, and we'll be back to witness your demise."

I was caught between a rock and a hard place. I was still sitting down on the seat, my hands and legs bound, and my body felt like a high-speed train had run over me. I swallowed hard, knowing that my options for getting out of this one alive were becoming thinner by the minute. I never believed in giving up. As my trusted friend Andrew Connors said, however, "There are always possibilities." There was a possibility that, when he said that, he was not tied down and sentenced to death.

Everyone left the room, and I found myself alone. I looked to my right and then my left, and there was nothing I could use to get myself out of this one. I knew that I was in bad shape; my uncle was going to kill the vice president of the United States, and there was nothing I could do about it.

I felt worthless and noticed that my shirt was wet with my own sweat. The fear I had wasn't about my pitiful situation but more about the good intelligence information I had in my possession, which if something happened to me, would go with me to the grave. I had to do something; the clock was ticking, and I was the only one who knew Mr. Lindberg and Dr. Harjo's plan.

It was my duty to escape. I had to use every ounce of my mind and energy to stop this Machiavellian plan, but how? *Think, Jack, think! I have to get out of here!* I could not allow Mr. Lindberg's plans to succeed; the thought of it consumed every inch of my mind and was driving me crazy.

***

The Anchorage Airport was busy; security and other key airport employees were dedicated to making sure that the vice president left Anchorage safe, sound, and on time. While resting on one of the corners near the stage, Special Agent Landis waited for the vice president to face him. He pointed at his watch, attempting to signal that it was time to go.

The VP's eyes sparkled with happiness, as if he was thinking that it was not a moment too soon. He took a minute to engage with the faces in the room and then began, "My dearest ladies and gentlemen, thank you for allowing me the pleasure to share this special time with you ..."

After his closing comments, VP Farmer willingly and diligently followed Special Agent Landis and Danny through the narrow corridor to the front entrance. As he walked past the many ladies wearing colorful hats, he carried a broad smile and shook hands with every delicate hand that passed in front of him.

Agent Landis guided VP Farmer to his limousine and, once inside, closed the door. He then got in the front passenger seat, fastened his seat belt, and asked the driver to drive.

As the limousine pulled away, it was followed by a marked, sparkling, shiny patrol vehicle, whose sirens let everyone in the immediate surroundings know that they were official business and to step away. In front of the patrol car, two police Harley-Davidson motorcycles led the way. Behind the limousine was another sedan, which Agent Landis called the chase car. This vehicle was to follow the limousine in case anything went wrong, with the purpose of being used as the backup car.

Behind the sedan was yet another patrol vehicle, helping to reinforce the vice president's security. This vehicle was followed by two other Harleys, which were roaring like they meant business.

The driver knew where to go. He navigated the limo toward Anchorage Airport. Agent Landis picked up his cell and placed it on his lap, and after punching a few keys, he sent a message to Special Agent McAllister at the secured hangar.

***

Agent McAllister picked up the phone and read the message out loud and clear: "Showtime in fifteen."

Everyone who was part of the security detail knew what that meant. The principal had left the event and was on his way. Everyone at the hangar got in position and readied him or herself like members of a well-directed orchestra.

Agent McAllister picked up his radio and shared with the pilots that the official VP jet would back up the Martin Mars, tailing it from Anchorage to Nome.

From inside the limo's front passenger seat, Agent Landis knew that phase III of his plan was drawing near. This phase was about bringing VP Farmer safely and soundly to Nome, and phase IV involved securing the principal and bringing him back to DC in one piece.

VP Farmer followed Danny to the holding room, where he took a couple of photos with the local crew and airport officials. The VP's break took nearly ten minutes. Agent Landis approached Danny and informed him and the VP that the plane was refueled and the pilots were standing by and ready to go.

The vice president looked at Danny, thanked his host, and followed Landis without hesitation. They boarded the limo again and slowly taxied toward pier number 12, where the Martin Mars was being caressed gently by the waves and was silently waiting for its precious cargo.

VP Farmer entered the plane, followed by Danny and Agent Landis, who passed next to McAllister without even acknowledging that he was there. As soon as the trio entered the plane, Agent McAllister stepped outside and remained at the door until it was completely closed from the inside.

Jimmy and copilot Phillips greeted VP Farmer, and Jimmy secured the door and said good-bye to McAllister. VP Farmer could not go to his seat until he checked the cockpit first. Agent Landis walked up to the cockpit and advised Jimmy that it was time to go.

From the window, Agent Landis could see the police cars' flashing lights. A shore police patrol and Coast Guard boat were keeping other boats who were trying to get closer to the plane to see the vice president at bay. It was, however, their right as constituents to be there; after all, DC government officials didn't visit Alaska every day. But it was also the duty of the Coast Guard to make sure that this plane departed safely and soundly and to ensure everyone's public safety. Shortly, the pier crew released the pier ropes holding the plane in place. Jimmy checked in with the tower and received an all clear for the Martin Mars to takeoff.

***

Agent McAllister stayed in place until he could no longer see the plane and remained at the airport thirty minutes after takeoff in case something went wrong and the plane had to come back to the airport. This protocol was not only for this visit but was considered standard Secret Service protection protocol, which Agent McAllister always followed to the letter.

***

From the Martin Mars's cabin, Jimmy was looking at VP Farmer, who was behaving like a kid at a country fair. He was admiring the interior decoration and enjoying the feeling of the plane on the water. Jimmy pushed the throttle forward as calm seas allowed for a smooth takeoff. Inside, the plane roared, screeched, and vibrated like a roller coaster at full speed, and as the plane gained momentum, the feeling changed from one of riding a jet ski to a sudden lift, which took the plane to the air. Now gravity took over, pushing the passengers deep in their seats.

Less than five minutes later, the plane was gaining altitude, and Jimmy and his new copilot were talking like chickens in a den. Jimmy practically had to explain to the young pilot each and every step he took to control the plane, from takeoff procedures to engaging the autopilot. Jimmy looked at his copilot, who was saying, "Jesus Christ! How in the world did you guys do it back then, especially when someone was shooting at you?"

Jimmy looked at him and said, "With patience, Captain, with a lot of patience."

The Martin Mars was gaining altitude at thirty feet per minute, not the usual speed that Phillips was used to in his modern jets. For him, it took forever to finally reach ten thousand feet into the open, blue skies. Jimmy was enjoying every minute of it; he felt like a school teacher, a mentor, and a grandpa. With a quick push of a button, Jimmy engaged the autopilot and set himself back to enjoy the flight.

***

Agent Landis glanced at the back of the plane to see Danny helping VP Farmer rehearse his speech. Already, the ride was not as smooth as the Boeing that normally carried the Air Force Two call sign. Landis observed VP Farmer trying to read, update, and tweak his speech the best he could. Landis sympathized with the VP, as he recognized that reading was not as easy in this plane as in the official jet. However, the VP's face was calm, and as far as Landis could tell, the VP was doing the best he could to survive the bumpy and noisy ride. The vice president was clearly trying to remain as normal as possible every time the Martin Mars dropped a couple of feet down and back up. But every time it happened, Farmer grabbed the chair's armrest hard and tight without even realizing he was doing it.

Agent Landis looked outside the window, and all he could see was blue; not a single cloud was in the sky. And although the plane was a little jumpy, Agent Landis knew that the Martin Mars was riding as smoothly as it was designed to do.

Agent Landis had a very good idea as to what was taking place at Anchorage's airport, with Agent McAllister's last-minute wrap-ups. Landis imagined that, by now, Agent McAllister was shaking hands with Captain Grimes and thanking him for a job well done. He also knew that Agent McAllister would be giving Grimes an official US Secret Service challenge coin—a longtime tradition of this organization and many others within the government. Challenge coins dated back to World War I, and many believed that the US Air Corps started the tradition. It was a way for pilots to remember their unit and served to rekindle the esprit de corps and boost morale and friendship. Today, all of the US government's military branches and almost all other agencies had their own challenge coins and closely follow the nearly sixty-year tradition.

Landis thought that having a gift as part of the visit would help boost relationships and keep doors open for them when it was time for the Secret Service to use the Anchorage police's services again. He pictured Captain Grimes looking at the coin, which displayed the USS five-point star on one side and the official US government eagle on the other, fascinated with its nice bronze color. The front outer edge displayed the words, "Department of Homeland Security," on the upper half and, "Worthy of Trust and Confidence," on the lower half.

Landis reached inside his back right pocket and pulled out his own coin, given to him by the head of the Secret Service right after he'd graduated from Quantico, Virginia, many years ago. Having this coin with him symbolized a lifetime achievement and the beginning of a new day toward achieving his ultimate goal to become the head of this prestigious organization.

21

THE LIGHT WITHIN

The room was quiet. I couldn't see or hear anyone around me. My wrists were bloody, and my legs bound so tightly that the binding was cutting some of my circulation already. I tried to release the binding, but all my efforts were hopeless. This chair was really made to hold someone down and to sever all desires of escape. And guess what? It was working as it was intended to.

The more I tried to escape, the harder it was for me to overcome my bindings and the tighter they got. In a moment of calmness, I wondered for a second how all those poor souls who Harjo had strapped here over the years could have handled this torture. They didn't have the luxury of the training I had; they didn't have the deep unbroken warrior spirit that comforted my soul and had, on so many occasions, kept me alive—the same spirit that had helped me keep my bearings in front of these two lunatics.

The many victims who had sat on this chair before me were just regular human beings made of flesh and blood. I had been trained to ignore pain, to look deeply into my enemies' eyes and dare them to harm me. One thing I was sure tonight that I would never give up, not for a second, not until the last drop of life was drained out of my body. Not because I was trained to think like that, but because it was my duty—because

I had made a promise, and nothing on this earth would keep me from fulfilling my word.

How was I going to do this? Although I had no clue how I was going to walk away from this chamber of torture, I continued to keep my mind busy and work on my bindings for as long as time allowed me to.

Suddenly, to my left, I heard a noise that I recognized even under these life-ending circumstances. It was the sound of a .45mm pistol discharged through a silencer; I knew the distinctive sound of the YHM Cobra .45 sound suppressors.

I then heard what appeared to be a body hitting the floor. I didn't know what to think. I braced myself and started counting every second I had left. I could see Colonel Harman approaching me like a predator, pistol in hand and looking at me like he wanted to put a couple of bullets between my eyes.

He got as close to me as he could and whispered, "Mr. Steele, if there's one thing I don't like, it's people wasting a perfectly good warrior and not being responsible for their actions."

When I heard this, I thought that my fate was doomed forever and that Colonel Harman was reciting my obituary. I said nothing. Years of training had taught me that, when someone has a weapon pointed at you and is in the process of philosophizing, you should listen and choose your rebuttal words with caution.

He pointed the gun at my head and said, "Mr. Steele, are you one of those men?"

I continued to look at him and said, "Colonel Harman, I have been and always shall be a warrior, just like you. I feel the years of military service blood running through my veins. I don't enjoy killing, but all those I have killed deserved it. I don't apologize for doing what I have done, and if I had to do it again, I would.

"Just like you, I have demons that come out at night; tell me, Colonel Harman, what was the turning point for you? Was it money, power, women?"

He responded back to me as dryly and coldly as an iceberg, "You don't know anything about me, Mr. Steele!"

Colonel Harman stopped for a second. I could feel the cold muzzle of his .45 pressing hard against my head. I swallowed hard, realizing that today I was meant to pay for the sins of Mr. Harjo, as well as those of Mr. Lindberg, at the hands of his trained assassin—a man who had once been a hero, a warrior who had become a puppet of a madman and who was holding a cold, steel pistol to my head with feelings of rage and vengeance running through his veins, and a man who was about to pull the trigger to terminate my life.

＊

Gertrud and her husband, Mayor John Stafford, startled Marie, who was watching the scenery below, from her deep trance.

"I am so sorry, Marie. Did I startle you?" asked the mayor. "I wanted to see if there was something we can do for you."

"Well, now that you mention it, yes, John, I am worried about my nephew Jack. He is missing, and on top of that, I am worried about Jimmy."

"Don't worry, Marie. I will ask one of my deputies to check on both of them and get back to us. Marie, I will take care of it. In the meantime, let's go through the agenda for today, shall we?"

"I'd like that, John; I'd like that," repeated Marie as she picked up the Fourth of July events brochure and perused through the agenda.

The mayor took the initiative and started reading the agenda items. "First thing first, are we positioned where we are supposed to be, Gertrud?"

"Yes, dear, we are. You see, in an hour, the town's band will pass in front of City Hall right in front of us, and then we will see the local merchants' parade."

Mayor Stafford continued line by line until he concluded

the agenda, but Marie's heart, mind, and soul were elsewhere; she was praying for her husband's and Jack's welfare. From the balcony, she looked like one of the town's elite citizens, an elder, or maybe a valued volunteer. But in her heart, she only felt like an abandoned, lonely, old woman. She wondered whether she would see her husband one more time and whether her nephew had survived the car accident.

The search had been called off by Sheriff Lindblom, who had been able to convince the mayor that he needed the manpower to supplement his security plan for the Anvil Run and the vice president's welcoming party. With little effort, Mayor Stafford backed up the sheriff's decision, and Jack Steele became another missing statistic in small town Nome, Alaska, USA.

"As I was saying," highlighted the mayor, "we'll be waiting for the vice president at Nome Airport. From there, we will escort him to Nome City Hall, where he will have a few minutes to refresh himself before the official start of the Anvil Run. Afterward, the vice president and I will enjoy a cold Midnight Sun Berserker and prepare for the ceremony for the run trophies and his final speech.

"Then VP Farmer, Gertrud, and I will drive with him back to the airport and see him fly away in the magnificent Air Force Two. Now, Gertrud, will you pass me one of those cold beers I like? You know that this is the only thing that really quenches my summer thirst."

"Yes, dearest, here you go."

22

AND I SAW THE LIGHT

D r. Harjo and Mr. Lindberg entered the research center's communications room. The security officer on duty stood up when he saw them. "What can I do for you, gentlemen?" asked the officer.

"Nothing at this time, apart from leaving the room," demanded Dr. Harjo. The officer cleared his post immediately, without challenging the order.

Dr. Harjo sat on the command chair and withdrew a black address book from his white coat. After flipping a few pages, he finally found what he was looking for—a frequency that he immediately dialed into the radio.

Right away, they heard Anchorage Tower giving directions to Alaskan Airlines flight 152.

Dr. Harjo looked toward Mr. Lindberg. "Based on the departure time and control-tower protocols at Anchorage Tower and knowing that Air Force Two has to calibrate altitude and direction, they should be contacting Air Force Two in a few minutes," he said.

***

From the Martin Mars cockpit, Jimmy and Captain Phillips were enjoying dancing through the clouds and the vast white

255

and green tundra below. The view was breathtaking. Copilot Phillips understood that his life while flying was just a mere gravity equation, but he loved every minute of it.

Jimmy was still struggling with his inner thoughts; there were moments when he would like to just end it all at once—the voices, the tension, the uncertainty. But deep inside his mind, there was something worth holding onto, and this was Marie. He looked to the front to see the blue sky and white and green tundra below. The voices—voices that on many occasions he had been able to shut out for a while—didn't want to shut up. Since yesterday, the voices had become louder and louder, making him even entertain the idea of terminating his life.

But what about the plane, what about my passengers?

These and many other demons were bothering Jimmy, not only at night but now on his conscious stage. And this frightened Jimmy the most. In his mind lurked the questions: When would they stop? And would ending it require him to terminate his life?

Jimmy was startled by a radio signal that came through the headsets. "Air force Two, this is Anchorage Tower, over."

Jimmy quickly picked up the handset and responded, "Anchorage Tower, this is, Air Force Two; copy you, lima-Charlie, over."

"Air Force Two, be advised that you are 150 miles away from Nome. We have you on radar. Please continue at the same altitude and engage standard approach procedures. We will get back to—"

The communication was interrupted and overcome by another strong signal and the words that both copilot Phillips and Jimmy heard were, "Time itself has no end, but it takes time to get there. You know that to fulfill your duty—"

"Air Force Two, this is Anchorage Tower. Acknowledge last transmission; acknowledge last transmission."

Jimmy moved the radio microphone next to his mouth and said, "Copy loud and clear. Air Force Two out."

And the radio went silent.

Jimmy looked at the altitude, speed, and map and then back at copilot Phillips, who was looking at him with his mouth open.

"Captain, did you just hear what think I heard?"

"What was that, Captain Phillips?"

"Someone else was speaking through the radio!"

"Nonsense."

"I clearly heard the second message. Look at the—"

And before Captain Phillips was able to finish his last word, Jimmy took advantage of the fact that his copilot was looking at the instrument panel and, with a furtive move, slammed Phillip's head hard with the cockpit's fire extinguisher and knocked him out cold. Jimmy quickly pulled Captain Phillip's head back and rested it on the seat, making it look as if he were asleep. Jimmy then reengaged the plane's autopilot program and walked back to the main cabin to make sure that the passengers saw him and to reassure them that all was going well.

VP Farmer was catching a power nap, while Danny was rewriting the vice president's speech and Agent Landis was looking seriously at him. The latter asked, "Mr. Steele, who is flying the plane?"

"Captain Phillips was so insistent on flying solo for a few minutes that I had no heart to say no to his indulgence. Phillips will like to be able to brag to his fellow presidential pilots that he flew this plane solo, and I didn't want to keep that away from him, even if it was only for a few minutes."

"I understand," said Agent Landis, "but I would like to have two masters in the cockpit rather than just one, no matter how good Captain Phillips is."

"Yes, I know, indeed," said Jimmy. "I wanted to let you know that we are 150 miles away from landing. Take care of last-minute details about the cabin because, when you see that green light come on, we will be preparing for a water landing."

Jimmy turned his back and started to walk back to the

cockpit, but he was interrupted by Agent Landis. "You could have said all that from the cockpit. Why trouble yourself coming all the way back here?"

Jimmy stopped right in his tracks, and without turning, his face to Agent Landis, Jimmy said, "As I mentioned before, I wanted to give Captain Phillips his solo flight time in the cockpit."

"Ah, yes, that's what you said before. Thanks, Mr. Steele," replied Landis.

Jimmy continued walking to the cockpit, and after shutting the door, he engaged the cockpit door's inner lock to prevent anyone from entering after him. He looked at Captain Phillips, who was still passed out. Jimmy looked again at his instruments and noticed that the distance dial was getting very close to fifty miles out. He could not get his eyes off the distance dial, and yet he didn't know why. In his mind, the thought of fifty miles was fixated in his mind like a bad smell; perhaps this number would be a distance the world would never forget.

***

"What are you waiting for, Harman? Pull the trigger! Or is it that a big warrior like you knows he shouldn't need a weapon to get rid of me? Untie me and let's settle this like two warriors. Or are you afraid that, if you release me, I can take you down like the big bully you are?"

"Ha, you make me laugh, Mr. Steele. I don't need a weapon to kill you. I can kill you with my bare hands. I was trained with Special Forces, and you are no match for me," said Harman.

"Then prove it, Harman. Stand by what you said, and let's settle this like the two warriors we are. Why pass up some fun beating me to death and feeling the satisfaction of breaking my bones and bloodying my face along the way."

I could sense the battle inside Harman's mind. I could also feel that the pistol was not pushing into my skull anymore. I whispered to him one more time. "Harman, I'll make you a bet. If I lose, I will kill myself in front of you. If I win, you get to kill me anyway you want and I won't even put up a fight. See, you have nothing to lose but some time; after all, you have to avenge Taylor."

"That's it!" he roared. "You want a beating, you'll get one." He placed the gun on a table next to the chair and untied my neck; he then untied my left hand and pulled away from me, allowing me to finish releasing my bindings.

Once I was on my feet, he looked at me like a devil who was getting ready to receive its first soul. I was not afraid anymore, as I had turned an imminent death to a fighting chance to live. I was not going to let the only opportunity I had to walk the hell out of here pass me by, once I sunk this stinking place.

I walked to the middle of the room, to a clearing large enough for us to fight in. Colonel Harman's eyes steamed with rage and vengeance. I suddenly realized that my fight for survival was going to be a lot more painful than I was bargaining for; this was going to be a battle that I would never forget. *So here we go.*

I waited for him to take the first step; usually rage and anger will make a man commit mistakes he would have never thought of doing. But today, I needed all the luck I could get to get out of this one alive. Colonel Harman was seven foot three, give or take, against my nearly six-foot-five frame, and I weighed probably half of the colonel's body mass. But what was on my side were the years of street-fighting experience under my belt, and I was counting on this advantage.

Harman finally got close to punch my head, and it felt like a sledge hammer pounding on glass; my jaw hurt like hell. I was not about to lose this fight, so I kicked him hard on his stomach and then placed my left punch to his jaw. And he didn't even blink.

Doom on me. Jack, be ready for more pain, I thought. But in a good fight, all is legal, so I used all the martial arts tricks I knew and started pounding hard on his body like my life depended on it. He got lucky on many occasions, taking me down to the floor in pain again and again. And I got up for more.

The colonel was in good, perfect shape and had a body to support it. The fighting went on for about ten long minutes, and by now our bodies had resisted a lot of abuse. Neither of us was in shape to keep it up any longer. I was standing because, if I dropped, I would never get up again, and the colonel was standing on his last fumes alike.

I mustered all the strength I could and made a very good roundhouse kick straight to the right side of his face. I could see his sweat spraying the wall and I felt like I'd just hit a brick wall. Nevertheless, Colonel Harman went down hard, bumping his head against the wall and landing next to an open flame that was cooking some type of formula. His suit caught on fire.

I went for the nearest fire extinguisher and quickly extinguished the flames. He was still conscious and knew what I was doing.

As I was holding Harman's smoking suit on my hands and was thinking that I had finished with this ordeal, Dr. Harjo arrived at the lab, in the company of another man, who, to my initial assessment, looked like his personal bodyguard.

The doctor looked at both of us with disrespect and anger and told his trained dog, "Kill them both. Neither of them are worth the air they are breathing."

Colonel Harman and I looked at each other and back at Dr. Harjo, who had a smirk on his face. At the same time, we both saw that his trained dog was slowly pulling the weapon from under his manicured, black blazer.

At this time, I remembered the pistol that Colonel Harman had left on the table next to the butcher's chair. I threw

Harman's suit toward the two who were standing in front of us. As the trained dog moved his eyes to look at the suit, I reached for the gun and shot one single bullet at him, which he managed to capture center mass like the trained dog he was. He dropped his pistol to the floor. His knees became loose, and he looked like he was trying to stand up, but his body's strength was leaving quickly. In spite of his efforts to remain standing, he fell forward and slammed onto the floor like ripe fruit falling from a tree.

Dr. Harjo, a coward, realized that he was in trouble as soon as he saw me redirecting my weapon toward him and firing a couple of shots. But unfortunately, the doctor ran away like a little girl and hid behind the wall, eluding both my rounds from personally meeting him.

I ran after him, but by the time I reached the door, he had disappeared like a ghost.

Harman looked directly at me; his face, like mine, was bleeding from the macho fight we'd just had. In his eyes, I no longer saw hatred or vengeance; the only thing I saw was regret. Since mind games were the issue here, perhaps the right words could help Harman realize that he was better off working with me than against me. So I softly and objectively said to him, "Would you have believed that not even twenty minutes ago, you were the master here and now you, as was I, were about to be shot like two stray dogs? Is this what you envisioned when you first joined Lindberg Research Corporation? I mean the only margin benefit I saw today was death, even to loyal servants like you. Is this the payment you want for servicing these bastards?"

Colonel Harman said nothing to me for nearly thirty seconds, which to me were like an eternity as he pondered the words I'd just said to him. Finally he mustered his warrior spirit and said, "I have finally opened my eyes after having them closed shut for a long time. I realized that, when you killed the security officer in cold blood, you were under Dr.

261

Harjo's spell, just like I have been for a long time. You are a soldier like me, and both of us have been lied to, programmed, and manipulated. Perhaps the pain and burning flesh helped me stop listening to the many demons deep inside my mind and realize that I had to put an end to this madness one way or the other before this job really kills me."

"Work with me, Harman, and together, we can take down this horrifying organization. You know that neither one us can take on Lindberg alone. But united, perhaps we may have a chance—a slim one, but today, slim is better than nothing. What do you say? Are you with me?"

"Perhaps you're right, Jack. We are the only ones who could have a slim chance of bringing down Lindberg and his inhuman empire. With my help and your skills, I believe we can put an end to Lindberg's terror."

I didn't know if Harman was just saying these words because I was holding the gun, the muzzle of which was still smoking, or because he really meant it. I figured that, perhaps, I should give him the benefit of the doubt and believe that the bump to his head or the smell of his own burning flesh could have awakened reason in him.

Either way, at this very moment, I didn't have time to worry about the veracity of his words; a helping hand in my current condition was a godsend, and I was not about to reject it. I had other, more pressing issues to deal with, and I could use all the help I could get. If this meant partnering with Colonel Harman, I was willing to take the risk; I mean, I didn't have any other options at this time.

I approached him and extended my hand and helped him up. Once he was up, he looked at me and said, "Let's go, Jack. We have a job to do."

Harman knew his way around and chose to use the small, dark corridors, where he knew we would not be monitored by cameras. Within five minutes, Harman was punching a digital combination into a locked door, which opened to reveal a full arsenal's worth of military detachment. I saw all the goodies one could wish for to start a small war, but for tonight, all we wanted was to harm and maim until daybreak.

I felt like a kid in a candy story as we entered the small room and started to fill two black, all-purpose nylon bags, which carried the Lindberg Research Corporation's logo on the outside. My heart jumped out of my chest when I saw a shelf full of military-grade explosives—C-4 plastic explosives and Semtex, which I recognized from back in the day. This is an explosive that was based on both an RDX and PETN combination. On the middle shelf was the old trusty RDX, which is a plastic explosive. And on the lower shelf was nitroglycerin, which is one of the world's most highly unstable explosives.

"Jesus Christ, Harman, what in the world were you guys up to here?"

"Jack, don't ask, and I won't tell," responded Colonel Harman.

I replied, "You guys are full of surprises."

"Thanks for the compliment, Jack. We like to be prepared, you know, just in case polar bears show up around here."

And both of us laughed out loud, as I very carefully chose the explosives we would need.

I selected several blocks of C-4 and Semtex. I then spotted another explosive, "Semtex-10," the latest and greatest in military-grade explosives. This explosive was preferred by most of the world's terrorists because it's light, versatile, and hard to detect when passed through X-ray machines. I took some of it as well, and as I was loading my bag, Harman looked at me with a smile on his face. "You know, Jack, I wish I had met you under different circumstances. You and I could have done real damage to the enemy!"

"We still can," I told him, "and have a lot of fun in the process."

"Without a doubt, my friend," Colonel Harman responded, "without a doubt."

To my left, I could see an array of military rifles, and one in particular stopped me dead in my tracks. It was the newest submachine gun UMP (Universale Maschinenpistole) or, in a plain English, the H&K MP-5 Universal Machine Pistol.

I looked at Harman and said to him, "You guys are maniacs! This is the latest firepower available out there, I would never imagine that you—"

"L R Corporation is very wealthy and can be very generous when talking about protection," Harman said, interrupting me. "This is why they always gave me what I asked for. You haven't seen our mortars yet."

"You mean to tell me that you have 8mm mortars?"

"No, Jack, we've got four-deuces."

"You've got to be kidding me, Harman. I think that I'm starting to like you."

We both laughed again as we continued to grab as many weapons and ammunitions as we could carry in the bags.

***

Back in the tundra, Sora was starting to suffer from the elements. She was still hiding behind a large bush, unable to move anywhere at the time, as the patrol vehicle was still parked closed by and the four men were still searching the area, taking trophy photographs of the burned-out Hummer and also a group photo in front of the downed helicopter.

Sora was miles away from Nome, in the middle of nowhere, without proper clothing, food, and water. She would not last too long, so she had to quickly weigh her options. She knew that she had only two options: either she turned herself in or she waited until the security team left and tried making it to town. She preferred the latter. However, town was still several miles away, and she didn't know if, under her current conditions, she would be able to make it. So she decided to go back to LR Corporation—back to the mouth of the bear.

Sora waited for an opportunity when the patrol team was taking another photo of the helicopter and their backs were to her direction and found her way into the patrol's Hummer's back cargo area, where she hid under a military half-tent shelter. She was a petite girl, and the half-tent was perfect to fully cover and conceal her body. Inside the Hummer felt warm and welcoming, but in her mind, she didn't know if her actions would actually seal her fate or if this was her last chance of surviving the night.

At least she thought that she'd have better chances of surviving a meeting with security people than with the harsh Alaskan night. A few minutes later, she heard the patrol approaching and made sure that she was as quiet and restrained as she could be. All four hunters entered the Hummer, and one picked up the hand mic and communicated with the base.

"Lima-Romeo 1, this is Lima-Romeo 5. Recovery vehicle never reached our location; waiting for instructions."

The LR Corporation security command center responded back, "Lima-Romeo 5, return to base to be relieved of duty. Your replacements are here and will continue recovery operations upon assuming their shift change, over."

"Roger that," responded the lead security officer, holding the microphone inside the Hummer.

Sora heard the Hummer's engine turn on and felt that she still had some hope of getting out of this one alive. She started praying to the spirits for strength, for her life, and for Jack's life all the way back to the LR Corporation. She made every effort to keep quiet and remain calm and still, despite the sexist, religious, and gender jokes being made by the four quasi-military Hummer occupants. If she had a choice, she would probably have stayed in the open tundra taking her chances than listen to their banter.

The trip was bumpy and hard, and on many occasions, she banged hard against the cold steel of the Hummer's cargo section. After what seemed like ages, she finally heard voices and saw a bright light, which told her that she was back at the LR Corporation's main entrance. Now the ride was smooth and slow. For a few minutes, the Hummer taxied and made a few turns, and all of a sudden, she noticed that the lights were dimmer. The vehicle slowly reversed and came to a stop. Sora was still as a stiff body. The four vehicle occupants left the Hummer, and she heard their steps fading as they walked away. When she could not hear them anymore, she lifted the half-shelter up and peeked out. There was no one around that she could see or hear. It was now or never to make a run for it and escape.

***

Mayor Stafford was halfway through his cold beer when he was approached by Sheriff Lindblom, who told him that it was time to depart for the airport. Nome Airport FBO had reported that Air Force Two was about thirty minutes away and would be landing soon.

Mayor Stafford stood up and asked Lindblom about Jimmy. Marie's eyes caught the sheriff's as he started to say that it had been confirmed by the Nome FBO that Jimmy Steele was piloting the Martin Mars out of Anchorage and the VP was his passenger.

Mayor Stafford smiled at Marie and treasured her facial expression as he told her that everything was going to be all right! He promised that, soon, she would be able to join her husband. He also promised that, if he could, he would be bringing him to her and asked her how she felt.

She thanked the mayor, but his words didn't nurture her; nor did they change the state of mind she was in. In her mind, she knew that nothing on this earth would calm her down until she saw that both her husband and Jack were alive and well.

Stafford smiled and excused himself from Marie. He held Gertrud's hand and walked away with Lindblom.

23

GAME TIME

Harman and I had filled the bags with goodies and left the room. Colonel Harman closed the door and, with his pocketknife, disabled the electronic keypad to ensure that, when the "shit hit the fan," none of his team members had access to this arsenal.

We started to walk down the back corridors and basement to prevent detection. We moved with caution and stealth, as we wanted to keep the casualties to a bare minimum. After all, the bad guys we were after were Dr. Harjo and Mr. Lindberg; they were the ones who needed to pay for what they had done to us. But first things first.

"Before we begin, we have to release the mental patients that are trapped and any other women in the stem-cell lab. They are innocent and don't deserve to be here."

"Fair enough," agreed Harman. "Let's take care of that first." Immediately, he led the way, and I followed.

We climbed a set of stairs and reached the first floor. The stench of death in the basement was starting to creep me out. On the first floor, we moved toward the north side of the building, where we found the elevator that took us down three floors below where Dr. Harjo held the captive human guinea pigs.

Before Harman entered, he put his hands in his bag and

pulled out some plastic handcuffs and gently placed them on my hands. I knew exactly why he was doing this, so I made all efforts to assist. Now inside the elevator, Colonel Harman swiped his electronic key and punched in a set of numbers, and the elevator started to drop down. One floor down, two to go.

As we moved downward, the elevator doors opened at the second floor, and a couple of orderlies entered the elevator, holding a female. Her eyes alone told me that she was broken, with no faith or will. She was not restrained, and the orderlies were enjoying how well they could manipulate her. One of the orderlies in the elevator, a tall, bold, muscular guy looked at my handcuffs and gave a smirk. *Hang around a few more minutes, and I will wipe that stupid smirk off your face*, I thought. But I didn't want to jeopardize the element of surprise, at least not yet.

I was disgusted by the way people were treated here. They were not treated as humans but as a means to gather empirical data. As soon as they were liberated and with proper care, they would be able to reestablish their lives—at least a few of them would.

The elevator announced that we had arrived at "floor three," and we all got out. As he walked away, the muscle-factory, bald guy stared at me like he wanted to beat me hard. It took everything I had to hold back, but I did stare back at him

That was when I felt Colonel Harman pushing me to walk forward. "Don't worry, turkey; your thanksgiving day is coming. Now move!" he said.

I complied and moved like a captive until we cleared the main room, where most of the scientists and orderlies were working.

Now deep inside the center, Harman cut my cuffs, and I started to place blocks of C-4, Semtex, and other goodies at the most vulnerable structural areas. Our plan was to take the house down. Colonel Harman stopped me to ask what I was doing, so I reminded him of how much pain and misery the LR Corp had caused. I was not going to leave anything useful remaining for the corporation's scientists to start their research again right where they left it.

"I am with you, brother, but first let us get these people out of harm's way, and then we can party."

"Fair enough," I said. "How long will it take us to get these people out?"

"I would say fifteen minutes if we hurry. We don't have much time. The day shift starts in an hour, and the staff will be double; there will be more casualties."

"What do you suggest?" I asked. "Let's place the timers for thirty minutes, giving us plenty of time to safely evacuate the people and get out."

"No," replied Colonel Harman, "that's not enough time. Let's place the timers to an hour and pull the fire alarm. It may take even longer to evacuate everyone without some motivation. However, if the staff's properly motivated, I can assure you everyone could be out of the building in less than fifteen minutes."

"Fair enough," I said, and we continued relieving our bags of explosives. We figured that we would level this place once and for all, as a reminder that evil can truly be stopped. Perhaps it wouldn't be for good, but it would be halted and delayed for a while.

***

Colonel Harman's phone rang. He picked it up, and it was Dr. Harjo. He was out of breath when he told Colonel Harman that I had somehow managed to escape. He was to find me and bring me back to him. Colonel Harman assured Dr. Harjo that he would do everything within his power to find me and bring me to him at once. Dr. Harjo didn't realize how efficient the colonel was and that he had already found me.

We set up all the necessary explosives where we wanted and set the timers according to Harman's recommendation. Harman approached the console and pushed several buttons. Following, all the glass cages opened at once. Some of the technicians and orderlies became aware of the situation immediately, and one who appeared to be the shift supervisor ran to Colonel Harman and challenged his decision.

Harman looked him dead in the face and said, "These are instructions from Dr. Harjo himself. Do you dare challenge my authority and actions?

"Initiate executive order five," he commanded.

The supervisor's face turned white, and he swallowed hard before he asked Harman, "Sir, are you sure?"

"Yes, do it now!" screamed Harman directly in the supervisor's face.

"Yes, sir," the supervisor muttered. "Sorry for the misunderstanding."

The shift supervisor immediately asked all the orderlies and other technicians to execute executive order five.

All the available personnel started to gather the patients and direct them to the elevator.

I looked at Harman and asked, "What the hell is executive order five?"

"It's the order to dispose of all evidence and patients. They are being directed to ground level to the industrial furnace for immediate termination."

"Are you out of your mind?"

"No, Jack, this is the safest way to get each and every one of them outside this room without arousing suspicions. Let's hope that Dr. Harjo and Mr. Lindberg don't get wind of the situation, and we can spare a few more minutes. Here, wear one of these."

I looked at Colonel Harman's hands to find a white robe. I knew what he wanted—to make me invisible to the eye. I took it and played along with it, but before I buttoned the robe, I pulled a 9mm HK pistol out of my bag and placed it at the small of my back. "Now I am feeling like a technician, if you catch my drift, Harman."

He smiled and asked me to hurry, as he had to get to the industrial furnace before the crowd did, to make sure no one was burned alive.

Although I was confident of my abilities, I knew that we only had something like fifty minutes left before the whole place was leveled to the ground. So we caught the service elevator and went directly up. Upon reaching the ground level, we headed toward the industrial furnace room.

When the doors opened, I saw hell on earth. Suddenly, something jumped at me and started hitting me hard. I pushed the person to the floor, and when I focused, I realized it was Sora.

I looked at her and said, "Sora, I thought you ..."

"Yes, Jack, me too. But I was able to escape and was looking for you and the exit." She then looked to her right, and seeing Colonel Harman, she switched gears. I saw fear cross her face before her instinct took over and she charged forward ready to attack Harman with all the strength she could muster.

I held her hard by shoulders and said, "Relax, Sora. Colonel Harman is on our side. He is here to help us, not to harm us."

Sora took a moment to internalize what she'd just heard from me. Then out of nowhere, she slapped him hard on his jaw. Right away, a thin red line found its way out of his lower lip.

I tried to hold her again, but Harman said straight to her face, "It's okay, Jack. I deserved this and more." He then cleaned the blood from his jaw as Sora stared at him without saying a single word.

Sweat began running down my head, confirming that the furnace was reaching its maximum heating point. It was a room designed to burn industrial waste. For a moment, I thought of how history repeated itself. I thought of World War

II, when the Nazis burned millions of captive Jews. Dr. Harjo may have considered himself the new Hitler. How poetic. And as Hitler was his hero, I would make sure that he died just like Hitler had, and that would be very soon. That was a promise I had made a while ago, and it was one I intended to keep.

The heat also reminded me that it was time to pull the fire alarm and get everyone out of the building as quickly as possible. I looked around and right to my left I saw the red box. I pulled the lever without hesitation, and seconds later, I heard the alarm echoing loudly in every direction.

In seconds, the first patch of white robes started to run, looking for the nearest exit.

Colonel Harman gave us instructions on how to safely get out of the building. I gave Sora a pistol and asked her if she knew how to use it. She pulled out the magazine, checked the chamber, pushed it back in, unlocked the safety catch, and asked, "Can I or can I not shoot?"

Not waiting for a reply, she pointed the weapon at the orderlies and, with the gun, motioned them to push the patients her way. The orderlies raised their hands as soon as they saw the gun. Some of the patients followed suit, though, for the most part, they raised their hands more warily; others simply stared ahead, seemingly confused or indifferent.

"We're going to get you all out of here," Sora said softly, her eyes momentarily wet. Then her attitude changed as she directed her attention back to the orderlies. "And you're going to help us," she snapped, waving the gun menacingly.

I asked Sora to take the rear, while Harman would take the lead; in the confusion, it would be hard to determine who was who.

As Sora, Harman, and the orderlies directed the patients to form a line, one of them, a woman between thirty and thirty-five years of age, left the pack and ran toward the burning flames, throwing herself into them before anyone could react. I could hear her screams and cries as the flames consumed her body.

I sympathized with her. Perhaps she couldn't comprehend that she would finally be delivered from the hell she'd endured; perhaps she'd been through so much that she could no longer fathom the concept of safety, and she preferred to kill herself before living another day under Dr. Harjo's reign of torture.

Clearly concerned that another desperate person may follow that patient to their death, Colonel Harman turned to the line of patients he'd been organizing. "You are free," he said loudly. "You are going home."

The orderlies had taken advantage of the confusion the woman's death had caused and were running toward the exits, abandoning their instructions to help Sora, Harman, and me guide the patients out. We did nothing to stop them; they were no more a concern of ours, as our efforts were directed toward saving the patients.

Those patients who were sane enough to understand started to walk behind Colonel Harman and to help others who, because of their advanced mental conditions, could not do so by themselves. As they moved past me, I recognized the woman I had seen in the elevator.

And all of a sudden, I felt like the building had collapsed on me.

It was the muscle-factory, bald guy from the elevator, who had smacked me from behind. I got up and realized that he recognized me, even with the white robe. He took his robe off to show me his massive muscle groups in an attempt to discourage me from fighting him.

Colonel Harman and I exchanged glances, and he said, "I know you can handle him. Sora and I will go ahead and clear these people out before all hell breaks loose."

"Roger that," I responded as the guy punched me once again on the upper left lip.

I felt and tasted warm blood dripping from my lips. "So this is the way you want it?" I said. "Okay, let's tango."

The subject came back at me with a left punch, and I

blocked it and hit him as hard as I could muster in his rib cage. I could feel cartilage and bones breaking as my fist hit his muscular torso. He bent down, which gave me an opportunity to hit him right on his left upper lip. "Just returning the favor, you know."

A splash of blood covered the upper front of my white robe. "Good, I hope it hurts."

He went down on his chest. I was so furious about this whole situation that I was giving no headway to this guy. But as I got closer, he played a dirty trick and pulled my leg toward him. I fell backward and hit my head on the hard floor. He pulled me from the floor and stood me up. Holding my head with both his strong hands, he bent back and hit my head with his forehead, and down I went again.

I had no time for bullshit. I had to end this, and I had to end it now, as the timers were still active and counting. I let him grab me again, and as I was straightening my body, I gave him an uppercut that he would never forget. With the impact he went down in sleeping mode. I took off the bloody white robe and noticed that the other orderlies had left. To me, they were not important; what was important was finding the cowards, Dr. Harjo and Mr. Lindberg.

I ran toward the command center and, on the way, encountered several security officers who wanted to kill me. Unfortunately for them, I had no time for delays, so I killed them before they could kill me. I had to warn Uncle Jimmy about Dr. Harjo's plan. I had to stop that plan. I stopped one man who was in a white suit and running out and asked him the way to the command center or communications room.

He didn't want to talk—until he met Helen and Kathy (the HK 9mm in my hands). Immediately, he pointed the way, after begging for his life. I had nothing against people making a living; what I hated were those giving the orders and hiding, so I let him leave.

Within a few seconds, I located the area and ran toward

the control room. Right before entering, I paused. The door was closed, so I checked the lock and it was locked. I had no time to waste, so I shot the lock three times and hid behind the concrete wall. I heard one, two, three ... all the way to ten detonations back at me. I knew that the HK pistols we'd seen in the armory room only held ten rounds in the magazine. I stood up and kicked the door wide open, to find the security guard trying to load his weapon under tremendous pressure. So my gamble was right—one guard, as I'd seen before, with one pistol added up to ten rounds.

Usually, security officers managing security cameras, alarms responses, and security systems are what we call geeks; they are technical support, and it's very rare that they are part of a specialized response team, who are constantly training, shooting, and practicing close-quarter combat. Thus, they don't react as aggressively or conserve ammunition like a disciplined shooter would.

When he saw the hole at the end of my pistol's muzzle, the guard threw his piece to the floor and raised his hands. "You see, this is what you should do when confronted with a superior force."

The security officer looked at me. Ascertaining that I was alone, he looked back at me and said, "Yes, sir."

"I love it when security is polite and service-oriented. Well, since we are on a first-name basis, give me the Nome FBO frequency now."

"Yes, sir, right away."

The security officer immediately turned around and adjusted the radio to the correct frequency and handed me the microphone.

I caught him lifting the panic bar he had under the security console with his left shoe. I smacked him on the forehead with the weapon, and he went down to the floor.

I clicked the microphone and called in, "Jimmy, this is Jack, do you hear me? Jimmy Steele, this is Jack. Do you hear me?"

When no response came, I tried again. And again, no response, and then doom came to find me. Out of the corner of my trained eye, I noticed a difference in the room. I was no longer alone. There was Dr. Harjo staring at me. "Mr. Steele, you are a man of incredible resources. You managed to do what no one else has been able to do in my many years of practice. I guess that congratulations are in order."

"Spare me your pleasantries, Harjo. How do I get Jimmy to respond to me? Quickly, tell me," I demanded, pointing the pistol at him.

Dr. Harjo, with a lot of confidence, approached me, getting close enough for me to touch his chest with the pistol muzzle. "Go ahead, Mr. Steele. Kill me; pull the trigger." His voice was calm. "Mr. Steele, what is going to happen is inevitable. You get to see it all from a front-row seat."

He looked at me and said, "Allow me the microphone, please."

I handed the mic to him, and upon taking it, he said, "Jimmy, this is Dr. Harjo. Do you recognize my voice?

Jimmy, who was at the cockpit answered. "Dr. Harjo, three minutes to mission time. Are there any new instructions?"

I took the mic away from Harjo and said, "Jimmy, this is Jack. Do you hear me? Please don't do it; you don't have to do this. You can resist. Jimmy, you don't have to crash the plane."

The line was dead, and Jimmy didn't answer.

"Dr. Harjo, I beg of you, call him off," I pleaded. "I'll do whatever you want, but don't kill Jimmy."

"I know you will, Mr. Steele. But as I mentioned, this crash and the vice president's death are inevitable.

I got closer and put the pistol to his right temple. "If it is inevitable, then I don't need you anymore," I said. "Prepare to die."

At that moment, I heard the Nome FBO asking me to get off the frequency and also instructing Air Force Two to stay on course. "Air Force Two, this is Nome FBO. You are losing altitude. Please return to the approved flight plan."

Jimmy's didn't answer.

I felt helpless; in fact I was about to be witness of not only the demise of my uncle but also of the vice president of the United States, and there was nothing I could do to make Dr. Harjo back away.

***

Inside the Martin Mars, Agent Landis observed VP Farmer holding the armrest tight as the plane started to drop. The fact that it was dropping was not of concern; the fact that it was dropping in a steep way was!

The other passengers were starting to look at each other with concerned faces. Agent Landis unbuckled his seat belt and started to walk toward the front cabin. It was now very difficult to walk, as the plane was now on a steep decline.

With difficulty, Landis reached the front cabin door and knocked several times. When no answer came, he knocked harder. Still he got no answer. He pulled out his weapon and tried to hit the lock opened, but the Martin Mars's cabin doors were constructed back in the forties, when metal was in abundance and planes were made to last. This metal door was not opening unless the pilot opened it from the inside.

Still, Agent Landis had to try something, so he aimed his weapon at the lock. Just as he was about to fire, the plane's inclination changed, and a briefcase, which had been stored in a compartment in the corridor, landed on his head, rendering him unconscious.

***

On the radio, a voice from Nome FBO came alive. "Air Force Two, do you wish to declare an emergency? Air Force Two, do you wish to declare an emergency."

My worst fears came to life; I knew that Dr. Harjo and Mr. Lindberg's plans would come to fruition. And worst of all was the fact that I was in the front-row seat and unable to change this Machiavellian plan.

My heart was pounding hard, and I was starting to sweat like a pig. I had to think of something and fast. But what? I was running out of time and options.

And then I heard a whisper coming from Dr. Harjo's mouth: "Time itself has no end, but it—"

Realizing that I had the microphone in my hands, I said to Dr. Harjo, "What did you say?"

And as he said the same phrase again out loud, I pressed the mic key, knowing Jimmy would be able to hear it loud and clear.

When I heard the phrase, my mind spun several times over. But why? I was a bit confused for a second about my reactions to these strange words but concluded that perhaps my confusion was a manifestation of the fuzziness threatening at the corners of my mind.

Then, adrenaline and, above all, my mental discipline took over the moment, rejecting the mental programming that was attempting to trigger a command in my mind.

Jimmy answered back, "Yes, Dr. Harjo. What do you want me to do?"

Dr. Harjo was about to speak when I hit him on the back of his head with my fist, and he went down to the floor. "Jimmy, it's Jack," I said.

There was no reply.

My head was running at a million miles an hour; my internal computer was remembering every inch of my training, knowledge, and the current events, looking for a solution. And all of a sudden, it hit me.

I reached for the mic and said, "Jimmy, think really hard about what you are going to do. Marie is waiting for you at home. Remember Marie—your wife!"

I waited but received no response.

Then I called to Jimmy and said, "Jimmy, this is Jack. Can you hear me? I want you to think about Marie. Picture her face right now. Say her name. Marie, Marie, your wife!"

"Jack, is it you?"

"Yes, Jimmy, forget about your prior orders and wake up. Wake up and fly the plane. You have to come back to Marie. Picture her face. She is waiting for you at home. Don't listen to Dr. Harjo! Focus on your Marie," I screamed, using the best persuasive tone I could muster.

"Oh my God, Marie, my lovely Marie. Jack, hold that thought. I'll get back to you. It appears that I am going to be a bit busy in the next few minutes. I have a plane to land."

I exhaled in relief, just in time to find that a cold muzzle had found its way behind my right ear.

"Very clever, Mr. Steele; you used an image that contained deep-rooted feelings to breach my programing," said Dr. Harjo, who had recovered and was now holding the security officer's weapon, which he'd recovered from the floor. "This is one of the few vulnerabilities I've yet to perfect. Your gamble momentarily worked, but it's still too late. Your uncle will never be able to regain control of the plane now. It's too late.

"Mr. Steele, I've won again," Harjo concluded.

I keep on missing these small details, I said to myself. *I should have secured the weapon on my person.*

"What happened to you, Mr. Steele? Has saving the second most powerful man in the world left you speechless?" Harjo sneered. "You have done tremendous damage to this operation, and the integrity of these facilities may be compromised, but tomorrow, we will open another in a remote location, perhaps China or India. And we will continue our studies because someone has to.

279

"We are at the brink of making a new human being—one who can tolerate pain, will follow orders without hesitations, and is not afraid to die. We have the answer to kidney failure, heart disease, and brain tumors. Do you hear me, Mr. Steele? You may have won this battle but not the war. I just wanted you to know this before I killed you. Now prepare to die."

"Go ahead, Dr. Harjo, be a man for once in your life and squeeze the trigger. I dare you to kill me." I could hear the anger in my own voice.

To my surprise, Dr. Harjo went for the trigger, and a loud noise shocked my body. I could feel the warm blood dripping from my head. Was I dead? I wasn't feeling anything.

"Jack, are you okay?"

I turned around to see Colonel Harman. "Harman, you don't know how glad I am to see you," I exclaimed warmly. I felt as if I'd just been reborn.

"Dr. Harjo was about to kill you, so I had to kill him. I had no choice."

I looked down at the floor, and all I could see was a dead man drowning in his own blood. His brains were splattered all over my clothes, and in his right arm was the weapon he'd tried to kill me with. I immediately picked it up and pushed out the magazine and found that it was empty.

"You see, Harman, I was in no danger," I said, grinning.

"Jack, please cock the gun," suggested Colonel Harman.

I pulled the slide backward, and a bullet was released and landed in my hand.

"Save it, Jack. That bullet was intended for you. I guess you owe me one after all."

"But I counted the bullets. Your officer shot ten."

"Yes, Jack, ten on the magazine and one in the chamber is part of our standard operational procedures."

I hesitated for a moment and looked him straight in the eye. "Yes, Harman, I definitely owe you one."

"Bullshit," said Harman, "you owe me more than that; you owe me your life!"

"There's no time to waste. Let's go now while we still have time."

I observed Colonel Harman open a compartment right behind the console and pick up a small black box, which he handed to me. I looked at it and knew exactly what it was.

Harman then moved to the front of the room and slapped the security officer to wake him up. When the man opened his eyes, Harman said, "Run out of here to safety if you'd like to live ... Now!"

The officer looked at me and touched his head and started to run, and we followed behind. We all three ran as fast as we could toward the exit.

***

Jimmy was trying like hell to level the plane. The commotion had woken Captain Phillips, and now Jimmy looked at him and said, "What are you waiting for? Help me stabilize the plane!"

Without hesitation, Captain Phillips started pulling at the yoke, and both could feel that they were making progress. They could also see that the deep blue sea was getting closer and closer. Jimmy thought that they would never make it, and Captain Phillips looked at him and said, "It has been an honor to fly with you, Captain Steele."

"Cut the bullshit and pull the yoke harder," said Jimmy.

Jimmy took a second to pull his headset off, as he was already tired of hearing, "Air Force Two, this is Nome FBO. Level your plane; you are on a collision course."

Jimmy pushed both his feet down and found his grip. He then started to pull slowly but surely. At this time, the plane was less than three hundred feet from sea level.

"We are not going to make it," yelled Captain Phillips.

And Jimmy said one more time, "Pull, Captain, pull now!"

This time, the plane leveled; it touched the water with one of its skis and bounced back into the air. Captain Phillips was amazed but thankful that Jimmy, with all his training, was at the helm. He would not have been able to save this old relic on his own.

Jimmy's immediate concern were his passengers, so he told Captain Phillips to level the plane and continue heading to Nome. Jimmy opened the door to find Agent Landis on the floor. Jimmy picked the agent up and woke him. "Are you all right?" he asked. "You have a hard contusion on your head."

Jimmy went for his pocket and drew a handkerchief and placed it on the agent's bloody head.

It took a moment for Landis to get his bearings, and the first thing that came out of his mouth was, "What the hell happened to the plane? Did you mean to crash this plane?"

"I don't know what you're talking about," Jimmy replied. "We were on autopilot making last-minute landing checks when, all of a sudden, I found the plane going down without control. The only explanation I can think of is that we went through a microburst that sucked the plane down into a dive. Captain Phillips is at the helm now, and the plane is fine. We will be landing in Nome in less than fifteen minutes. Let's see how our precious cargo is doing." Jimmy helped Special Agent Landis to his feet, and both went to the seating area.

SA Landis immediately approached VP Farmer, who had fainted. Landis called to him, "Are you all right, Mr. Vice President?"

VP Farmer woke up and said, "What the hell just happened? I thought that we were going to crash! It's been the longest five minutes of my life!" Then seeing Jimmy, he burst out, "Captain Steele, what happened?"

"Mr. Vice President, I honestly can't answer that." He told the others his microburst theory.

"Well, there is only one way to know for sure. Let's ask Captain Phillips," he added in a very convincing voice.

Agent Landis and Jimmy walked into the cockpit, opened the door, and saw Captain Phillips at the controls.

"Captain Phillips, will you please explain what just happened?" Agent Landis demanded.

"Agent Landis, the only thing I remember is losing consciousness. And when I woke up, Captain Steele was fighting to get the plane back on course."

"It is Captain Steele's theory that the plane went through a microburst. What is your opinion on this?"

Captain Phillips looked at Jimmy and took a moment to answer. "Yes, Agent Landis, I concur with the captain's assessment of the situation. I must have hit my head and lost consciousness the moment we encountered the burst."

Agent Landis looked at Jimmy with an expression that showed he was still having doubts. "One more thing, Captain Steele. Why did you lock the cockpit door?"

"Closing the doors is a standard operational procedure for all pilots to follow," replied Jimmy.

Agent Landis looked at Captain Phillips again. "Is this correct, Captain Phillips?"

"Yes, that is correct, Agent Landis."

Landis took his hand away from his head and observed the bloody handkerchief.

"You better clean that up. Go to the rear of the plane. There is a small restroom there," suggested Jimmy.

"Very well, but please, no more acrobatics for today. Alert Major Parker to change his course and avoid this microburst. We don't want to lose our ride home do we?" asked Agent Landis.

"Will do," replied Captain Phillips. He adjusted the radio channel frequency and sent a message to the jet flying behind them.

24

JUSTICE IS MINE

We ran like hell out of the command room and down a couple of corridors. Colonel Harman directed me to the nearest exit. It was a chaotic situation, and no one seemed to care who we were, where we were going, or whether we were escorted or not, as everyone was running for their lives. I guessed that folks took fire alarms very seriously in this corporation.

We finally reached the outside—I saw people running in every direction. As we ran away from the building toward the gate, we were cut off by a dark gray Land Rover.

We stopped in our tracks to see the dark, tinted glass lowering from the rear right seat, and I saw a flash coming from inside the vehicle. All of a sudden, a series of sharp sounds soon joined the noises generated by the general chaos.

Immediately, Colonel Harman reacted to his training and moved in front of me, followed by several bullets impacting his wide torso.

"You bastards," I yelled out loud. I reached for my pistol and returned fire, hitting the right door several times.

But the Land Rover accelerated, leaving a cloud of white smoke and the piercing smell of burned rubber.

I picked up Harman from the ground and pulled his face close to mine. With his last breath, he gasped, "Jack, do me one last favor and kill this bastard and bury his stinking business along with him." He then reached in to his front jacket pocket and handed me the jump drive he'd retrieved from the command center. With difficulty, he got out, "All you need to know …" Harman paused trying to grasp some air and collapsed in my arms.

I had no time to waste; Harman was still alive, and I wasn't going to leave him behind, so I picked him up and ran like a hare away from the building.

Adrenaline fueled my body. I felt no pain, no strains, and Colonel Harman felt as light as a feather. I ran for the next minute or so and crossed the main gate, passing many other people. If this were the Olympics, I would have won the 100-meter final race.

I heard someone calling my name. It was Sora. I looked to my right, and she was driving a large passenger bus. She screamed at me to get in.

I ran toward her, and she stepped from the driver's seat and helped me load Harman into the bus. She then put the bus in gear, and off we went. We hadn't driven more than a few yards before we heard the first explosion. The blast wave made the bus jump at least half a foot off the ground.

I knew what was coming, so I asked Sora to step it up. And as she did so, the second explosion must have detonated the rest of the charges in the sequence. As I looked back, I saw the Lindberg Research Corporation compound engulfed in a huge cloud of smoke and fire. A few seconds later, the entire structure imploded, and there was nothing more than smoke and a huge parking lot. Most of the people were still running away from the holocaust, but I could happily say that it appeared that the majority of those who had run after hearing the first fire alarm survived the explosion.

The explosion must have awakened Colonel Harman, who called me next to him. "The jump drive you have contains everything you need to shut down Lindberg and his enterprises for good. I am sorry I will not be here to see it through, but I am a bit tired, Jack." He signaled me to come closer and whispered, "Do your worst."

I extended my hands and closed both his eyes.

The LR Corp may have had some dirty secrets and nasty experiments, but from the ground level upward, it was all legitimate. What lurked within the three floors below ground was a crime against humanity, and for that, the passenger in the Land Rover would have to pay dearly.

As I held Colonel Harman's body in my arms, I was determined to finish what we had started. Harman's intrepid actions had saved this old skin of mine more than once today. In my book, he had redeemed himself from all the bad choices he had made in the past. We all make bad choices one way or the other; the true glory doesn't rest on the fact that you made them but on what you did when you realized that you had screwed up and how far you were willing to go make it right. I looked up and whispered, "Colonel Harman, you are all right by me, and I will give you the burial you deserve. I promise."

Once out of danger and at a safe distance, I could hear the town's fire engines approaching. I instructed Sora to stop the bus near some security patrol Hummers that were parked along the side the road. Security officers and staff were still watching the cloud of smoke and fire, as many of their dreams were going up in smoke.

I stepped out of the bus and commandeered one of the Hummers. I had to follow Lindberg, even if this took me to the end of the world. I opened the door and sat inside the Hummer; the keys were in the ignition, just the way I liked it. I stepped on the gas pedal and left the area with as much steam as this beast could muster.

I had to catch up. I was behind, but I knew I still had a chance. A coward like Lindberg would most likely be heading for the airport or a safe home. So I put all my marbles on the airport and headed in its direction with as much speed as this vehicle would allow.

***

Lindblom exclaimed, "God Almighty! What the hell happened? As if we didn't have enough problems!"

"What's up, boss?" asked Deputy Angel.

"You are not going to believe it, Deputy," Lindblom replied. "LR Corp just burned to the ground. All first responders are there now."

"Are you for real, boss?"

"Yes. Keep on driving and pay attention to the road," said the sheriff. Then he picked up his cell phone and hit speed dial number one.

"This is Stafford."

Sheriff Lindblom told him that there had been a major explosion at the Lindberg Research Corporation. He further reported that his sources had confirmed that most of the staff had survived the explosion. However, he didn't know the cause of the explosion yet. Unfortunately, the corporation's security department was not cooperating or ready to disclose any more details. The sheriff indicated that he would be sending a deputy to investigate and promised the mayor to keep him apprised of the situation.

Sheriff Lindblom's experience told him that this incident was not caused by an international terrorist organization or a disgruntled employee. However, he did mention to Mayor Stafford that he had a very good idea as to who might be behind it all.

Mayor Stafford instructed him that he'd better be right because he didn't want any leaks of this incident, especially when the vice president was about to land.

Sheriff Lindblom, as smart as he was, replied that he

shouldn't worry and that they would not make any assumptions yet. He asked the mayor to wait for the preliminary report.

The mayor asked Lindblom to keep him informed of any relevant developments. The mayor also dared to suggest that he wanted to keep this under wraps for a few hours—until the VP had left town, and he also instructed the sheriff to contain the situation after the visit, no matter what.

Sheriff Lindblom hung up and commented that he hoped that the many reporters in town didn't smell or see the smoke coming from the corporation's compound.

Following the conversation, Sheriff Lindblom pressed speed dial number ten, which connected him to none other than Secret Service Agent Mainer.

As soon as Mainer had answered the call, Sheriff Lindblom started the cover-up by saying, "I forgot to tell you that, in case you hear or see any commotions, we are conducting the annual fire drill at the LR Corp. It's very realistic, and many of my first responders are engaged in this exercise. Nome Police are participating as advisors and liaisons from the town. This event is handled by the corporation's security department. Just for your information ... Mainer," the sheriff concluded, "the drill is very realistic, so don't be surprised."

Agent Mainer thanked the sheriff and hung up the call.

During the rest of the trip to the airport, Sheriff Lindblom was giving out directions and instructions to his deputies now located at LR Corp's former headquarters. With the assistance of the local security department, Deputy Roscoe Adkin was keeping everything under wraps. He'd asked all staff members to go to their homes and stay there until they were contacted by the sheriff's office. The task was not as difficult as one may imagine, since this was a skeleton crew. Most of the regular staff was out on holiday vacations or at the Anvil Run enjoying a long holiday, and the day shift had been called and told to stay home with the same instructions.

***

LR Corporation's emergency team, under the direction of security shift supervisor Levi Thompson, was scrutinizing the access control roster, comparing the names of those who had survived or were dead against those who should have been in the facility. The team found that sixty-seven people were unaccounted for. Surprisingly, the dead were fewer than the injured but not fewer than the number of those still missing.

The team had moved as many of the dead and injured as possible to a nearby storage facility before the arrival of the local police; doing so was part of the corporation's original continuity plan, which was well known to LR Corp's security staff.

Maynard James Lindberg, in spite of several attempts, had lost all communications with both Colonel Harman and Dr. Harjo. He'd contacted Thompson briefly, simply reminding him that, as the highest-ranking security officer on site, he was now in charge and that he was expected to follow procedure. A situation like this was exactly why written emergency business continuity procedures had been created and rehearsed. The plans ensured that, in the absence of those in charge, the procedures were in place to continue operations.

Most of Thompson's time was engaged in calling a list of senior management and making sure that the written plan was followed to the letter, as per the many other times they had rehearsed this plan.

***

The dark Land Rover parked at the hangar. Two men exited the vehicle and headed toward the hangar. As they entered the hangar, they found the pilot waiting for them.

"Andre, let's get the fuck out of here. What are you waiting for?" yelled Lindberg.

"I haven't received the final approval for our flight plan, sir. I should be able to clear departure in a few minutes."

"Why is it taking so long?" Lindberg snapped.

"Sir, the plane carrying the vice president of the United States is about to land, and the pattern has been declared full," said Andre.

"What the fuck am I paying you for? I don't fucking care. Leave now, now, now," demanded Lindberg with authority.

"Yes, sir, I will see what I can do."

"I don't care to know what you'll do; don't tell me that! What you can do is get us the fuck out of here," insisted Lindberg.

Andre immediately asked his boss to enter the plane and secure his seat belt. He then reached out and closed the jet's door. Andre walked to the cockpit seat and started the engines. The whole hangar was operating on regular maintenance lights, and it was too dark to safely taxi. So from the cockpit Andre reached into his flight bag and drew a remote control, and in seconds, the massive hangar doors started to open. The light of the northern sun flooded the hangar, and Andre had to reach out and put on his sunglasses. He comfortably put on the headsets and pushed a button.

"Anchorage Tower, this is NLR-555. We are requesting permission to take off."

"NLR-555, the pattern is full. Skies are off-limits over Nome for the next thirty minutes. You do not have permission to leave. Stay in place until it is clear; you are the first in line."

"Anchorage Tower, this is NLR-555. This is an emergency takeoff. We need to depart now."

"Negative, NLR-555. Stand down until further notice; you are first to depart, but it will not be for another thirty minutes. Sorry for the delay, but these are orders from the FAA; out."

***

291

Finally, I saw the airport. It was early, and not a single plane was in sight. The main door was manned by an airport security police officer. I slowly approached him and stopped on his command, as of course, he was holding an M16 A-2 rifle. Years of experience and training told me that the person with the automatic gun always has the first word.

"Yes, can I help you?" asked the officer.

"Sir, I am Lieutenant McCabe. Colonel Harman sent me from LR Corp to personally deliver this package to Mr. Lindberg before he departs. It is imperative that I see him at once. It is a matter of great importance."

"Sir, the airport is closed for the next twenty minutes; there are no planes taking off at this time, so you can wait," said the officer.

"Officer, you don't understand," I said. "In twenty minutes, the jet carrying Mr. Lindberg will leave, and I will not have any time to deliver the package. Here, you can see it for yourself."

I picked up the package next to my seat, and when the officer came close enough to me, I opened the door and smacked the wind out of his ribs. I wasted no time. I jumped out of the Hummer, grabbed the officer's shirt, and knocked the officer down with a simple punch to his right jaw. My right fist hurt. I grabbed the M16 A-2 rifle and placed it on my passenger seat.

I opened the gate and started to slowly taxi around the private hangars. Only one had open doors. In the distance, it was welcoming me to enter. As I got closer I was able to clearly identify the hangar by the large letters at front that spelled out, "Lindberg Research Aviation." How I loved vanity! One thing that never changed, whether it was in the United States or abroad, was that billionaires and Fortune 500 organizations had to display their wealth, and they put their names on everything they owned. Today, this vanity was going to lead to Lindberg's own demise.

I continued over the clearly marked ground crew path;

after all, I didn't want to raise suspicions with the tower or any other ground personnel who would want to stop me to ask questions and prevent me from killing billionaire Maynard James Lindberg. In my book, this asshole reached the endangered species right about the first time I met him, when I realized that, under his command, hundreds of innocent people had been tortured, maimed, or killed.

He had deprived the love and affection of many husbands, wives, and children in this small town of Nome, USA. This asshole had almost killed me twice. And to put the cherry on top of the cake, he'd killed a good man—a rare warrior—in cold blood; Colonel Harman was a rare species, and for that, he had to pay.

The more I thought about it, the more I wanted to squeeze the last breath out of this bastard, but time was running out. I had the feeling that Murphy's law (when things go wrong), was not too far from showing its face.

As I was getting closer, I peered into the hangar and was able to make out the silhouette of a jet, which was slowly moving out. Was I too late?

This bird was not going to go anywhere. I accelerated the Hummer to top speed and moved the steering wheel to set it on course with the jet. What a rush came over me! I was about to damage several million dollars' worth of the greatest aviation technology with a piece-of-shit, four-wheel SUV.

But as they say, c'est la vie!

I extended the seat belt, locked the steering wheel with it, and placed the M16 I had taken from the gate police officer on the accelerator pedal to keep the Hummer going, and I jumped out.

The moment I opened the door, the Hummer lost control and deviated from its course, impacting the front section of the building and lodging inside. There was no explosion.

Shit, what the hell? This shit always works in the movies, I thought. Although I was disappointed with the Hummer's performance, I learned that this vehicle was safer than I'd thought!

I got up from the taxi lane and started to run toward the plane. To my surprise, the plane started to taxi and move away from the hangar, and then the Hummer exploded. Fire and debris covered half of the hangar. Unfortunately, while the plane had surely been shaken, I could not see any physical damage to the aircraft.

As I was getting closer, I could see a fuel truck, which I headed for. I opened it and started to look for keys.

Unfortunately, this time I could not find any, but by the time I looked up, I could see the plane passing me by. This was unacceptable! I could not let this asshole leave this airport. I searched behind the instrument panel and found the ignition switch. I pulled the cables and, bingo, I got the truck started. I drove it to the taxi area and started to chase the huge jet.

You are not airborne yet, motherfucker, and you are not going anywhere either. I was gaining speed when, all of a sudden, I could see and hear the airport emergency support services. I counted at least four fire engines and three large ambulances heading down the tarmac toward the burning hangar. *I guess they had to respond sooner or later.*

I looked up and saw a large, red plane I recognized as the Martin Mars making its approach to the nearby bay. I was glad that Jimmy had made it alive; that made one less problem I had to worry about! I continued chasing after the jet, which was now turning onto the tarmac and readying for takeoff.

This plane was not going to takeoff. As I was getting close, the plane started to move and pick up speed. I was about five hundred feet behind it—so close that I could smell the fuel. As I was getting closer, I realized that the Hummer explosion must have made a dent on one of the fuel tanks, as I could see the tank leaking through a piece of metal that was still protruding from the tank. Good, even if it manages to get airborne, this plane shouldn't get too far, and I had the intention of stopping it at all costs.

I accelerated the fuel tank to its maximum speed, but these dinosaurs were not made for speed but to hold loads and drive slowly. The plane was gaining speed, and I was losing it. Through my rearview mirror I saw the Martin Mars hitting the water. *Good for you, Jimmy; way to go*, I thought. I continued to follow the plane but to no avail. The jet was by far faster than this old truck.

In less than a minute, the plane was airborne, and as I looked to my right and my left, I was surrounded by airport police security officers. I smacked the steering wheel as hard as I could in frustration, watching the plane full of stinking human manure getting away.

But as I've said before, Mr. Murphy has a funny way of showing himself when you least expect it, and today he had chosen a front-row view.

***

"Nome FBO, this is Air Force Two taxiing to pier 2."

"Roger, Air Force Two, you are clear to dock. Have a nice day. This is Nome FBO. Over and out."

Jimmy took off his headset, looked at Captain Phillips, took a deep breath, and let it out slowly. Captain Phillips had been holding his breath and was finally able to breathe. "We made it, Captain Steele! I have to say—"

"Yes, you have to say that this was an extraordinary trip that you will never forget," Jimmy interrupted. "Am I right?"

"Yes, without a doubt," replied Captain Phillips.

Jimmy now followed the hand-signal directions of the Nome ground guy and parked right next to the pier. Once the air boat had died down, Jimmy shut down the massive engines and left the cockpit.

Immediately, he found Agent Landis waiting next to the door with a thankful smile. Jimmy understood and said to him, "You are welcome, Agent Landis." He then walked to the door and opened it.

A rush of fresh sea water and air commandeered the plane. Agent Landis asked his protectees to wait until all was clear. He was the first one out of the plane to see Agent Mainer waiting for him with the vehicle's door open, inviting the vice president to enter.

Landis keyed his radio and, after exchanging a short conversation with the person on the other line, left the cockpit and told the travelers that it was all right to exit. The passengers were still shaken by the trip's adventurous circumstances, and this kept them from engaging in conversations—well, at least for the time being.

When VP Farmer walked next to Jimmy, he looked at him and said, "That was quite a scare you gave us up there, Captain!"

"And yet, another safe landing, Mr. Vice President. Thanks for flying with us," replied Jimmy.

VP Farmer clearly understood what Jimmy wanted to say in layman's terms: "Be thankful that we were able to land, and if you wish, you can kiss the floor."

Jimmy, a war veteran and witness of many near-death experiences, was a bit shaken from the ordeal. However, he could see in Farmer's eyes that this microburst was a first near-death experience for the vice president, and Jimmy could bet that the VP would never forget it.

VP Farmer extended his right hand to Jimmy and said to him, "You are one hell of a pilot, Captain Steele. If you ever want a job flying my jet, don't hesitate to call me."

Jimmy didn't have to answer. He just nodded as he saw the second most powerful man in the world stepping down from his plane, followed by the rest of the passengers. Captain Phillips went past Jimmy, directly to the cabin, and searched each and every seat and compartment to make sure that no one had left anything behind.

When he walked out to the main door, he had with him a cellular phone and a notebook. He looked at Jimmy and said to him, "Captain Steele, I don't quite know what happened up there, but I am glad that I lived to say thanks." He shook Jimmy's hand and left the plane.

In less than five minutes, the caravan was already moving away from the pier. Jimmy looked up to the skies and noticed the Boeing C-32 that usually carried the Air Force Two call sign making its final approach as its pilot aligned it with landing strip one.

Jimmy looked inside his plane and knocked on the fuselage, saying, "Thanks, darling, for saving this old skin of mine one more time."

In the distance, Jimmy saw Soule driving the pull truck that would haul the Martin Mars landing wheels. *Well, back to work; this day isn't over yet*, thought Jimmy.

25

ONE WAY OR ANOTHER

A s Sheriff Lindblom's caravan was leaving the airport, the sheriff noticed two peculiar things that attracted his attention. The first was the landing of the official Air Force Two jet; the second was that his phone was ringing off the hook.

"Yes, what is it?" asked Lindblom.

"Sheriff, we've got a Jack Steele at the airport lockup, and he is demanding to talk to you," said the airport security officer.

"How about that?" replied Sheriff Lindblom. "I'll tell you what. Keep him there, and I will personally handle this within the hour." Without waiting for a response, the sheriff ended the call.

***

The caravan arrived and parked in the spaces that had been reserved next to City Hall. The people of Nome were happy to see the vice president. Most of the local residents were waving American flags, and others were wearing their country's colors on hats, shirts, or capes.

"My kind of crowd," said VP Farmer to Danny.

After parking the car, Agent Landis got out and moved

toward the VP's door. He grabbed the door handle but did not open it until he'd scanned the whole area. He made eye contact with Agent Mainer, and when he was confident that all was clear, he slowly pulled the handle and opened the door.

VP Farmer left the car on one side, and on the other, Mayor Stafford followed suit. Noise filled the streets, and the local band started to play "Hail, Columbia," which VP Farmer loved.

Mayor Stafford immediately walked behind the car and joined VP Farmer, and both followed Sheriff Lindblom, who was clearing the way for them to the City Hall. SA Mainer was already ahead heading to the second-floor balcony. VP Farmer stopped on a few occasions for photo opportunities and to shake hands with his constituents. Danny, as a good aide, followed closely behind VP Farmer.

After a few minutes of screams and pushing, VP Farmer and his entourage reached the second-floor balcony. Marie was sitting next to Gertrud, and upon seeing VP Farmer entering the balcony, both stood up. The police officers and Agent Mainer closed the door behind him to prevent other staff and town residents from entering the secured balcony. Marie immediately focused on the mayor's eyes, and Mayor Stafford understood what she wanted.

Mayor Strafford approached Marie and kissed her on the cheek. "Marie, Jimmy is all right. He just delivered VP Farmer to us in the Martin Mars. This is what all of this mystery was about. Jimmy was flying the VP to Nome. Your husband is a national hero."

Marie placed both her palms together in front of her chest and looked up to the sky in gratitude. She was grateful for not knowing what Jimmy was doing but because he was still alive, he was breaking the long-standing curse of the town. She felt like her blood was flowing again; she felt warm inside and could not prevent a single tear from running down her cheek. Gertrud approached her and hugged her tightly, and Marie once again found herself smiling.

***

This is not my day, I thought. *Back to a cold, isolated cell within twenty-four hours—what the hell am I doing wrong?* I found myself in a small airport security lockup cell. This cell was about ten feet by ten feet with not much space to walk about. I could not think of how to get myself out of this one. I was tired, sleepy, and beaten up.

These airport security officers didn't like people blowing up hangars or stealing their fuel tanks. I heard that they were going to fly me out to Juneau for a trial. I heard words I didn't like—like *murder, destroying government property,* and *domestic terrorism,* among others. These charges were a bit strong, but I guess that I was guilty as charged if I really thought about it. In a few hours, I'd killed half of the Lindberg Research thugs; I'd killed their terrorist boss, Dr. Harjo (*may he burn in hell*); exploded a major research center; and, yes of course, destroyed a corporate hangar. Had I missed anything? Oh yes, I wanted to add killing a Mr. Maynard James Lindberg. And in completing a wish list, I would like to stay alive.

As I was sitting down waiting for someone to talk to me, I remembered one thing that really disturbed me. While I was at the Lindberg Research lab, Dr. Harjo had said, "Good, just like the others" He had a plan B, an assassin who had been programmed to take Uncle Jimmy's place in case something went wrong and he failed. Shit, I had to get out of here and soon; the vice president was still in danger; this was not over yet.

Suddenly, a voice interrupted my thoughts. "Mr. Steele, you have a visitor."

I looked up and saw Sora, who was holding a tray with food.

"You are lucky, Mr. Steele. Someone out there likes you enough to send you food," said the airport police officer, smirking.

"Is this the prisoner, Stan?" asked Sora.

301

"Yes, Sora, this is the bastard who blew up half my airport."

"What a sorry-ass individual. Will you please hand this food over to him? I am a bit scared of him; he looks like he's got issues."

"Of course, Sora. Stand behind me."

Stan grabbed the tray and got closer to me but not before he asked me to stand back as he approached the cage. I complied like a good dog waiting to be fed. I took a few steps back and found myself against the wall. Officer Stan saw my action as an act of submission and felt confident enough to bend down and push the tray under the metal bars.

My trained eyes were focused on him. He lost eye contact with me as he was trying to push the tray inside the cell. With a surreptitious move, Sora took the desk phone and smacked him on the back of his head. Officer Stan went down to the floor without knowing what had hit him. I immediately asked Sora to grab the keys from the top right drawer of his desk.

Once outside the cell, I swapped clothes with the police officer, having already assessed that we were relatively similar in size.

Due to the commotion of the VP's landing, the burning corporate hangar, and pulling the Martin Mars out of the water, the under-resourced and overworked five officers at the airport police station were very busy carrying out their duties, and poor Officer Stan was now dressed like me and locked inside the cell. And I was dressed like him, armed, and walking with a purpose outside the Nome Airport Police Station.

It seemed that Murphy was slipping today and giving me some slack. My plan was simple. I had to get back to the action and take out a rogue assassin, save the vice president's skin, and fulfill my promise to Colonel Harman before sunset.

Sora pointed me in the direction of a Jeep, but as I started to walk toward it, I remembered that I'd knocked the wind out of the gate officer and that a familiar car might give me some leeway. I grabbed Sora by her hand and ran over to the

Yukon police car, which was parked next to the entrance. As expected, the keys were in the ignition. There was something very predictable about small towns. No one was going to steal a police car because the police would find it right away; no known roads led out of Nome, Alaska, so you had nowhere to joyride. There was no need to protect something that needed no protection. I loved the logic.

I turned the key in the ignition and also put on a hat, which had been left in the car. It was a bit tight for my big head, but it would do for now. As we approached the gate, I stuck my hand out and waved at the officer, and without hesitation, he opened the gate and out we went. He didn't make any efforts to look inside, but just in case, I'd had Sora sit in the backseat.

Once we were out of sight, she moved into the front with me, where she belonged. This local girl could pull her own weight and had earned my respect as a warrior.

I turned and looked at her with admiration and thought that this small-town waitress, who was insignificant to many of the local patrons, had saved the lives of many people today, including my own and possibly the life of the vice president of the United States. Over my many years in the intelligence business, I had learned not to underestimate the will and bravery that lie dormant in all of us. Sora's actions had made their mark deep inside my heart.

She looked at me and said, "Are we going or what?"

I smiled at her and pushed the pedal to the metal down the narrow road. As we drove, I passed a sign that read "Welcome to Nome, Alaska, population 3,731." I loved small towns.

The news crews were gathered near the finish line, waiting for the many brave athletes who were getting close to completing the Anvil Run. People threw water at the runners as they passed to cool their bodies. Some of the runners were actually asking for it but did not slow down, which didn't help the water throwers' accuracy.

Soon, we came across the first roadblock, and I had no choice but to ditch the car and start running to City Hall, where the action was. I was lucky that the police officers posted at the roadblock were more interested in the run participants than working their roadblocks. As expected, their backs were facing away from the roadblock, and all of them were watching the run.

Good for us, I thought as we continued to walk toward City Hall. I didn't want to raise concerns or questions or call attention to myself. If people saw a police officer running, they tended to expect that something worth watching had happened, and today, I needed to be like a ghost. I needed to work behind the scenes, not in front.

By the time we reached City Hall, the first ten athletes had arrived. These were going to be the only ones who would receive awards from the hand of the vice president. All the other participants would receive a certificate that they would have to collect later from City Hall at their leisure.

I found my way to the center of the action. After all, I was a respectful Nome police officer, so I did what I had been trained to do, which was to look for the target and then work my way through the crowd in the hope that my trained eye would be able to identify the bad guy.

I got as close as possible to the vice president, but I had to hand it to the Secret Service guys, who were alert and on their game today. What they didn't know was that an assassin was in their midst and that, today, they could return to Washington, DC, with their vice president inside a coffin. I positioned myself behind the mayor and the VP and was using my peripheral vision to look for anything untoward. I saw nothing out of the ordinary. I was becoming a bit nervous and started sweating like a roach at a chicken dance.

From where I was, I could clearly see the Secret Service agents moving in closer to the VP as he walked over to the podium to address the crowd. Something inside me triggered warning signals. A voice inside my head told me to move, to change my game, to move away from the podium to another position. At the same time, something also told me that I was right where I was supposed to be, and I tried hard to ignore these thoughts.

All of a sudden, something clicked inside me. I could hear Dr. Harjo waking from the dead and talking in my right ear. His words were so convincing, so reasonable, and so authoritarian that I felt compelled to follow them.

Something changed inside me, and I could no longer fight my feelings. To relieve the pain this mental conflict was provoking in me, I gave in and let go. I felt a great sense of relief as I began to comply with the instructions that were coming from within my mind. I asked Sora to wait there and to keep an eye open for me, as I was going to position myself as close as I could in front of the VP's podium, not behind.

As I got closer, I no longer cared about anything else; the only thought in my mind was clear. I needed to position myself in front of the VP's podium and listen to his speech.

"Constituents of Nome, I am very glad to be here today. The president and I believe that Alaskans are as important as constituents in DC. You are the true Americans, who keep our culture, hope, and way of life. You are the pioneers who've learned to break barriers, fight the elements, and embrace change like no other American citizens I know. You keep the American Dream close to your heart, and this makes us proud at Capitol Hill. Like many of your forefathers who crossed the nation to unearth the precious metals that this fine land has to offer, you are trying to make a better living for your families and for all of us in the process. I have some good news that both your president and I would like to share with you ..."

At this time, I found myself resting my hand on the 9mm automatic weapon holstered on my right hip. I had this burning desire to pull the trigger. I had to follow my instincts *because it's good for the cause and good for me.*

305

"So, my fellow Americans, this presidency has decided to ..."

In that moment, I pulled the gun and released five bullets, one behind the other, without stopping. I could hear voices in the background saying, "Gun, gun, gun." I think that they came from the Secret Service agents.

A lot of commotion and screaming soon filled the quiet afternoon. I remained focused. I had done my duty well. On the ground, I could see several bloodstains. A faint but steady line of fresh blood found its way between my shoes; all I could think was that shots had been fired, and someone was dead.

26

THE RIGHT TO RULE

S irens and red and amber lights filled the jet's cabin. Andre Emerson was scared out of his mind. He had always been surrounded by the best. All resources were placed at his disposal, and nothing he needed was ever denied him. The maintenance of his plane had never been his concern; he had the best mechanics taking care of it. He had never flown a plane that was more than three years old. In other words, he had never experienced any type of serious emergency. As a trained pilot, he knew procedures, but when a plane was losing fuel over the Alaskan tundra, there was no training that could have prepared him.

Andre radioed the nearest airport, which was White Mountain Airport, about sixty miles away from Nome. He knew that he would not be able to make it back to Anchorage, but as long as he could land without smashing the plane into pieces, he was okay.

Riding in the back of the plane was Maynard James Lindberg, who was unaware that his plane was on course to crash.

After requesting permission to land under an emergency protocol, Andre received landing clearance from White Mountain.

He also arranged for a local and fixed-base operator (FBO)

to have another plane ready to depart for Anchorage on their arrival. Once he received confirmation that this was good to go, he pushed a button and informed his boss about the change of plans.

Of course, Maynard James Lindberg was not happy. But he had no choice, and he knew it. The faster they could get away from Nome, the better, as this urge was in the best interest of self-preservation.

Despite the difficulty posed by the fuel fumes, Andre was able to successfully land the multimillion-dollar luxury jet. Upon landing, the driver, the tycoon, and the pilot were escorted to the hangar, where a small Cessna plane was waiting for them.

"What is this?" complained Lindberg to his pilot. "This is a kite, not a plane!"

"Sir, this is the only available plane in this small airport. My apologies to you, but if we want to leave now, this is our only option."

The FBO operator interrupted and indicated that he could order a jet from Anchorage or even Juneau, but it would take a day to get there.

"That won't be necessary; we will take this plane," replied Mr. Lindberg.

Andre told the FBO operator that they didn't need a pilot and that he would e-mail the location of the plane upon landing so that it could be collected. He also assured the FBO operator that money was not an issue, since he was going to be paying in cash for all the troubles and good graces.

The FBO operator said to them, "Gentlemen, enjoy the flight to Anchorage. You are clear to take off."

Andre opened the door for his two passengers, and once inside, he closed the door and opened a small, shiny metal briefcase. From there, he picked up three bundles of ten-thousand-dollar rolls and handed them over to the FBO operator, who, with a smile on his face, replied, "Do you need a receipt?"

Andre looked directly at him and said, "There will be another ten thousand under the seat waiting for you when you collect the plane if there are no questions asked. We were never here. This flight never took place. And you don't know who left the jet behind. Do you understand me?"

"Yes, Mr. Andre, I understand you. Rest assured, this flight never took place, and you and your passengers were never here."

Andre smiled and waved good-bye to his newfound acquaintance. He then entered the plane and closed the door. From his seat, he could see all six seats on the plane. Mr. Lindberg looked like he could kill someone in cold blood with his bare hands, while the driver was sitting deep in his seat, grabbing the armrest. Andre put his headset on, buckled his seat belt, and pushed the ignition on.

The Cessna Grand Caravan was not a luxurious plane but would suffice to take them to Anchorage. White Mountain Airport was a very small airport in the middle of nowhere. It was a state-owned airport that served as a stop-off for other local flights. No hotels or entertainment outlets were nearby in this place. The only runway had a gravel surface and was very short, at only three thousand feet long. You either knew how to fly, or you would end up in the middle of Fish River.

Andre didn't care, as long as they could get out of there as soon as possible. He taxied up the runway, pushed the brake down as hard as he could, and pulled the throttle as far as it would go. Fortunately for him, he had head winds, and this made him smile as he released the brakes and the Cessna ran forward with elegance and purpose. Shortly after, he heard his passenger whisper, "Jesus Christ," as the plane pulled up to the sky.

Andre followed flight protocol and climbed for a few minutes. He then leveled the plane and checked the instrument panel reading, and all looked very good. Traveling at top speed, the plane would take at least two and a half hours to get to Anchorage, so Andre used the microphone to let his passengers know the expected arrival time in Anchorage and told them to rest and enjoy the ride. He then placed the controls on autopilot and lay back in his seat and did the same.

***

Two and a half hours later, Maynard James Lindberg was rudely awakened by the static produced by the airplane speakers and the voice of his chief pilot, Andre, announcing their impending landing. From his seat, he could see Andre aligning the plane with the runway. Within minutes, the plane landed and taxied to Lindberg Research Corp's private hangar, where his staff was waiting for him.

Once the plane had stopped, Andre opened the door, and the ground crew received them.

Lindberg got out of the plane and into his trusted limousine, which was parked inside the hangar. Once inside, Lindberg searched the bar for his favorite drink, and of course, it was ready at the exact right temperature that he loved. Lindberg thought himself invincible and above the law. The deaths at the Nome research facility meant nothing to him; he felt no responsibility for any of them. In his mind what had happened at Nome was just a minor setback in the greater scheme of things.

In the front passenger seat was his trusted bodyguard, a Gulf veteran who had served three consecutives duties, two in Iraq and one in Afghanistan. He was a tall, Irish seasoned warrior who would give his life to protect his boss and his assets. Maynard J. Lindberg was back at his best; he was back in control, and nothing could stop him now.

His line of thought was interrupted by his PR manager who was calling him.

"What do you want?" asked Lindberg.

"Sir, we have a situation at our Nome facility. There has

been an accident. We need to discuss your strategy with the media." The public relations manager continued her spiel, telling him that the local news network had gotten wind of the situation and were waiting for an official statement from him.

Lindberg asked her to prepare the statement and have it ready for him at his desk in one hour. He also asked her to make sure that those bastards at the news station held off from releasing any news. He warned her that if any channel dare broadcast the news, they would pay dearly for not following his instructions. She responded that it would not be a problem and she would make sure things would happen as he wished.

Lindberg signaled his driver to start up the engine, and the limousine floated away toward his Anchorage mansion. Lindberg was already planning his corporate response to this "unfortunate incident." In his mind, the incident was caused by a radical private investigator who had delirious conspiracy theories as a result of his unbalanced and sick mind. He was able to confirm this allegation with the private session notes produced by the late director of research and psychologist, Dr. Harjo.

This private investigator's confusion and troubled mind led him unleash his revenge against Dr. Harjo, who was treating him. In a fit of rage, he not only killed Dr. Harjo but sabotaged his facility and burned it to the ground. Lindberg added that he would also present documents to the authorities to prove that, while taking part in Dr. Harjo's sessions, the private investigator had disclosed his intentions to kill the vice president of the United States before taking his own pathetic life.

Lindberg didn't worry, he had a plan, and he knew exactly what he was going to say. His plan was infallible. He would even recover most of the damages to his facility and start a brand-new research center with the insurance claim. Through this tragedy, he would also have enough public sympathy to continue his work, perhaps even in the same strategic place.

***

All of a sudden I found myself surrounded by weapons; Secret Service Agents Landis and McAllister were on top of VP Farmer. A body lay next to me; there was blood everywhere, and I realized that I had the smoking gun still in my hands. I raised my left hand and placed the weapon back in my holster.

Everyone who had a weapon was pointing it directly at me. I reached down and moved the body. I was distraught to recognize the body of the chief of police, Sheriff Lindblom, lying there. What had I done? I raised my face and suddenly, from the deep silence, I heard Sora scream out loud and clear, "That man saved the vice president! He saved us all."

All of a sudden, I realized that the reason I'd heard the voice in my head tell me to move in front of the vice president was because I had been programmed to be "plan C." If the sheriff failed to kill the vice president, I was supposed to kill VP Farmer myself. But my training and mental control had kicked in, and I was able to kill the man who was also programmed to assassinate the vice president and had been standing right next to me just a minute ago.

It made a lot of sense. Who in town could have access to a weapon? Who could get close to the vice president without raising any concerns or doubts? Who would have the least chance of failure? The sheriff of course. I had to hand it to Dr. Harjo; his plan was sound and could not fail, except that he messed with a warrior, and when you mess with warriors, you are more likely to fail, and dare I say, die.

The location and the instructions for the assassins were the same, but one thing that Dr. Harjo hadn't count on was my ability to control my thoughts, which kicked in when I needed it the most. I felt a lot of pain seeing a man of the law killed like that, but it was either him or the VP, and I had chosen to save the VP. I could not have lived with myself if I had chosen to do nothing and watch an innocent man murdered in front of me.

312

As for the sheriff, he was an honorable man, but unfortunately, he was a casualty of the Lindberg Research Corporation and for that Lindberg would pay.

Everyone started to clap for me. VP Farmer was quickly moved away from the scene by two trained agents, and a lot of confusion and panic between the local police officers and over what had just transpired seemed to ensue. Through the crowds, I saw a figure approaching, and when I looked up, I saw it was Aunty Marie, who came over and hugged me, like a mother would hug a long-lost son. The police officers in the vicinity took that as a signal to holster their weapons and began to clear the people away from the area.

Secret Service Agent McAllister pulled me aside and asked me to follow him. Inside a small bar located behind the podium, the doors opened, and there was only one person inside. As I entered the room Vice President Farmer stood up from his chair and started to clap for me, and then his aide Danny followed suit and began clapping. I didn't know how to react. My mind was still fuzzy, and many thoughts clouded my head. I moved my hands to signal that I'd had enough clapping for one day.

"Son, you are a national hero. You have prevented my assassination. I and this nation owe you our gratitude," said VP Farmer.

"Mr. Vice President, I am no hero," I insisted. "It all happened so fast, and I have yet to put all the pieces together. However, there are other, more pressing issues that I know you must attend to."

Agent Landis walked over to me and said, "Mr. Steele, we've known about an assassination attempt on the vice president for some time now. However, we didn't know the method, the time, or the resource. You've helped us prevent it. Thank you. You saved not only his life," he added, turning his face toward the vice president, "but also my career!"

"Don't thank me yet. There is another matter that I must

attend to, which is to prevent the mastermind behind this assassination attempt from getting away unpunished." I then told him that, if he really wanted to thank me, he could help me acquire certain items I needed.

"What are you saying? That you now who this person is?" asked the vice president.

"Yes, sir, I do, and with your help, I would like to bring this mastermind to justice. You don't want to deal with the administration being involved in anything that I am about to do. I just need a few of your resources to help me put closure on this issue, and I promise you, Vice President Farmer, that I'll be solely responsible in executing justice."

"Son, you can have anything you want, but I only have one condition," said VP Farmer.

"What is that, sir?"

"This bastard must know that he has failed."

"Mr. Vice President, in order for me to achieve our goal, you first have to die."

Agent Landis and McAllister pulled their guns out and pointed them at me.

I raised my hands and asked them to listen to what I had to say next. VP Farmer told them to stand down.

Both agents holstered their weapons but remained alert to what I was going to do or, rather, say next.

"The mastermind has to think that he succeeded in order for me to get close to him. He is rich and powerful and can disappear and never be found should he wish to. If he suspects that I'm still alive and that you didn't die, then it would be nearly impossible for me to get close enough to him, and he will attempt to kill you again." As everyone in the room listened, with full attention, I laid out my plan.

***

Shortly after our meeting, Danny stood at the Nome Fourth of July podium in front of several networks and gave his short speech:

"This administration has an important announcement to make. Today you witnessed an assassination attempt against Vice President Farmer. Our vice president was seriously injured and was transported to an undisclosed location. His condition has been deemed critical, as he has fallen into a coma, and according to the local doctors, he is not expected to survive the night.

"As for the shooter, the US Secret Service is partnering with the Nome Police Department to investigate this matter further. Police will not disclose the name of the involved until the family members are notified. In three hours Washington, DC, time, President Bill Mitchell will address the nation from the White House. I will not be taking questions. Let us pray together for his prompt recovery."

After Danny had finished his speech, several news crews approached the podium and asked questions about the shooting. The Nome Police officers did a good job of keeping the eager at bay.

After the announcement, Danny walked back to the small bar and whispered, "Mission accomplished."

27

THE RIGHT TO DIE

Maynard J. Lindberg was sitting comfortably in his study sipping his cognac and reading his news statement when he was interrupted by a call from his public relations manager, who asked him to turn on the television to Channel 2 KCVV. "Mr. Lindberg, there is a news report you should see right away."

Lindberg reached out for the remote control and pressed a button. A flat screen appeared from behind the bar wall. He then turned it on and switched it over to the right channel.

"This information was received from the vice president's aide, Danny Bedford, who just conducted a brief press conference," the reporter was saying. "He announced that Vice President Farmer has been shot and is not expected to survive the night. He was the victim of an assassination attempt, which took place while he was conducting a speech in Nome, Alaska. Local sources still haven't confirmed the identity of the shooter but can confirm that the assassin was also injured. They say his name won't be released until his family has been informed."

Perhaps the day was not such a loss after all, thought Lindberg. Lindberg still had his public relations manager on hold and told her that the statement was approved and to release to all news networks. She replies on the affirmative and then he hanged up the phone. He felt like he was the king of the hill—that there was nothing that his money or power couldn't do. He picked up his phone and pushed a speed dial key, and at the other end, Senator Whitmore, Chairman of the Committee on Appropriations to the United States Senate answered.

"Yes?"

"Mr. Senator, this is—"

"Yes, I know who you are. What do you want?"

"Have you seen the news lately?"

"Yes, I have," responded the senator.

"Well, there are no more obstacles in our way to stop us from moving forward with our little venture now, are there?" said Lindberg.

"I guess not, not anymore," replied Senator Whitmore.

"Then I expect nothing less than a Senate ratification to allow open stem-cell research. Do you agree with my vision, Senator? Do you agree that Lindberg Research Corporation will have a substantial contract to lead the project?"

"I really don't ..."

Lindberg heard the senator fidgeting and the sound of shuffling paper.

"But what choice do I have?" Whitmore finally said. "You leave me no choice if it's either stem cells or ruining my family."

Lindberg smile at the senator's obvious discomfort. "Well, I am glad that we have an understanding," said Lindberg. "It's always a pleasure to do business with you, Mr. Senator."

Lindberg hung up and whispered, "If you'd kept your pants on, you wouldn't have to worry. I love it when people do what I wish." He picked up his glass of cognac, raised it to his face, and observed the golden hue that told him the spirit was aged to perfection.

Soon stem-cell research will be as common as this drink, he thought. He would be the owner of the process, and this would make him billions of dollars, which would make him rich beyond his imagination. Stem cells would be his legacy, his signature for generations to come, well after he is gone.

In his large mansion, Lindberg was once again alone. His driver and pilot had both returned to their respective homes, and he trusted that his state-of-the-art security system would be resilient enough to alert his trusted bodyguard team, who were stationed above the mansion's garage, should anyone try to infiltrate his safe haven. The security team was composed of a team leader and four other executive protection agents. He could have had an army of agents working for him but he was like many other top tycoons in that he despised having security around—that was of course until he needed them.

He tolerated them because it was mandated by the board of directors. So he kept them as far away as possible. Lindberg was not a stupid man though and had the best electronic engineers design and install the security system, which he could control by pushing a couple of buttons strategically located throughout the mansion. He felt safe in his home, even when he was alone, because he had the best protection that, in his mind, would never fail.

Once Lindberg activated his security system, he went to his study, read, signed, and faxed a statement, which explained the cause of the unfortunate explosion at his Nome plant, to his public relations manager. The top of the message read, "For immediate release."

Lindberg entered his large master bedroom, which was connected to his exquisite suite; took off his bathrobe; stepped into his large and lavish restroom; and immersed himself in the warm, soapy, aromatic water. The whole room smelled like eucalyptus and cinnamon, his preferred aromas.

To his left, he had a lavish bar, from where he was able to refresh his favorite cognac drink. He then opened another cabinet door, which gave way to a fully stocked refrigerator. He drew from it a large, white plate finished with gold carrying a generous serving of red grapes and his favorite three cheeses.

He pushed a button, and a marble shelf came out of the wall. He placed on it his fruit and cheese plate and also his drink. He then immersed himself in the large, deep tub. As he started to relax, he pushed a button to his right, and a one-hundred-inch television came alive from within a mirror. The mirror was perfectly placed on the wall from the floor to the ceiling and was attached to the white-and-gold marble wall.

Lindberg switched channels until he'd found the local news; he wanted to enjoy dwelling on the media frenzy that focused not only on the current assassination attempt but also on the waves caused by Lindberg's accusatory press release. He felt that nothing could stop him from getting away with murder, deception, and extortion.

Lindberg lit a cigar and closed his eyes. He soon found himself so comfortable that he fell asleep. He was dreaming big; he was confident; he was the man who everyone was talking about. He had won.

All of a sudden, he heard a voice that scared the living hell out of him.

"Hello, Mr. Lindberg, did you miss me?"

He opened his eyes with disbelief and uncertainty as the voice he could hear was that of a dead man. And that dead man's voice was mine. "But you are dead. I heard ..." Lindberg dropped the cigar on the floor without even realizing it and said simply, "You cannot be here." He looked at his half-empty glass atop the marble shelf and quickly tried to rationalize the situation. To his disappointment, he was not drunk.

"Mr. Lindberg, I thought that you would be a lot more excited to see me again."

"But my plan ... I don't understand. How could you beat Dr. Harjo's mental programming? His techniques are infallible."

"Well, Mr. Lindberg, perhaps I am a ghost who came to

avenge all those souls you tormented over the years—all those innocent people you killed and all the families you destroyed in the interest of power, money, and self-gratification. I am the ghost who will put an end to your pathetic life." I stopped for a second, to flavor the moment, to make sure he was paying attention, and to choose my words carefully. Then I said to his surprised face, "Your reign of oppression ends today."

"No, Mr. Steele, it is the other way around. You came here alone. I know you. You are the type of man who wants to handle things with your own hands. So this is your weakness, as it will be your final destruction. Mr. Steele, allow me to shut down the television so we can discuss the problem at hand."

He reached for a remote control, pressed a couple of buttons, and the third was the one that shut down the television. I knew what he had done but didn't want to let him know that I knew that he'd pushed his personal panic button and that, in less than thirty seconds, his protective team would blaze through the doors, weapons in hand, to rescue him.

"Mr. Steele, you are an intelligent man; allow me to also make you a rich man. Remember what Dr. Harjo used to say in situations like this?

"Time itself has no end, but it takes time to get there. I could use a man like you in my organization; come and work for me, and in a couple of years, you will be rich beyond your wildest dreams."

I smiled and said to him in a very serious tone, "Don't bother, Mr. Lindberg, your mental games won't work with me, not anymore. You see, Mr. Lindberg, even when facing death, you're still trying to cheat, steal, and lie. I don't need your money, and I don't need your company. To the contrary, what I need you to know is that not only I am alive, but that before your programmed assassin was able to discharge his weapon, I was quick enough to shoot five rounds of bullets into his head. Does that number sound familiar to you—*five rounds.*

"Your assassin is dead, and the vice president of the United

States is healthier than you and I. He didn't even have a scratch on him. He wanted you to believe that you had succeeded so I could get close to you and end this charade of yours once and for all. VP Farmer gave me a message for you: 'Checkmate.'"

Lindberg's face drastically changed, as he realized in less than a second that, at this moment, he had lost one of his largest research facilities, his top scientists, the juicy government contract he'd believed he would be getting, and possibly his life.

As more than a minute had passed by, and no one had come storming into the room, Lindberg started to sweat. He soon realized that no one was coming to his rescue.

"In case you are wondering," I told him, "I took the liberty of disabling the alarm system and also your team. If you don't mind me saying, Mr. Lindberg, they put up a good fight."

Seeing his defeated face was absolutely intoxicating.

"Mr. Lindberg, I feel pity for you; here you are all alone with all the money in the world, and no one is coming to rescue you. You have no family, no friends, no love. The only close relative you have is your stinky, bloody money, and I promise you that today you will die alone. I will give you a gentleman's choice. Come with me and turn yourself in to the authorities and confess your sins, or you can use the last bullet in this pistol and kill yourself."

"Never, never; do you hear me, Mr. Steele? I will never surrender. And even if you were to take me in front of a court of law, I would never go to prison. I am too powerful. I have connections," said Lindberg.

"Very well, Mr. Lindberg, as you wish." I placed the pistol I had taken from one of the bodyguards with one bullet in the chamber on top of the table next to the bathroom door. "Here, Mr. Lindberg, it's up to you."

I walked away directly toward the main door. After clearing the porte cochere, I opened the door of my rental car. I heard a bullet whistling by me, breaking the rented car's driver's window.

Looking at the broken glass, I had no doubt that a coward like Lindberg could never take his own life. I turned and looked at his panicked face. He was standing at the center of his foyer, realizing that not even a gentleman's death was good enough for him.

I leaned my back on the car's side and locked my arms in front of my chest. I looked at my watch, and then at his puzzle face. I could tell when he saw me glancing at my watch that he had realized he was doomed. The pistol dropped from his hand and bounced several times over the polished marble floor. A couple of seconds later when my wrist watch second hand touched the top of the hour, I was thrown backward by the shockwave of a large explosion that decimated the front section of the foyer and quickly engulfed the rest of the mansion in flames.

I shook my head to the left and right, trying to get my bearings back. Everything was fuzzy, and my ears were ringing. Seconds later, I felt my strength coming back to me. I managed to stand up and was brushing away pieces of broken glass from my shirt.

I chose to leave Lindberg's last minutes of existence to his cowardice conscience. However, after seeing this bastard die, deep inside my soul, for the first time in my life, I could see the world through the many lives he torture, maimed and killed. After all, how could I have trusted that a man who lied and cheated for a living would have taken his own life? I was glad I had only given him one bullet and not the full magazine. But I guessed that everyone deserved a second chance at redemption, and I had chosen to give him one, and again I forgot to tell him about option two but I guess that he wouldn't have the heart to take the explosion either so I just allowed option two to run its course just in case.

***

I got in my car and drove away from the area before the authorities arrive and link me to this explosion. I had no time to waste. I had other affairs to attend to and loose ends to tie up before I felt comfortable enough that none of this would come back and bite me on my ass when I least expected.

Thanks to the expedient and comfortable ride provided by the vice president's plane, I arrived back in Nome in record time, where I personally delivered the news to VP Farmer and Agent Landis. The vice president assured me that my name would be cleared, along with the news of the vice president's miraculous recovery and Maynard James Lindberg's plot to kill him.

He also reassured me that the administration was going to continue to fight for dignity and humanity. The vice president would personally see to it to take a pro-life stand to prevent the atrocities of stem-cell research from tarnishing not only the scientific community but also the history of the United States.

Before I left, I spent some time with Aunty Marie and Jimmy.

When I left them in their small house in Nome, they were just as I remembered—a happy couple who could not keep their hands off each other. Marie knew that Jimmy was not entirely himself, due to the remaining side effects of the serum, but he was already starting to awake from a long and tedious self-absence, and she was over the moon with that.

Sora became their newfound best friend and promised me to keep an eye on both of them from now on.

She told me about her plans to enroll in the University of Anchorage Alaska, of course fully paid for with the compliments of the Unites States government and a very appreciative Office of the Vice President of the United States.

Upon finishing her degree, she was promised a job as head of the local tribal council. The first thing that she did was to convince the government of Alaska to proclaim the land where Lindberg Research Corporation had once stood back to local sacred land.

Sora promised me that the first order of business would be to honor the memory of a great leader, Sani-Shaman—a man who, like the phoenix, was reborn from the ashes through his heroic final hours, which did more for humanity than many of the top so-called world philanthropists I know today could do in a life time. I learned that, for his unselfish actions and heroism, the vice president of the Unites States and his boss had awarded Sani-Shaman the Presidential Medal of Freedom, which soon Sora would be accepting on his behalf in Washington, DC.

Three days later, I found myself in North Haven, Maine, paying my respects and fulfilling a promise to a fallen warrior. Finally, Colonel Tom Allen Harman was buried with full military honors under the presence of US Vice President Farmer; his Secret Service detail; and an old FBI friend, Director Nick Archer.

It was a small but heartfelt ceremony. Thanks to VP Farmer's participation, many news crews, local residents, and even the state governor attended the burial ceremony. Colonel Harman had no family and no relatives that could be there for him. He was buried next to his parents and in the same cemetery where his late long-lost love and mother of his only child rested today.

After our short adventure in Nome, Colonel Harman gained a new brother-in-arms, who not only honored his many accomplishments in life but also his last dying wish.

I made sure to remember all the good things we'd shared during our brief interaction in Nome and highlighted that, because of his heroic actions, we were able to save countless lives that tragic day.

I wanted no glory, no recognition, and no mention of me. I was only a man doing what anyone else would do in my shoes.

But without Colonel Harman, Sani-Shaman, and Sora, I would have never even got close to sinking the evil empire to its doom. So all the glory went to them, and I was all right with that.

After the final "Taps" note ended, I walked over to Director Archer and handed over all the evidence I had, thanks to Colonel Harman and Sani-Shaman. The evidence I'd acquired was powerful enough to finally put an end to Lindberg and its stem-cell and mind-programming programs.

Soon all the pain and suffering Lindberg Research had inflicted not only in Nome but also in Sierra Leone, West Africa, Berlin, and the northern Mexican region of Ciudad Juárez, among others, would be a painful memory for the American people and would stand as testament that we are not ready to play God yet.

These were just a few of the many other places in which the local government had welcomed the late Maynard James Lindberg with open arms, under the false promises of prosperity and wealth. They hadn't realized they were selling their souls to an evil man who would do all within his power to honor the contract, not in the best interest of science but, of course, in the best interest of making money and power.

With a handshake, Nick Archer promised me that he would assign the investigation to his best agents at "862 NC" and personally see to it that the Lindberg Research Corporation was dismantled, down to the last facility it owned. He would expose Maynard James Lindberg for the fraud, cheat, and liar he had really been. And that was all I wanted.

I thanked Nick Archer and the vice president right after the ceremony because I had to leave right away if I wanted to be true to my promise to pick up, at JFK International Airport, a red-haired, silky-skinned, beautiful woman returning from China.

THE END

REFERENCES AND CREDITS

1. Erik Lindblom: http://alaskamininghalloffame.org/inductees/lindblom.php
2. Range Rover: http://www.landrover.com/gl/en/lr/marketsel
3. Ford Bronco: http://corporate.ford.com/
4. Medeco: http://www.medeco.com/
5. Occam Razor theory: http://www.weburbia.com/physics/occam.html
6. Vince Lombardi Quotes: http://thinkexist.com/quotation/the_price_of_success_is_hard_work-dedication_to/149894.html
7. Project MKULTRA: http://all.net/journal/deception/MKULTRA/www.profreedom.free4all.co.uk/skeletons_1.html
8. Dr. Gorge Estabrook: http://www.youtube.com/watch?v=4vqr65ilHUs
9. Boeing 757: http://www.wgmd.com/?p=32092
10. Amphibious ARGO UTV: http://www.argoatv.com/recreational/rechome.aspx
11. Bell Helicopter: http://www.bell430.com/
12. Hummer: http://www.hummer.com/#/AMERICAS/us/en-us/
13. Harley Davidson Motorcycle: http://www.harley-davidson.com/en_US/Content/Pages/Police-Fire-Rescue/motorcycles.html?locale=en_US&bmLocale=en_US
14. YHM Cobra .45 Sound Suppressors: http://www.impactguns.com/yhm-cobra-45-sound-suppressor-with-nielsen-device-cobra.aspx
15. "Universal Machine Pistol" H&K: http://www.hk-usa.com/military_products/ump_general.asp
16. Jeep: http://www.jeep.com/en/?sid=1037056&KWNM=jeep&KWID=3543529755&channel=paidsearch

17. Cessna Grand Caravan: http://www.cessna.com/news/caravan/ dc_CES_EXT-dc_CES_MMG_Media_C-dc_CES-Layout-GenericMMGMedia_grand-caravan.html
18. Alaskan Amber Beer: http://www.alaskanbeer.com/
19. American University: http://www.american.edu/
20. Millennium Hotel, Alaska: http://www.millenniumhotels.com/ millenniumanchorage/
21. Rolls-Royce: http://www.rolls-roycemotorcars.com/
22. Remington Shotgun: http://www.gunsinternational.com/ Remington-SxS-Shotguns.cfm?cat_id=821
23. The EADS North America AAS-72X: http://armedscout.com/ about/capable.asp Armani: http://www.armani.com/ George Estabrooks: http://www.theforbiddenknowledge.com/hardtruth/ if_chapter4.htm
24. *Happy Days* Show: http://www.imdb.com/title/tt0070992/ Bruce Feirstein: http://answers.yahoo.com/question/ index?qid=20100813021046AAyEYg2
25. Eugène Viollet-le-Duc: http://www.britannica.com/EBchecked/ topic/629711/Eugene-Emmanuel-Viollet-le-Duc
26. Remi Martin XIII: http://www.louis-xiii.com/#/prehome
27. Or rather, "It is polite, and possibly also advantageous, to abide by the customs of a society when one is a visitor": http://www. phrases.org.uk/meanings/when-in-rome-do-as-the-romans-do. html